BURN ZONE

ANNABETH ALBERT

carina
press

carina press®

Recycling programs
for this product may
not exist in your area.

ISBN-13: 978-1-335-45949-7

Burn Zone

Carina Press
22 Adelaide St. West, 40th Floor
Toronto, Ontario M5H 4E3, Canada
www.CarinaPress.com

Printed in U.S.A.

To Oregon, home of my heart. I wasn't born here, but over the years you've made me the person I am today, in so many ways, both big and small.

BURN ZONE

Chapter One

Six years ago, September

"Fucking wind." Linc had been shit out of luck plenty of times in all his years fighting wildfires, but being quite literally up a tree, dangling like a puppet, never got any easier to stomach.

"Hang tight, buddy. I've got you." Retrieving the cargo that had dropped along with the members of their smoke-jumping crew, Wyatt prepared to climb up after him.

Linc had been treed, parachute tangled in the branches of a massive pine, when the wind had pushed him off course. Even his years of skilled landings under pressure-filled circumstances hadn't been enough to keep him out of the tree.

It wasn't his first time being treed and probably wouldn't be the last time Wyatt had to save his bacon. That was the nature of their work on the front lines of forest fires—they'd saved each other's lives so many times, he'd lost track of the number, but never lost sight of this feeling, being helpless, waiting for his best friend to come bail him out again.

"Careful," Linc called when a branch creaked as Wyatt started his ascent. "No stupid risks. May's counting on me returning you in one piece."

The fire season was winding down, lots of equipment checks and inventory for next year, and the occasional jump like this one, checking on reports of some spot fires from lightning strikes. Their job was to do what was necessary to prevent the spread of fire—hand digging lines, clearing brush, felling trees.

"She wasn't happy, having to take me this morning." Wyatt's voice was more strained than usual. Linc couldn't tell whether it was from the climb or the mention of May, who was pregnant with their first kid and had been full of worries all season long, the stress of being married to a smoke jumper getting to her. "Stupid truck's acting up again. She's on me to trade it in, get a four-door that can handle a car seat."

"Not a bad idea. Get me free from this mess and I'll come take a look at it tomorrow, see if I can get you running again for the short-term."

"Appreciated." Wyatt's tone was still clipped. Linc couldn't see him now, and he knew better than to twist too much. One wrong move and he could end up plummeting to the ground, which was enough of a drop to break some bones.

Ordinarily, Linc would be more proactive in getting free, but he'd tangled in a way that he couldn't get to the knife that was an essential part of their gear. Instead, he had to wait for Wyatt to reach him, trust that Wyatt wouldn't send him crashing through the branches, and that Wyatt would have enough sense to keep his own self safe. May—and Wyatt's mother, whom Linc loved almost as much as the memory of his own—would never forgive Linc if Wyatt went home with a broken leg or worse.

Working together this season was like shrugging into his favorite work jacket, worn and familiar, both of them more experienced this go-around. While Wyatt had stayed local after graduation, Linc had been gone as much as he'd been home, gaining experience on fire crews all across the West before finally duty called him back, roots as unavoidable as taxes. That Wyatt and this crew had been waiting was more than a reward for everything else he was dealing with.

Finally, though, he was free enough to grab Wyatt's hand, then use all his upper body strength to pull himself over the branch. Working together, they freed the chute. It was way too valuable and essential to their work to leave in the tree, so he breathed a little easier when it fluttered to the ground. Then they started their descent, tricky because of the weight of both of them. It was an old, sturdy tree, but Linc's attention remained on red alert for potential dangers until they were both on the forest floor.

Time to get to work, packing up the chute and rejoining the rest of the crew, digging fireline by hand, the wide dirt trails used to keep back any potential fire spread, until his arm and back muscles burned. This mission at least didn't involve an overnight in the forest, but it did have a long, arduous pack-out where they had to haul themselves and all their gear several miles to an extraction point.

"Careful!" Wyatt thrust an arm out right when Linc would have tripped over a large tree root. The others were some distance behind them, Wyatt setting a bruising pace as per his usual.

"Damn. You saved me. Again." Linc shook his head. They had been through hell and back, everything from fiery infernos side by side to pristine mountain mornings. Even in the years when Linc had been away for long stretches, they'd still shared every catastrophe and triumph from wading pools to wedding bells for Wyatt and every major life event in between. "What do I owe you?"

It was an old joke between them, but Wyatt's face darkened, eyes narrowing, voice hard. "Stay away from my little brother."

Fuck. Linc should have seen this coming, should have known that Wyatt had something more on his mind than May's worries. He'd probably been stewing all day, waiting to bring this up. That was how Wyatt got, even back when they were kids. He'd brood and brood and then his temper would flare.

"Me? What would I want with him?" Stopping, he turned to face Wyatt. If they were going to do this, he wasn't going to let Wyatt lecture over his shoulder like Linc was some ornery kid on a scout hike being called to task.

"Don't play dumb with me. I *know* you. Wasn't that me who didn't say a damn word when you took the number of that bartender New Year's Eve?"

Linc swallowed hard. He'd lay down his life for Wyatt, but he also wasn't going to let his best friend push him around either.

"Who I've taken to bed has zero to do with your brother. Zilch." On that point, he could be firm. That

Wyatt disapproved went without saying—they might be brothers of the soul, but that didn't mean they always saw eye to eye. His skin prickled, old wounds he tried his damnedest to ignore.

"Fuck yes, it does. He came out. Told the whole damn family yesterday at Sunday dinner that he's gay."

"Bet that took some balls, standing up to all of you." Somehow Linc managed a steady tone even as he wondered what in the hell Jacob had been thinking, coming right out and announcing that to his large, boisterous family which wasn't exactly known for open-mindedness, especially among the brothers. "Good on him, but again, nothing to do with me."

"Bullshit." The meanness was back along with a gravelly laugh. "He's been following you around two weeks now, doing all your crap jobs, ever since he got back from Vegas looking like a kicked puppy."

"He's been helpful." He kept his voice mild, not about to let on to any enjoyment of Jacob's presence, the way he lightened Linc's load far beyond hauling trash. And yeah, Jacob had been down, but some of that defeated air was starting to clear, leaving behind a guy with a quick wit, easy smile and strong back. "Not gonna deny I've been able to use him with the shit my old man left behind. It's a total—"

"Mess that ain't yours." Wyatt resumed their trek, not looking to see if Linc was following. Which he did. Like always. He might not like this conversation, but he owed Wyatt too damn much to just stalk off, even if part of him was tempted.

"I've been telling you," Wyatt continued as they crested a hill. "It's time you moved on. Let it go."

"Let it go to who?" This was an old argument, but Linc still took the bait, not liking the undercurrent of a message that maybe he should leave town again. "No real other family stepping up to the plate. Victor's dead. Dad's dead. Nah, man, it's on me. And Jacob's been a help. Stronger than he looks—"

Wyatt cut him off with a warning noise. "Did he tell you anything about whatever shit went down in Vegas? You wouldn't keep that from me, would you?"

"Nah. He didn't say shit about his love life." But actually Linc might have kept quiet if he had. Not maliciously, but Wyatt wasn't good with a secret, and Linc...well, he had enough of his own. He could hold on to someone else's for them until they were ready to share.

However, something had gone down in Vegas, something big to send Jacob home, away from all his MMA friends, tail between his legs, looking as heartbroken as Linc had ever seen a guy. And, well, it didn't take an engineer to piece together the facts.

"How's your mom taking it?" he asked. Of all the Hartman family members, she was least likely to cast Jacob out. He was her baby, and Linc couldn't see her hurling hate at him, no matter what she might personally believe. And as she went, so would the rest of the family, Wyatt's homophobic ass included.

"Ha." Wyatt snorted. "Mom's playing this like she's known for years, but Dad just got real quiet, then went back to the TV in their room. I'm worried about his heart, man."

"Him? Strong as a fucking ox." Linc was more worried about Wyatt's liver these days than his robust old man's maladies. He knew the Hartman family, knew how much they doted on Jacob, even if he did try all their patience from time to time. The way Linc saw it, they'd survive this shock.

Wyatt might not.

"He ain't gonna make a hotshot crew, not now."

"He wants that?" Dread gathered in Linc's gut that had exactly nothing to do with Jacob's announcement or Wyatt's predictable meltdown. Something in him didn't like the thought of Jacob out here, doing the work that he and Wyatt had done for years, fighting forest fires. Jacob in the line of danger didn't sit right with him, not at all.

"He said he did. Other night. Who knows though?" Wyatt shrugged. "Says he's gonna go out for the volunteer crew first. But he's also yapping about trying college. You never know with that kid. Can't stick to anything worth a crap."

"Any ETA on the extraction?" Garrick and Ray, their other team members, came around the bend, huffing as they hauled their share of the gear.

"Nope. Gotta haul ass to get us back for a late dinner." Wyatt managed to sound upbeat, but later, once Linc was dropping him off at the small house he and May shared at the edge of town, Wyatt had one more warning. "And I meant what I said. Don't you start messing around with Jacob. We might go way back, but I'll lay you out flat myself, you and him start carrying on."

"No worry of that," he said, pitching his own voice low and calm, no trace of the junk heap of emotions piling up inside him. "Go on now. Don't make May walk out and see what's keeping you."

"Fine. Some uncle you're gonna be, the way you hover over her. Between you and Mom, kid'll come out rolled in bubble wrap."

That Wyatt considered him an uncle for the kid on the way didn't make him warm with satisfaction, the way it might have earlier in the day. Now, it just added to his guilt and uncertainty, feelings that didn't evaporate as he headed home.

There was a shadow on the porch as he pulled up, and his heart knew what it was even if his brain didn't want to admit it quite yet.

"Linc. I was hoping they'd bring you back early." Jacob's voice was low and urgent as soon as Linc stepped onto the porch. It was old and sagging, one of the many things that needed complete replacing, not just repair. No light either, another thing he'd need to add. Off to the side of the house was a junk heap, smaller now thanks to Jacob's help. The whole place had gone to ruin while Linc had bounced around, sometimes here, sometimes out in Idaho or Wyoming, trying to outrun… everything. But apparently he hadn't run far enough, pulled back by his father's death to this box of uncomfortable memories.

"What do you think you're doing?" He wanted it to come out stern, but his voice was weary, energy bled out from the argument with Wyatt and the long shift. And now this. In his tiredness as he'd pulled in, he'd missed seeing the little compact parked on the other side of the junk heap. The car had belonged to one of Jacob's sisters and was currently held together with little more than duct tape and hope.

"Waiting. For you. Figured you'd show up sometime before midnight." It was too dark to see much of Jacob's smile, but Linc could *hear* it. The pleasure in Jacob's voice sliced him to the core, spoke to everything he'd been trying so hard not to notice the past few weeks, like the way his pulse sped up just sharing the same oxygen. Trying to steady himself, he sank down on a five-gallon paint barrel, carefully positioning himself away from where Jacob was perched on the rickety railing. "Invite me in?"

Oh, hell no. Linc ignored that potential stick of dynamite and went for the real reason Jacob had probably turned up. "Heard you caused a bit of a ruckus with the family last night."

"They'll get over it." This new all-grown-up, super-confident version of Jacob had plagued Linc ever since he got back to town. Jacob was the kind of guy who didn't let life get him down long, bouncing back from what had to be a hell of a hurt, and Linc couldn't help but admire that quality. He still managed to joke around, smile, get under Linc's skin. Especially that last one.

He wouldn't say he missed the little kid Jacob had been, because he'd barely known him at all. Back then, he'd been just another little Hartman kid roaming around, getting underfoot to whatever real business he and Wyatt were about. But then he'd turned back up, all lean muscle and short blond hair and a come-get-me grin, no trace of that annoying toddler, and a whole lot more trouble.

"Anything in particular bring this on?" He told himself that curiosity was the only reason he was keeping Jacob talking.

"Friends of mine were sharing memes about coming-out stories."

Linc tried picturing a universe where he might… *Nah.* Never happening.

Jacob's sigh was far worldlier than his almost-twenty years would seem to support. "It's a social media thing. I know, I know, you're not big on that, but news flash, there's a whole world beyond Painter's Ridge."

"I've been around, remember?" He needed to remind them both that he was a good ten years older than Jacob.

"Chasing fires all over the West hardly counts as *around*," Jacob scoffed. "No cities. No smartphones. No friends beyond your hotshot crew guys."

"Hey now." Linc might be something of a loner, but he had friends. Might all be local or seasonal acquaintances elsewhere, but he wasn't the cranky hermit Jacob was trying to make him out to be.

"I'm just saying, you don't even make it up to Portland much."

"No need. Anyway, these…friends of yours, they pressured you into coming out?"

"No one *pressured* me." Jacob sounded outraged that Linc would even think he could be swayed like that. And there was the backbone Linc admired so much— strength, not just in his slim, fighting-honed body, but in his character. "It was in the back of my head though, all day. And then at dinner, Wyatt started in again on why I left Vegas, saying I couldn't hack it in MMA, even as Tyler's sidekick. And I'd just had *enough.* Enough of the pretending. Enough of the lies and not a damn person around here knowing the truth. I was just so fucking tired of his bullshit."

"I hear you." And Linc did, heard his pain and loneliness loud and clear. He knew something of that isolation, and while maybe he wouldn't choose Jacob's way out, he got the desperation that had driven his outburst. "And that was a brave thing you did, standing up to him. Telling everyone."

"I'm not looking for a head pat here."

"And I'm not handing them out." Linc could meet his irritation head-on.

"Wouldn't turn down a beer though. Fuck. That was *intense*."

"Another year and a half, I'll buy you one."

Nineteen, he reminded himself. *He's nine-fucking-teen*. Even if Wyatt hadn't warned him off, he needed to remember that the kid couldn't even buy a drink yet. And thank the fuck that Linc had thrown out every last drop of alcohol in this place, first week back.

"Like you and Wyatt weren't drinking every chance you got, even in high school."

"Wyatt maybe," he allowed, stretching, trying to do something with the tension that kept gathering in his lower back, just from being here.

"Oh, right. I forgot. You're…like his guardian angel or something. Don't you ever get tired, being his designated driver? Cleaning up his messes?"

"Nope," he lied, far too easily. "He's my best friend. It's what friends do, take care of each other."

"I don't see him exactly returning the favor." Jacob flicked some stray leaf off the railing, narrowly missing Linc.

"You wouldn't know," he said testily, reminding both of them that he and Wyatt had a long history that Jacob had nothing to do with. "That man's done more for me than I can ever repay."

Jacob made a scoffing noise. "Maybe so, but you wouldn't know it from how he treats you sometimes. So, what's the deal? Can't believe Wyatt even told you about last night. He tell you to try to talk sense into me?"

"Fuck no."

"Oh?" Jacob's tone softened and he scooted closer. *Danger. Danger.* All Linc's proximity sensors pinged, brain squawking like a comm set when a fire wall shifted, coming straight at him. "I brought it up to make sure you were okay. That's all. Thought maybe you'd need to hear that your folks will come around. Give them time."

"Yeah." Jacob's sigh held a certain amount of wistfulness to it, which did something to Linc's insides, made him want to be stupid and take his hand or something else ridiculous.

"And for the record, I'm sorry about that Tyler kid. He's a fucking idiot, but you okay?"

"I'm fine." Leaning forward, he rested a hand on Linc's shoulder. "Totally and completely fine."

"Good." He didn't make a move to stand, couldn't, not with Jacob's warm hand pressing him down, dangerous sparks shooting all down his torso.

"But maybe I should make myself scarce for a few days, let everyone calm the fuck down. You wouldn't happen to know of somewhere with a spare bed now, would you?" His tone was light, but there was no mistaking his meaning.

"You're not staying here." Even if Wyatt wouldn't flay him alive, that idea was all kinds of trouble.

"No beer. No place to crash. You're no fun."

"Nope."

"I could be, though. Fun. The sort of fun you need. And you know it." Jacob's voice had all the brashness of nineteen to it, reckless confidence. "Don't tell me you haven't felt it, ever since I started helping you here. I've seen you looking at me."

Fuck. All those danger warnings shrieked again as the car carrying his sanity went over the cliff. He worked with any number of good-looking guys, had played four years of high school sports, had been around locker rooms almost two decades at this point, and it was going to be Jacob who called him on sneaking looks? And the worst, the absolute worst, was that he wasn't wrong. Linc had looked. And that Jacob noticed said he was either getting sloppy now that he'd hit thirty or that there was something about Jacob...

And fuck it all, there could *not* be something about Jacob. No way, no how.

"No idea what you're talking about." For the second time that day, he played dumb, knowing full well Jacob wasn't going to buy it any more than his brother had.

"I get it. You're not out yet. But I've heard enough of Wyatt's stupid jokes when he thinks you guys are alone to know you probably swing my way, at least sometimes. And like I said, I'm not blind."

The words to deny Jacob's assumption rose in his throat, but wouldn't leave his lips. Something about Jacob indeed. Linc could lie about this by omission or necessity to just about anyone else. But not Jacob. From the start of helping Linc, he'd earned Linc's trust. And maybe his truthfulness too, because he simply couldn't make the lie come.

"You're not blind. It's no one's business but mine though."

"Good." Jacob drew the word out, sinful and seductive and more dangerous than fraying webbing on a jump rig. "I can keep a secret."

If only. But no. His bones still remembered with breathtaking accuracy how it had felt, dangling above the earth that morning, little pieces of rope and webbing all that separated him and a broken neck. The view might have been nice, but the fall would have been deadly, save Wyatt's intervention. Not unlike this moment here.

I've got you, buddy.

Stay away from my little brother.

"Doesn't matter. You're barking up the wrong tree. I'm not letting you stay here."

"Why? You think I'm on the rebound from Tyler? Or you think I'll out you? Or…" His voice hardened and his hand tightened on Linc's shoulder. "It's Wyatt, isn't it? Did he threaten you?"

"No." This time the lie came easy, both because he had to and because he didn't like Jacob's tone, like he was ready to go to war with Wyatt on his behalf. That sort of concern, an almost protectiveness, made him shift against the plastic bucket. He didn't need anyone playing champion for him.

Jacob's grip softened, massaging Linc's neck with a touch that had him stifling a groan. His hands were strong, calloused from hard work and years in the gym and felt better than a hot shower after a long day in the field.

"He wouldn't have to know. It could be just an itch we scratch this one time."

"Ha." Oh, to be nineteen and so damn sure of himself. And that right there was the other reason why Linc had to turn him down. There wouldn't be any one time only for him, not the way Jacob pulled him in even when he knew full well he had to resist. Jacob, who apparently saw what hundreds of guys he'd worked with hadn't. Jacob, who made him laugh even while hauling mountains of moldy magazines, a feat not many could manage.

But Jacob had all but said it himself—he was nursing a broken heart from Tyler, and Linc had no desire to chance everything just to be the rebound fuck the kid forgot in a month.

"Not happening."

"Not tonight, maybe, but—"

"Not now, not ever. There's plenty of fish your own age to fry. Go find one." He forced himself to pull away from that delicious torment, to stand up because his body was that damn weak that another few minutes and he'd be making all sorts of stupid choices. Better to be firm now.

"Your loss." The hurt in Jacob's voice as he scampered off the railing pierced Linc like a dart, a sharp, swift pain he'd do anything to take away. Anything, that was, except the one thing Jacob seemed to want.

"I'm sure it is." He wasn't trying to be flip. He absolutely was sincere—both sure that he'd regret turning him down and sure that he was doing the right thing. Jacob was simply a risk he wasn't ever going to be able to afford.

Chapter Two

The Painter's Ridge Air Base parking lot was full, exactly how Jacob had expected it to be on this early morning. He'd anticipated the nervous flutters in his stomach as well, had skipped both coffee and cereal, too hyped to get here where all the smoke jumpers were reporting for orientation for the coming season. At least, it was easiest to tell himself it was hype, not try to name all the other things bumping around in his empty gut. And he'd also predicted the angry voice that greeted him moments after he entered the training facility.

"What the fuck are you doing here?" Linc looked like he'd spent the winter doing nothing except pumping iron, even more ripped and fierce looking than usual. And hot as fuck, because some things never changed. Short, dark buzz cut, similarly dark, trimmed facial scruff, forearm tats poking out of the rolled back sleeves of his flannel shirt. Menacing glare that would make weaker men than Jacob quake in their boots, but only earned a shrug from him.

"Reporting for training." He'd spent weeks now playing this moment over in his head, rehearsing both how cool and calm he'd be and how pissed Linc would be. Stepping to the sidewall, he freed the entryway for others. Linc followed, glower still fully in place.

"The fuck you are." If Linc was surprised, he had only himself to blame. He'd been scarce all damn winter, only surfacing in late January when May had Willow. The awkwardness at the hospital had hardly been the moment to tell him that he'd *finally* received the call to report to spring training here instead of with the hotshot hand crew he'd spent the past few seasons with, doing his time, waiting for this day. "When I saw your name on the roster this morning, I about choked on my coffee. And that was before the text from your mom."

"Sounds like a problem." Jacob continued to regard him coolly even as other people filtered in around them—fit men and women who would make up this season's elite forest fire fighting team. He was damn proud to be among them, and Linc was not going to ruin this for him.

"It is. Listen, there's a list of alternates a mile long."

"I *know*. I've waited five damn years for my shot. You're not talking me out of this."

But Linc continued, thoroughly undaunted. "This early in the season, you drop out, it's no big deal for them to bring in a replacement. Don't do this to your mom, kid."

"Not. A. Kid."

"You are when you act like one. This isn't a game or some extreme sport. You can get your adrenaline rush in other ways that won't break your mom's heart."

"She'll deal." Jacob refused to soften his stance, even

though he did hate how hard she was taking this. Not that he'd expected a parade, but not having a single person happy for him or even a little proud was damn depressing. "And this isn't some lark. I've paid my dues, done my time with engine and hotshot crews, got my certifications, worked my way up, same as you and Wyatt did."

"Wyatt would hate this." Linc stared him down, eyes daring him to say different.

"Well, seeing as how he's not here—"

"Can everyone find a seat? Go ahead and bring your coffee over, and we're going to get started." A grizzled older gentleman spoke over the din of the room. Witherspoon Alder, the base manager, was someone Jacob recognized both from the funeral and from his panel interview.

"We're not done." Giving him an ominous look, Linc stalked away, claiming one of the folding chairs in the back of the room.

Even without the warning, Jacob didn't doubt for a second that Linc had more to say. And maybe if he wasn't always such a hard-ass about it, Jacob might actually listen. But, no, Linc had always, always taken his marching orders from Wyatt. It was almost nine months since the fire that had claimed Wyatt's life, and Linc was still fighting Wyatt's battles for him.

"The next five weeks won't be the most arduous of your life. That's coming later this summer, the real deal." Alder addressed the room as Jacob took an empty chair on the opposite side of the room from Linc. "This is life-and-death serious business, and we lost three of our best last year. Make no mistake in what you've signed up for—we take pride in what we do, but we never lose sight of the dangers either. Look around you. These are the teammates who will keep you safe, and trusting them is as big a part of our training as anything else."

Jacob dutifully glanced around the room, noting the varied ages of the participants—returning men and women in their thirties and forties who'd stopped by the house with condolences and casseroles alongside newer trainees like himself. He knew a few of the other newbies from various hotshot and engine crews. Despite Linc's attitude, no one here was a *kid*—it took several years of experience fighting on the front lines to even get a shot at a smoke jumper slot.

Alder continued his welcome speech, introducing the various senior personnel who would serve as trainers over the course of the five-week period and outlining the skills they'd be covering. It included far more than jumping out of planes and all that entailed, with exit and landing procedures and all the maneuvering in the air. They'd also cover parachute and equipment maintenance, cargo retrieval, timber management, and tree climbing as well as the work they'd be doing on natural resource projects when not called out to a fire.

"In addition to the physical fitness tests, there are also several pack-out tests to show your readiness to haul gear long distances." A woman in her late forties with short hair and clipped speech addressed them after Alder was done. "We're going to start today with a baseline fitness assessment—no one's going home quite yet, but this will show any room for improvement. Failure to pass the fitness and pack tests at the end of training will, however, be grounds for reassignment."

Ever since his MMA days, Jacob had kept himself in peak physical condition, both during the fire season and with his various off-season jobs, so he wasn't too worried about passing the tests. He'd had the minimum requirements taped to his fridge all spring. The way more pressing concern was avoiding Linc so that he didn't have to suffer another public argument in front of all his new teammates.

To that end, he hung back when they were dismissed to the locker room to change into workout gear, waiting to pick a locker far from Linc, but his plan backfired when the only options were the two on either side of Linc, everyone else apparently giving him a wide berth.

Linc didn't waste any time before turning toward him, mid shirt change, scowl still in place. "Listen—"

"Save it. Not here." Jacob kept his voice low. And his eyes away from Linc's impressive chest, which he'd seen before, swimming and such, but still hadn't developed an immunity to.

"If you can't handle some criticism—"

"You really want to do this now? Thought you already had the hothead rep. It'd be a shame to make that worse."

It was a low blow, reminding Linc that the rumor was that there had been serious talk about not bringing him back for the season. It was Wyatt, not Linc, who had usually been the loose cannon with his mouth and quick temper with his fists, but gossip about a supposed shouting match after Wyatt passed that had resulted in discipline had reached the other crews. And there had been more speculation that Linc was washed, that maybe he couldn't hack it anymore, not without Wyatt and not after whatever had gone down out there that led to only one of them coming back. Which wasn't his fault, and Jacob knew that, but Linc wore his guilt like a cape, twisting in the wind for all to see. Plenty of people had thought Linc would never let himself jump again, but here he was, reporting for duty.

"Fine. Later." Linc finished dressing with anger rolling off him in toxic waves before heading out, leaving Jacob to do the same. But when he returned to the main room, Linc was deep in conversation with Alder and Sims, the woman in charge of the PT tests. Fuck. If he was advocating for Jacob's removal, they were going to have a lot more than words later.

He warmed up with some basic stretches while waiting for his turn at the pull-up bar. The minimum was seven, and most of the line rattled theirs off without issue. The guy ahead of Jacob though, an older returning smoke jumper, struggled.

"Come on, Ray!"

"You've got this!"

"Work it!" Several others in the returning crowd started calling out encouragement, Linc included. Funny how he could go from riding Jacob's ass to congenial teammate so quickly. After Ray finally got his chin over the bar for number seven, Linc was first to give him a high five.

Clipboard in hand, Sims summoned him forward. "Okay, Rookie. Let's see what you've got. Don't forget, there's more to come, but I'm looking for a quality ten from our rookies. Show me you've been working."

Ten with an audience was a little harder than the seven he'd been anticipating, especially knowing Linc wouldn't be cheering *him*, but he got a good rhythm going and reached the target without issue. He stuck around to cheer on the female recruit behind him who whipped off ten like she was in superhero training.

"Nice work," he said as she dropped down. "You were with the Winema hotshot team last season, right? Baker, is it?"

"Yup." Baker was tall and ripped, and Jacob liked her already—he wasn't expecting to make many friends with the old-timers like Linc's crowd, but it wouldn't hurt to have a few of his fellow recruits on his side as they went forward. "And you're Hartman?"

"Yeah, but you can call me Jacob. The whole last name thing gets confusing." He supposed he'd have to get used to it, as a lot of the firefighters he'd met went by last names or nicknames. However, to him, Hartman was still Wyatt—the name on his football jersey and letter jacket, the name on his helmet, the one known to firefighters all over the West as he'd built his rep as the best of the best.

"I bet. I prefer Kelley myself—last name makes me think of my dad. I heard about your brother. We all did. I'm sorry for your loss."

"Thanks." He'd gotten used to the condolences, gotten used to the sucker punch of grief that hit when he least expected it. *Wyatt should be here.* He'd wanted to serve together, damn it. Anyone who thought he was trading on Wyatt's death was wrong—the dream had always been to be here alongside him and Linc, proving himself as one of them, making Wyatt proud. If he'd still been around, stepping out from Wyatt's shadow would have been a challenge, but one he would have happily embraced.

Kelley's respect for Wyatt wasn't the last sympathy he was offered that morning as they rotated through sit-ups and push-ups and a two-mile run. By the time they reached lunch, he was exhausted, but not from the workout. Rather it was all the eyeballs on him. Everyone knew. It felt like they were all watching him extra closely, seeing if he could hack it. But he wasn't going to take his sandwich and go hide either. No, he forced himself to be social, sit with Kelley and some of the other recruits. This would get easier. It had to.

As one of the other recruits, a younger guy with a crew cut, droned on about his diet and fitness regimen, Jacob scanned the room, more than a little unsettled when his eyes met Linc's.

The rest of the space seemed to fade away, the distance between them the only important thing. And the worst part was still wanting Linc, even after everything that had happened. Life would be so much easier if he could shut off caring about Linc, but if there was a secret to doing that, he had yet to discover it. He needed to, though, needed to get his head on straight before Linc cornered him again with whatever lecture he had planned. No way was Jacob being talked out of the goal he'd wanted for years now.

Linc's next bite of sandwich turned to ash in his mouth as his eyes met Jacob's. He didn't look one bit ready to back down, defiant as always. But there was something else there beyond stubbornness that gave him pause—the same charged energy they'd had for years now, worse since…

No. He refused to think about that. No dwelling on *since.* Not here. Not now, and maybe not ever. Jacob was trouble, had always been trouble, and Linc's only focus now had to be on getting him to change his mind for the sake of his mother, who had already lost so much. Jenna was truly good people, and there wasn't much Linc wouldn't do to take away her pain. She didn't deserve this. First losing Big Mike to a heart attack three years back, then Wyatt, and now Jacob trying to break her heart all over again.

And fucking damn Jacob for letting him get blindsided by this news. He couldn't have been the one to text?

You know why he didn't. Fuck. There it was again. That voice reminding him just how badly he'd fucked up. And yeah, he knew he'd been scarce, doing what May and Jenna needed when he could, but also not hesitating to take a few gigs out of the area, just to put some miles between him and…

Fuck. *Get over yourself, Reid. Quit stewing about shit you can't control.* He forced himself to look away, take another bite of sandwich. He'd get his chance to talk sense into Jacob soon enough.

And maybe this was another sign that those out-of-area gigs were the way to go. He'd done it once before. He could do it again, bounce around the West, put distance between him and everything Painter's Ridge represented. He'd stayed after his dad died because fixing the place up, righting all his wrongs, had been a point of pride. That and it felt like the Hartman family had needed him. Wyatt had helped him get on with the smoke-jumping crew here again, after several years at other air bases, and it had felt like coming full circle to their teenage dream of being smoke jumpers together. Like maybe they'd have that and Linc could keep on ignoring Wyatt's asshole side in favor of being a part of something. But now that something was tattered, a few worn scraps holding everything together, and he'd been wondering for months now if he should just pack it in.

"Maybe the kids will work out." Ray nodded in the general direction of Jacob and the other rookies. "They've got some promise. Wyatt Hartman's brother has balls of steel, I'll give him that. No one would have blamed the kid if he'd yanked his application."

"Mmm-hmm." He knew better than to follow Ray's gesture by looking back in that direction again or to get started on the topic of the Hartman brothers. "You get enough PT in this winter? You wanna run together Sunday morning?"

Linc had enough equipment at home and usually worked out alone, but he was worried enough about Ray's ability to pass the fitness test to make an exception for his old buddy.

"Point taken." Ray sighed. "Yeah, I could have done more. Let's do it early, that way I can still get Betsy and the kids to church on time."

"Leave time for some weights," advised Garrick, another experienced smoke jumper who was sitting with them. Unlike Ray, the bigger man had easily churned out his exercises with his usual boundless energy. Friendly, he was on a first-name basis with darn near everyone, Linc included. "I'll join you guys, give Ray some form pointers so that when Sims sees you Monday, you're in fighting shape."

"Sounds good." Typical Garrick, inviting himself along, but Linc wasn't going to complain. He didn't mind the company. It was just weird, being back in the thick of team camaraderie after a long, too-quiet winter with all those thoughts of moving on plaguing him.

"Reid? A word?" Alder came over, his gait halting after decades of jumping had done his knees in, but his voice was as firm as ever. The base superintendent was an institution, and while he had plenty of capable staff under him, he ran a tight ship for the seventy-odd jumpers based out of Painter's Ridge.

"Sure thing." Brushing crumbs away, Linc stood and followed Alder to the edge of the room.

"I looked into that matter you brought up earlier. The Hartman rookie's certifications are all in order. He did extra continuing ed classes over the winter too. Exemplary rec from his hotshot crew chief from last summer. Why exactly did you think he might be missing paperwork?" Alder's shrewd eyes narrowed.

Damn it. It had been a long shot, but Linc had hoped Jacob's well-known dislike of the classroom and his changeable, impulsive nature would mean some required certification in his record might be lacking. Jacob had bounced around the past few years, and to be fair, he'd collected good experience on various summer crews. However, his winters had been spent trying on different college programs and job options, to the point that the family all joked about his inability to stay put in any one situation. And not that he wanted to impugn Jacob's character, but him missing one of the requirements would have been an easy way to get him kicked back to one of the safer crews. And now Linc was going to pay the price for questioning it, looking like an idiot.

So he went for the only other path that might work. Honesty. "His mother doesn't want him here. Wyatt's… It's just too soon."

Alder released a heavy sigh while he leaned against the wall. "I'm not unsympathetic to the loss of the Hartman family. Or you personally, for that matter. You guys went way back. Wyatt was a tragedy for us all. And I'm not discounting that loss, but this is one of the most qualified rookies in the class. He's applied the last four years running after putting in time as a volunteer and then later paid, racking up the hours. To my mind, he's more than earned his chance."

"I understand." Linc didn't have to like it, but he did understand. And Alder was right. Jacob had earned a chance through hard work and long summers, but that didn't mean that Linc was done trying to change his mind. Just meant that he wouldn't try to go through Alder to do it. He could respect the hell out of Jacob and still know in his bones that this was the wrong choice for him.

"How about you? You ready? When we pulled young Hartman's record, I couldn't help but notice that some of your own certs barely squeaked in by the deadline. You seem fit enough, but what about up here?" Alder tapped his temple. "No shame in admitting if you need more time."

"I'll be fine." Linc's voice came out harsher than he intended, so he tried again. "I appreciate the concern, sir. My head's in the game."

God, he hoped he wasn't lying, hoped he'd made the right call, sticking around here rather than moving on.

"See to it." Alder nodded at him, then lumbered away back to Sims, who was at the head of the room, ready to call them to attention.

The afternoon was an in-depth tour of the facilities for the rookies and equipment inventory for the returnees, getting everything in order for the start of jump training. It was boring but necessary work, checking every connection, every strap, every piece of harness and rigging that had overwintered in the equipment lockers. They made a lot of their own equipment, and the industrial sewing machines were checked as well. Plenty of time for his thoughts to wander to Jacob, but he forced himself to focus on the task at hand—people's lives depended on him doing a good job.

However, the effort required to do so had him crankier than usual. And fuck, when was the last time he'd been settled? Not even happy, just settled, not bristling around like a wounded bear. He missed that self, hated the thought that he might never get it back, at least not here, not now.

It didn't escape his notice that Jacob made a beeline for the door as soon as they were dismissed for the day, undoubtedly looking to get away from Linc and the black mood he'd unleashed on him earlier. Maybe he needed a different tactic, something friendlier and gentle, not that he knew how to be those things around Jacob, not anymore. As he stalked after him, he tried to summon that energy, but one sight of Jacob by Wyatt's old truck and all his resolutions to be more understanding fled. And it wasn't just the truck, all the old memories of the hours spent working on it with Wyatt, but also the newer, fresher memories of Wyatt handing the keys over to Jacob a couple of years back, of the afternoon spent teaching him how to drive a stick.

"You don't have to sit all the way over there." Somehow Jacob had found the station with a Springsteen fetish, and the music wore Linc down, almost as much as Jacob's relentless flirting.

"Eyes on the road. Careful not to stall out on that hill up ahead."

"Fine." Jacob took the hill a little faster than Linc would, especially for having been driving a stick less than an hour. *"And you owe me a beer."*

"I owe you a what now?" Linc had been distracted, both by the driving and by the cloudless blue sky, exact color of Jacob's eyes when they were happy, like now.

"A beer. I'm twenty-one now. You promised. I know a place in Bend. Wyatt won't have to know and none of his crowd ever goes there."

"We're not going out drinking."

"So we're staying in, then? Your place?"

"More like staying in trouble. You're something else."

Fuck. The sticky thicket of emotions conjured up by the old, battered red truck was enough to have Linc growling.

"Didn't I say we need to talk?" He kept his voice low, in deference to the other people getting in their vehicles around them. Luckily, Jacob had parked toward the back of the lot, but he still didn't want a public argument any more than Jacob did.

"Did I miss the part where you're in charge of me?" Jacob met him harsh whisper for harsh whisper.

"Not in charge, no, but I'm entitled to an opinion. I care—"

"Do you?" Jacob raised an eyebrow. Darker than his blondish hair, his expressive eyebrows always gave him a roguish appearance. "You care? Since when?"

Since always. Since the sun had caught Jacob's hair six years ago and… But he couldn't afford such fanciful thoughts, and sure as hell wasn't sharing them. "You're like family to me. All of you."

"Really? Family? Because if I recall there was nothing familial about what happened after the funeral. There hasn't been anything *family* about you and me for years now, and you know it."

"We're not talking about that." He was impressed at how firm his voice came out, given the way his insides were quaking.

"Yeah, God forbid we talk about *that*. Stop pretending—"

"Stop dodging the real issue. Unless…" His facial muscles tensed as he considered another possibility for Jacob's determination. "Is that what this is about? You trying to stick it to me? A giant F-U? Some sort of payback?"

"No." The fire in Jacob's eyes flared brighter, more dangerous. "And fuck you for thinking that. I've worked damn hard for this moment. Don't flatter yourself that I'd break my back to get you to finally stop polishing your halo and notice me."

I notice you. Every damn day. Of course, he couldn't say that, could only stay silent in the face of Jacob's fury. Jacob made an exasperated noise. Most of the rest of the crowd had cleared out, leaving only a few vehicles in the parking lot.

"I get it, okay? I get that everyone's still missing Wyatt. I miss him too. And now Mom's scared I'm going to go the same way. I didn't expect anyone to be happy for me, not now. But not a single person at least a little proud, that stings. Everyone assuming I'm some selfish brat of a kid and not giving me an ounce of credit for knowing my own mind, that fucking sucks."

The pain in his voice squeezed Linc like a vise. "Jacob—"

"Save it." With that, Jacob swung up into the cab of the truck. "Just save it, Linc. You said your piece. I'm still doing this."

But Linc hadn't said everything, not by a long shot, and as Jacob drove away, in a cloud of gravel and dust, he couldn't shake the feeling that he hadn't said a damn thing at all.

Chapter Three

"What were you thinking, contacting Linc?" Jacob's words were tempered by a sleeping Willow on his shoulder, a warm, sweet-smelling baby weight that made it hard to be mad at his mother. Not that he was that furious to begin with—his boots over by the door and fast reply to her summons for dinner bore witness that some of his earlier rage had settled.

"I was thinking that I couldn't sleep last night, thinking of you out there. I was thinking that I'm not ready to lose anything—anyone—else." The haunted look in her eyes as she turned away from the stew she was stirring stole his appetite and made him swallow hard. He hated knowing he'd cost her sleep, added to her burdens. May too. Usually friendly, she'd barely spoken to him when he'd arrived, disappearing to check on Junior and leaving him with the baby and his mother's disappointment.

"It doesn't help a little if I remind you that I've been training for this for years? If I promise to keep myself safe, not take any stupid risks?"

"You can be safe all you want, but all it takes is once…" Her voice cracked.

He squished his eyes shut, clamping down on the

emotion that surged through him. She wasn't wrong. "I know. But you can say the same thing about lots of other stuff. Driving even. Life's full of risks and un-certainties."

"Maybe so, but I don't have to like it." Her chin took on a stubborn tilt that he recognized from the reflection he saw in the mirror every morning. "And I'm not going to apologize for texting Linc."

"Fair enough." He hadn't really expected her to, just as he hadn't expected a congratulations for getting the call up to the smoke jumper team. But she was his mom, and she loved him, and she was dishing him up a huge portion of her famous stew, and right then it was enough. It had to be.

"You can set her in the playpen, you know." May came into the dining area that adjoined the open kitchen where his mother was working, trailed by Junior, who had his ever-present bear in one hand. "I didn't mean you had to hold her. You're spoiling her."

"Now, what good is an uncle if he can't spoil the kids?" Trying to soften her up, he gave her his best smile as he carefully laid the sleeping baby in the nearby playpen so they could all eat, not about to admit that he'd kept a hold of the baby to calm himself down as much as any other reason. He loved all the nieces and nephews, always had, but there was something about baby Willow that put everything into perspective.

"You're a good uncle." May gave him a half smile, which was more than he'd earned in a few weeks from her. She got Junior settled at the table before grabbing two of the bowls Jacob's mom had served up. "And thank you for cooking, Jenna. I feel bad that I didn't help more—"

"Nonsense. You know I love cooking for my kids. The more the merrier, and I love having you here."

May and her kids had moved in with his mom back in September, while May was waiting for the life insurance to clear and trying to decide what to do next. The plan for staying for a few weeks had turned into months, and Jacob knew his mom was hoping they continued to stay on with her.

"Speaking of a full house, what do you want for your birthday next Sunday?" he asked his mom as she joined them at the table with her own bowl and a basket of rolls. He wanted to get the conversation away from his first day at training, especially with May there.

"I'm not sure it feels right, having a party..." she demurred.

"You deserve one," he said firmly. "You said it yourself that you're happiest with a big gathering. Let us do that for you."

"Grandma needs a party! We can have cake!" Junior piped up from his spot next to May.

"Well..."

"Wyatt would want it," May said softly, studying her stew. "You know he loved a party as much as you. Let's get the other kids here, maybe a few of your friends. Fill the house."

"Yeah." His throat tightened at the mention of Wyatt, but May was right. "I'll help, come over early, help clean, do whatever you need done."

"I can order the cake," May offered. "A nice big sheet cake from that place in Sisters you love, Jenna."

"I can tell when I'm outnumbered." His mom laughed, a more world-weary sound than usual, but welcome nonetheless. "I guess we're having a party."

"Yup. Now what are we cooking?" He kept them on party planning for a while, deciding which of his mom's favorite party foods to serve, and going over who to invite and what to plan to keep the younger kids busy.

"We need to invite Lincoln," his mom said as May took notes for a to-do list.

"Of course." May didn't stop writing, but his mom looked at him like he was supposed to add something.

"What? Sure. Invite Linc." It wasn't like he could protest. The guy had been included in every major family event that they could drag him to for years and years.

"You need to ask him. I feel bad, asking him to talk you out of going today. Especially with things already... strained. He needs to know there are no hard feelings."

He sighed rather than rattle off a retort that maybe she should have thought of that *before* she texted. "Just call him. You know he loves you. He'll come if he's free."

It went without saying that Linc had turned down more invitations than he'd accepted in the past year, but pointing that out would bring up all sorts of issues better left unexamined.

"I will, but still you should ask him. Tomorrow at training. He'll be less likely to come up with an excuse if you ask him in person." His mom might be one of the nicest people in the area, but she could be downright commanding when she wanted to be.

"Okay, okay. Maybe I'll stop by his place on my way home. That way I'm not blindsiding him at work." And that way he wouldn't give him the opportunity for another public argument. He refused to admit he might have any other reason for stopping by Linc's house. And he wasn't lying—Linc's place was on the way back into town, just past Jacob's parents' property, and well before the town started. He passed that turnoff every damn day without giving in to temptation. He had no reason to change that now, no reason to go resurrecting feelings better left buried in the past where he stored all his other regrets. He'd deliver his message and be on his way, back to that headspace where every damn mention of Linc didn't hit him in vulnerable places he needed to protect at all costs.

"Sit down, you greedy mutt." Still toweling off, Linc stared down Bandit until he plopped his substantial ass on the kitchen floor next to the food bowls. Always calmer but no less eager for dinner, Shadow was already in position, looking eagerly at the large plastic bin where their chow was stored.

"Fine, fine. You win." He went ahead and fed them a little early because they'd been good while he'd been gone for the long first day of training. Later on in the summer when long callouts became inevitable, they'd get visits from the teenage twins who lived on the next property over. Linc paid them for help with the dogs and watering the garden when he couldn't get to it.

The evening was cool enough that he pulled on sweats after finishing a fast trim with the clippers, still unable to shake his restlessness. It was going to take more than a shower to clear his head after the stress of the day. He'd tried both a weights workout and a long

shower, and neither had been enough to banish Jacob
from his thoughts. Checking on the seedlings lining the
dining table was hardly enough distraction either, but it
was April, which meant time to get the hardier plants
ready for the cold frame if he wanted to eat come fall.

He chafed at people who called his gardening a
hobby. It was more of a necessity when dealing with
unpredictable seasonal income, a habit he'd picked up
from his mom, repairing her setup and ensuring that
he wasn't entirely at his dad's mercy or others' charity
when it came to groceries.

The sound of tires on gravel had him pausing mid-
spritzing, setting aside the water bottle and heading for
the front porch, dogs fast at his heels. Despite his usual
lack of visitors this late, he wasn't startled, and indeed,
had already resigned himself to who it likely was even
before Wyatt's—*Jacob's*—truck came into view.

His dogs, fickle things with no common sense, both
rushed to Jacob even before he was out of the truck.
Knowing they weren't likely to listen, Linc didn't bother
to call them back. And it was impossible not to appreciate the way Jacob crouched low, petting each one in
turn, doling out praise. He might well be pissed at Linc,
but he didn't take it out on the dogs.

"You change your mind about the job?" Not wanting to let Jacob's behavior with the dogs soften him
too much, Linc bypassed all the bullshit and potential
hemming and hawing and got right to what he wanted
to know.

"Fuck no." Jacob shook his head before he straightened. "Mom sent me."

Funny how three simple words could make his gut

churn, memories of the last time Jacob had been in his driveway bearing news swarming him, making it impossible to step off the porch.

"What are you doing here?" Only the fact that the dogs had raised a ruckus had brought Linc off the couch, and one look at Jacob's face had him wishing he'd stayed put, waited for him to give up and leave.

"Mom sent me." Jacob's face, usually so playful, was as somber as Linc had ever seen it.

"Oh." Fuck. He'd been expecting that. Didn't make it any easier. But he'd been expecting it. Best to just get it over with. "There won't be any trouble. I don't have to go. Last thing I want is her bothered."

"What the hell?" Jacob blinked up at him, eyes red rimmed and lines around his mouth that weren't there a few days ago. "That's exactly the sort of crazy talk she sent me here to put a stop to. Said you didn't answer her texts."

"Didn't know what to say."

"How about yes? As in yes, you'll be there. She wants you to be a pallbearer, needs to know you got the message, that you're not too injured to help, and that you've got a suit."

Humbled to his core, Linc sank to the porch steps, surprised when Jacob joined him, further shocked when Jacob threw an arm around him. "Don't know if I can do that," he whispered.

"Because you're injured?"

God, it would be so easy to lie to anyone other than Jacob, who always seemed to pull deep truths loose from Linc's chest. "Because it's my fault."

Nearly nine months later, and he still felt the truth of

those words, still the same humility that Jenna and the rest of the Hartman family wanted a damn thing to do with him. The official cause of death had been equipment failure combined with a bad landing—Wyatt had been treed due to high winds, and he'd come in hard, then a connector had broken, sending him plummeting before Garrick and Linc could reach him. Everyone said it was a fluke and part of the risk of doing the job, but Linc couldn't shake the guilt over not reaching him in time and over possibly missing something when cross-checking Wyatt's equipment.

"What does your mom need?" Somehow he got the question out in a normal voice.

"It's her birthday next week. Sunday. We're going to have a party for her. Food. Cake. The usual. And she wants you there." The porch lights danced off Jacob's hair as he came to stand in front of Linc on the porch. No way, no how was he letting Jacob in the house.

"Sunday? I might have plans. I promised to help Ray get in better shape." Of course that was scheduled for early in the morning, but Jacob didn't need to know that. But judging from how his eyes narrowed, he saw right through Linc's pretext anyway.

"All day? We're talking late afternoon. You can spare a couple of hours, make her happy. Hell, bring Ray along if you want. She likes his wife and kids. But she seems set on you making an appearance."

"I'll see." Crossing his arms in front of his chest, he tried to will Jacob back to his truck, errand completed. But Jacob didn't seem in any hurry, leaning against the porch rail and idly scratching Bandit's head.

"Linc. Can't you set aside how pissed you are at me for an afternoon?"

He didn't know how to tell Jacob that it wasn't him that he was mad at but rather himself, so he just shrugged.

"People are starting to notice how you never want to show up when I'm around. I swear that's why she insisted that I be the one to do the asking. And I get it, okay? Everything's awkward now. But it doesn't have to be."

But it did. He didn't know how to make it stop, all the snippets of memories that assaulted him every damn time he saw Jacob. And maybe Jacob could forget, but he couldn't.

Mouths. Hands. Desperate clutching need. Overwhelming grief.

"Don't send me away."

"I've got you."

Regret, sharp and swift.

The regret and recriminations tinged every replay, to the point that all he could handle were little flashes, and guilt that kept him away from the family. But he owed Jenna.

"I'll come." He forced out the words. Jacob was wrong, of course. There wasn't an alternative to awkward and stilted, at least not one he'd found.

"Good." Jacob's face softened, a vulnerability in his eyes that wasn't often there. "We were friends once, right?"

Fuck. Linc had to swallow hard. He really was an asshole of the first degree. It hadn't occurred to him that Jacob might have noticed his absence, let alone cared. And certainly not enough to hurt. Jacob was tough as they came. No way could Linc wound him. Except maybe he had.

"We were," he allowed, even though that was something of a lie. His traitorous body hadn't allowed him anything as benign as friendship with Jacob in almost six years, and he wasn't expecting a truce to make a lick of difference in that regard, but he also hated the idea that he'd hurt Jacob.

"Would it be *that* hard to try for, I don't know, maybe civil? Not avoiding? We're going to work together all season. It seems like the least we could do is try to get along."

"I'll do better." Trying might kill him, but he'd walk over glass before he intentionally harmed Jacob. "But don't ask me to be happy about you joining the crew. It's a bad idea, and you're not gonna sway me otherwise."

"Fair enough. You not acting like I'm radioactive would be a nice improvement, so thank you."

"I'll try." Linc couldn't deny acting like that. Truth was that Jacob was his kryptonite, always had been, and he was but a mortal man. So he'd done what felt like the only sensible thing and given him a wide berth.

"You're not going to ask me in, are you?" Jacob shook his head, resignation in his eyes before turning his attention back to the dogs, who were soaking up all the pats and head scratches. "Your owner's a big scaredy-cat, thinking I'm gonna drag him to the bedroom, relieve him of all that needless virtue."

"You tell yourself that." Linc matched him light tone for light tone, body remembering how good banter with Jacob felt even as his brain continued to churn. And actually, Linc was worried that *he* would be the one doing the dragging and the corrupting.

"Anyway, I said my piece. Don't let Mom down." Stretching, Jacob stopped playing with the dogs, waving them away.

"Wouldn't dream of it." With any luck and a whole lot of willpower where Jacob was concerned, he never would. "Surprised she's not madder that I didn't succeed in talking you out of this notion of yours."

"Oh, she saved all that mad for me." Jacob sounded weary, and Linc remembered what he'd said earlier about no one being proud of him. He wanted to be that person, wanted to tell Jacob how damn proud he was of the man he'd become, but couldn't get the words past the terror in his heart. And Jacob could tell himself that Linc's concern was all about Wyatt and Jacob's mom and their disapproval, but Linc knew the truth—he was scared of something happening to Jacob on a personal level that he didn't want to examine too closely and that he sure as hell wasn't ever giving voice to.

"You worked hard," he managed. Not quite praise or pride, but an acknowledgment nonetheless.

"Yeah, I did." Jacob turned toward the truck. Linc's mouth opened, about to say who knew what, something without permission from his brain, but then Jacob added, "See you tomorrow."

His mouth slammed shut. Fuck. Not only was Jacob as off-limits as they came, but he was now a coworker, whether Linc liked it or not. And that meant that everything—*everything*—would go unsaid. It was undoubtedly for the best, but he still couldn't stop the ache in his chest as Jacob drove away, the nearly overwhelming sense of loss.

Chapter Four

Damn Linc for getting in Jacob's head all over again, getting him rattled. Even on his drive to the air base, after a night of fitful sleep following their conversation, he was still antsy. He'd revealed too much, practically begging Linc to be friendly again, go back to how things had used to be. But if he was honest, things hadn't been good and easy between them in years. There was always this undercurrent of potential, something that could be and yet never was. But the past few months had been the worst of all, feeling Linc's absence like a scab that refused to fully heal. He'd missed him and hated himself for doing the missing. It made him feel weak, and there was nothing he hated more.

And still he'd gone to him, asked him to come around again, and not just for Jacob's mom. Almost like he was one of Linc's rescue dogs, pathetically grateful for any scrap of attention paid to him. So yeah, damn Linc and his ever-present fucking nobility. No one did guilt quite as well as him. And the worst thing was that it was that same nobleness that made him so damn attractive—he was as loyal and steadfast as they came, solid and dependable, thoroughly incorruptible.

"Come on, Linc. One drink. What's the harm, especially if no one knows?" He'd been on this quest ever since Linc took the time to teach him how to drive stick. He'd never been so grateful for learning to drive on his parents' automatics as those few hours alone with Linc. And maybe he needed to give it up, but he'd seen the heat in Linc's eyes too many times to let this drop.

"I'd know. And that's enough." Linc didn't look up from stirring the firepit.

"I'd rather have fun than sleep alone with my high-and-mighty principles."

"You might be old enough to buy your liquor these days, but you're still a kid. A man's only as good as his word." Linc's words landed squarely as a roundhouse to Jacob's jaw, enough to have him recoiling, needing to shake it off.

"Does it ever cross your mind that maybe you gave your word to the wrong guy?" he asked, hating the edge to his voice. *Fucking Wyatt. Always getting there first.*

"Nope." If Linc was lying, Jacob sure as hell couldn't tell from the set of his jaw or the way he stared straight ahead.

He tried to take some solace in the fact that Linc had said he'd come to the party, had said he'd do better, because Linc did keep his word. Maybe today wouldn't be so bad. Stomach more settled, he made a beeline for the free coffee at training, trying not to look around for Linc too much. Above the coffee table was the big board of names of the jumpers with the most jumps under their belts. Wyatt was way up there. Linc too. Jacob wanted his name up there in the worst way. He was going to make this work, no matter what anyone else thought.

Today's training would begin with class time in deference to a packed day of preparing the rookies for their first jumps.

"Quick. Look like we're friends." Kelley followed him to the rows of folding chairs, looking far more awake than him with shining eyes and short hair more spiked than the day before.

"Someone overstepping?" He didn't envy the harder road the women on crews always had. Not that he'd had the smoothest of rides as an out gay guy, but at least he didn't usually have creeps hitting on him or questioning whether he could do the work at all.

"Guy over there implied I won't be able to do the pack-out, saying 115 pounds might be more than I can handle over that distance. Suggested he give me private pointers." She rolled her eyes as they took seats together toward the back of the room. "I'd rather not have to tell him no a second time."

"Skinny one with the dark hair? That's Ross. He was a friend of Wyatt's from way back. You could probably bench-press him if you wanted. I might pay to watch you drop-kick him too."

"I know, right? That's what I'm saying." Laughing, Kelley gave him a grateful smile. "Later today they're assigning us to senior crew members as buddy jumpers for the duration of training. Lord, please don't let them give me the weasel. Word is we'll probably be paired up with them out in the field too."

The smoke jumpers usually operated in small crews of three or four, getting shipped out together to various fires and tasks, working as a unit for much of the season. Like Kelley, he wanted to end up on a good crew, preferably one without drama or assholes.

"Maybe they'll give you McKenna." He named one of the senior women on the crew. "She's good and she's been around years. Ditto Pope. But not everyone's like Ross. Plenty of good people. I can vouch for Linc—Reid—and Ray too. Their buddy Garrick Nelson's a player, but not obnoxious about it."

"Thanks for the heads-up. And I'll repay the favor—our fellow rookie Jimenez was on the Winema crew with me. Don't hook up with him—he talks."

"Not looking to hook up with anyone." It wasn't a total lie—he'd learned his lesson early on about fishing where he worked. Fire crews worked too many long hours together. Some dating around was probably inevitable from the close contact, but it almost always ended messily. But while he had no intention of making a move on anyone else on the crew, he knew himself, knew Linc was different. There had been a moment last night, right as Jacob was about to leave, when Linc had almost wavered. And even knowing it would be beyond stupid career-wise, Jacob still wanted him, had still held his breath when Linc's mouth had moved, had still known the sting when he'd said nothing.

And that blasted obsession reared its head again as soon as Linc took a seat a few rows ahead of them with Ray and Garrick. His eyes kept drifting over to Linc even as the lecture on basic jump safety procedures started. The instructor kept randomly calling on people mid-talk, just like this one history teacher he'd had in high school. Five other Hartman kids before him, and he alone was the one with the fidgety legs and restless mind that drove teachers crazy. And it wasn't that he couldn't pay attention—he could, hyper-focused at times, but other times it was like his brain couldn't decide which of the nine million pieces of information it was receiving to focus on. He'd taken ADHD meds as a kid, found some focus in martial arts as a teen, but still did best with active, hands-on learning and struggled mightily in a traditional classroom setup. Even McKenna's PowerPoint wasn't enough to hold his attention.

"Hartman? Hartman, did you have something to add?"

"I'm sorry. What?" Fuck. From McKenna's tone, she'd already asked him a question, and it had taken him far too long to realize she was speaking to him and that she needed a reply.

"I asked what you thought about the most important thing to remember for your first jump?"

Oh, hell. His mind went utterly blank, and he glanced around helplessly. He *knew* this, had reviewed the jump manuals, but such was the curse of his brain under pressure sometimes. As his eyes flitted around the room, they landed on Linc again, whose face was creased with concern.

"Calm," Linc mouthed. What the heck? He was supposed to calm down? Now? *Oh, wait.* That was part of the answer. Linc, for whatever reason, was trying to help.

"Stay calm. Don't panic. Listen to the person you're tandem jumping with," he said quickly, brain back online.

"Very good." She kept frowning at him, though. "Hopefully we're not putting you to sleep?"

"No, ma'am. I'm listening," he assured her. And he did try to do a better job for the remainder of the lecture.

On break he wanted to thank Linc for the assist but he was deep in conversation with Ray and Garrick and no way was Jacob pointing out Linc's help in front of them. They didn't need another reason to see him as Wyatt's flaky kid brother.

Linc took a long sip of coffee, and Jacob knew without looking that it was black. He wished that just once he could look at him without remembering. Because maybe Linc had forgotten in a rush of embarrassment and guilt, and months of avoidance to chase Jacob from his mind, but Jacob wouldn't ever forget, still wasn't able to drink coffee without remembering what it tasted like on Linc's lips.

"I need a ride back to my place. Don't want the dogs going nuts for their dinner." Linc threw away his paper coffee cup as he came over to where Jacob was standing outside the house. He was embarrassed to have to ask, Jacob could tell by the way his eyes darted away and his ears flushed pink. *"I told you this morning that I could drive myself."*

He had, but Jacob honestly hadn't been sure he'd show up without him dragging him there, and he'd been equally sure that he couldn't get through this hardest of days without Linc there. Simply sitting next to him shoulder to shoulder in the tightly packed pews had helped. But he wasn't going to admit that, so he just shrugged. *"Mom sent me. And I was right too—the church parking lot was packed."*

They'd arrived early and still had to park at the feed store on the other corner. Every seat was filled with *long-distance family, neighbors, people they'd gone to school with, teachers even, and firefighters from all over. Even now, a few hours later, he couldn't recall a word the preacher had said or remember which sad song his cousin had sung with her guitar. The choir had done "Amazing Grace," the refrain echoing in his ears as he drove Linc home in silence, neither of them up to small talk after the service followed by the meal in the church hall and then still more food and visitors back at the house, out-of-town mourners lingering.*

He didn't blame Linc one bit for wanting to be done and was actually damn glad for the excuse to head out himself.

"You need a hand with the dogs?" he asked as he turned down Linc's long gravel drive. It was the shallowest of stalling measures, but now that he was here, moments from being alone with his thoughts, he couldn't stand it. He had the idea of stopping on the way home, pick up some Jack, ensure he'd sleep at least, but the prospect of more time with Linc was far better than any liquor.

He expected Linc to turn him down, though, didn't anticipate his sharp nod.

"You might as well come in." Linc's voice was resigned. Maybe he was as reluctant to be entirely alone as Jacob was.

The low manufactured home that had been Linc's dad's was a humble gray, spruced up a bit by the green porch Linc had added a few years back. Linc bypassed the porch, went around to the back door, which led to a mudroom that gave access to a fenced dog run. As far as Jacob could tell, the dogs had a pretty pampered

*existence even when Linc was gone—big fluffy beds in
the mudroom, plenty of water, and a far more whimsical supply of toys than he would have expected from
their stoic owner.*

*He threw a rubber hamburger for them while Linc
changed out the water and dished up some dry kibble.
His mom hadn't had a dog in a few years, and Jacob
had missed the canine attention. Kinda like the little
kids at the funeral and all the after activities—meeting
their immediate needs was grounding.*

*"Your throwing arm tired yet?" Linc asked with a
weary smile. Despite his suit, Jacob had tossed the ball
for Junior and his cousins just to escape the house. Too
hot from the exertion, he'd left his suit coat in the truck.
Linc had taken his off to see to the dogs, shirtsleeves
rolled back now.*

*"Nah," he said as the dogs ran to their bowls, leav-
ing the two of them alone in the back doorway. He probably needed to head out, but his boots stayed rooted
to the spot.*

*"They got you dusty." In a surprise move, Linc
brushed something off Jacob's shoulder, putting them
face-to-face, inches apart. Linc's hazel eyes reflected
the grief that had dogged Jacob all damn day, an almost
visceral, physical ache, a heaviness he couldn't shake.*

*"Don't send me away," he whispered, putting a hand
on Linc's arm, keeping him there, not that Linc seemed
particularly inclined to retreat.*

*"Can't." Their eyes continued to hold, and he wasn't
sure who closed the gap. Maybe him. But suddenly they
were embracing, a tight hug.*

"Fuck. This is so fucking hard." His voice was thick,

muffled by Linc's neck, right there. He smelled like the
same combo of shampoo and classic aftershave he'd
used as long as Jacob could remember and felt so damn
solid and real in his arms. Eyes burning, Jacob held
on even as Linc pushed him against the wall. "Hurts."

"I know. Me too. Doesn't end. Keeps coming."

"Yeah." He had to swallow hard, trying to not give
in to the tears that had threatened all damn day. And
when Linc's mouth slammed down on his, he welcomed
it, water for his parched soul, soaking up the contact,
meeting him, desperation for desperation, desire for de-
sire. Linc tasted like the black coffee he'd been down-
ing all day and sweet like the cake foisted on them and
like five years of pent-up need. Or maybe that last bit
was all Jacob, relief and grief at war in his psyche as
he clung to Linc for all he was worth.

Now all he had was the memory of that taste, that
need, that desperation. And every time their eyes met,
he swore he could see memories of that kiss in Linc's
gaze, heat still flaring between them, brighter than ever.
Fuck. Why on earth had he thought that working together would be a simple matter? Seeing Linc like this,
every damn day, was going to be torture.

At least he had the hope of being paired with a different crew for the close work. Maybe if he only had to
see Linc here and there, in the locker room, at big meet-
ings, it wouldn't be so bad. And indeed, tuning Linc
out, focusing on the hands-on demonstration portion
of the pre-jump training was a good call as plenty of
important information was shared about all the steps
that went into being ready to jump. Planning. Prep.

Equipment readiness. Escape plans. Alternate options. Checks. And cross-checks.

Their first jump would be a very straightforward tandem jump, equivalent to a civilian sightseeing leap, none of their extra equipment and such yet, but still the instructors drilled them on each step of the process until a late lunch break. As they sat around the main training room with their food, several of the instructors passed out the afternoon's agenda and their team/ mentor assignments.

"Thank God." Next to him, Kelley smiled broadly as she looked down at her paper. "McKenna's crew. You were right. I don't recognize the other two names, but it's not Ross. Who'd you get?"

What he saw on his almost made him choke on his sandwich.

"What?" Kelley looked ready to whack him on the back.

"Linc. They gave me Linc." *Oh, fuck.*

Chapter Five

"Good. That worked out how I hoped." Garrick nodded as he folded his assignment sheet, neat creases that
would undoubtedly become a bird or rabbit. But Linc
was less interested in his origami than his words as he
gaped at his own sheet.

"What do you mean? You asked for Jacob?" He
shook the paper like that might make it say something
other than that Jacob was assigned to him, Garrick and
Ray for the season, the higher-ups apparently having decided to slot Jacob right into the spot Wyatt had vacated.

"Well, duh. How are we gonna keep him safe for his
mom if we can't keep an eye on him?" Garrick's tone
said that Linc was an idiot for not thinking of this idea
himself. "And we were going to need a fourth, one way
or another. Word is that they're going to move Ray into
more of the spotter role for us—keep him on the plane
this season, then see about him becoming a foreman
next year."

With each operation, one person always remained on
the plane, coordinating the jump from the air, selecting
the landing spots, relaying data from jumpers on the
ground about wind and terrain factors, dispatching ad-

ditional jumpers as needed, and coordinating the necessary cargo drop after the jumpers were on the ground. Last season, Ray had been their jumper-in-charge, relaying information from the fire back to dispatch and helping to establish safety zones and escape routes, so moving him to spotter was a natural progression, even if Linc didn't like it.

"Yeah." Ray nodded, setting aside his sandwich. "That's the talk Alder and I had yesterday. I'm getting old."

"You're not *that* old," Linc protested. Ray had maybe six years on him and Garrick, but Linc didn't like thinking of any of them as old or washed, even if he felt like it some days.

"I am. Staying fit enough for jump readiness is more and more of a challenge. I don't want to let you guys down, and management has always been my goal. God knows Betsy wants me off the fire line anyhow. You'll be jumper-in-charge when it's the three of you, then follow seniority for the larger operations. It'll work out, Linc. You'll see."

Linc, who had always tried to avoid management, was none too sure. "But Jacob? You guys actually asked for him?"

"Didn't think you'd have an issue." Garrick's forehead creased. "Lord knows you were heated enough about him being here to begin with. And it's not simply babysitting duty—he's one of the fittest rookies. Did you see him rattle off his PT test yesterday? He'll pass the pack-out, no problem, and he'll pull his weight. Might be nice if he listened a little harder, but we'll work with him, bust his ass when we need to, same as any other rookie."

He wished he had even an ounce of Garrick's confidence in this situation working out. And Jacob was far from any other rookie. Linc didn't get this terror in his heart over other smoke jumpers, didn't have the sense of crushing dread, and sure as hell didn't have inconvenient dreams remembering what they sounded like, tasted like, felt like. Garrick's approach made a hell of a lot of sense—keep Jacob as safe as they could for his mom—but nothing about how Linc felt toward Jacob made a lick of sense. And while he didn't exactly relish the idea of Jacob being on a different crew, maybe with people Linc didn't trust as much as Garrick and Ray, he sure as hell wasn't up for months of the closest proximity possible.

"Are we going to have a problem?" Ray asked in a low voice. "Alder might let us switch, but...he's already looking close at you, Linc. Might not want to appear too sensitive right now."

Fuck. All Linc wanted was to make it through this season. One last season here. The idea of moving on had never been so tempting, get away from everything and start fresh. Damn Jacob. And damn Wyatt too, leaving him in this pickle. And sure, he could quit now, try to catch on with another crew at a different base, but Garrick was right—doing that wouldn't keep Jacob any safer. At least he and Garrick could manage his load some.

"Nah. Like you said. We'll make it work."

"Good. We better decide who's tandem jumping with him today. Ray, buddy, you probably need the optional

PT run more than you need the jump." Garrick rubbed his hands together, clearly anticipating the airtime. But for a whole host of reasons, none of which had a damn thing to do with Garrick's jumping ability, Linc didn't want Garrick strapped to Jacob for the tandem jump.

"I'll do it," he said firmly. "You see if Alder will let you jump solo, get you your fix."

Garrick's mouth moved like he was going to object, but then he nodded as he stood. "I'll go try to catch Alder or Sims, talk myself into a spot on one of the planes. You can deal with our rookie."

He left right as Jacob headed their way, firm tilt to his jaw and stubborn glint in his eyes. He was spoiling for a fight, but Linc wasn't going to oblige him.

"I'll take our trash." Ray quickly scooped up both of their plates and cups before meandering away as Jacob came to stand right in front of Linc.

"So am I going to have to tell them we need a switch or are you?" Jacob glared at him.

"Neither," Linc said evenly. "Have a seat, Rook."

"You asked for this?" Anger flared in Jacob's eyes even as he complied and took the seat Garrick had vacated. "Think I can't hack it on my own? Think I need you and your crew playing guardian angel all season?"

"Simmer down. No, I didn't ask for this." He didn't rat out Garrick, though, wouldn't do that to a buddy. "But we'll deal, you and I. We don't want folks saying there's bad blood between us. Don't need that kind of gossip. And you know damn well I'm no one's guardian angel."

"Says you." Jacob all but rolled his eyes at him. But

then, that was always part of Jacob's appeal, the way he insisted on seeing the best in Linc, even at his worst.

"It's not your fault, Linc." Jacob's voice was raw but firm as he put his arm around Linc. *"You did everything you could. I believe that. Mom believes that. May believes that. Only one doubting you is you."*

"You weren't out there."

"Didn't have to be. I know you. This isn't on you. Ray and Garrick, they said it was an accident. That's good enough for me. Jump gone bad. Made worse by the fire and wind conditions. None of that's on you."

"I was the one who cross-checked his rig. Like I'd done so many times..." His voice went weak as his eyes burned.

"I know. Sometimes things happen." Jacob rested his head against Linc's.

The warmth of his skin and his words seeped into Linc's soul, burrowing beneath the layer of ice that had formed over his heart in the past seventy-two hours. *"Wish I could believe you."*

And even now, he still wished he had Jacob's faith in his own goodness. God, this was going to be a long damn summer, him so certain he was going to fail at the one thing that mattered now—keeping Jacob safe—and Jacob so darn sure that he could do no wrong.

"You'll listen to us." He got that Jacob had wanted this for years, that he was proud of his skills, that he'd earned the right to be here, but he still wasn't convinced this wasn't some big adrenaline rush for him. "That's all that matters. Not any...history between us. What matters is if we can count on you, if we can be a decent team."

"You can count on me." Jacob nodded, meeting his eyes with a seriousness that Linc didn't usually associate with him. "I mean it. And I'll listen. This morning…you know me, right? Lectures and classrooms and me don't always mix. But out there? I'll pay attention. Count on it."

"I get it. And trust me, I wasn't much better in school." Linc had to laugh because he knew Jacob's ADHD had given him a tough row to hoe, but he hadn't been much more popular with teachers himself, what with his dad's parental shortcomings and his own distaste for reading and being cooped up indoors. "Trust us and we'll trust you and the rest will work itself out."

He tried to sound like he believed that, tried to find confidence that this would be anything other than an utter disaster as the group came back together after lunch.

"I get to go!" Garrick crowed as he sat back down with them. "Sims said I can demonstrate proper plane exiting procedure when not in a tandem. Woohoo!"

"What was that you were saying about no thrill seeking?" Addressing only Linc in a whisper, Jacob raised an eyebrow. "All serious business, right?"

He had to shift in his chair because Jacob had him there. "Never said you can't take satisfaction in the work where you find it."

"Uh-huh. I take it that him going solo means I'm jumping with you?"

"Yep. And you remember that whole listening bit. Garrick, he's got years of jump experience. This is your first time—"

"I trust you to be gentle." Jacob had the nerve to bat

his eyes. No one was paying them any mind, but still he should know better than to flirt like that on the job. Drawn into Jacob's good mood as he so often was, Linc had to fight the urge to laugh, not wanting to encourage him more. And damn him for making Linc think about sex, wonder about experience Jacob had or didn't have, preferences in the bedroom, all the things he was supposed to have banished from his brain.

But he had to leave sex thoughts behind as they headed to the airstrip. He'd been at this enough years to know the pilot and the crew who would be taking them up, ten at a time, in the small plane. In addition to his group, they also had McKenna's group going up. Jacob and their rookie, Kelley, kept joking around while waiting, even as Linc grew more and more... Not nervous. He didn't do nervous and this wasn't his first jump since...

Okay. Maybe he was a little nervous, especially since it wasn't simply his own neck on the line. He checked all their rigging again, every connection point, and called McKenna over for another cross-check.

"Are you going to be okay?" she asked in a low voice as she verified his work. "I heard you did some civilian jumps over the winter. Good for you, getting back out there. We're lucky to have you again this season, Reid. Don't forget who you are."

Her pep talk wasn't unappreciated—she was one of the best they had, and if she believed in him, that went a long way. He wished he could believe as easily as everyone else did. She was right—he'd worked with a civilian outlet to get his legs under him again. And it had been a little extra cash, taking tourists up. In general, when he wasn't a wreck, he liked tandem jumping, enjoyed managing someone else's experience, giving them a good ride down, showing off his skills. It was far different than a jump for work where every second counted and precision mattered far more than any style points as they battled the elements.

That day was a mix of the two—clear blue skies, not a fire in sight, no two-minute warning to get geared up, and a bunch of rookies as eager as any tourists, the start of the many jumps the rookies would need before the real deal.

Finally, it was their turn, smooth ride as the plane achieved the right altitude near the landing zone. He'd grown used to this view of the mountains and valleys beneath them, so it was kind of neat, seeing Jacob and Kelley get more excited, pointing out the terrain below them and marveling at how far they could see in all directions. He'd always loved Jacob's ability to find joy in all situations from tossing a toy for the dogs to building a fire in the firepit to playing softball with the family. Heck, he even made working out and cleaning seem joyous, that infectious smile lightening any load.

But as they got ready to jump, true to his word, Jacob stayed still and at attention as Linc clipped them together and triple-checked everything one last time. His back was to Linc's front, and for once his nearness didn't affect Linc on a visceral level as he was more concerned with making sure the thick black webbing of the harness was secure.

"Watch Garrick," he ordered as Garrick went first, demonstrating how they'd need to learn to exit without hesitation, precise timing on the spotter's signal, his smooth movements and easy smile for the rookies the product of years of experience. Once he was away, McKenna and Kelley were next, Kelley doing a good job looking more excited than terrified as they leaped on the signal, not even yelling like most of the tourists he'd jumped with. Jacob was similarly calm as they waited for their signal.

You've done this before, Linc had to remind himself, taking a deep, steadying breath before adjusting his goggles. It being Jacob and being right now, after everything that had happened, shouldn't make any difference, except it did. For the first time pre-jump, possibly ever, his stomach roiled. Fuck. But there was no time to puke or even to hesitate as the spotter gave them their signal, and his training took over for his jumbled brain, leaping in unison with Jacob.

Then Jacob made a sound, not a yell precisely, but a noise of pure delight that cut right through all the fog in Linc's brain and loosened the stranglehold anxiety had on his chest. He didn't have to see Jacob's face to know that he was grinning. Jacob stretched his arms wide, enjoying the free fall, flying for the first time, and through him, Linc saw everything new and wonderful again—the trees and hills beneath them, endless panorama, pure blue sky, the rush of the wind coming up to greet them.

"About to deploy the chute," he shouted to Jacob after checking his altimeter. Because of the additional weight of a tandem jump, they used larger than normal main parachutes and deployed them sooner to decrease velocity.

"Already?"

"You're gonna fit in just fine." He had to smile himself as he pulled the rip cord. At least Garrick would have a new jump junkie for company this season. The jolt of the parachute pulling them up made Jacob whoop again. By the end of the summer, all this would be old hat to him, and the seriousness of the job would take over, but right then Linc let him have his fun, steering them in gentle swoops, drinking in Jacob's laughter until he was laughing right along with him, until they were truly doing this *together* in a way none of Linc's other tandem jumps had experienced, a synergy that left him breathless as they approached the landing zone.

They landed about as close to textbook as possible, a soft touchdown that got another pleased sound from Jacob.

"Fuck yeah. We did it!"

"Yeah, we did. You're going to do great for the solo jumps. Good job keeping your head about you." He'd praise any rookie jumper, but something about Jacob made his voice warmer, more intimate. Their eyes met as he unclipped them, and an unexpected closeness blanketed them. This was why he hadn't wanted Garrick to be the one to jump with Jacob. He was selfish, had wanted this all for himself, had wanted to be the one to put that look of awe on his face.

Only the presence of the others nearby, also laughing and shouting, stopped him from embracing Jacob. Even a backslapping hug felt too risky for all the big emotions churning inside him. Damn it. How was he supposed to get through a whole season of this? Maybe he wasn't as old and washed as he'd feared, but he sure as heck was screwed.

Chapter Six

"What do you mean I'm not ready?" Jacob had been looking forward to the first static line solo jump all week. The jump that enabled them to practice correct body positioning while still connected to the aircraft was supposed to be the capstone of the first week of training, prelude to next week's intense practices and more solo jumps with increasing autonomy. They'd have the weekend off, which was a good thing, what with Jacob's mom's birthday party. But right now, he wanted to jump more than he wanted two days off.

"I mean you're not ready." Linc stared him down.

Unfortunately, rookies needed their jumper-in-charge to sign off before they got to go. And Linc was being a damn pain in the ass. He and Garrick had been drilling him all morning on body positioning and how to deploy the reserve chute in the event of an emergency. That was the part he'd messed up on when they quizzed him, forgetting to mention cutting the main line, even though he *knew* that.

"You're too cocky." Ray, who would be going up with him as spotter, was usually quieter than the other two, but now wore a frown even deeper than Linc's. "This is way riskier than the tandem jumping. I'm with Linc on this one. We'll let the other groups go ahead of us. You need another run-through. Start by showing me your gear. Each part of the deployment bag assembly."

Fuck. This was typical of the past few days—the instructors gave them work and then his crew gave him double on top of that. All the rookies had stuff like extra inventory and hauling gear, but his guys in particular seemed to delight in keeping him busy. But he couldn't complain—he'd wanted this, and while he hadn't asked to be on Linc's crew, there were no guarantees that anyone else would be easier.

He started again, labeling the static line sleeve, pack opening loop, sliding sleeve, safety wire and other gear components. Then Garrick had him demonstrate cutting a line from a piece of old rigging—like Jacob couldn't use an emergency knife on his own. But whatever. Finally, finally he was in line for the plane. And the good thing about being irritated at the others was that there wasn't a lot of room to be nervous about his first time jumping solo.

"Do good work," Linc said, clapping him on the shoulder. Seeing as how he usually avoided touching Jacob when not strictly necessary, that was nice. It was weird—when they'd tandem jumped together, for those few minutes, Jacob had never felt closer to anyone, but most of the time, he felt further away from Linc than ever despite working right next to him. And then Linc had to go and ruin the warm tingle from the contact, leaning in to add, "Don't fuck this up."

"Thanks for the vote of confidence." He glared at Linc before following Ray to the airstrip.

"I'll be working your deployment bag," Ray reminded him as they waited for the plane to return from the previous batch of trainees. "Just keep a clear head and listen to your comm set. You've got this."

"Glad someone thinks so," he grumbled.

"Hey now. You need to stop butting heads with Linc. No one's making you be here." Tone impatient, Ray scanned the sky.

"I *know*. But it feels like you guys are just waiting for me to tap out. And that's not happening, no matter how much work you pile on me."

"Good to know. And hell, I'd say it's nice to see you treating Linc normally instead of that crush you had on him several years back, except all this snapping is getting old quickly. You gotta find a happy medium, kid. Figure out how to work together for the season or else you're both going to be miserable."

"I…what?" Jacob's jaw was currently taking up residence on the tarmac. He hadn't thought anyone had picked up on that crush, except maybe him at nineteen had been way less subtle than him at almost twenty-five. Because his feelings hadn't changed one bit even if apparently his behavior had. But fuck a duck on Ray noticing *anything*. "I didn't…"

"Sure you did." Ray shrugged. "And you'll find some guys here with issues with you being out. God knows your brother ran his mouth enough. But not me. I've got a cousin. Married to a SEAL. Good guys. But Linc's not like that…" He made a dismissive gesture with his hand that Jacob had no idea how to interpret. Linc wasn't what? Out? No shocker there, but Jacob was never entirely sure who knew what with Linc—Wyatt had known or suspected something, but he didn't know about the rest of the friend circle. And he sure as hell wasn't going to be the one to out him so he said nothing as Ray continued on. "Anyway, what I'm trying to say is don't go letting yourself get hung up on him again, but maybe stop with assuming he—or any of us—are out to get you. We just want to keep your ass alive for the season."

"Thanks." Jacob wasn't sure what else to say. Definitely didn't want to make things worse, protest too much, or reveal that his crush persisted like moss on a shady roof, never truly gone. And he couldn't promise to do better, not when Linc drove him up the side of the mountain with a single look.

Luckily, he didn't have to say much more because the plane arrived back at the airstrip and it was their turn to go. Even though he knew the dangers, he wasn't particularly nervous—more like the pre-fight jitters he'd had in MMA or the giddy anticipation of Christmas as a kid. It was another step closer to his ultimate goal, and with any luck, jumps like these would be routine soon enough. But he wasn't stupid either—he listened to Ray and the other flight crew, pushed out all other thoughts, including all those inconvenient ones about Linc, until he was leaping out into the perfect light blue spring sky, high above the world.

He didn't let the rush of free-falling distract him from the proper body positioning they'd been practicing, the arch of torso critical to maintaining stability, ready this time for the jerk back of the parachute as it deployed from the static line, then following the radio commands as he guided the parachute to the landing zone. Everything went from model-train-set tiny to larger than life rapidly, barely enough time to take in the scattered buildings below, the forest stretching beyond that. The whole enterprise took a matter of minutes—days of buildup to mere seconds really. But wow, the rush of adrenaline and satisfaction really was something, and the high lingered even as he did the remainder of his duties for the day. He wasn't intentionally slow, but his crew had heaped a lot of fiddly tasks on him, so he was one of the last to leave the facility, only a few vehicles left in the parking lot.

And somehow he'd known, known the whole time he was floating down to earth and then stowing gear and doing end-of-the-day chores, that Linc would be here, waiting by his truck. Linc's own truck was conveniently three spaces over. He'd parked in the back of the lot again, by the trees, out of view of the facility, but still rather open for an argument if that's what Linc was spoiling for.

"So." Linc regarded him coolly. "You didn't die. Or fuck up."

"There is that." He met Linc's gaze, didn't waver. What was it going to take for Linc to believe in him, really *believe* that Jacob could do this? Not having an answer to that made his back muscles tense and his voice testy. "Ray was a good spotter. No problems there. Well, other than the fact that he seems to be under the impression that I once had a hopeless crush on you."

A sputtering noise escaped Linc's pursed lips, expression damn near priceless, all wide-eyed horror. "He what?"

"I know. That was my reaction too, only inside. Man. Your face." He had to laugh, keep from flipping out like

Linc. "I kept it cool in front of him, but what the hell? He even warned me to not get hung up on you again."

"As far as advice goes that ain't terrible." Rubbing his jaw, Linc looked away. He didn't seem particularly shocked by the crush thing, only that Ray had known, not that Jacob had expected anything different. He *had* been damn obvious when he'd first returned from Vegas. And afterward too, the years that followed, all his flirting and innuendo, not all of it as private as it probably should have been. It was easy to forget sometimes that this was a small town and people talked. "He say anything else worth noting?"

"That we need to get along. Apparently, I'm being a pain in the ass."

"He's not wrong there either." Linc breathed hard, like he was working overtime to convince himself this was no big deal. But Jacob wasn't having any of Linc shoving all the blame on him.

"Come off it. You know damn well I'm not the entire reason things are weird. It's not all on me being stubborn."

"No, it's not." Exhaling like he'd just been gut punched, Linc slid in closer, stealing the last of Jacob's oxygen as he yanked him close, bringing their mouths together.

Their last kiss had been tense from the start, grief-fueled, regrets seeping in even while they were still lip-locked. This wasn't that.

No, it was raw and hungry and more than a little angry, like Linc wanted to use his mouth to extract something from Jacob. Maybe a promise to be nicer. Or to give up smoke jumping. Something. It was impossible to think with Linc kissing him so thoroughly that it was a wonder there weren't scorch marks in the gravel at their feet. It was coffee and cinnamon and a hot, questing tongue that sought to singe his every last nerve ending until all he could do was gasp and hold on.

"Jesus, *Linc*," he managed when Linc finally let him up for air. "Were you that damn sure that I was going to fuck up the jump?"

"No. I…uh…" Linc stepped back, looking down at his hands like they'd betrayed him, reaching for Jacob. "Not sure what the hell came over me. Sorry. That… Damn. That was inexcusable. Sorry."

"Well, could it come over you back at your place?" Even though his mind was still spinning, Jacob put on a light smile. *Maybe…* "For a not-out guy who wants no drama on his crew you sure know how to take a risk." Gesturing at the nearly empty parking lot, he licked his lips, tasting Linc there.

He'd expected Linc's recoil, so it didn't hurt, much, when Linc stalked several paces away, looking stricken. "Fuck. I didn't mean… This is why it's crazy, us working together. The things you do to me…"

"Oh, it's all me, huh? Like I'm the mountainous equivalent of a mermaid, luring you to your doom? Damn it. This is not all me seducing you."

"I know it's not." Linc's voice was more subdued now. "The kiss is on me. And like I said, I'm sorry. It's not that I don't want…" Shaking his head, Linc shifted his tone even before Jacob could revel in him admitting to wanting Jacob. "But we can't do this."

"I take it that's a no on heading back to your place, working this out between your sheets?"

"Fuck. Is everything a joke to you? This isn't some game."

"No, it's not." Hadn't been a game in years, and Linc damn well knew that. He met him hard stare for hard stare before Linc turned on his heel, undoubtedly ready to go sulk somewhere and blame Jacob for all this when he had been the one doing the kissing. Again.

"Night," he called, determined that this wasn't the end of things, not by a long shot. "Don't forget about Mom's party Sunday."

Whirling around, Linc made a very ungracious noise. And it was a low blow to be sure, but it felt good to land the hit nonetheless, watching as Linc went pale then flushed, opening and closing his mouth a number of times.

"I'll be there," he ground out at last.

Jacob gave him a mock salute. "Counting on it."

Linc had seldom been so reluctant to have a day off, and not even a long run with Ray and Garrick early Sunday morning settled him. He didn't bring up Ray talking to Jacob while they worked out. First because he didn't want Garrick involved, but also because he didn't even know where to start. It wasn't that much of a surprise—anyone with eyes probably had noticed Jacob's behavior after Linc's dad died and Jacob was around helping him, a near daily thing. Then Jacob had come out and everything had gone to shit with Wyatt. Jacob had toned it down some over time, kept the flirting private, but Linc had been deluding himself if he'd thought Wyatt was the only one who had figured out Jacob had a crush back then.

Although, as he pounded out the miles along the back roads in companionable silence with his friends, dogs at their heels, he had to be honest with himself, admit that calling it a crush was maybe not the fairest to Jacob. That implied that Linc was blameless, like he hadn't eaten up the attention right up until Wyatt warned him off. Jacob at least had had the excuse of being nineteen, horny and on the rebound. Linc was supposed to be the older, wiser one, but even now he could recall exactly how Jacob had looked helping him move mountains of crap out of the house, muscles flexing right along with that damn dimpled grin, sun in his eyes, sweat rolling down his neck, a trail that Linc had wanted to trace with his tongue. Then Wyatt had reminded him where his loyalties lay, and he'd boxed up all those impulses, tried to forget the moments spent working side by side, Jacob a bright spark in one of the darkest of times in his life.

At least Ray thought all that was in the past, small mercies. Both his friends seemed oblivious to Linc's inner turmoil as they headed back toward his place. Which was how it should be. No one knew about that... *collision* after the funeral. And if Ray had a suspicion about Linc himself, well, he wouldn't be the only one of Linc's friends to know. Wyatt had, mainly because they'd been kids together and he'd told him everything once upon a time. Garrick knew. Linc had never been particularly good at faking attraction with women, bumped along here and there with some ill-advised short-term relationships, but mostly he'd just lived his life as he saw fit, privately as possible. It wasn't a state secret or anything, just something Linc preferred to keep away from work and stupid people.

Bigger issue was this thing with Jacob. Not that there was a *thing*, but Ray thought he sniffed smoke, and Linc needed to be damn sure there wasn't a fire for him to find. Hell, he didn't know how to admit to himself let alone Ray that neither of them had ever let that long-ago attraction lie in the dirt where it belonged. No, it had merely shifted. Become a private game almost where Jacob tried to get him in bed, a score he was determined to settle, and Linc resisted, and not just because of Wyatt and having a healthy love of his own skin. No, he'd resisted because those old feelings, those moments, they weren't a game to him, not ever. Not even when they drove him to do desperate things like after the funeral and again on Friday when he'd lost his damn mind, kissing Jacob in the parking lot, when he didn't even have the excuse of grief and guilt.

Nope, this one was all on him. And if he replayed that kiss, over and over while he showered after the run, well, that was between him and the hot water. He'd tried rationalizing the kiss all weekend as relief that Jacob had come back in one piece from his first solo jump. That was why he'd waited around, thinking he might as well tell Jacob he'd done well, give him some of that praise he always seemed to be seeking. But that was a lie. He could have simply sent a quick text, told him "good job." No, he'd waited around because he'd needed to touch him, needed proof that he was okay. Need, not relief, had driven him. He'd needed Jacob, needed the touch and taste of him, until nothing, not even news of Ray's warnings could stop him from kissing Jacob like a drowning man clinging to the last buoy.

And now he had to go to Jenna's party, act normal,

and most definitely not lose his head like that again.
Which meant getting ready, even if he didn't particularly want to. Because he'd been the hungry Reid kid
showing up empty-handed to Hartman family gatherings too many years when younger, he refused to do it
now. So after his shower, Ray and Garrick long gone, he
made a plate of deviled eggs to take to the party. Mrs.
Billups, a widow he helped from time to time, had had
extra eggs when he fixed her fence the day before. He
wasn't one to let food go to waste. So eggs. All fancy,
his mother's recipe from a cookbook older than he was.
And a clean shirt, one with buttons, and him showing
up at the party only a little after the appointed time.

"Hey! It's Uncle Linc!" Jacob greeted him at the
door, holding baby Willow in one arm, Junior right
behind him.

Linc's heart did that funny thing it always did when
he saw Jacob with the nieces and nephews. Stupid heart
had damn near beat out of his chest at the hospital after
Willow was born, when he'd seen Jacob holding the
baby while Jenna held May, who was crying because
Wyatt wasn't there to see.

"Here." Like back then, Jacob passed him the baby,
who was bigger now, a warm weight to settle in the
crook of his arm while he handed off the eggs to Jacob,
a trade-off as easy as if they did it daily. The baby didn't
even protest the change, snuggling into Linc as they all
trooped toward the open kitchen.

"I found Uncle Linc," Junior announced in a carnival-
barker-loud voice. Looking at him was a flashback thirty
years ago to Wyatt in kindergarten, faded memories of
a little blond boy with a big family and a long ride into

town on the school bus filled with shared sticks of gum and crumbled trading cards. A friendship born of convenience but forged in blood nonetheless.

"Find a seat," Jenna called, so Linc took a chair next to some older boy cousins playing on tablets at the table, transferring the baby to his other shoulder.

"Do you need me to take her?" May flitted over, thinner than he'd seen her last, but somehow less fragile, not quite stretched so tissue-paper thin. Maybe living here with Jenna suited her. And maybe too it was the passage of time, the relentless march forward that Linc tried not to dwell on.

"Nah. She's fine."

"Thanks, Linc." She gave him a pat on the shoulder before heading back to the kitchen.

"You're always the baby magnet. We need to find you a wife." Jon, one of the older Hartman siblings, slapped him on the back, giving a meaningful glance in May's direction.

"Gonna nip that bad idea in the bud right now," Linc said in a low, firm whisper. Jon was only a year younger than him and Wyatt. They'd all hung around some, had their first beers and plenty of other adventures together.

"What? I'm just saying—"

"Well, don't. And don't let her catch you at it either." Even if Linc were so inclined in that direction, May was so far off-limits as to be wrapped in barbed wire. Luckily, the feeling appeared to be mutual, with her always cordial but cool, the way she was with all Wyatt's buddies. But the last thing he needed was the all-too-helpful Hartman clan playing matchmaker.

Across the table from him, Jacob said nothing aloud,

but his eyes spoke volumes. *Tell him. Just set the record right. No wife for you.* He shrugged, like it was no big deal, while Linc went cold at the very thought.

Nope, he shot back with his own eyes. The family might have all dealt okay with Jacob coming out, but there had been some rocky years in there. And Linc didn't doubt that Jon would have a similar warning for him regarding Jacob. It would change things, and not for the better to his mind. Wyatt had intimated more than once his theory that it was Jacob's crush on Linc that had "turned" him. Like such a thing was possible.

And there was that old ache again, the bruise that never faded, Wyatt's ability to flip on a dime, temper flaring, hurtful words flying, especially when he'd been drinking. Then in the morning, he'd be sober, saving Linc's ass at work again, all forgotten, except not really.

Even knowing Wyatt was wrong, Linc didn't want to risk hearing that same accusation from Jon or one of the other siblings, or even Jenna herself. She was the closest thing he'd had to a mom since his own died when he was eleven. He couldn't bear it if she pushed him away, if he lost this family too, right along with losing Wyatt and everything else.

For all that he didn't much care for parties, he'd always loved being in this house, all the happy people and commotion. A baseball game was on in the living area while kids played outside, patio door wide open as they raced back and forth. The women were in the kitchen, gossiping and setting up food. It was familiar and comforting, but he didn't know how much longer he'd have it, especially with that urge to move on that he couldn't seem to shake. Even if he pulled up stakes, he'd still be drawn back here if Jenna asked, heart still called to the family that wasn't his.

"So." Jenna plunked a plate of finger foods down in front of him. "How much trouble is Jacob giving you?"

It took him a moment to realize she meant on the job and not the memories of the kiss keeping him up at night.

"He's working out." He kept his voice guarded. She undoubtedly wanted Jacob to not pass training, but Linc wasn't about to lie to her. Instead, he added, "I'm doing my best to keep him safe."

"And who's keeping you safe?" Jacob rolled his eyes, clearly already over Linc feeling responsible. "I swear all of you guys need to remember that I'm not in diapers anymore."

"Trust me, I'm not in danger of forgetting." Linc tried to tell him with his eyes that he was well aware that Jacob was fully grown.

"Good." Jacob's eyes sparkled with a mischievousness that made Linc's stomach churn, equal parts arousal and alarm. Linc was almost relieved when Jon called Jacob over to see something on his phone.

Linc made small talk with Jenna until she went back to the other women, then rocked the baby and ate his food and let the party swirl around him. Eventually, May claimed the baby back for a feeding. Jon motioned for him to come join the sports fans on the couches, but Linc wasn't in the mood for more uncomfortable suggestions so he wandered a bit, playing trucks with Junior and some of the other younger boys. When they got bored, Linc ended up heading outside to the firepit like he hadn't known all along where he was headed. Jacob was just working on lighting the thing as the evening temperatures dropped.

"Need a hand?" he asked, squatting down next to him.

"Yours? Always." Jacob was far too flirty for his family being close by, but Linc liked the warmth in his tone too much to call him on it.

"Here." Linc handed him some kindling. Same as with the baby, they worked together silently, doing this task like they'd done it a thousand times before, when the reality was that the firepit had always been Wyatt's domain, not Jacob's. He liked working alongside Jacob, something that had both annoyed and buoyed him the last week, the way Jacob could often read his mind, anticipate what he was about to ask.

And somehow once the fire was going, they ended up the only two out there in the big wooden chairs, alone but not really. They sat in a companionable silence for a while before Jacob shifted, leaning forward, voice a bare whisper. "You know, I've been thinking—"

"Please don't." Linc wasn't trying to be funny. The look on Jacob's face, at once mischievous and earnest, so damn appealing, both turned him on and put him immediately on edge.

"We need to get this—" Jacob gestured between them "—out of our systems. Once and for all."

"No." It didn't work like that, and it spoke to how damn young Jacob still was that he thought it did.

"Hear me out. One night. Then we can concentrate on work after. Put it behind us. Take away the mystery maybe."

Linc snorted. It might be simply curiosity for Jacob, but it sure wasn't for him. "It wouldn't work."

"Maybe not, but I at least want to try. You don't?"

"I'm not an itch you scratch once."

"That sure of yourself, huh?"

More like he was that sure of Jacob, but he said nothing, just stood. His no might be firm now, but he wasn't made of iron either. Enough wheedling from Jacob and he might get twisted up enough to agree to that ridiculous plan.

"Night. You have a nice time now with your family. And see you tomorrow. At work." He chose his words carefully, reminding them both about the two big reasons they couldn't do anything foolish.

"Just think about it," Jacob urged.

"It's cake time!" someone called from the house, saving Linc from answering. But he would. He'd think about it all right. He'd think about it tonight, alone in his bed. And probably tomorrow, in the shower. And he'd want it, just like he had for years now, every cell in his body aware of what he could have but wouldn't allow himself. Lord, how he'd want it, especially now that Jacob had made this diabolical little offer. *One night.*

And it didn't help that a small piece of himself kept whispering, *It might work. Never know. It could work.* That part was wrong, of course, but it spoke to his want, wormed its way into his thoughts until he wasn't sure how long his willpower could hold out.

Chapter Seven

Jacob guessed he was supposed to regret his proposition to Linc, was maybe supposed to be embarrassed and contrite that Linc had turned him down. Again. But he wasn't, not even when Monday morning rolled around and he had to face another week of training with the guy. No matter what Linc thought, fucking wasn't a terrible idea at all. They had something hanging between them, had for years now, and if Linc wasn't ever going to come down from his high horse and give things a real go, getting it out of their systems made the most sense. A sexual exorcism or something. Anything was better than all this pointless wanting and not having.

And Linc had kissed him, taken the initiative, twice now. He'd as much as told Jacob that he wanted him. That coupled with the fire in his eyes when he thought no one was looking made Jacob bolder than he'd otherwise be. And he'd persisted in large part because Linc's reasons for not giving in to what they both wanted were so damn flimsy, especially now.

"You got a bed, Linc?" he'd asked when Linc had finally pulled back from the kiss, just enough to rest his head against Jacob's. Calling that fireball a kiss was

a disservice to all the sweet, gentle kisses out there, but damn if Jacob didn't want more. They'd ground together, fitting together like gears finally sliding into place, and he'd been just this side of coming in his suit pants when Linc pulled back.

"A what?" Linc blinked, still looking every bit as grief-stricken as before the kiss.

"Bed. Let's go to bed." He rubbed Linc's shoulder, the need to touch and soothe every bit as strong as the lust. "Let me make you forget...everything. At least for a little while."

Maybe it was the tenderness that Linc didn't want, the sympathy and understanding. Or maybe it was the need to be decisive, to actively choose to go to bed with Jacob as opposed to more or less falling into that kiss. But whatever it was, Linc stepped all the way back, shaking his head. "We can't."

"Sure we can. What's the point of holding out anymore anyway? Wyatt's gone and—"

"You need to leave." Linc's voice was low, a tone that brooked no further arguments and had him feeling small and ashamed. He hadn't meant he was glad about Wyatt, not at all, but more that all this wanting-but-not-doing was stupid and pointless and had been for years.

And now it was months later, and the memory still made him the same mix of horny and guilty and frustrated. Linc needed to listen to reason, at least once in his life. But Jacob had said his piece at his mom's party, made the offer. The ball was in Linc's court now, and Jacob wasn't going to keep pushing, especially not when they had work to do.

At least they had a busy week in front of them—

more jumps, more team building, pack-out practice with hauling gear long distances, and some actual forest work too, the other less exciting but no less important part of their job as they worked to prevent the sort of large-scale fires that necessitated emergency operations. Controlled burns, tree removal, brush piling, construction and other maintenance jobs were a big part of what they did. Which meant he wasn't surprised when a good chunk of their drizzly Monday was spent with chainsaws whirring, out on assignment, practicing some of their skills on an active forest management project.

"This is key because later this week we're practicing cargo drops and some jumps with gear. We'll do some tree removal in a remote drop site, then pack out to a rendezvous point, a light version of what we'll do during the fire season," Linc explained as they packed their equipment into forest service trucks before heading to the project.

"Trust me. I'd much rather cut timber than be in the classroom."

"Yeah, well, don't get ahead of yourself." Linc was borderline gruff, but Jacob ignored him and climbed in back of the truck, next to Garrick. If he acted normally, Linc would too. Eventually.

And he was right because Linc settled down when they were out there, scaling trees and hauling branches and doing the other work that needed doing. Linc and the other guys had worked together so long that they had a natural rhythm, a steady patter of inside jokes and good-natured insults that kept the day moving and the work from getting too boring. Of course, it would be far different in the middle of an active fire, but Jacob enjoyed the tree climbing and other arduous tasks. He didn't even mind the teasing that the others sent his way. It was worth it if it meant getting to hear Linc laugh and if it gave him a better shot of fitting in.

"Damn. You're fast." Garrick whistled low as Jacob made fast work of returning to level ground after a preliminary ascent to prepare for felling a tree. The praise felt good, even if he did wish Linc were the one acknowledging his skills.

"Guess we can use you when we have to do some demos like we do for the school groups sometimes. Less waiting around for the kids." Linc picked up his chainsaw.

"Is that the same thing as 'good job' in Linc-speak?" he teased as soon as the others were out of earshot, heading down the trail to the next spot.

"Good job ensuring that Sims and the higher-ups will give you extra work all season long." Linc's voice lightened. "But, then you always did seem part cat, leaping from branch to branch like that. What were those obstacle courses you used to do when you were training on the regular?"

"Parkour. I still do them some, especially in the winter. And when Tyler or some others from the old squad are in town and want to work out."

"Thought he stayed in Vegas pretty much full-time these days," Linc growled.

Oh, good. Nice to see he wasn't indifferent to jealousy. Jacob didn't even bother trying to hide his smile. "He is. But he's still got family here. And all that old shit between us...over and done. It's easier to be friends now, forget there was ever anything else there. He's still fun to spar with."

"He broke your damn heart," Linc said in an urgent whisper, almost like he wouldn't turn down the chance to lay Tyler flat himself. That was cute.

"Hearts heal." Jacob shouldered his gear. Truth was, whatever he'd felt for Tyler had faded like the summer sun, mellowing into a sort of cool regard where he could appreciate being crazy kids together but not get worked up over old hurts. However, not even Tyler worked him up like Linc did, which was why he hurried to keep up with the others, keep the temptation to flirt at bay. Linc would either take him up on his offer or not. Most likely not, but Jacob would deal with that disappointment in due time, away from the job. He didn't want to spend the rest of his life with a pointless crush, but at the same time, he wasn't quite ready to give up all hope.

For the rest of the week, he managed to keep his distance. The work was grueling but with each successive jump and task he was even more sure that this was the work he was supposed to be doing. He didn't stop wanting Linc's praise, but he tried to focus on the things he could actually control. Wanting Linc wasn't one of those things, but there was also no point in making both of them continuously miserable.

Not when the job was still so new, and his life was very literally on the line with each new skill and mission. By Thursday, he was ready for their first cargo drop and pack-out. He'd had several successful jumps that week and was ready to finally feel like a functional crew member at last.

Getting the chainsaws and other equipment ready to

drop was much more complicated than he had thought. Everything had to be packed exactly right and loads balanced to ensure that the cargo arrived at the same place they did. They'd even take MREs and other rations down with them. With a real deal fire, they would take at least forty-eight hours' worth of supplies on their person and in the form of cargo drops. Even their own weights had to be balanced—him taking on more since he was the lightest of their four, something Garrick delighted in pointing out.

"Come on, Rook. Doesn't anyone feed you at home?"

"I burn it all off. Unlike you. And we can't all be giraffes." He wasn't *that* short—only a little shorter than Linc, perfect for when they…

Not the right time. See? He was doing better, turning off the memories, especially at inopportune times. Couldn't be thinking about kissing right then anyway, not with tons of others milling around, waiting for their assignments. Or in the plane, on the way to the jump. He had to be one-hundred-percent focused on the job, which meant tuning out any potential distractions while they waited for Ray's signal to jump, trying to tune his focus inward, the same way he had with MMA matches.

The jump was into the forest, trees stretching to the horizon, undulating green waves. Even as he juggled multiple data sets that needed his attention like his altimeter, he had to take a second to appreciate the gift of such a stunning view. The canopy of trees was dark green now, surrounded by a crisp blue sky, not a fire in sight. The sight made him feel their mission in a bone-deep way he hadn't before, not even on the front lines of the hotshot ground crew. This was what they were protecting for future generations, these centuries of trees, this endless beauty.

He landed a little hard—nothing he couldn't handle, but a tooth-rattling jolt nonetheless. But he remembered the training, letting his butt rather than ankles absorb the impact, rolling with the momentum.

"You okay?" Linc rushed over, more mother hen than usual. Jacob got it—Wyatt's death was always going to hang over Linc, but even knowing that didn't mean the hovering was always easy to take.

"The rook's fine," Garrick answered for him, brushing off his shoulders with a quick, impersonal touch that was nothing like Linc's. "Let's get going."

Ray had stayed on the plane, radioing information down about the cargo drop coordinates and other relevant information for their assignment. That left the three of them to go find the cargo drop, do the necessary tree removal, and then pack out.

The revving of their chainsaws broke through the stillness of the forest. Linc and Garrick did a better job than the classroom lectures of explaining how strategic cuts would make a difference in fire management and how working quickly and safely was key in accomplishing their job. He had to climb a few more trees, resisting the urge to show off for Linc.

"Damn." He turned his face heavenward, drinking in the spring sunshine when they took a break for food and water. "Sure is a beautiful day. We're damn lucky to get to do this, you know?"

"Yeah." Linc's voice was gruff, a strange, confused look on his face, almost as if he were seeing Jacob for the first time. "Be sure and hydrate before we start the hike out. You're going to handle the compass for us."

"I am?"

"Yeah, Rook, don't get us lost." Garrick slapped him on the shoulder. "There's often no groomed trails out where we work. We've got GPS devices, but if they go out, we need to go old school. If you don't know your compass skills, you're fucked. And you can't rely on Linc or me to be the one to navigate you out or for the comm sets to work. So get to work."

"Will do." He maybe should have paid more attention to the compass lecture earlier in the week, but he wasn't about to admit that to the other two. Following Ray's directions over the comm set, he set off in a southeast direction, all three of them loaded down with equipment.

"Better not make us double back," Linc huffed as they trudged through the forest.

"I'm trying." Pausing, he checked the compass again. "This way."

Right when he was about to give up and admit compass reading defeat, they hit the old logging road they'd been aiming for. "Fuck, yeah!" He fist pumped as they emerged from the dense forest. "Told you I could do it."

"You did." Linc shook his head, a half smile teasing his lips, clearly amused at Jacob's happiness. "Good job."

Hell. Jacob had it even worse than he'd thought. Only that small bit of praise was enough to make a happy shiver race up his spine. Maybe there was some sort of vaccine he could take to make him immune to Linc because this was getting ridiculous.

Resolved, he tried harder to keep his distance, both

physically and psychically, as they tromped toward the rendezvous point. But then all those good intentions fled when he ended up next to Linc for the truck ride back to headquarters. He was intensely aware of their thighs touching, the brush of Linc's wide shoulder, the warmth radiating from him.

And maybe Linc wasn't oblivious himself because as they exited the truck, Linc dropped his voice. "You win."

"What?" Jacob struggled to follow. Did they have some sort of bet?

"You. Win." Still barely a whisper, Linc enunciated more clearly. "I give. Uncle."

"Hey, Linc, where did you want this stuff?" Garrick called, removing any chance of Jacob getting clarity as Linc hurried away.

He won? Won what? What did Linc mean? He hadn't been bugging Linc for—

Wait.

There was one thing. *The* one thing.

His proposal that they get this out of their system. Heat licked at the base of his neck. If Linc meant what he thought he did, they were *both* about to win big, and he couldn't wait to find out if he was right.

Linc had expected the crunch of tires on gravel that evening, but he still couldn't stop the mix of dread and anticipation and lust at war in his gut as Jacob's truck pulled into view. He let the dogs out as Jacob parked, making his way to the front porch slowly, trying to tone down his own eagerness. Shadow and Bandit could handle the foolish devotion for him. They both danced around Jacob, mesmerized as usual.

"Who's a good dog? Is it you?" Jacob dispersed lavish amounts of praise and pats on the way to the house, coming to stand in front of him. Like Linc, he'd showered since work, arriving with unstyled damp hair and a fresh blue hoodie that advertised one of the local ski resorts. His smile, however, was far less cocky than Linc had expected. He'd won. He should be strutting.

And Linc wasn't even sure what part of the week had made him give in to Jacob's crazy idea. Jacob's increased competence, taking on new tasks and skills with an ease that settled some of Linc's nerves about his ability to do the work, was strangely appealing. Working alongside him did something for Linc's soul that he'd never really been able to explain, but it was deeper than lust, more than the physical appeal of watching his muscles flex. It was the appreciation and joy with which Jacob approached every task. With each jump, his enthusiasm was infectious, making Linc see the mundane with fresh eyes. And perversely, there was also the way he'd been nothing other than professional all week. Distant even. Making Linc crave his usual flirty closeness and making him more restless with each passing day even as he respected the hell out of Jacob not continuing to push.

Finally, there had been this moment out there today when Jacob had looked like an angel disguised as a lumberjack, an almost reverent expression on his face as he'd taken in his surroundings. Maybe that was the moment Linc had known. He wasn't ever getting over this through sheer force of will. There was want, which he had denied years now, and then there was *need*, this new level of attraction bolstered by the knowledge of what Jacob smelled and tasted like. Need didn't listen to reason, cared not about well-thought-out rationale, and need continued to grow, wild and frantic. It was all kinds of ridiculous, giving Jacob's plan a try, but he was simply that desperate.

"You're not sending me away. Not this time." Jacob sized him up, determined eyes, stubborn tilt to his chin.

"Nope."

"Good." One step. Two. Three, and they were face-to-face on the porch. Long inhale as their eyes met. Held. They'd kissed in grief, and they'd kissed in frustration, but Linc still hadn't kissed him deliberately, in full control of his judgment and knowing exactly what was likely to happen the moment Jacob crossed the threshold to the house. The moment dragged on, charged, neither of them backing down, but no one taking that last step.

"You should come in." Linc swallowed hard. If Jacob was waiting for some sort of signal, that might be the best Linc had in him, suddenly as unsure as a teenager. But maybe that invitation was all he needed to do, because Jacob grabbed his wrist, tugging him into the house, dogs rushing ahead of them. He swiveled to get the door, and when he turned back, Jacob was on him, pressing him into the wall. He might be younger, but there wasn't a damn thing timid about him, and hell if that didn't rev Linc even further.

Stretching, Jacob claimed his mouth with more of that intoxicating aggression. His lips were warm and soft and everything Linc had tried so hard not to remember. But his body did, each note of his taste and scent a familiar melody until he was welcoming Jacob like a long-lost lover with a groan. He let Jacob have his fun, plundering Linc's mouth with an eager, needy tongue, until the last shred of his control snapped, and he had to take over. Nipping and sucking at Jacob's lips, he drank in every moan and gasp. Fuck but he loved how Jacob didn't back down one inch, sucking hard on Linc's tongue, until Linc was no longer sure who was leading, only that it was all better than it had ever been because it was Jacob and he was right here, right now.

Jacob showed off some impressive multitasking, pushing Linc's thermal shirt up while they continued to kiss, hands roaming all over Linc's sides and back. Two could play at that game, so Linc worked a hand under Jacob's layers of hoodie and T-shirt, connecting with warm, bare skin for the first time. He tried to memorize the planes of Jacob's back, the smooth muscles, the scoop of his spine, the definition of his shoulders.

"Fuck." Nuzzling Linc's neck, Jacob licked his way across Linc's jaw to his ear, a spot that was usually more ticklish than turn-on for him, but right as he opened his mouth to tell him that, Jacob raked his teeth over the tender flesh and proved him dead wrong.

"Do that again," he commanded, voice rough.

"What? This?" Jacob repeated the gesture, making Linc shiver. "Bet I can do you one better."

Before Linc could figure out what he was about, Jacob sank to his knees in a smooth movement. Right there on the tile entryway floor. Jacob on his knees, hands already undoing the fly of Linc's jeans. It was a wonder Linc didn't come from the sight alone. He hadn't bothered with a belt, something he was grateful for right then as it meant faster access for Jacob's deft fingers.

"Hell. I always figured you were hung, but *damn.*" Jacob whistled under his breath as he withdrew Linc's cock, shoving his jeans and boxer briefs out of the way. "This cool?"

"Like I'm gonna say no." Head falling back, Linc groaned, a sound which deepened as Jacob licked all over his shaft. Little teasing flicks which drove him crazy and had his hips rocking even before Jacob reached his cockhead. Keeping with the light approach, Jacob laved it all over with the broad side of his tongue making Linc curse. "Fucking hell. Do it already."

"I am." Jacob batted his eyelashes, all false innocence as he continued torturing Linc with the lightest of flicks and strokes of his calloused fingers, which felt a thousand times better than Linc's own familiar touch. He needed to come before he passed out from wanting, but he refused to beg, settling for soft moans that he couldn't hold in.

Taking it to the next level of warfare, Jacob sucked little kisses all over the shaft, almost, but not quite, taking the head in.

"Okay, okay." Linc gave in with a full-body shudder. "Please. Fuck. Jacob. Please."

"Well, since you asked so nicely…" Pulling back, he grinned up at Linc. He knew exactly what he was doing, damn it. And he didn't seem in all that much hurry, taking a moment to undo his own jeans. But all was forgiven when he finally took pity on Linc and took him deep, a wet, hot suction that was as close to perfect as anything else in Linc's life. No teeth, but a devious, active tongue that made every retreat a revelation. A slight brush against his calf made him glance down to where Jacob was stroking his own cock with lazy, left-handed strokes while he sucked Linc.

"Holy fuck." He groaned as he watched the unex-pectedly hot show—Jacob's mouth stretched around his cock, eyes squished shut, hand on Linc's hip steadying him, other hand stroking his tasty-looking cock. "Swear I'm good for returning the favor if you slow down. Or hell, let me get you off first."

"Nuh-uh." Jacob pulled back long enough to protest. "I want to come with your cock in my mouth. I thought about it the whole way over, you fucking my face until we both come."

"Jesus. You keep talking like that and me going first isn't going to be an issue."

"Yeah. Knew you'd like that idea." Jacob managed a confident laugh before diving back onto Linc's cock, switching hands on his own so that his strokes were more purposeful now, matching the bob of his head. Experimentally, Linc rocked forward. Plenty of guys *said* they were cool with face fucking, but in his admit-tedly not huge experience, most liked to stay in control of the depth and speed of thrusts.

But Jacob made a needy, hungry sound, yanking Linc's hip, exaggerating the movement until Linc got the idea and started thrusting in earnest. Jacob moaned around Linc's cock on every upstroke, little sounds that were every bit as devastating as the action of his mouth. At a certain point, Linc gave up trying to control this or even hope of trying to time things perfectly, instead simply riding the wave of sensations. Jacob's mouth, hot and urgent. The bite of his fingers on Linc's waist. His sounds. The slap of his hand on his dick. Linc found the more he let go, the easier it was to read Jacob's signals, tell when he wanted more air or when he wanted Linc to go harder, his moans intensifying, carrying Linc closer and closer to the edge.

"Close," he warned, which only seemed to embolden Jacob, getting him to suck harder, like he was getting graded on his ability to get Linc off in the next thirty seconds. Then he made a noise, a little hitch to his breathing, like he was close himself, and knowing he was that turned on from blowing Linc pushed him over into the hardest climax of his life, great waves of release that he didn't surf as much as get towed under until he was shuddering and breathing hard. He got his eyes open right in time to see Jacob come, erupting all over his fist even as he kept right on sucking Linc through the aftershocks.

"Damn. You have gills I haven't seen?" Linc's words were as rubbery as his knees, and when Jacob finally released him, he sank down next to him on the floor. He'd managed the joke, but he lacked words for how… awe-inspiring that had been. Humbling even, from Jacob's obvious enjoyment and generous nature.

"Nah. Just an oral fixation I can't shake." Jacob bumped shoulders with him, shifting around so he could rest his head against Linc's neck while he licked at his swollen lips. And despite the world-shaking orgasm moments ago, Linc's pulse pounded like his body wouldn't mind a second go right that damn moment.

"Fuck." Shaking his head, Linc braced for a wave of regret and guilt that never came. He'd done it. He'd broken his word, and he should be wrestling with what that meant as a man. But maybe all those brain cells were still offline because instead, all he felt was a burning need to kiss Jacob senseless until he wasn't the only one thinking second helpings. "Fuck it all. That didn't work."

"It didn't?" Jacob yawned. "Pretty sure your taste in my mouth says it worked plenty."

"You know what I mean, fucker." Linc hauled him closer into an awkward embrace. "You said that would cure us, but it didn't cure me of a damn thing."

Shrugging, Jacob gave him a wry grin. "I never said it would be instantaneous."

Woof. Woof. Apparently done being ignored, the dogs pranced over, inserting themselves between them.

"Ew. No." Jacob scrambled to his feet before Bandit could lick his hand. "Can I clean up in the bathroom before you kick me and the failed experiment to the curb?"

"I'm not kicking you out." Groaning, Linc hauled himself up.

"You're not?" Jacob's surprise made shame lick at Linc's cheeks, heating his skin. Was he really that much a bastard?

Yeah, you are. He'd been as much surprised as Jacob by his words. But the longer Jacob stayed, the longer those recriminations could stay at bay. A reckoning was coming, but he wasn't ready. Not yet. Not when he had a chance at a little more of Jacob first, not when there was so much he'd waited years to do.

"Nah. Maybe you're right. Not a miracle cure. Gonna need a repeat application." He offered what he hoped was a smile. His humor was so rusty with disuse that he no longer trusted his ability to joke, especially when Jacob didn't laugh, but instead gaped at him.

"You want a round two? Now?"

"Not right this damn minute. Not all of us are twenty-five. But I figure I might as well feed you, see what trouble we can find after."

Jacob studied him for such a long moment Linc worried he'd grown a third eye. "Okay," he said at last. "Okay."

"You sure? You don't sound very enthusiastic for the guy who tried to sell me on this whole get-it-out-of-our-systems plan."

"Oh, I'm still down with that plan." Jacob offered him a smile that still seemed a little strained around the edges. "I'm for damn sure not turning down a repeat. And hey, you never know, maybe another few rounds, and my idea will still work."

"Here's hoping." Linc was pretty sure it wouldn't, but hell if he could send Jacob away. Seconds. Fifths. No number of repeats was going to be enough for him. But he had him here and he wasn't going to waste the opportunity. Tomorrow could be all about regrets and guilt. Tonight was for storing up every second he could.

Chapter Eight

As Jacob cleaned up in the small hall bathroom, he studied himself in the mirror. Skin still flushed. Lips kiss swollen. Breath newly minty thanks to some mouthwash he'd found by the sink. He didn't look like his world had shifted on its axis, but it totally had. Kissing Linc, blowing him, hadn't felt new and exciting like he'd expected. No rush of an illicit encounter, frantic to get it while it was good. No, instead, it had felt like coming home, like a long-awaited reunion of bodies and souls.

Sure, he loved oral, always had, but there was nothing routine about doing it with Linc. Every moment had felt charged, and he'd had a hard time reminding himself that this was a one-off, as his brain kept suggesting things about next time. Next time he wanted a bed. Next time he wanted to play with Linc's balls. Next time he'd take Linc up on the offer to reciprocate. Next time, next time. Except there wasn't going to be a next time, no matter how much this felt like a homecoming. All they had was this one night, and seeing as how it had been his idea, he needed to make the most of it.

And apparently that included dinner, something he had neglected in his rush to get to Linc's after work.

Somehow, emerging from the bathroom to find Linc cooking was almost unbearably domestic, a level of intimacy they'd never had and probably wouldn't ever again. Linc hummed as meat sizzled in a skillet, giving him a nod as he came into the kitchen.

"Steak okay? I got half a steer on the cheap after I helped a buddy with some brush hauling. You want to pick some greens so we can have salad?" Linc gestured at a line of plants in the dining area, little seedlings in neat rows on the table and more mature plants in planters in front of the window.

"Wow. Talk about farm-to-table service." Grabbing an empty bowl from Linc, he headed to the plants. Luckily for him, neat white labels identified what each was, same cramped handwriting Linc used on equipment labels at work. "It looks great in here. Nice job with the cabinets and stuff."

"Thanks. It turned out okay." Once upon a time, this had been a dark tiny house forever trapped in the seventies with cramped rooms that stank of cigarettes and wet dog. Jacob had hated it the few times he'd had reason to be there, dropping off Wyatt or some food from his mother or whatnot. Helping Linc clean it out after his dad died had been immensely satisfying work. Sometime in the past few years, Linc had finished transforming the place, knocked down a few walls to open up the kitchen, living and dining areas, installed better lighting, and used light wood details to make the small space feel bigger. Nothing was high-end, but the overall effect was super welcoming and homey.

"Hey, you have the same bar stools as Mom." Maybe that was why it felt so good here—there were a fair number of similarities to his mother's much larger, more gourmet kitchen.

"Guess I spent enough time over at her place that it crept into my design choices." Linc's neck flushed like Jacob had called him out for doing something shady.

"I didn't mean it was *bad.* It's sweet." And it underscored just how important his family was to Linc, how deep the bonds went, promises Linc wouldn't ever break no matter how much he might want Jacob. "Although Mom always gets her vegetables at the store. Doubt you could pay her to take up gardening as a hobby."

"It's practical. That's all. Nearly free food is a win even when it's work." Linc accepted the bowl Jacob had filled with baby salad greens from one of the planters. "And no store-bought tomato can compete with mine in August."

"I bet." Jacob's throat grew tight with the knowledge that he likely wouldn't be invited back to taste the summer harvest.

Linc divided the greens between two plates, then plated sliced steaks on top, as effortlessly as a line cook at some upscale restaurant, drizzling the salads with some sort of homemade olive-oil based concoction. "Is it okay if we eat at the counter? I don't want to move all the seedlings from the table."

"Sure. Let's not disturb your babies." He laughed as the dogs followed them to the bar stools at the breakfast bar. "And you poor guys. Doesn't anyone around here feed you?"

"Ha. Twice a day like clockwork. Don't let them fool you into handing out scraps." Linc leaned down to pat the bigger of the two dogs on the head. Both mutts, one had a shaggy brown coat, some sort of overgrown shepherd mix, while the other had short speckled black fur like a lab and a dalmatian found a hound lurking in the family tree.

"Damn. I miss our dogs growing up. We had some great ones."

"Yeah. I remember that big chocolate lab you guys had for years. Sparky, right? And I'd say you could borrow these mutts whenever you want but…" Looking sheepish, he trailed off with a shrug. Jacob got it. There weren't likely to be many opportunities after tonight, no more chances to play with the dogs or their stubborn owner either.

"Maybe I'll move out of the trailer soon, get a place big enough for a pet." He currently occupied Wyatt's old Airstream trailer at an RV park near town with cheap space rent and decent utility hookups.

"Eh. Get yourself a hamster or something." Linc's teasing didn't feel forced, felt more like they were settling into something they did all the time, talking and eating. "Making arrangements for the dogs at the height of the fire season is complicated. And last I heard, apartments were stupid expensive."

"Good point." The cramped quarters weren't perfect by any means, but it beat living at home with zero privacy or trying to figure out pricier rentals. With everyone wanting to make money off the tourist traffic, locals could easily find themselves priced out of housing. "It would probably be a better idea to convince Mom and May to take on a dog for the kids."

"That's an idea." Linc rubbed his chin. "Junior's the

right age for a dog. Guess I could ask May if she'd let me pick out one for his birthday later this year."

"Way to ensure you'd be Uncle of the Year." Jacob laughed before eating more of his salad. The steak was good, nice sear on a generous portion of medium rare meat, simple but balanced seasonings. Linc could cook, something Jacob should have anticipated but hadn't. It was nice, this domestic side of him. "Nice food. Thanks."

"No problem."

They finished the food with more easy talk—about the kids and Linc's garden plans, carefully avoiding all mention of work. Talking with him had always been comfortable, even with all the unresolved attraction stuff that lingered for years. Maybe that was part of why he'd persisted so long—it wasn't simply that Linc was hotter than fuck. He liked hanging out with him, liked the intent way he listened, liked the way a funny story about the kids could coax out a rare deep laugh and make Jacob feel like a rock star simply for making Linc lighten up. And each contribution from Linc felt like earning secrets, even if it was simply gardening tips.

Linc moved to clear their empty plates, but Jacob beat him to it.

"Let me. You cooked. I'll get the dishes."

"Okay. Shouldn't be too hard because I've got a dishwasher now." Linc followed him around the island to the sink, lounging against the counter while Jacob loaded the plates and washed out the skillet. His hooded gaze made Jacob feel like a rabbit off in the hills, easy prey for a hungry bobcat. Anticipation gathered low in his gut, even before Linc tugged him against his front.

Without even giving him a second to dry his hands, Linc wasted no time in raking his teeth against Jacob's neck. Not enough to leave a mark, but still more aggressive than a quick kiss, and it made Jacob instantly hard.

"I was thinking—"

"I thought we weren't supposed to be doing that." Jacob had to laugh.

"Behave." Linc gave him another soft bite. "The whole time we were eating, I was thinking that maybe we didn't do enough to test your theory."

"Is that your way of asking me how I feel about fucking?"

"Yeah." Linc held him tighter, letting him feel how aroused he already was himself. "Do you like getting it? Because I'm not saying I won't...but damn I really want to fuck you."

Jacob liked how Linc didn't automatically assume that because he was younger or shorter that he liked to bottom but that he also wasn't scared to show how much he wanted it either. That sort of want was undeniably appealing, even if it wasn't Jacob's usual. And it wasn't like he hadn't spent *years* wondering what it would be like with Linc.

"Yeah, we can do that." He sank into the embrace as Linc inhaled sharply. "Do you have stuff? I won't go bare."

"Need to check some expiration dates." Chuckling, Linc pulled him toward the hall that led to the bedrooms, but into one of the smaller rooms, not the master.

"You didn't take the master for yourself?" The room was small, dominated by a queen-size bed with a plain blue comforter and an older nightstand, with the remaining floor space devoted to two dog beds.

"Nah. Made that my gym. The attached bathroom is handy after a workout, but also…" Trailing off, he shook his head. "Too much baggage, I guess. Taking over my old man's space…yeah. I was fine with keeping this room for sleeping."

"I can see that." Feeling bad for making Linc think about his asshole of a father, Jacob wound his arms around Linc's neck. "Now about those expiration dates…"

"Okay, okay. Let me dig." Linc pulled loose. There was something endearing about him not even knowing where his supplies were. Logic said he had no hold on Linc, but the jealous, primal part of Jacob's brain liked knowing that Linc didn't do this very often. Indeed, everything about the simple room said he didn't entertain many guests at all. Rattling around in the nightstand, Linc came up with a bottle of lube in the top drawer and a strip of condoms two drawers down and tossed both on the bed before pulling the comforter back. "Dates are good."

"Thank goodness. I sure wasn't driving back into town." The nearest convenience store was still a good fifteen minutes away.

"We'd just get creative." Coming up behind Jacob again, Linc pulled at his shirt while nuzzling his neck. "But either way, I wasn't gonna pass up my chance to get you naked."

"Yeah." Jacob swallowed hard at the reminder that this was their one chance. Linc didn't need him, not on the same level Jacob did, and he needed to remember that, be careful to not make more of this than it was. Maybe Linc was good at seduction, the little touches and kisses, but that didn't mean he was entertaining any romantic thoughts. With that in mind, Jacob shed his own clothes quickly, not sure how much more tenderness from Linc he could take.

Linc took the hint, removing his T-shirt and jeans. And *damn.* It was one thing to know the guy was ripped and hot as fuck and another to have it all on display, defined muscles, dark ink of his tattoos, smattering of chest hair. His tats were an eclectic mix—geraniums on his upper shoulder with his mother's name under them, geometric cuff on his biceps, flames and a helmet on the other arm, and one he didn't remember seeing before on his back—a Celtic cross caught in flames with "all give some, some give all" around it, and he knew without asking that that one was for Wyatt.

"I want to get one too." He gestured at Linc's back. "A memorial one for him and my dad both. So far I've been chicken."

"Yeah? I've got a woman over in Bend, does nice work. But it's a big decision. And you look plenty good without the ink." Linc's exaggerated leer said he wasn't up for heavy discussion around tattoos, and Jacob was glad for the out. He flopped onto the bed, making himself grin up at Linc, not let any talk of Wyatt ruin this before it even got started.

"This is me hoping those condoms are the extralarge variety," he said as Linc skimmed off his black boxer briefs. He picked up one to examine it, but Linc plucked it from his fingers, set it aside before straddling Jacob.

"Don't get ahead of yourself." Balancing his weight

on one arm, he claimed Jacob's mouth in a thorough kiss that made all jokes and inconvenient thoughts flee, leaving only burning need in its wake. Linc's free hand explored Jacob's torso while they kissed, lighting up nerve endings Jacob had forgotten he had. He pushed Jacob's arms over his head, stretching him out, making him even more at Linc's mercy before dipping his head and licking Jacob's neck like he had in the kitchen.

"You have some sort of neck fetish?" he asked, trying to distract himself from how damn good it felt.

"More like I've got a *you* fetish." Linc laughed.

"Good." He liked knowing he was under his skin, that the big, tough guy wasn't any more immune to this thing than Jacob was. "Do your worst."

"Oh, I will." Linc waggled his eyebrows before sobering. "And don't worry, I won't leave marks."

"Darn. But yeah…smart." Under any other circumstance, he'd love to wear Linc's bites on his skin, but he was hyper-aware of having to change at work the next day in the locker room and not wanting questions or teasing. Sighing, he stretched, trying to chase away work thoughts. And thinking about tomorrow, when this would be a memory, was damn depressing. Better to yank Linc up for another kiss until nothing mattered except them and this right here, right now.

Linc used his tongue to fuck his way into Jacob's mouth, a deliberate rhythm that had Jacob writhing against the sheets, desperate to get on with the main event.

"Come on, come on," he urged.

"So damn impatient. We're getting there." Pressing another openmouthed kiss against Jacob's neck,

Linc managed to sound like they had all the time in the world.

"Not fast enough." He tried to reach for the lube bottle, but Linc stayed his hand.

"Not yet." The stern expression on Linc's face had him shivering.

"You're just trying to pay me back for teasing you earlier."

"Maybe." Shifting his weight, Linc fisted Jacob's cock, a light touch that barely grazed the shaft but had Jacob groaning all the same. "Or maybe this is just fun, making you beg."

"Oh, fuck. Please. Please." If it was begging Linc wanted, it was begging he'd get, especially when Linc dipped his fingers lower, teasing Jacob's balls and the sensitive skin behind them. Their mouths met in a lengthy kiss as Linc continued his gentle assault, fingers dancing everywhere but never lingering long enough for Jacob's taste. "Please. Need it."

Apparently those were the right words, because Linc growled and blessedly grabbed the lube bottle at last, coating his fingers. Jacob wanted to protest that he didn't need a ton of prep and that Linc should just get on with it, but Linc's touch felt too good to protest the attention. Even wanting it so much though, his body still tensed as Linc's blunt fingers pressed against his rim.

"Fuck. You sure you've done this before?" Linc's forehead creased as he pulled back to make gentle circles with his slick fingers that felt amazing and went a long way to getting Jacob's muscles to relax.

"Yeah." They weren't going to discuss how rarely as he could already sense Linc about to offer to get off another way. Now that they were here, Jacob wasn't losing out on his one chance to experience this with Linc.

Moving with even more glacial slowness, Linc moved so they could kiss again while he rubbed and teased and reminded Jacob of all the reasons he wanted this. Gradually, he worked a finger in, but way too gently for Jacob's tastes.

"Come on. I promise I'm not going to break."

"You got somewhere you need to be? Some curfew I'm not aware of?" Another of those stern looks had Jacob rocking his hips, trying to get more contact where he needed it most.

"No, I'm here."

"Good. Be here then. Quit rushing." Linc punctuated his words with another hard kiss.

I'm afraid to slow down. The thought arrived before he could push it away. But it was true, he was afraid of what he might find lurking in the dark corners of his emotions if he truly gave himself over to this, let himself fully experience it. He didn't slow down for much in life, and somehow he knew that sinking into Linc might do him in.

But Linc didn't seem willing to accept anything less, kissing him with an almost lazy regard, leisurely exploring his mouth while he worked his finger deeper. He waited until Jacob was panting and breathless before he added more. Every time Jacob tried to push the pace, chasing the kiss, fucking back onto his fingers, Linc slowed down more, to the point that Jacob would be pissed if it all wasn't so damn sweet, every kiss almost drugging. So damn good.

And at a certain point, he simply stopped fighting,

went from clutching at Linc to stroking his arms and back, wallowing in the warmth of his bulk above him. He stopped trying to control the kisses and let Linc have his way because little in his life had been this good. When Linc finally connected with his gland, electric waves of pleasure had him moaning, eyes squishing shut.

"That's it." Linc's words were hot in his ear. "God, you are something else when you finally let yourself take your foot off the gas for a damn minute. Fuck. Look at you."

Jacob was actually a little glad there wasn't a mirror, not sure if he wanted to see his desperation—or his bliss.

"Now?" he asked, voice fuzzy like he'd pounded back some shots of Jack. "You proved your point. Slow doesn't suck."

"Yeah. It's good." Linc's eyes were glassy, and maybe he was closer to losing control than it seemed because he rolled away to take care of the condom. He was overly generous with the lube, and it was touching, the way he was so reluctant to cause Jacob discomfort. Which was funny because as far as Jacob had figured out that was what fucking was all about—uncomfortable fullness, a deep burn, and it could feel decent especially if the pressure lined up with his spot, but that was far rarer than porn made it seem. The closeness could be nice if it was with someone he liked as well as the accompanying adrenaline rush, but there was a reason he didn't do this very often.

Rolling him to his side, Linc pushed in from behind him, and as his body tensed up again, he worried that

Linc was about to be disappointed. All those efforts to get him to relax and same predictable outcome. But maybe that was for the best. It took away the mystique and the longing and reminded him that this was fucking, not transcendental poetry.

"You can go," he gritted out, trying to not let on how intense the stretch was.

"Shh. Slow. Remember?" Linc kissed his neck and stroked his torso as he rocked in, slow and steady. The first couple of shallow strokes burned, but then Linc shifted, some minute adjustment to the angle and—

"Fuck. That." Okay, not poetry, but damn close. It might be fleeting, but his body lit up like a scoreboard, and his dick took renewed interest in the proceedings.

"Yeah? Better?" Linc repeated the thrust, and as things turned out, he was some sort of fucking savant because he did it again and again, finding the exact pressure needed against his gland to have Jacob moaning.

"Fuck, yes. More." He pushed back, trying to get more, totally willing to reconsider his opinions on fucking if he got to come sometime in the next decade.

Trying to make that happen, he reached for his cock, but Linc beat him to it, hooking one arm around his chest, plastering them together as he stroked Jacob in perfect rhythm with his strokes. Slow but devastating, until it felt like he was cracking from the inside out, little fissures at first, then big hits of emotion and pleasure until he was legit falling apart, broken moans and whimpers and wordless pleas.

He wasn't sure whether he was begging to come or begging it to never end. Maybe both. All he knew was that he had nothing left to hold back, giving everything to this moment, everything to Linc, even the things he'd tried so hard to hold back. No more rushing away from his feelings, instead drowning in them, every stroke a fresh wave of sensation that went far beyond the physical.

"So fucking good," Linc growled, tipping him back so they could kiss. He sped up, both his hand and thrusts, his moans joining Jacob's.

"Please." He'd never once needed permission to come, but somehow his body had decided on its own to wait for Linc, to need him that intensely.

"Yeah." Linc made a pleased noise as if he'd been waiting for that final surrender, going harder and deeper now. "Come for me. Get there."

Yup. That was exactly what he needed, body surging, fucking into Linc's tight grip, taking everything he had to give. And then he was coming, hard spurts that almost hurt in their intensity, body hanging on to awareness, waiting for Linc's shout, dishing out the last of its pleasure as Linc came too.

Holy fuck. He'd pretty much assumed that simultaneous orgasms from fucking were a trick of porn editing, but damn if they weren't both breathing hard, collapsing into a sweaty heap. His muscles protested as Linc withdrew, too sensitive now, but Linc rubbed his arm, more of that unbearable tenderness from him.

"Damn," he groaned, not pulling away even though he should. "I should have known you'd be too good at that."

"You thought I'd be bad?" Yawning, Linc rolled away

to discard the condom, then pulled Jacob back into his embrace.

"Hoped, maybe." God, it would be so easy to leave this in the rearview had it been terrible.

"Ah. Well, sorry to disappoint." Linc didn't sound particularly apologetic as he yawned again. "Fuck. You wrung me out. Gimme five and I'll shower with you. Promise."

However, Linc's soft snores soon called him a liar as he held Jacob tight in his sleep, far more content than Jacob with his racing mind. He'd made a promise of his own, told Linc that one night would be enough, that it was possible to get beyond this thing between them. He'd been dumb and naive, thinking like that, thinking he could have all this and let it go again. But he had to. He owed Linc.

He waited until Linc was deep asleep, slipping from the bed, covering Linc up and setting his alarm clock for him. Then he showered alone in the hall bathroom, not wanting to risk smashing into a weight machine in the dark in the master. Even the dogs were sleepy, barely rousing from the couches to investigate what he was up to as he penned a fast note on paper he found near the plants and left it in front of the coffee maker. There. He wasn't being a dick and sneaking out. He was doing what needed to be done, heading out into the chilly darkness of the night, taking with him the memory of every touch, every moan. The memories weighed him down, so much worse than any crush because now he knew, deep in his soul, what he'd be missing for the rest of his life.

Chapter Nine

Linc found the note by the coffee maker. He hadn't been surprised when he'd awoken alone. Holding on to Jacob wasn't ever happening, not even in his dreams. He had, however, been startled by his alarm going off. Apparently, he'd slept straight through to the clock going off, someone having helpfully turned it on for him. The same helpful person had left the bathroom pristine, towel neatly on the rack, not even a fogged mirror to indicate Jacob had ever been there. And he didn't blame Jacob for not having woken him up for what was sure to be an awkward conversation.

It wasn't like he could expect morning cuddles, breakfast together, and then driving into work. Wasn't ever happening no matter how cozy the image was. Likewise, neither of them needed to rehash all the reasons they couldn't do that again. And chances were high that any shower would have simply led to a round three and not anything productive. But even knowing all that, he couldn't stop the churning in his gut. More disappointment than regret if he was honest, much less guilt than he'd expected.

Maybe it was because the sex had been that damn

good. And he could tell himself that it was only that he hadn't had it in a very long time, but he knew that was a lie. It was Jacob, his scent and taste and reactions and sounds. It was the way he'd resisted slowing down, held back, right up until he didn't, until he'd let go, like a caged bird finally allowed to soar, whole body transforming. It had been nothing short of a privilege to watch and experience, and damn, he wanted it again already. He jerked off to the memories in the shower, not bothering with any embarrassment, because he had a feeling it was going to be the only way he could get through the morning without being half-hard at every stray thought of the night before. And besides, he was entitled to a little self-pleasure after the way Jacob had snuck out like a thief.

Except he hadn't. Not really. He'd set the alarm, left the coffee maker ready to go and left a note in his usual blocky scrawl that gave Linc a tight throat.

It didn't work. I know. Not sure either of us really expected it to, but it was my idea and I'll own that. I just wanted to say that I won't bug you about it again. You don't have to worry about me being weird at work or hanging around. You can trust me. I said one night, and I'm not going to beg you for something you can't give anyway. Take care. I mean that. Despite everything, I can't bring myself to regret tonight, so you don't get to beat yourself up over it either.
J

It wasn't a *Dear John* letter as much as a sad statement of the reality they were living. It didn't matter if

Jacob's idea of one night to get it out of their systems hadn't worked. It wasn't like they could have anything else. And he should be feeling relieved that Jacob had thought to reassure him that he wouldn't make things hard at work. But all he could manage was sadness, deep and pervading, a loss he hadn't seen coming. Like Jacob, he couldn't make himself wish away the night either—it might hurt now, but he'd rather have had a few perfect hours.

That he was willing to trade a few hours of pleasure for the honor he'd prided himself on for decades, that said something about who he was as a man and he didn't like it. Part of him kept expecting Wyatt to show up, fists at the ready. But that wasn't going to happen. Wyatt was gone, exactly as Jacob had tried to point out. There wasn't any ghostly spirit coming to lecture him on breaking his promise. His gut ached, a new level of grief that felt that much more final. No Wyatt to hold him accountable. No, that task was going to fall to his own conscience. And he might not want to erase the night, but Jacob deserved better than a guy who couldn't be trusted to keep his word.

Knowing all the reasons why this had to be a one-off didn't make him any less confused as he drove into the air base, so he was already cranky even before they started the day. He ran harder than normal with the PT, outgunning Garrick and Ray but not joining the lead pack with Jacob and Kelley at the front, keeping to himself. He kept to himself for the debriefing of the mission the day before too, which worked well until the direct questions started.

"And how did your rookie do?" Sims asked as they

reviewed how the jump portion had gone. Her voice was clipped as usual, and she paced in front of the four of them.

"Fine. Kept his head about him." Linc kept his voice even, sticking to the same sort of praise he'd use for any rookie. "Landed a little rough, but he can work on that."

"Hartman? Do you have any questions or concerns?" Sims turned her attention to Jacob, who was doing a far better job of paying attention than Linc, leaning forward, hands on his knees, posture respectfully alert.

"Nah. Like Reid said, it went well. I'll work on my landings. And my compass skills."

"Sounds good. See that you do. I've got a light day for your crew today—some brush hauling in preparation for a controlled burn next week."

"When's our next jump?" Jacob sounded as eager as Garrick, who nodded.

"Next week. Enjoy your weekend off as we won't see many of those later in the season."

Linc was probably the only one not looking forward to the weekend, to the endless hours for rehashing the night before, only the dogs for company.

"Who's up for a run Sunday?" he asked as they made their way to the truck to head out. Getting Ray back in shape would be a good distraction, but he shook his head.

"The youth group is having a lock-in Saturday night. I'm going to be bushed and lucky to make it to church with the rest of the family."

"Look at you, Mr. Chaperone." Garrick laughed as he took the back seat next to Jacob. "Man, old age comes up on you fast. Seems like just yesterday we were the ones getting locked in. I had my first kiss at one of those. Good times."

"Me too," Jacob shared, which made all three of them cough with varying degrees of surprise.

"No kidding?" Ray took the passenger seat next to Linc, who was driving. "Damn. Here I thought keeping the genders separate would ensure I got some sleep tomorrow night. Thanks for giving me new worries."

"No problem." Jacob laughed.

"And I can't run either." Garrick stretched in the cramped space. "My neighbor lady is possibly more nuts about her plants than Linc. I'm building her some raised beds this weekend."

"Neighbor lady, huh?" Ray swiveled to waggle his eyebrows at Garrick.

"Ha. It's not like that. She's probably in her seventies now. Guess Linc and all his good deeds have worn off on me." Giving a lopsided smile, Garrick shrugged.

"Okay, fine. Leave me to run alone." Linc backed out of the parking space and headed for their assigned location.

"Hey, you didn't ask the rook," Garrick pointed out. Damn it. Linc had *not* meant the invitation for him but now he couldn't exactly exclude him without raising questions.

But before he could figure out what to say, Jacob sighed, casual as could be. "Nah. I'll text you if I get free, but I'm on yard work duty for Mom myself."

That was so deftly handled that Linc almost whistled under his breath. He was good. No sign of the guy who had been panting and begging in Linc's arms, no extra interest in him at all.

And why that made him sad, he couldn't say. He needed to be relieved, not wistful.

"Well, let me know," he managed, trying for the same carefree attitude, but not sure he got there.

"Will do." Jacob kept up the casual distance even when they were out in the field, nothing other than professional, one of the guys. He joked around when Garrick or Ray started it, neither pensive nor withdrawn, but mainly he got down to work. How the fuck did he stay so normal when Linc could hardly breathe from wanting him so damn bad? And he had how many more months of this to get through? He seriously might not make it in one piece.

Garrick and Ray didn't seem to pick up on his internal distress, but Jacob did, casting him a speculative glance when the other two were occupied with hauling some deadwood.

"You okay?" he asked when Garrick and Ray were busy some distance away, chopping up branches too big to move by hand.

"Fine."

"Good." More of that professionalism. Jacob didn't press, which was again oddly disappointing.

Not that he wanted Jacob's concern, but… Fuck. He was a mess. He tried following Jacob's lead, throwing himself into their tasks, but it only worked so much, especially when Ray and Garrick ended up out of sight, fetching more tools from the truck, leaving him alone with Jacob.

"Look, I'm only going to say this once." Coming closer, Jacob spoke in a whisper as he wiped the sweat off his forehead. "Do you need me to ask for a switch?

I'm not here to make you miserable, Linc. And I think
I could do it in a way that wouldn't throw anyone under
the bus. Kelley's chafing at McKenna's leadership. They
seem to have some sort of oil-and-water thing going. I
could frame it as doing her a favor, switch with her. Is
that what you need me to do?"

"Fuck." The smart thing would be to agree, get Jacob
off his crew, out of sight and hopefully out of mind.
But Garrick and Ray had gone to some trouble to get
him where they could keep an eye on him. He'd be letting them down if he let Jacob move crews. And okay,
that was a pretty slim excuse, but it was all he had. But
maybe also it was that he'd be letting himself down
too. "No."

"Seriously? You think you're going to be okay all
season? You've looked like you're a couple of heartbeats
away from a stroke all day. You have a better idea of
how to make this work?"

We're not done yet. The answer came to him in desperation, born of hours of frustration. *Need a repeat
application.* Wasn't that what he'd said? Maybe once
wasn't enough. Or twice. And he'd already broken
his word. Had already proven himself to be untrust-
worthy. Had shown himself yet again why he needed
to be thinking about moving on after the season. This
thing still had no future for a whole host of reasons, but
maybe there was something to Jacob's theory of working it out of their systems. Or so he needed to believe
if he was going to have any chance of clinging to sanity the next few months.

He could hear Garrick and Ray approaching, indistinct chatter coming through the trees, meaning he had to speak fast. "My place. Tonight."

Jacob's eyes went wide, but he nodded. And strangely, that agreement was all Linc needed to relax and get back to work, shoulders unknotting, spirits lifting as he tossed branches around. He'd get to see Jacob later, and maybe, just maybe there was a way to work this thing out that wouldn't leave both of them charred and useless, devastated trees after the fire of whatever the hell this was between them rolled through.

Jacob took the long way to Linc's place, as in not the way that passed by his mom's place, not that he expected anyone to be watching the rural road for his truck, but he wasn't taking chances. Similarly, he was grateful for Linc's long, winding drive that hid the house and parking area from view. He still didn't know what Linc was up to, ordering him to come over, turning down Jacob's offer to switch to a different crew. An offer he'd meant sincerely. He wasn't out to make either of them miserable, and if Linc didn't want to be around him after last night, he'd understand. Hell, he was having a hard time playing it cool himself with all the flashbacks and frustrations.

And if he was smart, he wouldn't be returning here so soon, a kicked dog looking for another scrap, but he'd never been particularly wise where Linc was concerned. As it was, he'd had to force himself to slow down, go home to his trailer first, take a shower, play on his phone awhile, anything to appear less eager. But judging by his galloping pulse as he turned down the drive, he'd failed miserably in that regard.

Speaking of dogs, Linc's pair greeted him with their usual enthusiasm. These two were neither mistreated nor lacking in attention, more like spoiled rotten, and it was undoubtedly stupid to be jealous of them. But he was, mainly because the dogs were proof that Linc could attach to things, that he had a heart, a deeply kind side, that he wasn't simply some aloof, emotionally distant loner incapable of affection. Hell, even his plants were a testament to him having a hidden domestic side, being more than a tattooed, hard-living badass who had no use for other people.

Jon had teased Linc about needing a wife, but he wasn't entirely wrong—Linc had every sign of being the sort of guy who settled down, the sort of guy anyone would be lucky to have. But of course thinking of Jon reminded him that Linc still wasn't out to everyone, still had a pile of misguided notions of honor and loyalty, and wasn't likely to be setting them aside any time soon.

So why the hell was Jacob here? Why had Linc summoned him? Linc's face as he leaned against the porch rail gave nothing away, stoic as ever, coolly assessing Jacob as he walked to the porch.

"You came," he said with a nod.

"You thought I wouldn't? Pretty sure that was an order, not a request."

"Sorry." Flexing his hands, Linc looked away. "It wasn't an order. More like invitation. If you'd rather—"

"Linc." Reaching out, Jacob forced him to meet his gaze. "I'm here. Not about to turn around and leave. It was a joke, okay?"

"Yeah." Exhaling, Linc didn't shrug away from Jacob's touch, instead stepping closer. "This is crazy."

"The craziest," Jacob agreed as Linc tugged him into a tight embrace. His eyes were troubled, but his mouth was hot and urgent as it claimed Jacob's, hands sure on his back.

Not about to let Linc have all the fun, Jacob gave as good as he got, meeting Linc kiss for kiss, using lips and tongue and teeth until they were both groaning and stumbling toward the house. They bumped into the porch rail, righting themselves with another kiss, only to crash into the door frame, dogs racing back into the house ahead of them. But still they kissed, even as the dogs almost toppled them over. Linc broke away long enough to pull the door shut, returning to push Jacob into the entryway wall for another brutal kiss as they ground together.

"Fuck. We're insane." Linc didn't give him much room to answer before he raked his teeth down the jaw Jacob had shaved earlier. Snaking a hand up under Jacob's hoodie, he held him in a possessive death grip, like Jacob was in danger of running off.

"Crazy's not supposed to feel this damn good," he managed to gasp as Linc continued his assault.

"I know. And we're...supposed...to be talking." Linc explored more with his hands, broad touch lighting up each muscle group.

"Talking?" he groaned. "You brought me here to talk? Because it sure as hell feels like you asked me over to get off."

"Both. Need both." Linc captured his mouth for another desperate kiss. "Talk first. Then fuck."

"Uh-huh. Good luck with that." Jacob sucked hard on his questing tongue, loving the way it made Linc growl and shove him toward the nearby couch, them stumbling together in a sort of zombie waltz.

"Damn. Can't think with you like this." Linc pushed him down on the couch, sinking to his knees in between Jacob's spread legs. Jacob had been blessed with some amazing sights in his life—sunrise at Crater Lake, family trip to Yellowstone, old growth forests and countless mountain sunsets. But none of those were as awe inspiring as Lincoln Reid, on his knees, looking like his sole goal in life was sucking Jacob as he undid Jacob's belt and fly.

"This gonna help with the thinking problem?" He couldn't resist joking even as Linc withdrew his cock, eyes hungry, lips parted.

"Nope." Linc gave a tight smile before ensuring that neither of them was going to be doing much thinking at all by swallowing Jacob to the root in one smooth movement. He was pretty darn proud of his own oral skills and certainly enjoyed showing them off, but there was something about Linc's greedy mouth that was utterly devastating. Maybe because he managed to still be just as dominating as ever, one hand keeping Jacob firmly in place as his other teased Jacob's balls in time with the smooth, steady strokes of his mouth, each movement seemingly designed for maximum pleasure.

"Fuck." Jacob was already breathing hard, body way closer to the edge than he liked. "If you're serious about fucking, you might wanna slow down."

"You're giving *me* lectures about speed when I've got your dick in my mouth?" Linc pulled back to speak, jacking Jacob with his hand. "Mr. Faster-Faster-Faster? You want slow?"

He tortured Jacob with featherlight teases from his fingers and a few well-placed licks undoubtedly designed to ensure he had no brain cells left to answer with.

"Just…saying…if I come quickly…too sensitive to fuck…need time." At least that had been his experience in the past, but then Linc had gone and made all his past experience with fucking totally irrelevant the night before, redefining what good felt like.

"Noted." Linc went right back to sucking, same speed, same rhythm, even deeper suction now, intent clear. And hell if Jacob could continue to hold back. His head fell against the soft gray fabric of the couch, legs spreading wider to give Linc more access. Unlike how he'd jerked himself off while blowing Linc, here he got Linc's undivided, single-minded attention, and it made it impossible to hold anything back. Every sensation was magnified—the bite of Linc's fingers into his hipbone, the heat of his mouth, the friction of his tongue, the deviousness of his touch, delving lower, finding still-pleasantly-sore nerve endings from the night before.

He reached for Linc's head but received a stern look before his hands even connected. "Hands behind your head. I'll get you there."

"No worries there." Jacob's voice was shaky now, as wobbly as his insides. He complied, not sure how he felt about the strangely vulnerable posture, except his cock seemed plenty on board with the command, dick pulsing as soon as he laced his hands behind his neck.

And Linc was as good as his word, doubling down, fingers rubbing, mouth pulling hard and approving noises escaping as Jacob let go of everything other than this right here. Every doubt, every uncertainty, all replaced by need and moans, until climax was slamming into him, not able to do much more than a muttered warning. Linc didn't stop, sucked him right through the aftershocks until the attention was just this side of too much. But still he held the position, didn't shove at him, waited to see what Linc wanted. Trusted Linc not to push him too far.

Wise decision, because Linc released him with a series of gentle licks and touches that only magnified the last waves of pleasure. Then Linc flopped down next to him on the couch, cock already out and in his fist.

"I can...help." Jacob licked his dry lips, tried to find more of a voice.

"Good." Still in bossy mode, he grabbed Jacob's hand, brought it to his cock, but kept his own there too, guiding the rhythm and pressure. It should have been stifling, but instead it was hot, the way Linc kept all the control for himself, even as his head tipped back, low growls and grunts filling the room.

"Later...gonna fuck you...right here." Linc's voice was a raspy promise.

"Yeah, you are. Come on," he urged, his own body responding to the tension in Linc's.

"Fuck, fuck, fuck." He squeezed Jacob's hand tighter, increasing the pace as his body stiffened and came all over their joined hands.

"Mmm. Damn." Jacob stretched when Linc released his hand, bumping their shoulders together, not exactly a cuddle, but needing to keep contact with Linc, not break this spell. But then Linc groaned and pulled off his T-shirt, used it to clean off both their hands and gave him a pointed look, evaporating a lot of those good feelings.

"Now we talk." Linc's tone was resigned and his eyes were distant.

"Do you have to sound like I dragged you into getting off? Pretty sure that was you enthusiastically participating."

"It was." Linc sounded pained. "But we've gotta get a few things straight. Can't keep fucking around and hating ourselves after and still doing it again."

"Speak for yourself. I don't hate myself." Jacob scooted away as he zipped up his fly. God, could Linc make him feel worse? The last thing he wanted was Linc upset. "It's just sex. Sex we're long overdue on having. And okay, I was wrong about once being enough to get it out of my system, but I'm not going to beat myself up over that, not going to feel guilty for wanting you, for ending up here. There are plenty of things I regret, plenty of shortcomings I'd like to correct, but not this."

"Fair enough." Linc exhaled hard.

"But you do." He didn't make it a question. "You hate yourself for wanting me, and for what? Some promise you made more than half of a decade ago?"

It was dicey, even alluding to Wyatt, but it had to be done. However, that didn't stop the sour feeling in his gut or his sudden need to study Linc's bare white walls.

"It's more than that, and you know it. Yeah, I broke my word. That happened. And you're not wrong about him being gone, much as that kills me. But that doesn't make it any better of an idea. Can't change that I broke a promise, but I can still do my best to do right. There's also the job now and your family and a whole lot of other factors that make us being together long-term a losing prospect."

Jacob didn't see how any of that was insurmountable, but if Linc wasn't willing, he wasn't going to plead with him to feel shit he simply didn't. It was one thing to beg in bed, to need Linc for that release, and another thing to become a needy brat out of bed, demanding things Linc couldn't or wouldn't give and building resentment on all sides.

"So? You turned down the idea of me finding a different crew, getting out of your hair."

"Yeah." Linc groaned like Jacob had punched him. "I did. And I've got reasons for that too. But I've been thinking…your idea about working this out of our systems, it wasn't *terrible.*"

"Except for the part where it didn't work."

"Well, maybe we didn't give it enough time. We've got an awful lot of wanting at this point. Maybe it's going to take more than once or twice to be able to move on."

"So you propose fucking on the down low until one of us doesn't want to anymore?" He couldn't keep the skepticism out of his voice.

"You make it sound crass."

"It's not?"

"It wasn't in my mind. Not like that. Not like using you." Linc managed to sound outraged and hurt at the same time, like using Jacob was simply unthinkable. "More like…using each other. Working this thing out, figuring that it'll run its course eventually. If we can do that, maybe the rest of it will get easier—work and everything else. We can be normal around each other finally."

Jacob snorted. They were many things around each other, but normal unaffected acquaintances probably wasn't ever going to be it.

"And it's not like I'm gonna be here come fall anyway."

"What the hell? What do you mean you're not going to be here?" Jacob pushed off the couch so he could loom over Linc for once, show him how stupid his talk was.

"I've been doing a ton of thinking. All winter. Maybe I miss when I was traveling around. Taking jobs as they came. I figure me and the dogs, we can find a fresh start somewhere. Maybe near one of the other air bases. Alaska even. Somewhere where it doesn't ache so damn much."

Jacob's heart broke for Linc's pain even as frustration with his logic made his muscles tense.

"Oh, well, at least you're keeping the dogs. You'd really sell this place? After all you went through to keep it? All the shit you had to deal with about your dad's debts? You'd just let it go?"

Linc let out a pained huff. "Too much damn baggage around here. You. Wyatt. My folks."

"I get it. But you think it will hurt less, not being around here, and you're wrong. You can't outrun yourself."

"Maybe not. But maybe I gotta try. Anything to lose this…funk. Fucking sucks."

"You think I'm not sad? This year's been depressing for all of us." Maybe he hadn't realized until this moment exactly how sad and depressed Linc likely was. And he'd do anything to take that from him, but he wasn't sure that encouraging him to get some sort of fresh start was the answer. "But you can't run away. And what, you'll fuck around with me up until you pull up stakes? And you'll hope that makes you… I dunno… immune to me or something? No more what-ifs?"

"Exactly. One way or another, it'll burn itself out, but there's no reason to drive ourselves crazy all summer with avoiding each other. Not when I'm leaving anyway. And you're the one who said getting it out of our systems would help."

"Yeah. I did." Defeated, Jacob slumped back onto the couch, next to Linc. Was he really going to turn down more sex with Linc simply because he was pissed that Linc found him so expendable? Especially when he'd done nothing other than encourage Linc to see him that way. And if the choice was more months of tense and awkward interactions or a secret affair, was there really a choice at all? Not when he still wanted Linc so damn bad. It wasn't like he could simply turn it off, not after this long. Linc might be able to delude himself into thinking he'd be able to walk away, unscathed and guilt-free, but Jacob knew the truth. Losing Linc was going to suck no matter when or how it happened. So he might as well enjoy it while he had it. "Fuck it. Okay. Okay. Fine. Have it your way."

"It's the only answer I've got." Linc sounded as resigned as Jacob felt, which strangely strengthened his resolve. Linc was hurting, and if this helped, then Jacob was powerless to say no. "Only thing that makes sense, not that any of this does, not really."

"Well, either way, we're screwed. Might as well be the fun kind." He forced his voice to be light, knowing that was what Linc expected of him. He wasn't supposed to be the emo, pensive one. He was supposed to be leaping at the idea of more sex with Linc. It wasn't enough, wasn't ever going to be enough. But whatever. He'd take what he could now, worry about the autumn and what was sure to be left later.

Chapter Ten

"Yeah. Might as well." Linc gave Jacob a tight smile. It was possibly the stupidest plan he'd ever had, but it was the best he could manage. The alternative was to quit now, hit the road, hope to catch on with another smoke-jumping base, but he'd be leaving a lot of people in the lurch. And the dogs. They made everything more complicated, but it wasn't like he was leaving them behind either. No, it was better that he see the season out, then find a situation for him and the dogs that better suited them, away from all these blasted memories. Close enough so that maybe he could see Jenna and the family every once in a blue moon. If they'd have him. If this thing with Jacob didn't blow up in all their faces first.

And yes, the smartest thing would be to get Jacob moved to a different crew, but apparently lust had addled what remained of his brains. Because right now, the best plan seemed to be to get through the summer, keep Jacob alive at work, carry on with him enough in private to loosen this hold they had on each other and make the work easier and the moving on more realistic. He wasn't being cutesy—he really did think Jacob had a point. Maybe if they fucked around enough this… fixation would end.

And maybe Bandit and Shadow would start flying around their dog run. But it was worth a shot. And at this point, anything that got him more Jacob was worth all the rationalization and justification.

"If that's settled…" Jacob glanced over his shoulder at the door. He seemed to be as reluctant as Linc to continue the deep talk. "I believe I was promised couch sex, but you've got old-man recovery issues and I don't want to overstay my welcome—"

"Simmer down." Linc forced himself to smile, to reach for the lightness that was never that far away when Jacob was around. "I'll feed you. We'll get to the other."

"I don't want to keep taking your food," Jacob protested even as he followed Linc toward the kitchen.

"Sorry. Pizza won't deliver this far out, and I'm hungry. You can cope with your guilt by helping me cook." Both dogs followed along to the kitchen, undoubtedly sensing that human food was in the offing. After washing his hands and getting his clothes back to rights, he turned back to Jacob. "You wanna start by helping feed these beasts?"

"Sure." Jacob threw a few toys for them while Linc changed out the water and set out the chow.

"Go get it! Come on! You can do it!" Jacob's laughter filled the crisp spring air. He was so good at being playful with the dogs, and they ate it up, chasing down the toys and dancing around in front of him. As he watched them, Linc's chest grew uncomfortably tight. He was used to the bolts of lust where Jacob was concerned, but these other, softer emotions always took him by surprise, made him simultaneously want to run but also to wrap the moment up, tuck it away in his memory banks.

Back in the kitchen, Jacob helped him decide on hash—homegrown potatoes from his bin, onions, left-over meat and some of the eggs. It felt way too cozy, cooking for two, Jacob taking his directions on chopping, hips and shoulders bumping in the small kitchen, dogs still making pests of themselves as the two of them worked and talked food, him giving Jacob ideas for easy suppers and Jacob waxing poetic about the diner food he didn't often allow himself.

It felt suspiciously like a date, not that Linc had had a ton of those. They were supposed to be fucking. Not dating. But as with the night before, feeding him felt... *right.* Talking together was almost as good as fucking, simply hanging out together, doing what he'd denied himself anything other than small tastes for years. Much as he didn't want to admit it, maybe he needed these quieter moments too.

"So..." Jacob paused as he set the plates on the breakfast bar. "If I show up to run on Sunday...you gonna kick me to the curb?"

"You want to work out together?" That too sounded rather date-like and not like the purely physical affair he'd been intending, but he couldn't deny the way his pulse hopped at the mere thought of more time like this.

"You made the invitation. In public. No one will think anything of it if they see us out jogging. And what we do back here when we're cleaning up...well, I figure that's just between us."

As he took the seat next to him, an image of Jacob in the large shower in the renovated master bath crept into Linc's brain and took hold, water dripping down Jacob's muscles as Linc licked… *Yeah. That.* He had to shift on his stool, force himself to think of other things.

"Yeah. We can do that," he said gruffly, more turned on than hungry now, cock overriding brain yet again. Body liking the idea of having both—time together and sex, the full package he wasn't supposed to want, but hell if he could stop the warmth coursing through him. "The pack-out test is coming. You'll want to do some weights in addition to the run."

"Right. And your setup is more convenient than my gym in town." Jacob gave him a wink that he felt all the way to his balls, new set of images flooding his brain of a shirtless Jacob lifting and straining.

"You're welcome to it." Shaking his head free of the distracting visions, he tried to focus on the food. But Jacob ate like he kissed—full of gusto, lots of approving noises and pleased sounds that had sex right back on Linc's brain.

"This is really good. How'd you get so good at cooking anyway?"

"Self-preservation." Linc took a bite and swallowed before continuing. "After Mom died, it was all crap food around here all the time, and that's when there was food, when Dad could be bothered to get to the store. Sometimes Victor would make me something easy—grilled cheese, pancakes, spaghetti—when he could be troubled, before he headed down the same fucking path as Dad."

"Fuckers." Jacob's eyes narrowed. "You were only a kid when she died. Feeding you shouldn't have been an afterthought."

"Yeah, well, I didn't exactly choose that fate. And not liking to live on frozen burritos, I learned to cook. And wonder of wonders, I didn't burn the house down in the process. In high school, I had a job bussing tables at that old diner on Fir Street in town. Cook there taught me some things that have come in handy."

"I'm glad someone was there to help you. But seriously, fuck your family." Jacob looked ready to kick ass on his behalf, and he didn't even know the half of it.

"Eh. I lived through it." He wasn't sure how he felt about Jacob as a champion. Tough and fearless, he'd always been ready to fight, but seeing him all indignant on Linc's behalf was…something. Made his back tighten. "You, though, you've got no excuse not knowing how to cook. Your mom's stuff is always tasty."

"Ha. She had four other kitchen helpers, plus Dad. It was easy enough to get out of cooking chores. I guess I was spoiled that way. And even now, it's easier to drop her some hints than to try to do a big meal on the little stove in the trailer."

"She likes feeding you, likes you coming around." He ignored the kick of wistfulness that often came when thinking of Jenna and the Hartman brood. For the first time though, he wasn't sure which he envied more—her kids for getting to have her or her for having so many people she loved to feed and take care of, even now after so much loss.

While they finished the food, they talked some more about the family and dishes Jenna made particularly well, heading down memory lane to memorable parties and holiday gatherings. Somehow, the memories didn't sting quite as much as usual, all the places in his soul where Wyatt still lurked. Maybe because Jacob shared them, had his own bittersweet remembrances and his own reasons for missing Wyatt. And maybe because Jacob made it easier to focus on the good parts, the memories that didn't hurt so much. Making each other laugh with the stories was a lot more fun than sitting here alone stewing, that was for sure.

"Dude, you have cake!" Jacob grinned at him as they put the food away, crowing like a pirate discovering hidden treasure. "Did you make it?"

"Nah. The lady I get eggs from, sometimes she gets a mind to do some baking. I fixed a leaky faucet for her Wednesday, and she had that spice cake for me. You want some?"

"Uh-huh." Jacob cut a single large hunk of cake and grabbed two forks before heading to the living room.

"What do you think you're doing?" More curious than irritated, Linc followed behind him.

"Netflix and chill. Duh." He patted the couch next to him. "With cake."

"You wanna watch TV?" Linc struggled to keep up.

"Well, that and the couch sex you promised me. But I figured that stripping down in your kitchen as soon as we were done eating might shock the dogs. Besides, this is classier."

"Yeah," Linc agreed even though he could usually give a fuck about class. But it was also more of that "date" feeling that he was still coming to terms with craving, more romantic, what with a single plate of cake to share, sitting too close, one of Jacob's legs draped over his thighs, fighting over what show to pick.

But he couldn't argue with how much sweeter Jacob's

lips tasted when they finally got around to the kissing,
partway into a show about jungle survival, after they
finished off the cake and joked around about the fake
parts of the show. After Jacob bumped his shoulder,
clear intent in his eyes, and after Linc hadn't been able
to resist another second.

"See?" Jacob laughed against Linc's cheek. "I am
capable of slow. You should be proud of me."

"Gold star for waiting." Linc growled as he was the
one to go fast, shoving Jacob's shirt up and off, at-
tacking his collarbone as he pushed him back against
the couch. They wriggled out of their clothes between
kisses, T-shirts and jeans and boxers all raining to the
floor. He'd had a notion of bending Jacob over the back
of the couch or maybe having Jacob ride his dick while
sitting, but now that they were here, being pressed together like this, skin-to-skin, felt like everything he'd
ever needed.

Show forgotten, they made out like a pair of horny
teens, hands and lips roving with more enthusiasm than
finesse. Even little sensations were thrilling—the rub
of their bare stomachs together, the rasp of their fuzzy
legs dragging against each other, the strain of his biceps, stretching to wrap Jacob up even tighter. Their
cocks bumped and rubbed, random glancing contact,
not purposeful grinding, not yet, but it was enough to
have them both moaning.

"Fuck." Jacob's long fingers dug into Linc's ass, pulling them tighter together. "Kissing you is a fucking
drug. I shouldn't be this close…"

"Good. Love you close." Linc started more deliberate thrusts, rewarded by Jacob's head falling back, eyes

glassy, lips parted like another kiss was the one thing he wanted most. And Linc could give it to him, could kiss him until they were both breathless all over again.

"Wait…" Jacob panted. "Aren't we supposed to be fucking?"

"Are we?" Linc carefully nibbled on Jacob's neck. He wasn't sure what his obsession was with that particular patch of skin. Maybe it was how Jacob always shivered. Or maybe it was how he smelled and tasted so perfectly *Jacob* right there.

"Don't…want to…leave you hanging."

"You won't. We'll get to the fucking." And they would, a fresh thrill racing through him at the realization that they didn't have to cram everything into tonight. They'd have more chances. Shower sex on Sunday. Maybe some late-night hookup next week. More chances to do everything he'd craved for years. "Right now, I want this."

Linc shifted his weight so he could get a hand between them, stroke them both off. Catching on, Jacob's hand joined his, creating a tight channel for their dicks.

"Not opposed to this plan," Jacob groaned, body surging upward to meet their joined hands. "Fuck. Everything about you gets me off."

"You're telling me." Watching Jacob's face was almost hotter than fucking, a feast for the senses—the heat in his blue eyes, the flush on his pale skin, the tightness around his mouth, the softness of his mouth as he moaned again.

Needing something slicker but not wanting to dash for the bedroom, he brought his hand up to Jacob's mouth. "Lick."

"Oh, yeah." Jacob got his fingers and palm good and slick, each movement of his mouth a reminder of the way he'd sucked Linc off the day before.

"God, that feels good." His whole body exhaled as he returned his newly slick hand to their dicks, stroking faster now, enjoying the slide of their flesh together. For all his raving about how hung Linc was, Jacob wasn't that much smaller, maybe not quite as wide, but with a plump oval head that felt amazing against the underside of Linc's cock.

"Linc." Jacob's eyes squished shut. "Wanna come."

"Yeah. Get there." Linc had to groan right along with him when Jacob tightened his grip, increasing the slick friction.

"Kiss me," Jacob demanded as if Linc would deny him that. As if he could *ever* deny him more kisses. Their mouths met like it had been years since they'd kissed, not a matter of moments. Jacob's combination of aggression in the way he sucked on Linc's tongue and softness in the way he seemed to sink into the kiss allowed Linc do what he wanted, but he met him half-way for all of it. His enthusiasm was enough to have Linc panting, body hurtling toward release.

Then Jacob broke away from the kiss, body stiffening, and Linc was done for, the way pleasure transformed Jacob's face, and the sounds he made that just egged Linc on, making him stroke faster and harder until he was coming too.

And just as good as the climax was the laughter that seemed to descend on both of them afterward, a different sort of release.

"Fuck, that was something." Linc couldn't stop chuckling.

"I know. Damn. Fast too. It's still on the first episode." Jacob gestured at the TV.

"So it is." Linc scooted back so Jacob could sit up too. Felt like eons had transpired while they'd been kissing, but apparently it was less than thirty minutes, dogs still snoozing, bored on the other couch.

"Any chance of you showing me your remodeling work in the other shower? And maybe letting me stay for a second episode before I hit the road?" Still laughing, Jacob snuggled into his shoulder, head falling against Linc's neck as perfect as if the spot had been made just for him.

"You can stay," Linc said thickly, trying to ignore the part of him that wanted it to be far more than just another hour. So much for more sex working to decrease his need for Jacob. All that last round had done was make him need more than either of them could give. *Stay. Stay right here.* But of course, Jacob wouldn't. Couldn't.

Chapter Eleven

"It's Monday. Time to run those weekend donuts off," Sims barked at them as they assembled in the cold, gray, drizzly morning. Even with the dreary weather, Jacob had to hide a smile. He hadn't had any sweet treats all weekend, unless one counted the Friday night cake at Linc's place. And he definitely hadn't had any Sunday donuts, instead getting a punishing workout in with Linc, who'd missed his calling as a drill sergeant. He'd give even the most hard-nosed MMA trainers a run for their money. And not that that wasn't fun—he'd always liked being pushed physically, liked being exhausted in body and mind both, and working out with someone who was more than his equal was always a nice treat. Something he could easily get used to.

Still, one would think that the prospect of getting his dick sucked would make Linc go easy on Jacob, but he'd put them both through their paces until Jacob was convinced he'd forgotten all about the promise of sex afterward. However, then he'd redeemed himself in a spectacular fashion, making out in the big shower off his home gym, then stumbling down the hall to his bed where he'd proceeded to make Jacob forget his own name until it was time for lunch. So, yeah, he didn't really need the Monday PT or the lecture about staying in shape for their jobs, but he was in way too good of a mood to let either the rain or the work bring him down.

As usual, he ran next to Kelley in the lead while Linc hung back with Garrick and Ray, nowhere near as hard on his buddies as he was on Jacob.

"My weekend was so *slow. Boring*," she complained partway through the long run, not breaking stride. "Tell me yours was better."

The best. But of course he couldn't share that, couldn't even smirk. "Nah. Yard work for my mom. Working out. Streamed a new survival show that's not too bad. But otherwise, it was pretty damn boring."

"What do you say we head to Portland this coming weekend? We're not likely to be able to leave the area once the fire season starts in earnest. We should take advantage of the chance to get away, find trouble."

"Uh." He focused on running, trying to find a good way to hedge. As far as Kelley knew, he was a single gay guy who should be chomping to get to the Portland club scene. He couldn't exactly confess that he was hoping to convince Linc to make their weekend workout a regular thing. And not that Linc would probably care, but he had no desire to pursue another hookup, risk upsetting this tenuous connection they'd only now established. "It's a long drive."

"Three hours," Kelley scoffed, undeterred. "And if we stay over, it's not like trying to cram it into a single-day turnaround. I've got friends we can crash with. You'd like one of them—cute as heck shy guy a little younger than you who'd probably like nothing better than to worship your muscles."

"I don't need a setup." He kicked up the pace, hoping to wind her into dropping this, but she kept up easily.

"It's not me playing matchmaker. Honest. More like incentive to split the driving with me."

As they turned the corner back to the base, he searched his brain for a non-Linc-centric way out of this because ordinarily he'd be in favor of getting to spend a weekend in the city with cute, uncomplicated guys who had nothing in common with a certain stubborn, tattooed hard-ass.

"I should probably stick around here," he said as they came to a stop, rear groups starting to catch up. "My mom was making noises about getting a new play structure for the little kids." It wasn't a lie—she had been talking about exactly that on Sunday, but he hadn't been the most enthusiastic about a weekend spent wrangling power tools and fiddly small parts. However, it was a good, solid excuse. "If the weather's good, I might as well build it for her."

"Fine. Miss out on Portland." She sighed dramatically, but her eyes stayed friendly. "Go build your toys."

"What are you talking about building?" Linc came to a stop right next to them, wiping his face on the edge of his T-shirt. Jacob studiously avoided looking at the strip of bare skin he revealed because Garrick and Ray were right behind him.

"Since May and the kids seem like they're staying through the summer, Mom wants some sort of souped-up swing set for Junior. You know, the type with the climbing wall and big slide and little hideout fort? Looks to be a pain in the ass to build, but fun for the kids."

"Sounds like a two-person job. Tell your mom I'm free Saturday afternoon. Suppose I could come by and give you a hand." Linc's voice was completely casual, no hint of strain, simple as an old friend helping out. Putting it on Jacob's mom, not Jacob, was a nice touch too.

"I worked at that big home improvement store over in Bend over the winter. I can probably swing you a discount if you want," Garrick contributed. "I've got Saturday plans or I'd help out myself, but I've got an extra drill if you guys need it."

"Sounds good." Jacob was pretty impressed at himself—not only had he gotten out of the Portland trip, but now he had a friend-approved reason to spend time with Linc that weekend. "I'll tell Mom that we take payment in brownies. See you Saturday."

"Why are you planning your weekend when it's still Monday and we've got work to do?" Sims barked.

"It's for Hartman's widow. Play structure for their kids, not some wild party." Garrick frowned at her, and she immediately softened.

"Sorry. We do need to get on with it, but that sounds like a great plan. It's a good idea to take advantage of the slow time." Her usual stern face was replaced with something approaching sympathy, and she patted Jacob's arm as she headed into the building.

And now he had his boss's approval to spend his weekend with Linc. Things were definitely looking up.

Well, except for the part that their planned controlled burn was delayed because of the weather, and the remainder of the day was spent indoors, going over more slides about fire management and various situations they might encounter in an active fire. Things like wind conditions and coordinating efforts with the various hotshot crews on the ground. All important stuff, but keeping his focus was as hard as usual, his mind continuing to wander to his favorite parts of the weekend along with all sorts of other random stuff his rabbit brain found more interesting than the PowerPoint.

Twice, Linc tapped his chair right before Sims called on him, the briefest of warnings before he was put on the spot, but enough so that he didn't look like a total idiot.

"Thanks for saving my bacon," he said in a low voice at lunch. Garrick was joking around with Kelley, and Ray and McKenna were deep in conversation and not paying them any attention.

"No problem. Your bacon's worth saving." Matching his whisper, Linc offered him a lopsided grin and one of the first purposefully flirty jokes he'd made. Something warm unfurled in Jacob's gut. This was only sex. He knew that. Hoping for anything else would be stupid, and still...

"You gonna come with me to Bend to collect this play set for the kids with Garrick's discount?" Setting up more non-sex time together was undoubtedly a mistake, and still he couldn't help hoping Linc said yes. His body tensed, and he tried not to stare too hard at Linc, waiting for a reply.

Taking another bite of his sandwich, Linc was silent for a moment, then finally nodded. "We'll take my truck. It's bigger, and there's sure to be a lot of boxes.

Friday? After work? That way it's ready for us for Saturday."

"Yup. Might as well get dinner on the way." He went ahead and pushed his luck. "You owe me a drink, you know."

Linc did an admirable job of not choking on his sandwich, instead looking thoughtful. Which was nice, him not looking spooked at the idea of something date-like. "So I do. Work it out with your mom for us to do the building and pickup, and get back to me so we can work out the specifics."

"Will do." To anyone listening, it was just two guys agreeing to do a nice deed, maybe with a side of some beer and food because that was only practical. Not a date, even if Jacob did have every intention of leaving his truck at Linc's as another practicality—one that made hooking up that much easier. But while there wasn't anything romantic about this conversation, little sunbeams of hope still danced around his gut, giddy and restless all at once, already counting down to the weekend. And maybe all that would come of this would be a new swing set for the kids and some hot sex on the down low for him, but it was more than he would have hoped for, even a week ago. It would be enough. It would have to, because wanting anything more would be a lesson in futility.

"The rook's getting better," Garrick said as he handed Linc a box with a drill, some spare batteries, a few wrenches and assorted bits. The late Friday afternoon sun winked at them, promising a sunny weekend, one he was apparently spending building a play structure with Jacob.

"He's not doing too bad." Linc put the box in the cab of his truck. He'd stick it in his garage when he met Jacob back at his place for their trek to Bend to pick up the parts for the play structure. He owned plenty of tools himself, but everyone seemed eager to take an interest in this project of Jacob's from Garrick arranging for the discount to Sims producing a large plastic steering wheel to add to the fort and some little curtains for the windows.

"His last several landings have been way better," Ray added as he brought over a bucket of sand toys for the digging pit part of the structure. He'd said his kids had contributed the toys, but they looked suspiciously new. "And he kept his head during the controlled burn. Now he's just got to pass the pack-out test."

"*He* will." Laughing, Jacob came over to them, his truck parked not that far from Linc's. His hair was still damp from a shower in the locker room, and he'd changed shirts. Not like dress clothes, but still he looked nicer than a trip to the home improvement store warranted in a blue shirt with buttons. "You guys don't have to sound so surprised that I'm not flaming out of training."

"Now, don't go getting a big head." Ray clapped him on the shoulder. "You're doing okay, but you still gotta put in the work."

"I know." Jacob didn't roll his eyes, but his tone said he was tempted. "We've got more jumps next week. Bring it on."

"That's the spirit." Garrick added his own light

punch to Jacob's arm. "I'm heading out. See you guys Monday. Bring pictures of the swing-set thing."

"Will do." Jacob answered first. Linc was still trying to wrap his head around their whole social network conspiring to ensure that he and Jacob spent much of the weekend together. And sure, most of it was going to be either in public or under the watchful eye of Jacob's family, but Linc still found it surreal.

And for all he told himself that this wasn't a big deal, it kind of was, deliberate plans that had nothing to do with sex. Sharing dinner simply because they wanted to and not as prelude to getting all tangled up on Linc's couch as they already had twice that week.

After saying goodbye to the guys, he drove home, trying to quiet the thrum in his veins when he saw Jacob already there, waiting for him. He helped Linc see to the dogs before they headed back to the truck. Part of Linc was disappointed that Jacob hadn't tried for a quickie back at the house, what with his spiffy shirt and smelling extra good all of a sudden thing, but they did need to pick up the parts, so he restrained himself from being the one to nail Jacob to the mudroom door. Again. *God.*

"I'm already hungry. Here's to hoping we can be fast at the store." Jacob stretched, more of that new shampoo of his filling the truck, as Linc headed for the rural highway that led south to Bend, heart of shopping and such in central Oregon. "Do you want me to suggest a place for dinner? I know a few places where you're not likely to run into anyone you know and where two guys sharing a meal isn't a big deal."

"This isn't a date," Linc protested, even though it sort of was, and he knew it.

"I didn't say it was. I was thinking of your comfort at being seen with me." Jacob sighed like Linc was insufferable and maybe he was. "And when was the last time you were on a date anyway? Maybe you've forgotten how they work."

"I've…" Linc started to protest, then paused. He honestly wasn't sure. Some double dates with Wyatt back in his twenties, painful setups with fresh-faced girls who deserved better. But on his own? It had been a while. "If we're defining date as sharing a meal at a restaurant knowing sex is probably on the table after, then yeah, I've had a few of those. Probably fewer than you and not as much around here, but when I was bumping around from crew to crew, it wasn't an unheard-of situation."

"Well, I'm a sure thing for later, and you know it. And we're sharing a meal out. So…"

Linc groaned because Jacob had him. "Fine. It's a date. Happy?"

"Ecstatic." Jacob sounded exactly the opposite.

"And I'm not a total country bumpkin over here. I know the sort of inclusive places you mean, and shocker, I actually know people who eat there. I'm not expecting us to stay anonymous no matter where we eat."

"You're not?"

"*No.* I'm not ashamed to be seen with you or something. Guys at work heard us make plans to go out to eat after getting the parts. It's not a big deal." Maybe if he said that enough, he might believe it. "Pick a place you like with red meat on the menu and decent portions, and I'm fine."

"Good." Jacob's tone was far more pleased now. "You know, I've always been curious why you don't just come out. Wyatt's homophobic high school squad notwithstanding, you mainly have open-minded friends, some of whom already know. You're not cringing at the idea of strangers maybe thinking you're on a date. You've had same-sex encounters prior to this..."

Hills rolling by, Linc let a few more miles tick away before he answered. "You're way more into labels than me. I don't see it as being closeted, not anymore. My dad...he was a bastard."

"I know." Jacob sounded all willing to be his champion again, making warmth bloom in Linc's chest.

"Anyway, he made Wyatt and his crowd look downright tolerant. I didn't want any part of him knowing, not when I was still bailing out his messes. But now... it's complicated. And I'm not sure it would make any difference. Not like I've got someone at home."

"True. Not like you're in a relationship where it might matter." With a wounded sigh, Jacob slumped in the seat.

Linc hadn't meant to hurt Jacob, and a heaviness settled over his shoulders. Not wanting to make it worse, he let Jacob stew as they started to approach more clumps of houses on the outskirts of Bend.

Finally, he couldn't stand the weighted silence anymore. "Out or not, it doesn't change things between us."

"I get that, thanks."

"Fuck." Linc was mucking it up, exactly as he'd feared. "Listen, even if I was staying, even if we didn't work together, it would still be..."

"Complicated. Your favorite word. Yeah. I know. Because you want to be noble or some such shit. And you made some promise to Wyatt a million years ago for God knows what reason."

Linc's fists tightened on the steering wheel. "It's not just the promise. Arguing over you almost tanked twenty plus years of friendship. He accused me of 'turning' you. More than once. If we were…a thing, a public thing, he wouldn't be the only one to think like that. I'm older. Too much older. People—your family—might start to wonder…"

That earned him an actual eye roll as he pulled into the store parking lot, Jacob huffing like he was running a hill. "And they'd be beyond stupid. Ten years is nothing. I've got a friend in Vegas with a leather Daddy more than twenty years older than him, and they are stupid in love."

"Good for them." Linc's jaw ached from clenching his teeth. He parked the truck but made no move to get out. "And say what you want about your family—I think you're wrong—but the fact remains that Wyatt saved my life. Maybe I didn't keep my word to him, and that's on me, but I still owe it to him and all the rest of them to do right by you. Keep you safe."

He didn't simply mean safe at work either. Safe from saddling himself with someone like Linc long-term, a guy who was too much older despite Jacob's protests otherwise, who couldn't manage to keep a promise to his best friend, a guy who had itchy feet, needing to outrun his past. And yeah, carrying on like this, it wasn't necessarily the smartest way to meet that goal, and it continued to weigh heavily on him, knowing he was risking a lot for both of them.

"Fuck." Jacob let out a tortured sound, head thump-

ing back against the seat. "This isn't how I wanted tonight to go. Because I get it—you're leaving, we work
together now, and you've got your own reasons, even
if I don't like them. I don't want to fight."

"Then let's not." Linc reached across the console,
squeezed his knee. "I know this is fucked up. And crazy.
And ill-advised. We've established all that. Us fighting
isn't going to change that, but there's also no reason why
we can't enjoy the night like you wanted."

"Okay." Shifting, Jacob laid his hand over Linc's,
keeping him in place. "But you *really* owe me that beer
now."

"You're on." Linc forced himself to smile. He got it,
putting up with him was no picnic, and Jacob was understandably frustrated. Honestly, he was probably only
a couple of weeks or so from deciding Linc was more
trouble than he was worth, this thing burning out, just
as he'd predicted. His shoulders knotted up, but his gut
knew it was true. And rather than fall to pieces over
it, the best thing was to simply make the most of the
time they did have. "Now, let's go pick a kick-ass play
structure for the kids."

The play structures were set up outside the store,
so they wandered about, considering the variations
and optional add-ons. Linc was more concerned with
the number of pieces and the types of connectors, but
Jacob, large kid that he was, was more into the "cool"
factor—pirate flags, twisty slides, climbing nets and
weird-shaped teeter-totters. He was cute, and despite
their earlier heavy talk, Linc found himself enjoying
watching him inspect each setup. They settled on a de-
luxe model with a little picnic table by the digging pit,

a bucket swing for baby Willow and a real roof on the fort part that made it more like a tiny house. And a pirate flag, which was totally worth the price of making Jacob smile.

"You guys must be the best uncles ever. Or...dads?" The young sales associate tossed her long silvery hair like either option was the same to her. And maybe it was. Not everyone was as accepting as Jacob wanted, but the truth was that the world was changing and plenty were. Unbidden, an image crept into his brain of the perfect clearing for a play structure behind his house, near the dog run and vegetable garden, visible from the kitchen window. The picture was so bright and crisp that he had to blink several times to get it gone.

"Sorry, didn't mean to offend." Finishing ringing them up, the salesclerk reminded him that he hadn't answered her inquiry.

"You didn't." Linc drew in a deep breath, trying to keep that vision of a future that wasn't to be away. "And he's the uncle. I'm just..."

"The other uncle." Making an exasperated noise like Linc was overcomplicating things again, Jacob pocketed his wallet. He'd refused the idea of letting Linc pay, saying he'd already worked it out with his mom. "Now, let's load up."

That took some work, all the boxes and timber, but finally they were back in the cab of the truck, Jacob messing around on his phone.

"Feed me," he demanded, setting the phone where Linc could see the GPS. "This place is newer, but fabulous reviews. And all the pictures look like giant portions. You'll be happy."

I'm with you. That's a given. Linc bit back the cheesy reply. "Sure. Sounds good."

It was weird, all the smiling and sentimental thoughts he had around Jacob. Felt bubbly, like some forgotten vintage of happiness. And he couldn't remember when he'd last been this happy. Before Wyatt's death for sure. All winter, he'd been sure he'd never laugh like this, and yet here he was, ribs and loaded mashed potatoes, laughing as Jacob did impressions of various blowhards at work.

The brewpub Jacob had picked was packed—Friday night, not quite to the summer tourist season yet, but enough hungry locals and out-of-towners to fill every table of the renovated brick building downtown. Mixed crowd—families, twentysomethings in groups, adults clearly on dates and more than one table with two men or two women. The busyness gave them a sort of privacy that he liked, made it possible to smile at Jacob however much he wanted, steal some of his fries and not have to worry about standing out.

I could get used to this. Even more insidious than his thoughts earlier, this one snuck its tentacles into soft, fleshy spots he'd forgotten he had. And for the first time, he'd found something worse than the misery of the last few months—hope. Hope that maybe he didn't have to hurt so damn much all the time. But hope when he should know better was fucking dangerous. Even so, he couldn't stop his smile, couldn't make this stop feeling so damn good. So damn right. And so very, very wrong.

Chapter Twelve

Even the sun beating down on Jacob's back wasn't enough to cut into his good mood. Wiping the sweat from his forehead with the edge of his T-shirt, he accepted an ice water from Junior, who'd come out with May to check on their progress.

"Is it done yet?" Junior was apparently oblivious to the stacks of timber and packets of screws still littering the side yard.

"Nope. Soon." Jacob patted his head. "Thanks for the water, kiddo."

"I wanna help," Junior demanded, apparently in no hurry to get back to the house.

"Let the big people work," May said, voice weary. She'd probably been preaching patience to Junior all morning.

"It's okay." Linc held out a hand for the kid. "You want to leave him out here? He's big enough to sort screws for me, hold some boards."

"Really?" May's eyes brightened, the same way Jacob's sisters' always did at the prospect of some kid-free time.

"Sure. I'll watch him too," Jacob offered.

"That would be great. Junior, you be good for your uncles." Step lighter, May headed back to the house.

Jacob was supposed to be shingling the clubhouse portion of the structure, but he kept getting distracted by watching Linc with Junior, the patience he displayed as Junior's arms wobbled holding a cross-brace for him.

"That's it. Great job. Soon this'll be the monkey bars." Voice encouraging, Linc worked quickly with the wrench. "You'll get to test everything out."

"Before Brayden and the other cousins?" Junior's eyes went wide as he forgot again to keep holding on, but Linc didn't get mad, just steadied the board himself and went on with his work.

"Yup. You'll be first."

A few minutes later, sorting piles of screws, Junior looked up with a pleased smile. "We make a good team, huh? Don't we, guys?"

"Yeah, we do." Jacob's throat was strangely tight. But he'd had the same thought himself several times already that day. Like on the job when Linc wasn't freaked out, they worked well together, no awkward power struggles or bumping into each other, rather each of them doing what was necessary, often without needing to talk it out. Linc was great at instinctively figuring out what Jacob wanted next, and Jacob liked to think he wasn't half-bad at that either. Despite the hard work and often obtuse directions, they hadn't argued at all. And now, they'd incorporated Junior into their tasks, easy as if the three of them did things together every weekend. "Thanks, buddy."

Easy was the last word he'd ever thought he'd be able to apply to Lincoln Reid, but it simply fit the past

twenty-four hours. After their contentious talk in the
truck on the way to Bend, they'd settled into some sort
of truce, where they didn't talk about the future. Instead, no matter whether it was a date or not, they'd had
a truly pleasant dinner followed by a dessert of sex, Linc
seeming way more driven than usual, keeping Jacob in
his bed until sleeping over was only practical.

"If anyone asks, I'll say I had too many beers with
dinner, slept it off on your couch," he'd offered as Linc
had made them both scrambled eggs in the morning.

"Sure." Linc didn't seem particularly concerned,
which was a nice change. And that same easiness had
kept up all day.

"You regretting turning down Portland now?" Linc
laughed as Jacob straightened yet another shingle.

"Not one bit," Jacob answered honestly, even with
Junior right there. "Nowhere I'd rather be."

"Well, I'd rather be watching TV." Junior stretched
like he was eighty, not five. "I'm going back to Mommy."

"You do that." Linc gave him a fond look before hol-
lering back at the house that Junior was coming back
so that the women knew where he was. Dropping to his
heels, Linc watched him walk away with a strange expression that Jacob couldn't quite make out.

"What?" he asked.

"Nothing. Just…he looks so much like Wyatt sometimes."

"Yeah. I forget that you guys were around his age
when you met. Before my time." He laughed and tried
not to get jealous over all the years Linc and Wyatt had
had that he wasn't a part of, stacks of memories that

forged the bond that Linc refused to break. "I need to hunt down a kindergarten pic of the two of you."

"Ask your mom. Anything like that at my house got ruined or thrown out after Mom died."

"That sucks. But we might have some old videos even—I remember Dad getting an old-style camcorder at some point, and I know Mom kept the tapes. You were around here so much that I'm sure you're in at least some of them."

"That I was." Returning to his part of the monkey bar assembly, Linc had a wistful air about him, voice sounding far away. "I owe your family a lot."

"Not *that* much." Jacob didn't particularly want to resurrect their argument from the day before, but he was damn tired of Linc playing the martyr. "You've done a ton around here too. I doubt there was a major remodel project after you were thirteen that didn't have you helping. You've done more than Jon probably, and more than the sisters and me for sure. We're the ones who owe you."

"It's not the same thing. I wasn't kidding the other day. Wyatt saved my life." Linc looked away, off into the horizon.

"On the job?" Finally done with the shingles, Jacob turned his attention to helping Linc tighten the rungs on the monkey bars.

"That too. There are plenty of stories I could tell you, but I'm thinking of one particular day when we were twelve, maybe. Mom had been gone about a year then, place had gone to shit, but we still hung out there some. Less pesky toddlers around." He gave Jacob a pointed looked.

"Hey, I can't help the fact that I'm age-challenged."

"Anyway, Wyatt and I, we're playing some game in the living room, and Dad comes in, already lit and on a tear. Doesn't like us there and doesn't like the mess of the board game even though the rest of the house is awful. Starts going on about my shortcomings—now remember, I was a skinny kid. Didn't really grow until late high school. Wyatt was bigger than me back then."

"I've seen pictures. You were shrimpy." Jacob didn't laugh because he had a feeling he wasn't going to like the rest of this story.

"Anyway, Dad, he'd been…mean. Knocked me around a lot. I hadn't told Wyatt much, but he knew. And that day, Dad didn't really care that he had an audience. He thought I was talking back, and he wasn't going to have it. He comes in and backhands me, and I stumble toward the wood stove—the one in the corner of my living room—and only Wyatt catching me saves me from falling into the hot stove."

"Wow." Jacob whistled low, wishing Linc's father wasn't already dead so he could give him a piece of his mind—and fists.

"But that's not all," Linc continued, still not meeting Jacob's eyes, rocking back and forth on the balls of his feet. "Wyatt stands up in front of me, puffed up like a rooster, and says to my dad that if he ever lays a hand on me again, he's telling his dad and mom on him, and your dad will make him sorry. Dad wasn't scared of much, but your dad intimidated most, and he knew he wouldn't stand for someone beating a kid. He started to cry and said he was sorry he was so drunk. And it didn't stop the drinking, but that was the last time he laid hands on me."

"Good." Jacob wasn't really sure what else to say—it was a side of Wyatt he hadn't seen all that often, loyal, protective, doing the right thing, standing up for someone who needed it. "I guess Wyatt did have a heart."

"He did." Linc nodded, returning his attention to the bolts he'd been tightening. "I know he wasn't always easy, especially as he got older. But he was one of the best guys I knew. If he hadn't caught me that day—who knows what could have happened. And that wasn't the only time he stood up for me. So when I say I owe him, I mean I *owe* him."

"Yeah. I get it." And he did, even as his back ached and his hands tightened on the metal pole he was holding. He got it. He couldn't argue with that kind of bond, the deep loyalty that Linc had, even in death, to his best friend. He was still just some pesky kid compared to that. Sure Linc liked banging him, but he wasn't ever going to inspire that kind of commitment from him, wasn't going to come close to replacing Wyatt in his heart.

"I'm glad he was there," he said as they moved on to the next task, attaching the monkey bars to the main structure. And he was glad, glad that Linc hadn't been alone back then, glad that he was alive now. Any other feelings he had like the bitter disappointment of knowing he'd never measure up to the legacy of Wyatt, well, that was his burden to bear, not Linc's.

Another question prodded at him, one he'd had for years. "If he had your back so much, shouldn't he have been more supportive when you came out to him?"

Linc snorted, pausing to shake his head. "There was no coming out. He caught me kissing the visiting team's running back behind the school senior year. And he was pissed."

"I can imagine. Not sure where he got his toxic views from, but he sure did like to run his mouth."

"That he did. Some of it was his crowd. Coaches we'd had in sports. Hell, even comedy he liked. I'd thought maybe us talking would change...but no." Linc looked so worn down that Jacob could easily picture his younger self, desperate for his best friend's approval. "Anyway, we had ourselves an awkward few years. We'd always planned on smoke jumping together, but it was...tense. I got on with a crew in Idaho first then I bounced around the West. Stayed gone a lot, thinking it might help. And I guess it mellowed him some. He'd worked his way up fighting fires here locally, and when we ended up on the same crew at last, it felt...right."

"Except for the part where he was still a dick about your sexuality. If I caught him in a couple of stupid wisecracks, I can imagine there were a lot more when you were alone."

"Some." Linc's expression became tight and pinched. "We didn't really talk about it much, but it was always there some, a tension that hadn't been there before. But for whatever reason, he kept it between us. Didn't let it keep him from asking me to stand up at his wedding. I don't pretend to understand how his brain worked, but you painting him as all...toxic isn't the Wyatt I knew."

"I get that." And he did. He wasn't ever going to know the Wyatt that Linc had cared so deeply about, wasn't ever going to be able to make sense of all of Wyatt's contradictions. The bully and the mean drunk. The best friend and the lifesaver. He'd known one a little too well and the other not at all. And that made his jaw clench, made his shoulders tense with a loss he'd never really considered that much, the loss of a guy he'd never get to know, the loss of a future where Wyatt might have redeemed himself, been the brother Jacob had needed and the friend Linc had deserved.

Nodding, Linc resumed the work, sliding into more of the thoughtful silence that Jacob liked almost as much as their deeper conversations. He liked that they could tackle heavy shit as well as just hang out, no obligation to make small talk. Working together, building something real and tangible together, was immensely satisfying, as was the way Linc respected his interpretation of the directions and asked his opinion about equipment placement. Similar to at work, feeling like Linc finally saw him as an adult equal made his shoulders lift and step lighten, a deep contentment settling over him.

"How much more do you think we've got to do here?" he asked after a while.

"You sound like Junior." Linc teased, easiness between them fully restored, at least for now. "Honestly, we might have to finish up tomorrow morning if we run out of daylight tonight."

"That's okay. And I can do it if you've got other things to do."

"Nah. I'll be here." Linc shrugged.

"Don't worry, the next time I want to spend the weekend with you, I'll figure out something with fewer screws."

"Oh, I don't know about that. Screws aren't *all* bad."

Linc raised an eyebrow and all of a sudden Jacob was right back in his bed the night before, panting and begging, the good kind of sweaty and desperate.

"I think I left my hoodie at your place last night. Could I stop by after we finish up here?" They were alone, and there was no reason why he couldn't just come out and ask to hook up that night, but using the excuse gave them both an out, didn't require him to look quite so needy.

"Suppose you could." Linc's eyes flashed hot and dark, full of promise for another late night. Good. Maybe he'd never be Wyatt, but he could at least be *something* to Linc, something he wanted and craved, even temporarily. And maybe that would be enough. It would have to be.

He was about to continue their little flirt when the sound of footsteps gave him pause.

"Food break!" Jacob's mom called from the patio, and they dutifully set their tools aside and headed in. She and May had set out more water, brownies and fixings for sandwiches.

As they finished eating, the baby started fussing in her playpen, and Linc scooped her up before May could. Taking her back to the table, Linc bounced and patted the baby while Junior peppered him with more questions about the construction process. Jacob went ahead and cleared the table for his mom, taking the dirty dishes to the sink, where she was already washing up.

"Now, that's nice to see," Mom said in a low voice, eyes darting back to the dining area. "He's so good with them."

Hell. Not her too. Jacob stifled a groan. "Don't go getting ideas."

"Who me?" Her expression was too carefully innocent to be believed. "I'm just pointing out the obvious."

God, what a mess. He desperately wanted to tell his mom that any matchmaking was likely to be futile, but it wasn't his place to out Linc or even insinuate. And it wasn't like he had a hold on Linc himself. That much was painfully clear.

"Way too soon," he said instead, trying to force his jaw to loosen up.

"Yeah." His mother's shoulders deflated. "You're right."

He was. But maybe Linc had a point too—maybe there would be disappointment and hurt feelings if Linc ever did come out. Jacob didn't think anyone else would make stupid accusations like the nastiness Wyatt had spewed, but what did he know? He hated to admit it, but Linc was right that him coming out would change how people saw him. He couldn't completely discount those worries. And behind all that was his own worry— no, not worry. Certainty. Certainty that whatever he had with Linc wasn't ever going to be enough to tempt Linc into anything other than knocking boots on the down low.

But then his eyes met Linc's from across the room and Linc gave him a lopsided smile over the top of the baby's head, and that was all Jacob needed to know deep in his bones that he'd keep taking whatever Linc wanted to give him as long as he possibly could. Fuck pride. He wasn't letting Linc go, not yet.

* * *

"I'm gonna need photographic proof that you guys weren't screwing around all weekend." Garrick laughed, but Linc still almost choked on his coffee as he took a seat for the Monday morning briefing. There *had* been a fair bit of screwing, both the literal and the figurative kind, and he didn't need Garrick catching on to the weekend having been anything other than a chore.

"Here." Much calmer, Jacob passed over his phone, picture gallery already open. Curious, Linc looked over Garrick's shoulder as he thumbed through, dread gathering in his stomach that Jacob hadn't done anything stupid like get a picture of him sleeping. But so far, the pictures were just of the progress of the play structure, from collection of boxes to the finished structure with Junior and some of the other cousins playing on Sunday. Plenty of Linc working, but all clothed, thank God.

Still, the snapshots made his stomach weirdly wobbly, what they revealed. Him lifting timbers. Him smiling, something he thought he'd forgotten how to do. Him with Junior. Nothing goofy, but still…personal. And he wasn't one for pictures. After his dad ruined most of his childhood mementos, he'd learned not to get sentimental about much. As an adult, he didn't see much point in a collection of snapshots, but the pictures Jacob took of the weekend made him ache in an unexpected way, wanting to be back there in the memory, working side by side with Jacob, wanting to be the guy Jacob saw when he snapped the shutter.

"You guys should hire yourselves out." Kelley too leaned in for a look. "Pretty impressive stuff. Still

though, Jacob, you missed a heck of a party in Portland. Next time?"

Jacob made a noncommittal noise. "Maybe."

All the warmth the pictures had inspired in Linc fled,
replaced by a niggling reminder that this was temporary. Someday, probably soon, Jacob would be back to
the party scene, back to screwing around, and there was
nothing Linc could do about it. He certainly couldn't go
getting jealous of the Portland pretty boys waiting for
Jacob's attention. He had no hold on the guy, even now.
Didn't matter how primal and crazed he made Linc, all
that possessiveness was as futile as trying to bottle up
smoke. Waste of energy. And yet...

Don't go. The growl vibrated in his throat, close to
escaping, right as the meeting began, saving him from
his stupid self yet again.

"We're about to the halfway point of the training period, so it's a good time to evaluate your pack-out test
scores." Sims paced at the front of the room. "If you fail
the pack-out test, you'll get another chance when we repeat it, but failure to pass at the end of training means
you won't be jumping with us this season."

They were scheduled for more unseasonal warmth,
which would make the test a miserable slog. Three miles
seemed like twenty when loaded down with over a hun-
dred pounds of gear, and each year, the pack-out test
was Linc's least favorite part of spring training.

The designated course was at least nominally level,
but level at altitude was still hard work, and there were
still some softer inclines and declines to navigate. Gearing up, Linc took time to make sure he was hydrated—
he'd been at this enough years to know that was key.

Figuring that Jacob would be in the lead pack as usual, Linc settled himself at the rear, appointing himself the human equivalent of Ray's pace car. They'd probably let Ray slide into the spotter role even with a borderline score, but it was also a point of pride to pass.

"You've got this. Come on," he huffed. They'd lost sight of the front group, but that was okay. They only needed to finish under the time limit. Stopping to suck down more water, he adjusted his gear. Somehow this was easier when it was out in the field, adrenaline pounding, time of the essence, crew counting on them to make it to the extraction point. Out here, sun beating down, no fire in sight, the urgency was in short supply.

But he forced himself to keep moving and to stay upbeat for Ray's sake. At least there was a slight breeze, but still he was drenched in sweat by the halfway point. Finally, time ticking down, they entered the home stretch.

"Go ahead," Ray panted. "Gotta get your time."

"Nothing doing. We're in this together. You can do it." Linc adjusted his pace further, aware of the minutes passing, but trying to keep his focus on Ray and getting him to the finish.

But right as they made the final turn, higher-ups with clipboards in sight, Ray slowed further.

"What's up with them?" Ray pointed to a clump off to the side. Garrick and McKenna loomed over two figures seated on the ground. Sims was there too, which couldn't be good.

Jacob. Somehow the internal homing beacon he had for Jacob warned him even before he figured out that Jacob and Kelley were indeed the two on the ground.

They were both pale as copier paper, and Jacob had his hands on his knees.

"What happened?" Ray came to a stop by the group, giving Linc an excuse to stop too.

"Overheated," Garrick explained in grim tones. "Pushed too hard, too fast. Kelley's probably dehydrated, but our rook's not much better, puking his guts out."

"I can finish," Jacob said weakly.

"No way." Sims shook her head. "You'll get another shot at this, but I'm not letting you risk real injury. We'll handle your gear. I want you to get some fluids, then when you feel up to it, you can either bunk down back at base or head home, but you're taking the afternoon off, and that's an order."

"I'm not sick," Jacob protested, even as Kelley nodded. Her shoulders were slumped and even her usually spiky hair drooped. And Jacob's voice was even saggier. "Who hasn't puked while exercising before? It happens."

"Yup. But you don't want to spend all week miserable." Leaning down, Garrick clapped him on the shoulder. "You need to rest up. Lingering dehydration is no joke, and there's always the chance you picked up a bug on the weekend."

Weekend. Fuck. Was this Linc's fault? Too many late nights? Too little sleep? Had Jacob drunk enough during the building? Had the sex worn him out too much? His own gut churned, guilt and concern bubbling up like toxic sludge. He knew how much Jacob wanted this. He had to be truly hurting to tap out like this.

Garrick helped Jacob to his feet, steadying him when

his legs wobbled, and the urge to reach for him was so strong that Linc had to clench his fists and plant his feet to keep from moving.

"Reid. You guys need to finish." Sims gestured at him and Ray. "We've got this."

The last thing he wanted to do was leave Jacob hurting and unhappy, but an order was an order. He trusted Garrick and McKenna to take care of the rookies, but that didn't cancel out the urge to be the one hovering.

"They're right. You both need rest." He didn't let his eyes linger on Jacob too much, not wanting to risk giving too much away. "You take care. You don't want to miss out on the jumps later in the week."

"Exactly." Garrick dropped his voice, saying something to Jacob in low tones that Linc couldn't make out.

"Let's go." Ray sounded as resigned as Linc felt, but he didn't want to give Sims reason to repeat her order either.

Reluctantly, he finished the course, mind churning. Not long after they finished, an ATV pulling a small cart came by loaded down with Jacob, Kelley and their gear.

"He says he's good to drive back to his place," Garrick reported. He'd apparently finished the course himself before doubling back to check on the rookies, and the extra mileage showed in the tight lines around his face and sweat dripping down his neck. "One of us should maybe check on him after work."

"I will." Linc kept his voice firm, not too eager, but not allowing Garrick to talk him out of it either. He'd already been planning on that himself, distracting himself on the finish to the course with thoughts of electrolyte beverages and soup for Jacob.

"Good." Garrick shook his head. "Never thought I'd see you as the mother hen, but you looked almost as sick as him out there."

"It's not that." Linc made a dismissive gesture. "More that I know how much he wants this. Failing training would gut him."

"He's not gonna fail." Garrick sounded a lot surer than Linc currently felt. "He's in good shape. Just had a bad morning."

Because of me. Shit. Maybe he'd have had an easier time of it had he gone to Portland. Again the guilt took hold of Linc, made it hard to breathe.

"He'll get it." He tried to make himself believe the words.

"Tell him we're all pulling for him," Ray added. "And it's good to see you guys friendly again. Nice work on that play structure. You make a good team."

Yeah, we do. Linc's throat tightened. He liked them better as friends too, liked being a team more than he should. And as much as he didn't want to care, didn't want to be this concerned, he was. He wasn't going to rest easy until he saw for himself that Jacob was okay.

Chapter Thirteen

A loaded cement truck had nothing on the weight bearing down on Jacob's shoulders. His head felt like a wrecking ball had smashed into all his logic centers, making the world fuzzy. After protesting that he didn't need rest, he'd slept most of the afternoon, first time napping since he'd had the flu several years back. But he wasn't sick. Just stupid.

He'd fucked up. Hadn't modulated his fluid intake right. Had pushed too hard, wanting to show off with one of the best times, hadn't calculated for the effect of all the excess weight of the gear. And hell, Kelley at least had the excuse of being slightly hungover from her weekend fun. He was simply a dumbass. And her getting ill was at least partly his fault as well—he'd set too brutal of a pace for both of them. And now look at what had happened. Everything riding on the retake. Fuck.

A knocking at his trailer's door cut through his still half-asleep brain. And somehow he knew even before he stumbled to the door who it was.

Linc.

His breath hitched as he opened the door to reveal

the man himself standing there, two grocery bags in his arms.

"What are you doing here?" His voice came out all croaky.

"Checking on you. And from the way you sound, you need it."

He swallowed, trying to get the cottony feel out of his throat. "I'm fine."

"Yeah, right." Linc shook his head, apparently not buying it. He held up the bags. "Can I come in? I brought you some stuff that might help."

"Yeah. Okay." He stepped aside so that Linc could come into the small space. The trailer had never felt as small as it did with Linc standing in the entryway. "Aren't you worried about being seen here? People talk."

"Eh." After he set the bags on the narrow counter, Linc made a dismissive gesture. "Garrick told me to come. And Sims told me what brand of electrolyte beverage to get for you."

"Oh, well, if you got permission, by all means." Making a sweeping arm movement, he pointed at his small built-in couch at the rear of the trailer. "Make yourself at home. We wouldn't want to waste your Get Out of Jail Free card."

"It's not like that," Linc protested as he unloaded the bags, ignoring Jacob's unspoken order to sit. "I would have come anyway. I just meant we don't have to worry. Which I would think you'd want. Thought you were all about convenient excuses."

"Only when they don't backfire." Stretching, he groaned. And even if Linc wasn't going to sit, he was.

He sank onto the bench seat in the tiny eating nook opposite the kitchen area.

"So, it *was* the work this weekend? Overdid it, you think?" Sounding defeated, Linc uncapped a bottle of a popular sports drink and passed it over.

"You don't need to go blaming yourself. Honestly, I think it was my stupid ego. Pushed too hard, too fast. Forgot to pace myself and to drink water slowly. The sun this weekend probably didn't help, but if you're thinking it was the sex, you're nuts."

"I kept you up late." Apparently intent on making himself at home, Linc rustled around in Jacob's limited kitchen until he came up with a pot.

"And I loved every minute." The beverage was helping him feel more human and put more oomph in his voice. "Real talk, I wouldn't change a thing about the weekend."

"Good." The tips of Linc's ears turned pink, and he looked away. "Me too."

"So what are you cooking me?" Still feeling foolish for earlier, he probably wasn't the best company, but he also wasn't turning down Linc's cooking. Or *him*.

"Soup. The canned stuff is crap—full of sodium and other stuff you don't need. This will sit right with your stomach."

That Linc cared enough to make him something from scratch was better than any pain reliever at removing some of the weight from his shoulders.

"Thanks. Can I help?"

"You can take a shower." Linc's nose wrinkled. "I'm betting you just came back and collapsed?"

"Something like that." Jacob gave a self-conscious

laugh. "And I'd invite you to join me, but it's barely big enough for me. Your master shower has spoiled me."

"Well, I'm glad someone appreciates it. Tiling in there was a bitch." As usual, Linc shrugged off the praise. "Go. Shower. And we'll see what you're up to after the food."

"Is that a proposition? Please?" He grinned at Linc as he grabbed a towel.

"We don't want you worn out for tomorrow…"

"Then you can do all the work." Winking, he headed for the shower before Linc could come up with more reasons why they shouldn't fuck. Now that Linc was here, he was feeling way better, and sex sounded like the perfect distraction from all the ways he'd screwed up.

Despite the cramped quarters, he took his time in the shower, not jacking off, but doing plenty of thinking about what they could do after dinner.

"Are the dogs going to be okay?" he asked Linc when he emerged, not bothering with clothes beyond a pair of briefs. If his lack of dress bothered Linc, so much the better.

"Yeah, I stopped off there for some herbs for your soup and fed them early, checked the water, and made sure they had access to their run. They're fine." Linc dished up the soup into the only two bowls Jacob owned, both castoffs from his mom, one with snowflakes and one with superheroes. "Eat slow, okay? I don't want you puking up my hard work."

"I won't. You really brought herbs for me?" Somehow that touched him even more than the rest of it.

"Didn't trust you to have dried stuff on hand." Linc

shrugged. "And it's nothing that special—chicken breast, couple of vegetables, a little rice for body."

"Well, it smells great." He took the seat opposite Linc at the table. "I'd praise you for figuring out my kitchen setup, but this probably wasn't your first time cooking here, right? Is it too weird being here?"

He hated bringing up Wyatt, but he didn't like dancing around the fact that this was his old place either.

"I probably made a hangover cure here a couple of times. Not sure. We didn't hang out here a ton—I was gone a lot back then. And it's cramped. Wyatt was always one for having his whole crowd together. Can't really fit more than two in here."

"Not comfortably at least. I've tried." Jacob laughed before tasting the soup. Linc was right—it was simple, but good. Creamy with the rice, subtly seasoned with rosemary and onion, and soothing on his stomach.

"Don't tell me that." Linc made a sound that might as well have come from a prissy maiden aunt for all its self-righteousness.

"I didn't mean an orgy. God. Just friends hanging out." He took another bite, then added, "Honestly, you're the first date I've had over in a long time. I'm not nearly as wild as you seem to think I am."

"This isn't—"

"A date. Yeah, you tell yourself that, but generally a guy shows up to cook for me, brings a beverage and doesn't mind me being in my underwear, it's a date."

"A sports drink is hardly the same as wine."

"That's your defense? You brought me four flavors. Come on. Admit it. This is a booty call with a side of you wanting to check up on me."

Linc cared, Jacob knew he did, and with his eyes, he tried to dare him to admit it.

"I told you. Everyone was worried about you. Me included. We can't afford to be down a person, not this late into training."

"Oh, come off it. You'd be relieved if I dropped out, and you know it." Now he was back to the same exasperation, knowing full well that Linc wouldn't shed any tears if he couldn't pass the test on a second try.

Huffing out a breath, Linc took his time answering. "That's not fair. Yeah, I'd rather you not put yourself in danger, especially when your mom's been through so much. That hasn't changed. But I also know how much this means to you. I get it now. You're not simply being a reckless kid here. You want this. And I respect that. Not saying I like it, but I respect it."

"You do?" Jacob's chest pinched, Linc's respect even more satisfying than his praise, soothing a need he hadn't even known he'd had.

"Yeah. And I'd be lying if I didn't admit you're good at the job, today notwithstanding, and you're hardly the first rookie to tap out on their first pack-out test. Like you said, puking with extreme exercise isn't that uncommon. I've done it myself and battled heat exhaustion more than a couple of times."

"I'm going to pass the next time," he said firmly.

"Yeah, you are," Linc agreed with a sigh. "And so I'm trying to make my peace with you being on the job. I didn't come here to gloat or to try again to change your mind."

"Then why'd you come? Really?" He kept his voice soft, wanting to coax out a real answer.

Groaning, Linc set down his spoon and pushed his bowl aside. "Fine. I needed to see for myself that you were all right. I knew I wouldn't be able to sleep until I saw how you were doing. That okay?"

"Yeah." Jacob liked knowing Linc was there for his own reasons, not just because the others at work were worried or because he felt responsible. But he cared. And maybe Jacob wasn't ever getting him to admit that, but he did. "I'm glad you came."

"You just like my cooking."

"That and I want to get laid." Jacob let himself make light. He knew the truth, and that was enough for now.

"I noticed." Linc dropped his eyes to Jacob's lap and his red briefs, desire clear even if he refused to say it.

"You like it and you know it."

"Maybe. Finish your soup."

"Yes, sir." Jacob gave him a mock salute before digging back into the soup. "I promise I'm feeling better. More than up for work tomorrow. And you tonight."

"Don't wear those to work." Linc's eyes still hadn't left his briefs.

"You like them." He preened and let his legs fall open as he took the last bite of his soup.

"You look ready to accept tips at some Portland go-go bar."

"Ah. You're worried if I wear them to work, people might start slipping fives in my waistband?"

"Fine. I like them. Happy?"

"Thrilled." He grinned up at him as Linc stood, collecting both their empty bowls.

"You go lie on your bed while I wash up." He gave him a purposeful look, but Jacob didn't move.

"You cooked, so I should help."

"Nope. You said you wanted me to do all the work."

"I meant—"

"Yeah, and if you want that, you'll rest up."

"Fine. Evil taskmaster." He headed for the bedroom that was essentially only a bed, a door and some built-ins. Pausing at the door, he turned. "Linc?"

"Yeah?" Linc looked braced for more argument from him.

"Thank you. For coming. And for cooking. And for... just...thanks. That's all."

"Any time." Linc's expression softened and he looked like he wanted to say more, but then he sighed. Making a shooing motion, he returned to the dishes, leaving Jacob to ponder what he'd been about to say while he arranged himself on his bed.

He didn't bother with the TV on the wall—no sense in pretending they were going to do anything other than fuck. And he'd barely had time to scroll through his phone messages before Linc was kicking off his shoes and joining him on the bed.

"Kelley says she's feeling better," he reported as Linc plucked the phone from his hand.

"Good." Linc set his phone back on the shelf, crawling toward Jacob.

"I feel bad. I pushed the pace too hard on her. And it's my fault she had to do all the driving on her own this weekend."

"A very wise guy once told me that guilt is pointless. It's not your fault, but if it makes you feel better to apologize..." He held Jacob's phone back out.

"I did." God, he certainly didn't deserve either Kelley's forgiveness or Linc's kindness, but he'd do his best to be grateful for both. "Right now I just want to forget about my own stupidity for a while, you know?"

"Been there. And you're not stupid." Linc rubbed his shoulder, voice reassuring before his touch turned more seductive, trailing down his arm. "But I'm happy to help. Roll over."

"Yes, sir." He loved how Linc's eyes turned feral. Hungry. And Jacob was only too happy to be dessert.

Pulling off his shirt, Linc stripped down to his black boxer briefs. "You got stuff?"

"Drawer next to you. Expiration date is good—"

"I'm sure." Linc's arrogance was going to land him out on the steps, neither of them getting what they wanted.

"*Because* I just bought them. Last week. After we started fucking around."

"Sorry." At least he had the grace to look contrite. And instead of yanking off Jacob's underwear as he'd expected, Linc straddled his hips, thumbs digging into Jacob's neck.

"What are you doing?"

"Work. As requested, I believe." He kept up the firm massage, strong hands loosening long-held knots in Jacob's neck.

"Ass. You know what I mean. This isn't fucking."

"Nope. It's not. Good that you noticed." Still moving with maddening slowness, he worked over Jacob's shoulders and biceps next, all the muscles that still ached from hauling the heavy gear that morning. "Settle down. You'd think you'd never had a massage."

"Not from you." And if he was honest, not one in

a bed like this. Sports medicine ones, sure. But not a lover. Felt…strange. Intimate. Especially coming from Linc, who was usually so careful about keeping his distance on all levels.

"First time for everything." Linc gave his ass a gentle slap, and a snippet of an old fantasy flashed in Jacob's brain. Not that his actual first time had been that traumatic or anything, but there was something about the notion of it being Linc, not Tyler, that was particularly seductive. Linc wouldn't have made him flip for who was bottoming and then made him feel bad for "losing." And Linc would have lasted more than two minutes. But mainly, Linc would have been *Linc*.

"Oomph." He couldn't hold back a groan as Linc worked a particularly tense muscle around his shoulder blade. "Okay, you're good at this."

"Good." Linc laughed. "Kinda winging it, to be honest."

His humbleness was endearing to the point that Jacob had to turn his face into the pillow, reluctant to reveal how this gesture made his insides all gushy. But then Linc leaned forward, adding kisses to the mix, and Jacob's inner marshmallow roasted as lust replaced sentiment. He already had plenty of evidence to say that Linc was almost as oral as he was, and the guy was definitely obsessed with Jacob's neck. But tonight, he took it to another level, raining kisses down Jacob's spine, licking over his shoulder blades, tongue even more devastating than his hands had been.

And right when Jacob thought he might be about to melt into the sheets, Linc scooted lower, hands knead-

ing Jacob's ass as his mouth teased all along the waistband of his briefs.

"Are we doing that thing where I have to beg you
to fuck me again?" His voice managed to sound both
sleepy and impatient.

"Maybe." Linc lightly bit his ass before peeling down
Jacob's briefs, mouth following the path of his fingers.

"You don't have to—*oh, fuck.*" Whatever gallant
protest he'd been about to make died on a rush of pure
pleasure as Linc spread his ass, wasting no time in at-
tacking Jacob's rim.

"You were saying?" Chuckling darkly, Linc pulled
back long enough to ask.

"Didn't mean *that* kind of work. *Damn.*"

Linc didn't even let him finish his thought before he
was back, teasing and torturing him with his lips and
tongue. Jacob had played around with rimming before,
but never with someone who seemed so determined to
make it a fucking meal. For all his humbleness, Linc
clearly knew what he was doing with this, flicking and
licking and sucking.

"Linc. Fuck. Linc." Jacob wasn't even aware that his
hips were rocking until the friction on his dick went
from pleasant to oh-fuck good seemingly in the space
of seconds. But the hoarseness in his throat said Linc
had probably been at it awhile, him moaning and shame-
lessly humping the bed the whole time.

"Stop," he managed to grit out. "Stop. Gonna come."

"Fine. Take all my fun." Sitting back on his heels,
Linc dug around in Jacob's drawer, coming up with the
lube and condoms. "Damn. You're fucking sexy that

way. Tempted to get you off with nothing other than my mouth."

"But you won't." Jacob wasn't above whining. Or begging. "Fuck me. Please."

He bumped his hips up, trying to make his point, but Linc pinned him to the mattress. "I do the work, remember?"

"Yeah." Fuck but Linc pushy like this, all dominating, was the sexiest thing ever. And it was way more intense this way, flat on his front, letting Linc move him around, no choice but to take whatever it was Linc wanted to give him. It was tighter too, even after all that rimming, Linc's lubed fingers feeling broader than usual.

Breathing deep, he tried to relax into the stretch. Even after having done this together a few times now, this was the part he still wasn't crazy about, the needing to let his body adjust. The actual fucking was glorious. But the getting there made him impatient, made him want to rush.

He tried again to push back. "You can—"

"Nope." Linc held him firmly in place. "We do this my way."

"You're getting off on this power trip," he complained, even as he kind of did love Linc like this.

"Hey, you're the one who needs to rest up," Linc said right as his fingers connected with Jacob's gland and oh-fucking-kay, all the waiting and adjusting was worth it.

"Just fuck me," he begged, all chill lost in a rush of blinding need and want.

"Mmm. That's more like it." Linc's voice was like

the purr of a classic car, the seductive sound of a lot of horsepower about to get unleashed.

Jacob had something to say about arrogant, bossy men, but whatever flip response he'd been planning fled as Linc shifted, condom-covered cock dragging along Jacob's ass, teasing. Then the blunt pressure at his rim made him gasp.

"Easy." Linc ran a hand down Jacob's back, easing forward slowly, giving Jacob almost too much time to adjust.

"Just go," he urged. Somehow the more Linc took his time, the more he took care of Jacob, the harder it was to focus on the fuck, the harder it was to convince himself that the fuck was all there was. Soft touches and murmured praise felt perilously close to affection, and affection was too close of a cousin to everything he'd ever wanted from Linc.

"We'll get there." Not surprisingly, Linc didn't listen to his pleas, continuing to work in with shallow thrusts that stole Jacob's breath. Finally, Linc's balls brushed his ass, and they both moaned. The position itself was as intense as all the emotions it inspired, every nerve ending sensitive, body tight even as the angle let Linc go deep, every stroke nailing his gland.

"Fuck." He wanted to fuck back, get more of that delicious pressure, but Linc held him fast. This level of letting go was something new, nothing to do but lie there, taking everything Linc wanted to give him, completely at his mercy. And hell if that wasn't a metaphor for his whole damn life. But at a certain point, he stopped holding back, gave in to the urge to meld into the sensations, feather in the wind, along for the ride, no longer trying to control it.

Above him, Linc was groaning and muttering praise, sounds almost as arousing as his thrusts. He'd never come from fucking without a hand on his cock, but the more the tension in his muscles built, the more likely it seemed that the friction against the sheet was going to be enough.

"Oh, fuck. I think I can…" He more than half expected Linc to tell him no, make him wait, but Linc made a satisfied growl, speeding up.

"Yeah, you can." Linc's voice was strained and his arm shook against Jacob's back. Maybe he wasn't quite so iron-control after all. And knowing this was getting to him too pushed Jacob further, let him chase the climax that kept teasing the edges of his awareness. Then Linc shifted, going deeper and harder, giving Jacob just enough room to writhe against the bed, cock dragging against the sheet, and the prospect of coming went from nice possibility to absolute certainty.

"Coming. Coming. God." He probably didn't have to announce it as his whole body went stiff, everything clenching before he collapsed in giant shudders, a sticky, sweaty mess. And Linc didn't have to say a thing for Jacob to tell he was there too, hips hammering hard, as he made a low, pained noise.

"Fuck." Linc dropped kisses all across Jacob's shoulders, more of that caretaking as he eased out. "You're something else."

"Something good?" Sleepy, he snuggled into Linc's side, mess be damned.

"More like trouble." Linc groaned and held him close.

"At least I'm good at it." He kissed Linc's arm as he snaked his hand down Jacob's chest.

"The best." Linc buried his face in Jacob's hair. "Promise I'm not sleeping over, but—"

"Sleep. I'll kick you out later." Simply having Linc here, in his space, his bed was enough of a novelty that he didn't join Linc in drifting off, instead luxuriating in the rare quiet moments of closeness. Not sex. Not guilt. Not obligation or misguided duty. Only...intimacy. The sort of familiarity he'd never had before and already craved more of. He liked to think that few others had ever seen this side of Linc and that this was something only for them. Special.

Fuck. He had it bad. He'd waited years to be special enough for Linc to make an exception for, and now that he had this, it wasn't enough. He wanted more. Wanted everything. And that sort of want could only lead to pain, but that didn't stop his chest from tightening and his hands from pulling Linc in even closer. He wanted, and he wasn't letting go.

Chapter Fourteen

"Burn boss wants to see you, Reid." McKenna's voice crackled across the radio.

"On my way." Linc was ready to get this show on the road. Nodding at Garrick and Jacob, who had been waiting next to him, he headed toward the makeshift command where the person in charge of that day's pre-scribed burn waited. It was easier these days to walk on by Jacob, not have to deal with a racing pulse or galloping thoughts. He'd see Jacob alone later, and that made it easier to be professional on the job, get done what needed doing and trust Jacob to handle his duties.

Something had shifted the past few weeks, especially once Jacob had passed training along with the other rookies. Yeah, he didn't want Jacob in danger, was no more comfortable with that than he'd been years ago, but he respected Jacob's goals.

In short, he cared. Far more than he'd ever thought possible. Of course, in the background everything else still swirled—all the reasons this was a bad idea like the whole business of sleeping with a guy he worked with, something he tried not to dwell on too much. When he was a rookie himself, bumping around from crew to crew, he'd fucked around some, and it had almost always gone badly, no getting around the awkward no matter how much on the down low the hookup had been. Here, the awkward would be off the charts if their repeated hookups came out, but even so he couldn't seem to quit Jacob, even when ending badly seemed more and more inevitable.

They were *supposed* to be working this...whatever it was out of their systems. But it had been weeks now, and Linc's lust showed no signs of burning itself out, and miracle of miracles Jacob kept coming around, hadn't gotten tired of Linc and the secrecy. If anything he'd damn embedded himself in Linc's life, eating his food, playing with his dogs, watching his TV. Hell, he'd even brought groceries last visit when he'd helped Linc transplant several trays of seedlings to the garden. They spent as much time out of bed as in it, talking and hanging out, each encounter another cozy layer Linc would eventually have to peel away. But not yet.

"We ready?" he asked Morrison, the burn boss who had spent weeks planning for that day's fire. One thing outsiders seldom understood about smoke jumping was how much hurry up and wait there was, and how much time was spent on other forest management projects designed to ensure that their emergency services were needed less. Today they'd been loaned out to help with a prescribed burn project east of Prineville. May had given way to early June, and the risk for fires increased with each sunny week, especially as fireworks season crept up on them. But so far they'd had limited emergency callouts, mainly working on planned projects.

This was a larger controlled burn, so several hotshot

and engine crews were assisting along with the crews from the smoke-jumping base. Their job would be to keep the fire within the designated boundaries. Back at base, another crew stood ready to parachute in if things got out of hand and their services were needed. But the objective was to not get to that point.

"I'm not liking this wind." Morrison frowned. "I want your crew to move into position ahead of ignition, get us some additional data on how the fire is moving. We're going ahead with the burn, but we need to be smart."

"Absolutely. We're on it." This sort of complex management was exactly why they were involved—their years of experience and training would help the other crews do their jobs more effectively. After sorting out more of what the burn boss needed from them, he took Garrick, Ray and Jacob with him to talk with the firing boss—the person in charge of all the planned ignitions.

Their plan was worked out, so they geared up, checked their communications set, and trudged out. While they waited for the ten a.m. ignition start, Linc checked all the readings on their equipment while Jacob and Garrick were deep in conversation about something. And if Linc was jealous about how close they stood or how animated their voices were, he quickly dismissed that as being pointless. He'd get Jacob all to himself soon enough.

"Are we keeping you guys from book club or what?" Ray teased.

"Nah." Garrick laughed and pointed at Jacob. "I was just convincing the birthday boy here that it would be rude to not let us take him out after we're done here."

"It's your birthday?" Damn. Linc had totally forgotten that Jacob's birthday was this part of June, and now he felt stupid. Even so, he modulated his tone, trying to not sound entitled or hurt. But it would have been nice for Jacob to drop a damn hint on one of his many secret visits.

"I know." Garrick slapped Jacob on the shoulder. "He kept mighty quiet. I wouldn't know if Kelley hadn't said something. She and McKenna and a bunch of others want to go out, but he keeps putting us off. Hedging his bets for a better time or something."

"It's not that." Jacob shot Linc a helpless look, shoulders slumping. Heck. He must have been hoping for some Friday night alone time, same as Linc. But Linc couldn't keep him from his friends, especially not on his birthday.

"Then it's settled," Garrick said firmly. "You're going. Ray, you in? Surely the wife can spare you an hour?"

"One beer," Ray allowed, keeping his gaze on the horizon, same as Linc should be doing, no doubt scanning for the start of smoke. "You in, Reid?"

"Yeah," Garrick answered for him. "You're even worse than the birthday boy here about going out lately. A single beer isn't going to kill you. Or hell, make it a soda, but you're coming too."

The absolute last thing Linc wanted was to be social with the work crew while having to act like Jacob was simply another coworker. It was hard enough at work, when he had all the distractions of the job. And now that Wyatt was gone and that circle was scattered, he couldn't seem to find his bearings socially. Hell, there were plenty of days where Jacob was the only real friend he cared to see, the only thing truly grounding him.

And that was why when Jacob said, "Yeah, you should come," he nodded automatically.

He wouldn't go for himself, but for Jacob there wasn't much he wouldn't try. "I've got to get home, see to the dogs, but I'll come out after that."

"Good." There was a message in Jacob's tentative smile, but Linc didn't have a chance to decipher it before the radio crackled with the countdown to ignition. And then it was on, them studying the fire's progression, gathering data for the burn boss and other crews as everyone worked together to keep the fire to the planned low-intensity burn. The ignition crew changed their approach based on their reports, minute adjustments that kept all the ground personnel safe.

A few spot fires crept up on the perimeter of the controlled burn, but the holding crew quickly dealt with those. The day was tense but familiar, an energy he always enjoyed, everyone working in concert and on high alert to avert disaster. And not surprising, everyone was in a celebratory mood after the burn boss declared the fire completed and dismissed the various crews. Seemingly half the personnel headed out to drink, successful fire and Jacob's birthday as good a reason as any.

Linc took care of the dogs and showered and changed as he tried to come up with a plan for Jacob. Not a present exactly and sure as fuck nothing public, but it was the guy's birthday, and Linc couldn't help but feel a little sentimental himself. Luckily, a decent idea came to him, one he thought Jacob might like, and he found himself almost eager on the drive back into town.

The bar and grill was popular with the firefighting crowd, an older building near downtown with a worn sign, large covered patio and music spilling out into the parking lot. Kelley, Garrick and a bunch of others had pushed several tables together on the patio. Jacob was penned into the far corner, surrounded by friends, no chance of Linc getting a word with him, so he didn't try.

Instead, he sent a fast text. Don't leave without your present. It was direct without being too flirtatious, but he was nevertheless gratified when Jacob checked his phone, smiled and nodded. That smile was worth all the risk, as was getting to watch him from a distance. He'd always known that Jacob was popular and well-liked, but watching him with his friends like this was different somehow. He had a natural way of putting people at ease, making those around him laugh and have a good time. Pride coursed through Linc, like when Jacob had passed training, chest light, mouth unable to keep back a smile, body almost gloating that he alone would get Jacob by himself later.

"See? This isn't too hard." Ray stuck a soda in Linc's hand.

It took Linc a second to figure out that he didn't mean the watching-Jacob thing, but rather this, being out, being social. The Wyatt-not-here thing.

"Yeah," he agreed, even though now that Ray had said it, Wyatt's shadow loomed over the patio. There by the door to the main building was his favorite summer table. That beer Jacob was drinking was his favorite brand. The song filtering in was one he'd sung along to off-key.

"I know it's difficult, losing your best friend," Ray was continuing. "But he wouldn't want you holed up at your house months on end. Alone. Too serious, even at work. He'd want the old you back. We've been worried about you."

Ray undoubtedly had a point, but all Linc's brain latched onto was *Wyatt wouldn't want...* Hell. What Wyatt wouldn't want was Linc standing here watching his baby brother with hungry eyes, knowing full well his plans for later. Every kiss was a betrayal of what Wyatt would want. And hell if Linc could stop now. He was in too deep, wanted too much. He might have made his peace with breaking his promise, but still he couldn't deny the hurt, the way it sliced deep, knowing Wyatt would never forgive him.

Further, the guilt wasn't only for Wyatt. Here Ray was worried for him when the truth was that Linc wasn't alone, hadn't been truly alone for weeks now. Words rose up in his throat only to die as another work friend came over to say hello to Ray. Oh, well. It wasn't like he would have told him anyway. Would he? For the first time he'd been tempted, his long list of reasons momentarily retreating before it slammed back into him full force.

This is only temporary, he reminded himself as he watched Jacob continue to hold court over at his table. But it was getting harder to believe that, especially when Jacob's hold on him only seemed to increase. All those reasons, all the guilt over Wyatt weren't enough to keep him away, keep him from counting down until they'd be alone, and he could show Jacob his birthday surprise.

"So? Where's my present?" Finally, heart hammering way more than it should have, Jacob freed himself from his various work friends and made his way to Linc, who was picking at a basket of sweet potato fries. Alone, because Ray and some others had left a while ago, and he hadn't left this spot. Still Jacob had felt his presence, felt his eyes on him, a mountain lion stalking his prey without moving an inch.

"Depends. How buzzed are you?" Linc kept his voice low as he studied Jacob, making him have to fight the urge to squirm. Instead he grabbed one of the empty seats at Linc's table, helped himself to a fry.

"Not that much," he hedged. He wanted in on whatever Linc had planned, but he couldn't deny being a little tipsy—his beer had been refilled by helpful people and Kelley had insisted on a birthday shot. "I walked over if you're worried about me driving."

The bar was only a few blocks from his RV park, and he hadn't wanted to bother with finding a parking spot. Plus, if he was honest, he'd been hoping for a ride home, another chance to have Linc's big body filling his little trailer.

"Hmm." Linc's mouth twisted. "Guess you shouldn't have to walk."

"Nope." Stealing another fry, he grinned over at Linc. "Don't worry. I'll put it around that you did me a favor, nothing more."

"Luckily, I'm not planning on parking at your place."

"You're not?" Jacob hated how disappointment hit him like a dart, deflating all the fun out of the evening.

"You'll see." Linc gave him an arch look, one that worked like a patch over Jacob's wounded hope. Maybe all wasn't lost. "Go on, now. Make your goodbyes. No more shots. You drunk isn't part of my plans."

"What is?" He resisted the urge to lean forward,

close the gap between them. His minor buzz made it that much harder to not flirt or touch.

"That's for me to know. Meet me at the truck." With that, Linc stood, giving a little salute in the direction of the others, leaving Jacob to go make excuses for leaving.

"I could give you a ride." Kelley pouted.

"You're not driving either," McKenna said firmly, using her jumper-in-charge voice, which made Kelley nod meekly. Interesting. The two of them had been getting along better since the end of training, but Jacob couldn't get a read on what exactly was going on there. "Go on, Hartman. Glad to hear you've got a ride."

There. He'd practically been ordered to leave with Linc. And if he wished they didn't need to dance around the truth so much, be so darn careful to not rouse suspicion, he quickly pushed that aside. He got to see him. That was what mattered right now. Bad idea or not, there was no drink, no drug as powerful or addictive as Linc's pride, as his praise, as the feeling he got in his embrace, and he wasn't giving it up.

And that delicious curl of anticipation about what Linc might have planned didn't deserve to be extinguished by pointless thoughts about what could be. What it *was* was plenty.

Linc was waiting in the truck, some country station on the radio, female singer crooning about hard-to-love men. His slow smile when Jacob opened the door though had the polar opposite effect on Jacob—this man was too damn easy to like. Too easy to fall for, too hard to get over.

"So, what's the plan?" he asked as he buckled up.

"You'll see." Linc headed toward Jacob's place but then turned before they reached it, taking one of the rural roads out of town. Because it was June with its long days, it wasn't all the way dark yet, but getting there, a pretty pink twilight settling over the craggy rocks lining the curving road that led toward one of the nearby state parks.

"Bit late for hiking," Jacob joked.

"And you're not sober enough for that either." Linc's voice was stern, but there was an affection there that warmed Jacob even as the outside temperatures dipped. "I'm not letting you slip down one of the rocks."

Linc left the rural highway for increasingly smaller roads until they were truly in the middle of nowhere as the last of the late evening light fled, but not before they got a spectacular view of a rocky canyon with mountains in the distance, not a trace of civilization outside of the gravel path that had led them here.

"Well, if night hiking's out, you must have brought me here to get up to no good. And since I don't think you're a serial killer, I'm betting I get a birthday kiss." Already anticipating, he turned in his seat as soon as Linc parked.

"Maybe. If you behave." But Linc didn't offer a kiss right away, instead getting out of the truck, leaving Jacob to do the same. Linc went around to the bed of the truck, sitting on the tailgate, dragging a bag close. "Come here."

"What's all this?" he asked as Linc shook out a thick blanket.

"Nothing much." Linc finished making a little nest

of blankets, then withdrew a six pack of Jacob's favorite beer. "I owe you a drink. That's all."

Jacob's chest grew painfully tight as he hefted himself up next to Linc. Six years now, give or take some, he'd tried to get Linc to give in to what was between them. And now he had, weeks of perfect memories capped by this moment right here, gorgeous vista, sunset, twinkling planets starting to come out. The stars would be a while, but this far out of town, the sky was likely to be spectacular and he couldn't wait. The man might claim to have no use for romance, but this was possibly the most romantic moment of Jacob's life. He was almost nervous to speak, to ruin this magic.

Linc pulled a plastic container from the bag. "And I know your mom's probably doing a better cake this weekend for you—"

"Sunday. Brunch. I'm supposed to be reminding you. She said she left you a message."

"Yeah. I'll try. Anyway, it's not a birthday without some cake. This is just something from the grocery." He offered Jacob the container that had one of those mini-cakes in it. Exactly enough for two. Jacob had to swallow hard. He wasn't ever going to deserve this man.

"Thanks." He took the container and one of the plastic forks Linc held out. "This is…maybe my favorite birthday ever."

"Better than the year you got a mountain bike? Or one of your mom's chocolate cakes?" Linc scoffed. "Doubt that."

"Maybe I appreciate things more now. And if you want her cake, you need to come Sunday. I told her I want German chocolate this year. Surely you can put up with being social twice in a weekend."

"Yeah. I suppose I can. For you." Linc looped an arm around Jacob's shoulders, pulled him close. He was warm and solid and smelled like his usual classic soap with a tangy undercurrent of shaving cream. Liking the idea of Linc getting ready for this, like a real date, Jacob's blood rushed south. He pressed a kiss to Linc's smooth neck, trying to do a better job of showing Linc how much this meant to him.

Linc plotting all this out had to mean he felt some of what Jacob did every single time their lips met—that this was more than convenience, more than scratching an itch, more than some secret fuck-buddy arrangement or whatever the hell they were telling themselves that week. This was real. And big. Bigger than either of them alone. Bigger than Jacob wanted to admit, even now.

Instead he put all of that uncertainty and want into a kiss, claiming Linc's mouth with a new desperation. And Linc met him fully, needy sigh and grasping hands, pushing the cake and the beer aside. Darkness fell in earnest. Temperatures dipped. The first flickers appeared in the sky, and still they kissed. They kissed sweet and they kissed slow and they kissed dirty. Their mouths and tongues and lips met every way two people could meet and still it wasn't enough.

Not breaking the kiss, he unbuttoned Linc's shirt. Soft blue cotton, vaguely Western styling, and it looked a hell of a lot better on the truck bed floor than on Linc and that was saying something. Linc was equally deft at getting Jacob out of his T-shirt, and then their bare skin met, chilly air, warm flesh, soft quilt under them as they tumbled backward. Their pants were next to go, leaving them in their boxers, Jacob wriggling into Linc for warmth as they continued to trade kisses.

"Tell me that magic bag of yours has stuff," he panted as Linc moved from his mouth to his neck, soft little licks that wouldn't leave a mark except on Jacob's soul where he felt every tender gesture, every touch.

It wasn't even that he needed to come as much as that he wanted to be with Linc, every way possible, dragging this out until the sun rose again, still kissing, still needing, still together.

"Yup." Linc fumbled around, came up with a condom and small bottle of lube, pressed them into Jacob's hand.

"What? You want…" His brain struggled to make sense of the gesture.

"Happy birthday." Linc pressed another kiss to his mouth, swallowing Jacob's gasp.

"You don't have to…" Although he'd made passing comments about getting fucked before, Linc always seemed to have a single-minded focus on getting inside Jacob when it came to actually doing. Not that Jacob was complaining because he'd gone from ambivalent about fucking to downright craving that with Linc. This, though, was something else, less craving and more a hopeful wish, a long-held fantasy that he hadn't ever truly thought he might get.

"Want to." Kissing him harder, Linc drew him back down into the blanket nest. "Want to with you. Right here."

And as Jacob followed him down, his pulse sped up.

Maybe some wishes really did come true. And fuck, he hoped he had it in him to make this good for Linc, make him feel even a fraction of everything coursing through him right then. *Don't let me fuck this up.*

Chapter Fifteen

Linc tugged Jacob back down, but he was still tense. Which, honestly, wasn't at all the response Linc had been expecting.

"Can we please not do that thing?" he asked.

"What thing?" Jacob's voice was too cautious to be entirely ignorant of what Linc meant.

Linc couldn't hold back a groan. "That. That thing where you ask me if I'm sure a dozen times and tell me that I don't have to. How about you believe me when I say yes, I'm sure. And yes, I'm well aware that I don't have to. But I want to. Don't make this more than it is. I want to get fucked. That's all."

"Okay." Jacob wasn't any less tense, but he at least didn't ask again.

"Rumor says you're good at this, so maybe try relaxing?" Linc teased.

"You've listened to rumors about me?" Jacob sounded vaguely pleased as he finally stretched all the way out next to Linc, feet tangling as they lay on their sides.

"Only the ones you've bragged about nonstop," Linc lied, not wanting to admit how closely he'd paid attention over the years—or how deeply he'd felt the weird mix of curiosity and jealousy over Jacob's hookups. "Now, can we get back to where we were? We've got cake for after, and you trying to talk me out of the fun parts wasn't part of the plans."

"I like your plans." Jacob licked his way across Linc's jaw. "All of it. The drive. The cake. This."

And then they were kissing again, no more awkward talking. This they were good at. This he could count on, solid and real and reliable, the way it heated him up from the inside out.

They rolled slightly, giving Linc a view of the sky over Jacob's shoulder. The stars were starting to come out in earnest now, a glittering canopy that dwarfed them, making Linc feel like little more than a speck of dirt on a soccer ball. But also wide-open, full of endless possibilities. He'd always loved this place for that reason. Far from the light pollution of any city, even the moon seemed closer, the sky that much bigger and brighter. But he'd never brought Jacob here, never had it to where what was in his head and heart was every bit as awe-inspiring as the sky itself. In the past, he'd come here for perspective, but with Jacob kissing him, everything got jumbled up in his brain, making him feel more significant, not less, and more alive than he had in years.

"Man. The stars really are something." Jacob pulled back, wonder in his voice.

"Thought you might like it." Maybe Linc didn't have the first clue about birthday presents, but he could give him this, could share this place.

"I do." Jacob's mouth was more purposeful now, and

Linc found himself surprisingly content to let him lead. Usually he liked to keep control, set the pace and be in charge regardless of who was doing the fucking, but with Jacob he was able to let some of that go.

They'd been at this enough weeks that he knew he could snatch the reins back at any point and Jacob would happily follow. And Jacob was hardly the type to take more than Linc wanted to give. Letting him explore and tease was freeing, allowing him to drift and watch the stars as Jacob kissed his mouth, then his ears and neck, all sorts of nerve endings Linc had forgotten he had.

"I can do whatever I want, right?" Jacob's mouth ghosted across Linc's collarbone as his fingers toyed with the waistband of Linc's boxers.

"I'm yours." Linc had meant to give a more trite "it's your birthday" response, but the truth slipped out instead. And he was. Jacob owned him in almost every way that mattered, had Linc's head and heart both.

"Good." Jacob's kiss was firm and decisive as he shoved Linc's boxers out of the way. He shifted, a momentary rush of cool air before his warm mouth swallowed Linc's cock in a smooth move.

Linc's mouth opened, him about to tell Jacob that he didn't need anywhere near this much prelude, but all that came out was a low groan cutting through the still night air. Usually when it came to fucking, he got in a mood, got fucked, simple as that, but of course nothing with Jacob was simple. He made complicated fun, long drawn-out encounters magical. Jacob inspired him to try all sorts of foreplay he'd previously ignored—massages, shared showers, kissing for what felt like hours. And apparently Jacob enjoyed returning the favor as well.

Now, with Jacob's mouth working him with its usual practiced ease while his fingers grew more adventur-
ous, Linc had to exhale, take a moment to appreciate the slow road he was always advocating to Jacob. Slow was good. Delicious even, the way Jacob easily paired the methodical, deep deep strokes of his mouth with gentle explorations of his slick fingers against Linc's rim. He sucked harder as his fingers pressed in, a devilish move that Linc filed away for later. Not able to stay still any longer, he tangled his hand in Jacob's thick hair, body surging toward Jacob.

"More," he demanded and mercifully, Jacob com-
plied, going for a second finger and faster pace with more tongue action on the underside of Linc's cock. "Fuck. Damn, you are too good at this…"

"I try." Jacob chuckled before diving back down, mouth sinking all the way to the root, fingers going deeper, firm pressure against Linc's prostate that had him moaning louder.

"Now. Come on. Don't wanna come this way." Un-
like Jacob, he didn't entirely hate getting fucked after coming, but that wasn't what he wanted right then, wanting to drag this out longer, let it build even more.

"Always so bossy," Jacob chided even as he shifted backward. The sound of foil tearing and more lube being applied had Linc's body tensing with more of that delicious anticipation. To his surprise, Jacob didn't have him flip, instead pushing Linc's legs up and back as he moved between them. Huh. Being on his back like this wasn't Linc's usual preference, and he almost asked to switch, but then Jacob was kissing him again, mouth hot and needy. Linc swallowed back his objections. The position might make him more vulnerable than he liked, but this was Jacob, and if Jacob wanted him like this, then Linc would give it to him, would give him everything he had within him to give.

Jacob pressed in, broad cockhead stretching more than his fingers had, but Linc willed himself to relax, knowing the initial burn would fade into something worth the momentary discomfort. And it did, his body remembering what it liked about this, moving with Jacob to find a rhythm that had them both groaning. As they moved, Jacob kept returning for more kisses, sweet and dirty and lingering, driving Linc every bit as crazy as Jacob's cock.

He got a hand on himself, stroking slow, matching their pace, still not ready to come, but liking the way that magnified the sensations, liking the rub of their bodies against his fist as Jacob loomed over him for another kiss. It had been so long since he'd even thought about doing this that he'd forgotten how good this could feel, how all-encompassing, not unlike the stars and their surroundings. He reveled too in Jacob's strength—the flex of his lean muscles, the firmness of his kisses, the way he balanced on his forearms.

"Oh, fuck. Linc. Need you to get there." Jacob's voice, rough and ragged, slid over Linc, another caress, one that ramped him up, knowing how turned on Jacob was.

"Yeah." He didn't speed up his hand, though, instead letting the sensations wash over him, letting Jacob's intensity be the thing that got him closer.

"Fuck. It's too good. Tell me…what you need. Anything." Jacob begging always did it for Linc, and this was no different, the way he was both totally in control and still dependent on Linc for his pleasure.

"You. Need you. Go hard. Hard as you want." Linc knew what he needed, what they both needed. And even more than the pressure and friction, he needed to hear and feel Jacob lose control. Hell, simply his moans were almost enough to push Linc over. He sped up his hand. "That'll get me there too. Promise. Want to see you go."

"Yeah. Fuck. Oh, God." Jacob's hips stuttered, losing the rhythm but gaining intensity. Him not holding back was a thing of beauty, the way he went deep even as his head tipped back, totally lost to his pleasure.

"That's it, baby. Go fast."

"Can't…hold back." Voice breaking, Jacob pressed another desperate kiss to Linc's mouth.

"Don't." Trying to match him, Linc went fast and hard on his cock, letting each of Jacob's moans carry him higher.

"Right there. Fuck. Right there." Going deep, Jacob's whole body shuddered, climax so intense that Linc swore he could feel him pulsing in his ass, even with the condom.

"Yes." The word felt ripped from his lungs as feeling Jacob come tipped him over the edge too, exactly what he needed. Jacob. Always Jacob. Always what he needed and yet never enough either.

"Linc." Jacob collapsed against him, still shaking, even as he laughed. "What the fuck even was that?"

Linc's body shuddered in wordless response. It knew what it was, knew the right words to describe what had happened, what simmered between them. But it didn't matter what truths his body knew—there were some words he simply couldn't afford to ever give voice to. Instead, he forced himself to laugh and press a kiss to Jacob's sweaty forehead.

"Damn good. Not sure, but man…*damn.*"

"Exactly." Jacob's head fit perfect against Linc's shoulder, all those words he wouldn't say right fucking there. The night air was cool, but their bodies were still warm, muscles well-used. The stars twinkled, framing this moment like a million glittery flashbulbs, but no matter how crystal clear the memory was, Linc knew his brain would never do this justice. Nothing was ever going to be as good as this. And it wasn't simply his well-fucked body. It was everything churning inside him, the surety that whatever else came into life, nothing was ever going to equal Jacob and this moment right here.

"No joke, this really is my favorite birthday ever," Jacob said as he leaned against Linc. Still in the back of the truck, they'd pulled back on some of their clothes and snuggled into the blankets to enjoy the birthday cake Linc had brought. Jacob's insides felt bright and glittery, like the stars that seemed almost close enough to grab.

"Grocery store cake that good? Or is that a compliment for my ass?" Linc laughed, the deep chuckle of a content guy, and Jacob was never getting tired of inspiring that reaction.

"Both." Fucking him had been a revelation, a chance to give Linc a little of the attention and affection he always bestowed on Jacob. And as much as he'd started out focused on what he could give Linc, he'd ended up being blindsided yet again, feeling so much more than simple release. "But...uh... I'm down with next time being our usual too."

Much as he'd enjoyed fucking Linc, that different sort of connection and closeness, the sexiness of watching Linc let go, he'd also had an urge to switch places. In the past, he'd always loved topping, showing off his ability to make the other person feel good, but there was something about being with Linc that made him lust for Linc's power and domination. He'd loved every bit of the sex, but damn if his body wasn't already counting down to the next time. He wasn't quite as relaxed as Linc either, a certain thrum of restlessness that said anything this good couldn't last. And a drive to prove that voice wrong, squeeze in a second round before they were forced to leave this place and this magical night.

"We have a usual?" Linc teased. God, Jacob utterly loved him like this, all light and warmth, warmer even than the quilts and sweeter than the chocolate cake. "Remind me to change it up more often. Can't have you getting bored."

"I'm not." He tried to keep his tone as casual as Linc but wasn't entirely sure he managed. Because they did have a usual, a past now, a pattern of encounters, little things he was going to miss so damn much when this was done. And even memorizing this moment—taste of the waxy chocolate icing, crisp scent of Linc's fabric softener on the quilts, soft night sounds—wasn't going to be enough. He wanted more, wanted every damn thing Linc had to give and then some.

"Summer's going fast," Linc mused, almost like he could sense the direction of Jacob's thoughts.

"Says you. It's not even the twenty-first yet—not

even technically summer." The cake turned to clay in his mouth. *Slow down, time. Slow down.* He needed this to last, needed all of this so damn bad. But maybe… Taking a deep breath, he gave voice to the thought that had plagued him for weeks now. "And it doesn't have to end."

"What do you mean?" Linc's tone was cautious, but not outright dismissive, which Jacob would take as a win.

"You don't have to leave. Don't have to find something new. You could just stay. Nothing has to change."

"Jacob…" Linc groaned, and his shoulder moved against Jacob, undoubtedly from a vigorous head shaking. "Things always change. They just do."

"But they don't have to." Jacob was prepared to be stubborn about this. "Come on, Linc. Your house will miss you. You don't really want the hassle of packing everything up, moving, just to outrun…what? This? Some memories? The dogs love it here. You don't *have* to start over away from here all by yourself."

It was as close as he could get to saying that he would miss Linc desperately, that he loved him here in town and on the job both, that he needed him, and that they could start over together if that was what Linc truly needed.

"Fuck." All the lightness left Linc as he scooted away. But Jacob wasn't letting him get too far. Not yet. Instead, he pinned Linc to the side of the truck, straddling his thighs.

"I miss Wyatt too. Every day. But you leaving town… it's not going to cure a damn thing."

"Maybe not." Linc sounded defeated. He also didn't

move to remove Jacob, instead resting a hand lightly on Jacob's hip.

"Then why do it?" Emboldened, Jacob placed a hand on Linc's shoulder. "Stay. Do you *really* want to leave?"

"It's not just about Wyatt. Not now. We can't keep going indefinitely." Linc ignored the meat of Jacob's question, exactly as Jacob had expected him to. But even expecting it, Jacob's muscles still slumped, disappointment weighing him down, a heavy pack without the promise of a parachute ride down.

"Says who? I'm not suggesting we march into brunch at my mom's on Sunday holding hands or anything. I'm just saying there's no need to hang up a good thing, not when we're both enjoying ourselves."

"Guess the whole burn-itself-out plan was fucked from the start." Linc's laugh was a bitter thing, knocking over Jacob's stockpile of private hopes.

"Yeah. But I'm not regretting a damn thing."

"Not saying you should." Linc's hand tightened on Jacob's skin. "And I don't either."

Hope flared anew. "Then why stop? Why put an expiration date on something so good?"

Linc groaned like he had another round of objections in him, but Jacob cut him off with a swift kiss, trying to reinforce that this truly was the best thing he'd ever found and that he wasn't giving it up without a fight.

"Damn it. Can't think straight when you kiss me like that." Linc rested his forehead against Jacob's.

"Then don't think right now. I'm not asking for a decision or a commitment or anything like that." Jacob was proud of how level he kept his voice. No way was he throwing everything they had away by being too demanding when Linc was hell-bent on being stubborn. "We've got the rest of the summer here. All I'm saying is consider staying as an option."

"Maybe this isn't fair to you." Linc ghosted his lips along Jacob's neck. "You deserve—"

"You. I deserve you." Jacob actually wasn't sure he *was* worthy of Linc, but he'd go to the mat for the chance to try to prove himself.

"I don't want to hurt you." Pulling Jacob close, Linc's grip was firm, resolute, a stark contrast to the tenderness of his lips against Jacob's mouth.

"You won't," Jacob lied, knowing full well that come fall he was likely to be in a cold, barren world of hurt, a life without Linc in it. But he wasn't giving it up even a second before he absolutely had to.

"I will." Linc sounded so sad and full of regrets that Jacob had to kiss him back, trying to push some of his certainty into Linc. What they had was *good.* And special. And worth fighting for. And all he needed was for Linc to see that.

Stay, his heart asked as they kissed. *Stay with me. Fight for us. Don't be such a fucking coward.* The words were all right there along with other even scarier declarations, the contents of his heart spilling out in every caress, every touch, every sigh and groan. His body was far braver than his mouth, willing to risk what Jacob himself couldn't, not yet, maybe not ever.

With his lips and hands, he demanded more from Linc, demanded his full participation until Linc was tumbling him back into the nest of blankets, hand cradling Jacob's head like he was something rare and precious. Something worth protecting. And maybe that would have to be enough, the stories their bodies were able to tell each other. Maybe he wouldn't ever get anything more than these stolen moments from Linc, maybe it was unfair to both of them, and maybe it was foolish, courting this kind of pain. But then Linc moved against him, deepening the kiss, and Jacob knew it was all already too late for him. Linc owned him, body and soul and heart, everything Jacob had in him to give.

And he refused to believe it wouldn't be enough, refused to give in to the sadness and frustration, refused to give up on this, on the future that was right there, as sparkling as the night sky, and every bit as hard to hold on to. But Linc was here now, and he was *real*, a bulwark against the chilly air and unwelcome reality. So fuck the future. He was clinging to the *now*, to Linc, and to the hope that it would all be worth it in the end.

Chapter Sixteen

Linc was in hell. A sunny, pleasant hell filled with Hartman family members and chocolate cake and coconut-caramel frosting, but hell nonetheless. He arrived at the birthday brunch for Jacob somewhat after the appointed time, and instead of Jacob answering the door, he got his relentless matchmaking brother, who was seriously barking up the wrong tree.

"May's outside," Jon said as he led Linc into the house, helpfully and way too damn casually, pointing out the window at the play structure. "With the kids. You could go help. Junior sure loves you."

"I should put this in the kitchen." Linc gestured with the dish of pea salad he'd brought. He figured the bacon made it nominally a brunch food, and he'd had a bumper crop of peas, some local cheese and a promising-looking recipe.

"And you cook." Jon laughed exactly like a dude who was proud of barely being able to make toast. "Like I've been saying, you've secretly been a family man all along. You just need the right—"

"You came!" Jacob appeared, all wide smile and backslapping bro-hug that had zero in common with their one-more-kiss routine the night before when they'd been tangled up on Linc's couch. Yup, Linc was *secretly* something all right, but it sure as fuck wasn't a straight bachelor needing a ready-made family. And no offense to May, who deserved a whole lot better.

I'm not suggesting we march into brunch at my mom's on Sunday holding hands or anything. Jacob's words from Friday night echoed back to him. Would it be easier? Would even the absolute worst be better than this torture of being right next to Jacob and unable to say a damn thing?

"There's three types of French toast casserole. I think it's a competition of some kind. You can come judge." Jacob steered him away from Jon and toward the kitchen, plucking the bowl of salad from his hands.

"Here's a card to add to your collection." Linc pointed to the envelope on top of the plastic-wrapped bowl. Didn't matter what private present he'd given Jacob Friday night—he knew enough to come to this thing with a bland cartoon card and a fast-food gift certificate. And if he'd seen a card he liked better, one with a vivid sunset and a line of poetry, well, maybe he needed to work on being a little less fanciful. Getting sentimental would serve exactly nothing and no one.

"Lincoln. Come fix yourself a plate." Jenna greeted him with a huge hug, clucking over his attempt at a salad and shoving a plate in his hands. Jacob was dragged away by two of the nephews, but she continued to hover as he dutifully served himself eggs and bacon and some of each casserole. A three-layer cake stood at the end of the buffet, undoubtedly tasty but the uneven icing and haphazardly placed two and five candles gave it a homey air.

"Junior helped." Jenna laughed as he studied the cake. Her love for Jacob shone through with each dish, each little detail of the gathering. *Maybe...*

"So, I have a bone to pick with you." She leaned against the counter, and just like that, his stomach sank and any last whimsical impulses he had fled. "You still haven't talked Jacob out of this whole smoke-jumper phase."

"Uh..." Linc didn't really have a good answer for that as he hadn't truly tried to change Jacob's mind in weeks, more wrapped up in other concerns like keeping their affair private and trying to hoard their limited time together.

"I mean, don't get me wrong, it's lovely to see you guys getting along again. But, I was counting on you. I thought for sure he wouldn't make it out of training. And now fire season is here and..." Wringing her hands, she gave a helpless-sounding sigh.

"You're worried," he finished for her. And he couldn't help but wonder if she'd be as happy about them getting along if she knew the full truth. "I get it. And I'm sorry. Sorry if I've let you down. He does seem rather hell-bent on this career choice."

"You haven't let me down." Closing her eyes, she took a long sip of her orange juice. "Just promise me that you'll keep him safe."

"I..." Fuck. Could he really promise that? When he had failed with Wyatt? It didn't matter how many times people said it wasn't his fault. He wore that failure on his soul, a scuff mark that wasn't ever going away. "I'll do my best."

And that best might not be enough. And that sucked. Hell. He'd managed to not dwell on the risks in weeks, not think about what it would mean if Jacob was hurt on his watch. What it would mean to this family. To him, personally. It would be like losing the sun. Impossible to go on. Merely thinking about it made his sternum ache, shoulders tensing as he tried to hold back the impulse to curl up, let the anxiety take over. It probably wasn't healthy, but the only way he was managing to cope was to pretend those risks didn't exist. But Jenna's shrewd gaze and nervous eyes wouldn't let him now and the pain—literal, physical pain—was almost more than he could stand.

"I know you will." Reaching out, Jenna patted his arm. "I trust you. Always have."

Knife. Heart. Twisting. She *trusted* him. And how was he repaying that trust? Hell, he hadn't even tried that hard to talk Jacob out of the job. He'd been way too preoccupied with getting in Jacob's pants and not nearly focused enough on his obligations to this family, to Jenna specifically. She was trusting him to do the right thing. And hell if he even knew what that right thing was anymore. But whatever he'd been doing clearly wasn't it—fucking around with Jacob, knowing full well that they were both going to be hurting come fall. And the right thing definitely wasn't continuing despite knowing there wasn't a damn soul who'd approve of what they were doing.

He needed to—

"Whoa! Come back here!" Jacob sped through, chasing after one of the toddlers, stopping long enough to grin at Linc and his mom before he scooped the little girl up. "Prisoner escaped. Gotta return her to Jon, but are we going to do the cake soon? Please?"

"You always get your way." Jenna laughed, affection clear in her eyes.

"Yup. And you love me for it." And he clearly meant his pouting look for his mom, all pursed mouth and puppy dog eyes, but Linc had to stop his hand from clenching his fork in two. He was powerless to deny this man anything. Hell, Jacob didn't even need to turn that look on Linc. He had him. Completely. And therein lay Linc's entire problem. He didn't want to let go, didn't want to listen to logic, and even guilt and obligation might not be enough to make him quit Jacob.

"Finally! Some real action!" Garrick sounded far too gleeful given the circumstances.

"Thought we weren't supposed to celebrate a callout." Not that Jacob wasn't also hyped, but he was trying to rein in the adrenaline and also have the necessary respect for what the job and the situation required.

"There's no shame in loving our work." Garrick winked at him, good mood contagious enough that Jacob had to smile back as they worked on assembling their gear. A fire was raging to the south and west of them on state lands. An unattended campfire had led to the situation, and the ground hotshot crews had been at it all day. Another smoke-jumping crew had already been deployed, and now Jacob's group was preparing for their turn. They needed to be ready to fly with only a five-minute warning once the command decided where they could do the most good.

"Ready?" Unlike Garrick, Linc was all business, no joking around, as he worked next to Ray on assembling the cargo they'd be dropping.

"Yup." Jacob could be professional too, not even glancing in his direction. Linc had been this way, all work, for days now, even before the latest fire broke out. Something had changed after Jacob's birthday and not for the better. They'd been closer that night than Jacob had ever been to anyone, but then Linc had been distant at the brunch, hanging more with Jacob's mom and the kids. And Jacob had figured it was probably to avoid suspicion, but then Linc had kept up the pensive front even when they did get some stolen moments together.

He had undoubtedly made everything worse by asking Linc to think about staying, but he wasn't going to apologize for the request either. It was as close as he could come to saying that this was far more than simply sex for him. What they had was too good to toss away, and he needed Linc to accept that. Like really *accept* it, because he did see it. Jacob knew he did. He had to feel it. It was there in every kiss, every long look and every late-night conversation where *good night* were the hardest two words ever and *five more minutes* a lifeline.

"I hope you guys are ready." Sims bustled into the hangar, clipboard in her hand. "We've got jump coordinates for you now."

Once they were fully briefed on the mission at hand, they had only a few minutes to finish their prep before they were loading up the plane and cross-checking each other's parachute rigging. Linc had his usual pre-jump scowl firmly in place, and he was even more dictatorial than usual. Jacob was willing to concede some control in deference to his nerves, but it was still irritating, the way Linc *still* seemed unable to trust him, even after all these weeks.

And he should. The jump went fine, Jacob landing correctly, hitting the target zone without issue and not landing too hard either. The start of their work was also straightforward, no need for Linc to be barking orders like Jacob was inches from screwing up. If anything, Linc being tense made Jacob even more so, made him more aware of each movement. Each tree he felled, each action, each reaction felt more weighted with Linc's scrutiny. Thus, it was probably inevitable that he did screw up, sliding down a tree he was supposed to be climbing, narrowly avoiding a tumble.

"Watch it!" Eyes narrowed, Linc looked more angry than concerned. "I said go slow. Those branches look weaker than I like. Damn it."

"I'm fine." Testing, Jacob stretched, grateful his shoulders didn't seem too worse for the wear.

"Let me do it."

"I can handle myself." Jacob brushed himself off, even as Linc was scrambling ahead of him, completing the maneuver himself. And from that moment on, Linc kept coddling him, rushing to do things before Jacob could, shouldering the lion's share of the work, and generally making a pest of himself. But Jacob couldn't call him on it, not with Garrick right there. And Garrick was just as bad. Any remotely dangerous task and one of them was there first, almost like they'd coordinated ahead of time. And maybe they had. But he couldn't demand answers, not with the fire bearing down on them, every minute critical. They didn't have time to waste arguing.

So, he pushed it down, but by the time they were packing out, heading to the extraction point, he was seething, emotions thicker than the smoky air surrounding them and temper hotter even than his sweat-soaked skin. Their gear and exertion and weather had combined to make him count down to his shower. But not before he could speak his mind.

"Would it be so awful if you guys let me actually work?" he finally asked, unable to wait any longer, immediate danger past as they met the old logging road that would lead them up and out of the path of the fire.

"Yup." Garrick gave him a good-natured pat. "You did good, Rook. But don't get ahead of yourself."

"Felt like you guys were babying me. If it's a matter of experience, you have to let me gain some."

"All in good time." Garrick couldn't have been more fake-nice if he were a Hollywood talent-show judge, and Linc was ominously quiet, letting Garrick do the justifying. "We've got you here to keep you safe, and that's priority one."

"Wait." Jacob whirled on them, eyes locked on Linc's. "You've got me here? It wasn't just luck of the draw? You asked for me?"

Damn it. Linc had strongly implied it was simply shit luck. And if Jacob couldn't trust him to be honest, then who could he? He'd figured that at the very least Linc could be straight with him. But it totally fit that he'd have some sort of rescue complex about keeping Jacob out of harm's way. Hell, he'd probably promised his mom too, and that promise likely meant more to Linc than anything with Jacob. And fuck but that left him feeling like he'd downed a gallon of pickle brine, all sour stomach and bitter mouth.

"Yeah, we asked." Garrick rolled his eyes like this was no big deal. "And don't get me wrong, you're not bad for a rookie—you've got the stamina of five veterans, but you've got to get over this stubborn streak. You almost fell because you weren't listening to Linc to go cautious. If you're not going to listen, then yeah, we're gonna take over. Turning into the Dark Knight solo act might have worked back on the ground crew, but we're—"

"A team. Exactly. We're a team. I'm not trying to go it alone, but you're not using me. You're coddling me. All for what? Some obligation to Wyatt? Feeling like I can't hack it?"

"That's not—" Linc started to talk but was cut off by the arrival of the trucks that would take them back to the fire command.

Damn it. Jacob was still angry as he climbed in the truck, not caring which one of them rode next to him. Fuck them. He was pissed that Linc had all but lied to him about how he landed on their crew. Pissed that Garrick was acting like some entitled big brother. Pissed at himself for almost screwing up.

Linc ended up the one next to him, but Jacob let him stew in silence. He didn't need to let the firefighters driving the trucks in on their business, and he wasn't sure he trusted himself to not bring the personal into it, not with how mad he was.

"We going up again?" Evidently in no hurry to finish their argument either, Linc headed right for Sims at the fire command, helping to coordinate all the various efforts.

"Nope. Fire's looking fairly contained for now. Ground crews holding the line. Good work." Sims nodded at all of them. "We're sending you back to catch a shower and some sleep. If we need you to go again, it'll be tomorrow, but we're optimistic that the worst is behind us."

Cue another tense ride, this one back to Painter's Ridge with other smoke-jumper crews that had completed their jumps. He took advantage of the chaos to catch a ride in one of the other trucks with Kelley, listening to her recount a thrilling jump and close call with a chainsaw. But he made damn sure to catch up with Linc in the base parking lot.

"So much for you not asking for me to be on your crew, huh?" He'd waited until others were out of earshot, but his anger had run out of patience. They were having this out.

"I said I didn't ask. Wasn't a lie." Eyes hard, Linc kept his voice even. "What Garrick or Ray did...that's their business."

"But you didn't tell them no. And you seem to have had some sort of... I don't know...*pact* to keep me safe. Which means not letting me do my fucking job."

"I told your mom—"

"I knew it. Fuck it, Linc. Why are your promises to everyone else more important than me?"

"It's not like that." Linc's eyes shifted, more pained than angry now, not that Jacob gave a fuck right then about his pain. "I owe—"

"Me. How about you owe *me*?"

"You? What promises have I made you?" Linc's whole face pinched like he was thinking extra hard. But apparently not hard enough.

"If I have to tell you… Forget it." Jacob threw up his hands. "But maybe you could start with basic respect. The same respect you'd give anyone else on the crew. You wouldn't be rushing to do their work for them. Wouldn't be freaking out with each jump either. Why am I different?"

With his eyes, he dared Linc to tell him he cared. That Jacob was different because of who they were to each other and not any stupid promises he'd made other people.

But Linc merely shook his head. "Told you. I owe—"

"Fuck what you *owe*, Linc. I'm done with being Wyatt's little brother. So fucking *done*."

"Hold on—"

"Save it."

"Damn it, Jacob. This isn't the place for this talk." Gaze darting around the nearly empty parking lot, Linc dropped his voice. "How about you come over later?"

"I don't think that's such a good idea. Not tonight." If he went to Linc's, they'd end up fucking. And fucking meant feeling things he didn't want, not right then. Fucking meant not fixing a damn thing. And it let Linc off the hook too damn easy. Linc had been the one throwing up walls lately. He didn't get to play peacemaker now. He could damn well wait for Jacob to calm down.

"I suppose you're right." Linc nodded sharply. "Probably for the best—"

"Fucking hell, Linc. You that eager to see the last of me? I'm taking the night off. Not the whole damn summer." Although part of him knew that would be the sane thing, just let it end here, but he couldn't. Wouldn't. He might be pissed but he wasn't giving up on Linc until he was forced. But fuck it all, it looked like that point might be sooner rather than later.

"Okay. Guess I'll see you when you cool down." *Sorry* must not have been part of Linc's vocabulary because he continued to regard Jacob warily, like he was angry for no good reason, and that just made Jacob that much more upset, back muscles tensing and head pounding.

"Yeah. You will." With that, he strode away to his own truck before he could say something he'd truly regret. He wasn't giving up on Linc, wasn't giving up on them, but it wouldn't kill Linc to fight back, to fight for them. And to maybe see Jacob as anything other than Wyatt Hartman's annoying little brother and a fucking *obligation.* Damn it all. Jacob might as well wish to lasso the moon than to think he could change Linc.

Chapter Seventeen

Linc wasn't going to stop caring about Jacob. He couldn't. And caring about Jacob meant caring about the promises he'd made others. Simple as that. And yet, as Linc passed a long, sleepless, Jacob-less night, his principles were miserable bedfellows. One couldn't exactly snuggle a moral certainty that keeping Jacob safe was more important than making Jacob happy. But damn if Linc didn't wish he could have *both*. Both Jacob safe and Jacob right here, next to him, smiling the way he always did when sleepy and satisfied.

And Jacob had said it was only for tonight, not a permanent thing, but it sure felt permanent when Jacob still hadn't answered a text Linc had sent hours ago.

You okay? You get some food? And don't forget to hydrate after that long pack-out.

Not apologizing. Linc couldn't do that, not when he wasn't sorry about wanting to keep Jacob safe at all costs. But he'd tried to extend a hand anyway. Fucking lot of good it did. Ignoring their mats, the dogs were both occupying Jacob's half of the bed, and he didn't have the heart to kick them out. And how the hell had he gone from never going to touch Jacob to him having a side of the bed?

Right when he was about to give up pretending he might sleep and go hammer out some exercises, his phone buzzed.

I ate. Soup from a can. You can lecture me about it later. And yeah, tanked up on the fluids.

Linc seized the opening like a kid trying to catch butterflies, dashing off a fast and probably pointless reply, but he couldn't not send anything.

Good. Maybe if we don't have a callout tomorrow, I can make you that chicken you liked last time?

The wait for a return message felt like decades, but was actually gratifyingly quick. The one with rosemary?

Smiling for the first time in hours, Linc typed faster. That one. Got some potatoes to use up too.

Guess we can't have them go to waste. Jacob's reply buzzed a few moments later, not exactly enthusiastic but as close to a yes as Linc was likely to get.

Nope. Dogs will be happy to see you. His chest hummed, an almost electric sensation, a giddiness at knowing he hadn't fucked things up with Jacob beyond repair. Even if the sane thing would be to let it end here, he simply wasn't ready.

Just the dogs? Jacob added a head-scratching emoji. And Linc almost had to literally scratch his, trying to figure out how to answer. He didn't want to be desperate or needy, but damn, he *did* miss Jacob, and couldn't lie.

Not just the dogs.

Jacob sent him another emoji in response, this one sleeping. Just checking. Get some sleep.

And finally feeling settled for the first time all damn day, Linc was able to follow orders, falling asleep to thoughts of cooking for Jacob sometime soon, making things right the best he could. But the next day, on the drive to the air base, the doubts returned. Were they back to normal? Was Jacob still pissed? How the hell was he supposed to both keep Jacob safe and give him the respect he demanded?

Still deep in thought, he almost bumped into Garrick on the way into the headquarters building.

"Sorry."

"No problem. The rook still pissed?"

"Not sure." Linc had to work hard to keep the defensiveness from his voice. And no way was he sharing the late-night text exchange as proof of Jacob's mood.

"Well, he'll just have to get used to us caring." Garrick clapped him on the shoulder.

"Yeah," Linc said, but his mouth twisted. He wasn't sure which way to feel about being lumped in with Garrick. Because he did care, too damn much, but it sure wasn't the same as whatever casual meaning Garrick was giving the word. Garrick cared about everything—his elderly neighbor, the people they worked with, his friends—but nothing terribly deeply. Nothing in common with this soul-deep ache Linc got at the mere mention of Jacob's name.

"Speaking of rookies…" Garrick steered Linc into an empty hallway that led to the offices. They were both a few minutes early for the morning meeting. "Have you heard the latest? Apparently, it's a-okay to hook up with crew members now."

"What?" Linc legit sputtered the word, and his knees wobbled. What the fuck had Garrick heard? Who had talked? Or worse *seen*? His mind raced, trying to think of a response that might do some damage control.

"I take it that's a no." Garrick laughed. Fucking laughed. Like this was no big deal. "Apparently, Mc-Kenna and Kelley have been hooking up on the sly. And so since *apparently* that's the thing to do—"

"What?" This time Linc had to blink. This wasn't about him and Jacob? Just idle gossip?

"Yeah. That was pretty much my reaction too. But they must have hooked up the night of Jacob's birthday party. And kept going. Anyway that's not what I wanted to talk about."

"It's not?" Damn. His pulse sped up.

"No. I've been thinking… If Sims and Alder let McKenna and Kelley get away with it, maybe I might see what the rook is up for. After the season of course. Because I'm not looking for *that* much trouble."

"You want to do what?" Linc swallowed hard. Garrick wanted to date Jacob?

"Life is short. He's out. And it's been less of an issue than I would have predicted. Doesn't hurt that he's damn good at the job. Even if he is stubborn."

"And that makes you want to hook up? With *him*?"

"You don't have to look so shocked. You know I'm pan. He's hot. Which you can't claim not to know. Which brings me back around to why I'm even having this conversation with you. Wanted to make sure I'm not encroaching on any...*plans* you might have in that area."

"I don't have plans," Linc said reflexively as his mind spun. Since when was Jacob being hot the answer to Garrick's boredom or whatever the hell this was? His fist tightened, gut roiling at the notion of Jacob as a convenient good time.

"Great. I mean, you guys have been dancing around each other for years. I can't be the only one who's noticed that. And you can't tell me you're blind to it yourself. But lately you guys seem more like friends."

A strangled laugh escaped Linc's mouth. *Friends.* He might not have plans, but he for damn sure knew they weren't friends.

"Oh, fuck. Are you guys...?" Garrick's eyes went wide.

"No." The harsh denial was out even before Garrick finished the question. His already agitated stomach burned now, a caustic pit of guilt and shame. This was Garrick, whom he'd known for years now, almost as long as Wyatt, and had trusted him with his life more than a few times. If anyone deserved his truth, it was Garrick. But he couldn't confess. Not now. And truth was, he'd be gone come fall. If Garrick and Jacob wanted to hook up... God, he couldn't even form the thought without bile rising in his throat.

"Well, okay then." Garrick's head tilted, expression saying he didn't quite believe Linc. "So okay if I sniff around?"

"I—"

"Sims wants to see us."

He whirled around, and oh, holy fuck. Jacob was right there behind Linc. And judging by his winter-storm eyes and pursed mouth, he'd clearly heard more than he should.

"Jacob—" He reached for his arm but Jacob shook him off.

"Save it. We've got a job to do." Jacob pushed by both of them, disgust rolling off him in toxic waves that almost choked Linc.

"Well, now. *This* is a mess." Garrick shook his head, but before Linc could speak, Sims called down the hall at all three of them.

Probably just as well. He didn't know how he'd planned to try to explain something he had no good answers for, what he could say to Garrick that might correct whatever conclusions he'd jumped to. And fuck, *what a mess* was right. Honestly, though, he was less concerned about Garrick and more about catching Jacob, trying…

Trying what? To make this right? Or was this where they ended? Line in the sand, their heat finally extinguished, this time for good by Linc's own stupidity. *Fuck.* Doing the right thing for Jacob might damn well kill him.

Somehow Jacob got through his shift without having to talk with Linc or Garrick beyond the bare minimum necessary to do the work. With Linc, there seemed to be an unspoken agreement that they were having it out after work in private. And with Garrick…who the fuck knew? He hadn't overheard his whole conversation with Linc, but he'd heard enough. Enough to be beyond pissed with both them. Far too angry to stop and marvel at the revelation that apparently Garrick was pan and not opposed to banging him. Which might be flattering if it wasn't comical. Garrick was too tall. Too much of the sort of dude-bro top Jacob usually steered clear of. Too casual, nothing ever serious. Too not Linc.

Mainly that. Garrick wasn't Linc, wasn't ever going to be, and so his interest was more funny than anything else. All these years of not finding much in this town and now the only opportunity he truly wanted was the one he wasn't supposed to have. With the dude who didn't even care enough to speak up for him, who couldn't even admit for a second that what they had was significant, worth fighting for. Hell, he couldn't even admit that they'd been seeing each other at all, even casually, or even suggest that he might be interested in Jacob in that way. Nope. Only a flat denial of every damn one of Jacob's hopes.

And so Jacob seethed as they worked. The fire on the state lands continued to burn, ground crews working round the clock. They had another long day—early morning cargo drop to crews already on the ground, then a jump themselves, working through thick smoke and heat to carry out the mission before packing out.

Unlike the day before, he was quiet on the pack-out. His muscles burned with more than exertion. If he started in on everything churning through him, he might never stop. Might say things he couldn't take back. But more importantly, he didn't want an audience for what needed saying between him and Linc.

Garrick was simply a complication he didn't want to deal with right then.

He trudged on in the hot, smoky air, listening to the comm set, letting Ray's directions guide him, tuning out Linc and Garrick's continued efforts to play kindergarten teacher and keep him from the hardest of the tasks. Whatever.

It was well past dark when they finally made it back to Painter's Ridge, under orders to rest and hydrate and prepare for another long shift. And he was pretty sure no one would advise heading to Linc's, spoiling for a fight, when he should be resting. But still, here he was, unable to be anywhere else but turning onto Linc's long drive, gravel crunching under his tires.

The dogs weren't out to greet him, and for a moment, he worried that Linc might not be home. Had he gone to Jacob's trailer? But then he emerged on the porch, still no dogs, arms crossed. The night temperatures had dropped, but Linc was still in the same T-shirt he'd worn earlier.

"Where are your sidekicks?" he asked as he approached Linc.

"Out in their run."

Great. Apparently, they were back to porch conversations and clipped responses. "I take it I'm not getting a chicken dinner."

"You really interested in food?" Shoulders slumping, Linc shook his head, answering his own question. He still had traces of soot around his face. "Figured I'd let you say your piece first."

"More like you'd already said it for me without me

even saying a word yet. Already made up my mind for me? Doing my work for me again?"

"You didn't say a full sentence, the whole shift. Didn't even look my way. I don't need it in skywriting to tell that you're pissed at me."

"With good reason." Resigning himself to not getting an invitation into the house, he leaned against one of the porch supports. "Seriously, what the fuck, Linc? Giving Garrick the green light to get in my pants? I had no clue the dude was pan."

"Wasn't my information to share." Linc regarded him coolly, porch light making his eyes glow like iron embers in a forge.

"Yeah. You've got a real talent for secrets." His voice came out snappish with his temper already getting the best of him and he still hadn't reached his real complaints.

"What did you want me to say?" Dropping his arms to his sides, Linc paced away.

"How about the truth? That you'd rather I not hook up with him? Hell, you didn't even have to confess everything, just admit for freaking once that you care. But you can't do that. Can't risk a single person knowing how you really feel. Even me."

"I never said I don't care." Linc swiveled, scowl still firmly in place. "But I'm not sure what that has to do with anything."

"Maybe everything? If you care and I care, what the hell does it matter who knows? Especially someone like Garrick who already knew your sexuality." A bitter, caustic thought barreled into his brain. "Oh, hell. Tell me you and him never…"

Linc shrugged in a way that did nothing to ease Jacob's mind. "Way back when we first were friendly, we sorta felt out that possibility. But we just aren't compatible like that. So, not that it's any of your business, but no."

Making an exasperated noise, Jacob moved to stand directly in front of him. "Of course it's my business. Come on. You can't keep pretending that we don't have any hold on each other."

"You were the one who said this was simply fucking." Linc met him hard stare for hard stare. "An itch we scratch until it's out of our systems."

"You know perfectly well it's more than that by now."

Linc's silence was damning.

"Hell, it's *always* been more than casual between us. You've just been too stubborn to admit it."

"What do you want from me?" Linc threw up his hands before lacing them behind his neck, like he needed restraint to avoid touching him. Jacob understood the impulse—his own damn body couldn't seem to make up its mind whether he wanted to shove Linc or kiss him until he saw sense.

Fuck. Ignoring those competing impulses, Jacob sagged against the porch pillar, letting it dig into his shoulder, not that the pain provided any comfort or courage. "Everything."

"Don't be flip." Linc's tone was biting, and he resumed pacing after making a disgusted noise.

"I'm serious. I want *everything*. I'll settle for what the fuck ever you want to give me, but I'm done pretending." And he was. He'd buried this truth all spring and summer, shoved down real demands in favor of getting his dick's needs met, all to have a stolen sliver of Linc's time. And it wasn't enough. "I want everything. I want a real relationship. The one we're actually already having—date nights and staying in and doing stuff for the family and memories we make together. Say what you want, this isn't just sex. It's not. We've got something good going, and I want it *real*. Not secret. Not temporary. I want the future we deserve."

"We can't have that." Scrubbing at his buzzed hair, Linc closed his eyes.

"Says who?" Screw Linc's obvious discomfort. Jacob was done taking his fast denials. "Your conscience? Your fears? Some ancient promises?"

"I don't expect you to understand." Linc's long-suffering tone torched Jacob's last shred of patience.

"Oh, I understand. A little too well. Like I said yesterday, everyone else comes first for you." And probably always would, a realization that left Jacob breathless and more than a little dizzy, world shifting on him despite his best efforts at denial the last few months.

"That's not fair." Stopping his pacing, Linc actually had the gall to sound offended.

"Oh? How about you try making *me* some promises then? Or yourself? Why did Wyatt get the best of you? He's gone. Not coming back. Not here to spew his hateful positions and theories."

"You don't get to talk like that." Angry Linc was back, the mad, hard man who had banished Jacob after the funeral. Guess that answered where his loyalties lay.

"No? He was my goddamn brother." Jacob could meet anger with anger if that was what Linc wanted. "And he's been between us for years now. I sure as hell think I get an opinion on you hiding behind some promise you made a homophobic bigot—who yeah, had a nice side too—but you've used him as an excuse for years instead of admitting what's right in front of your face. What's in your heart."

"What do you want me to say? That I care? You know that." Linc made it sound so obvious when it was anything but, Jacob relying far more on his actions than his words. "But it's not simply Wyatt. I've been wrestling all damn summer with letting him down, but it's not just that promise. There's the rest of your family. I can't risk losing them too. Not with everything else gone. Not if it might mean them mad at you too. I promised your mom to keep you safe. You and me shacking up on something approaching a permanent basis isn't what she or any of them want for you."

Despite everything, hope flared, a little hot spot in a cold forest of lost chances. Linc even *thinking* permanent was a start.

"So why not test it and see? God knows I love my family, but if they want to follow Wyatt's stupid theories or get mad about something minor like an age gap—"

"Ten years isn't minor—"

"It is too. Screw them. If they cut us off, at least we'd have each other. Or am I not enough?" The flicker of hope faded as quickly as it had arisen. His anger was an almost palpable, prickly thing because he was pretty sure he already knew the answer to that question, and it pierced every soft part he had left. Linc had considered a future together and found it lacking in some fundamental way, had decided that others were worth more than Jacob, had determined that old promises trumped any fresh potential.

"It's not that—"

"Save it." Turning away from Linc, he rested heavily on the porch rail, fighting the urge to simply pack it all in right then, head for his truck.

"It's that you deserve more than me. You do." Linc's voice was pained, but Jacob couldn't bear to discover if his face matched.

"These are tired, tired reasons, Linc." He spoke to the scrubby little bushes on the side of the porch. "Truth is that you just don't want me as much as I want you, and I'm the stupid fuck who took six years to figure that out. You care, but not enough. You like what we have, but not enough. You trust me, but not enough. Whatever this is, it's not enough to keep you. And that fucking hurts."

"I'm sorry." It was the worst two words Linc could have chosen. Not a quick denial. Not an explanation. Not a fumble. Just a quiet apology. "I'm a bastard—"

"No shit. You know what you really are?" He didn't wait for Linc to answer. "A coward. We could have… so much. But you refuse to choose it, and your reasons all fucking suck. Which leads me to think that you're a cowardly bastard. And I'm an idiot."

"Jacob—" Linc reached for him then, placing a warm hand on Jacob's chilled arm, but he shrugged it off.

"Unless you're about to tell me that I'm all wrong, don't *Jacob* me." *Please tell me I've got things wrong.* Unspoken wish clogging his throat, he stared off into the cold, dark night.

Not surprisingly, Linc said nothing. Still, though,

his silence sliced through Jacob, made it hard to take his next breath.

"About what I figured. I'm done here." With that, he jumped the porch rail, not even wanting to brush by Linc to use the steps, not caring as he stumbled on his way to the truck. He heard the sound of his name, but he didn't turn around. Couldn't.

Once in his truck, he spent several long minutes with his head resting on the steering wheel. Long minutes where Linc could have come after him but didn't. Instead, when he finally looked up, the porch was empty. *Fuck.* How had this gone so south so fast?

As he drove home, his brain kept churning with that question, replaying their last two arguments, trying to figure out how they went from sneaky and happy to… nothing at all. Shattered pieces of an illusion. The only real conclusion was that it had all been fake. He'd seen what he'd wanted to see, believed Linc capable of more than he was, read more into things than was real. And even if it wasn't fake, it didn't matter. If Linc didn't care enough to fight for them, it didn't really matter what he felt about Jacob. Whatever it was, it wasn't enough. And that meant that all Jacob's certainty for *years* that there was something potent and important between them was now a lie. It wasn't simply a matter of getting Linc to give in to their attraction. *Not enough.* It all came back to that. Jacob and what they had together wasn't enough for Linc and fuck all what the reasons were.

His insides had been sandblasted, everything dry and crackly, one stiff breeze away from turning to dust. His eyes, too, burned, and only muscle memory ensured that his truck actually made it to his trailer in one piece. The clock flashed an absurd hour, a reminder of how they were supposed to be sleeping so they could—

Work. Damn it. Somehow he was going to have to drag himself and his half a heart into work in the morning, face Linc again, and try to not crumble with the force of wanting someone who had never been his to begin with.

Chapter Eighteen

Sunrise was a little after five, a lightness to the sky that Linc took as permission to give up pretending sleep would come and to go check on his plants. The garden would produce most of its bounty in August, when the tomatoes and cucumbers and peppers came on, but there was still watering to be done, weeds to pull, herb seedlings to coax along. It was mindless, methodical work, the sort he could do in his sleep. Or in his sleep-deprived, grief-riddled state with only the faint light for company, as the case might be.

He'd had the notion that the weeding might center him enough so that he could start his shift without the worry of falling apart the second he saw Jacob. But maybe falling apart was inevitable because the more he worked in the vegetable beds, the less together he felt, skin and bones rattling like an old Ford on a gravel road. The dogs had come with him to check on things, giddy with the freedom outside their run, sniffing and wagging and generally making pests of themselves, but even they weren't enough to replace this heaviness in his heart.

Letting Jacob go had been the right call. He was sure

of it. Continuing on meant an even greater likelihood of hurting him. Jacob said it himself—he wanted *everything.* Everything that Linc wasn't sure he could ever offer anyone, let alone Jacob, with whom he wasn't supposed to have *anything,* let alone the everything Jacob apparently wanted. Jacob, who wanted a future. How had he put it? *Memories we make together.*

Linc already had too many memories burned into his neurons. Jacob's birthday. Building the play set. Their first kiss. Each one after that. The satisfied tilt to Jacob's mouth after really good sex. His playful smile in the shower. His furrowed forehead when he concentrated, trying to help cook. His too-long eyelashes on his pale cheeks when he slept. The smattering of freckles on his shoulders. More memories than his heart could hold right then.

And he had an obligation to not steal Jacob's future in the pursuit of more of those moments.

The way he saw it as he ripped out more prickly weeds, he was either a man of his word or he was nothing at all. And he hadn't kept his word, a concrete pylon of guilt weighing him down all summer. Jacob deserved more than him, and even if Wyatt had lived, had somehow found his way to more tolerant views, Linc couldn't believe that he would have condoned him being with Jacob. And maybe he'd stumbled with the whole "get it out of our systems" plan, but he couldn't give Jacob what he wanted without feeling like he was letting down Jacob's family, letting down an obligation to keep Jacob safe, give him the best possible future, which wasn't Linc.

Everything he owed the Hartman family, Wyatt es-

pecially, plowed through him, guilt and grief in equal
measure.

"*Saved you a seat, Linc.*"
"*It's okay. You can share my lunch.*"
"*Easy there. You almost fell off the edge.*"
"*I've got this.*"
"*Stay away from my little brother.*"

All the echoes of Wyatt through the years wound
through his thoughts like tendrils of pea shoots. Wyatt,
young and fearless. Wyatt, gangly and giving. Wyatt,
hard and mean. Wyatt, gone. He knew Jacob missed
him too, but it was different. He'd never known the
Wyatt Linc had grown up with. Never seen the guy
who'd saved Linc's ass so many times in the field. He
hadn't been there at twelve when Wyatt brought extra
lunch for a solid six months because Linc was so often
without. Or at fifteen when Linc almost took a one-way
trip down one of the rock faces. Hadn't been there the
night Wyatt met May, seen his whole body light up.
No one could infuriate Linc more, and no one could
take his place.

But who's going to take Jacob's place? The niggling
question poked at him, thorn to every one of his good
intentions. Instead, fresh grief kept smacking into him.
Goodbye to more sleepy smiles and lingering touches
and jokes he only made with Jacob. Wyatt might be ir-
replaceable but so was Jacob. The way Linc figured it,
Jacob would get over this, the way he had that Tyler kid.
He'd find someone to take Linc's place soon enough,
someone he could be proud to take home to his family,
someone without complications. And—

Fuck. Without thinking, he'd moved, crushing a

young tomato plant under his knee. It was toast now, crumpled beyond saving. Damn it. It had been a new variety of cherry tomato, one he'd hope to share with—

Breathe in. Breathe out. He'd known better than to go building castles in the air. Future plans were a one-way trip to disappointment. Planting vegetables for the guiltiest secret he'd ever kept was the height of stupidity. And yet, here he was, all wilted hopes and broken stems.

And fucking hell, if there wasn't an active fire to worry about, he'd call in today. He'd had time off pushed onto him when Wyatt died, but otherwise hadn't ever missed a shift, had worked through twisted ankles and summer colds and wrenched shoulders, but this, this *hurt*.

Left with no other option, he showered, headed to the air base. And such was his fucking luck that the two people he least wanted to see were deep in conversation with each other, Garrick and Jacob, standing over by one of the towering trees near the headquarters. For several long minutes, he sat there in his truck, watching them.

This was going to be his life now. Watching Jacob move on, move away from whatever they'd had, knowing he had no pull over him, no right to demand he stay away from Garrick and anyone else who might be interested. He had to force himself out of the truck, each step feeling like a solid mile of a pack-out test.

Say what you want, this isn't just sex. It's not. Jacob's pained words echoed in his ears. And God, like Linc had needed that declaration to know in the very marrow of his bones that this was the very opposite of casual, no matter what either of them said. The certainty he'd had back in the garden returned, a smothering blanket of loss. He wasn't ever getting over Jacob.

Jacob's gaze left Garrick, darted across the parking lot, landed on Linc. The pain in his eyes was enough to make Linc stop, take a step back, like that could fix anything. *Am I not enough?* That question still lingered between them. That he'd come to that conclusion was entirely Linc's own damn fault. Hell, one might even say it was by Linc's design, part of the necessity of pushing Jacob away for his own good.

But not enough? Truth was, Jacob was *everything.* Everything Linc could ever want. Ever hope for. And more than he deserved. More than he'd get to keep. Too much, maybe. But not enough? Never. He was the embodiment of Linc's heart and—

Fuck. He was Linc's heart, and Linc had squashed him, sure as he had that tomato plant. The hurt was there, open and undisguised, in Jacob's eyes. But fuck it. Linc didn't know the first thing about how to heal it. Some things simply stayed broken, no easy solution. Giving Jacob everything he wanted might be the worst thing for him, and Linc simply didn't know how to reconcile his urge to give in with his duty to protect him. *You're doing a bang-up job of that, Reid.* He hadn't been able to save Jacob from this pain, a guilt he'd carry to his grave.

But still he stood there, tethered to the spot. If only he could believe he was worthy of Jacob, that being together might not cost Jacob more than he should have to give. Then he might march over there and...

And what? Did it even matter? Because he wasn't and he wouldn't. But hell, how he *wanted*.

Somehow Jacob broke the sad symphony his eyes were busy conducting with Linc and returned his attention to Garrick, who had stopped him to make sure he was okay. Which he wasn't. But he could pretend. Could smile and nod and act like this was just a temporary blip, nothing worth getting upset over. Could deny that there was anything between him and Linc, not that Garrick seemed inclined to believe him. But Jacob could insist, could dig in his heels, could repeat again that he wasn't hurt or offended. Could brush off Garrick's concern.

But later, alone at his locker, his muscles trembled with the effort of holding it all together. Faking it was damn hard work. As was ignoring Linc. God, if only one *look* had gutted him, how was he going to make it through a whole shift? Linc had looked like shit, which wasn't helping anything. Deep lines around his facial features and tired eyes said he'd possibly slept even less than Jacob had. Misery had rolled off him, thick waves of regret and guilt, which served no purpose. This was Linc's damn fault, what he'd wanted. If he were miserable, then *good*.

Except for the part where Jacob had wanted to run to him, make him feel better, but hell if he even knew how to do that. By getting the most stubborn man on the planet to reconsider his stance? Not happening. And Jacob had his pride too. He wasn't going to beg Linc to feel something he didn't.

Merely thinking about him seemed enough to conjure him as he sensed Linc come into the locker room, large frame lurking far too close. Head bowed, he stood in front of his locker, making no move to start changing.

"I think Sims will have a jump for us sooner rather than later," Garrick said, already in the first layer of his gear. They'd add the heavier protective gear right before they jumped. "Jimenez and his crew deployed at dawn. McKenna's is on deck next. We'll be up soon. I'm going to see if Ray's clocked in yet."

"Sounds good." If Jacob was smart, he'd go with him, but he couldn't seem to make his muscles move faster.

"You might want to hit the coffee hard." Garrick clapped Linc on the shoulder. "You look like deer droppings, man."

Linc muttered something that sounded pretty close to "fuck off," but Garrick paid him no mind, laughing on his way out of the nearly empty room. Someone was showering in the far corner, but otherwise it was only them, left staring at each other, strangers who could have been everything.

"He's right. You do look awful. You gonna be okay for the shift?" Despite everything, Jacob still found himself being the first one to speak, concern seeping into his voice despite his best efforts to sound detached.

"I'm fine." Linc didn't put any force behind the words, hardly sounded like he believed himself.

"Liar."

"Like you'd know." Shaking his head wearily, Linc rolled his shoulders. "And like you're in any better shape."

"Actually, yes I would." He ignored Linc's second

claim. "I know you far better than you seem to want to give me credit for."

Linc visibly deflated at that, upper body curving in. "I know. Damn it."

His voice was pained, as if their very closeness was a wound or maybe a shortcoming he was trying to get over. And Jacob took umbrage at that, drawing himself up taller.

"You don't have to sound so offended. It doesn't have to be a bad thing." He liked knowing Linc. Liked knowing that there were stories that maybe only he had heard, sides of him that few others got to see. But now instead of special, it simply made him more frustrated. "That's all on you."

"Yeah, it is." Linc groaned then, scrubbing at his head. "Fuck, I hate this."

"Me too, but again—"

"It's on me. I *know*. Trust me, I know. And I'm sorry. So fucking sorry. This isn't how I wanted things to go at all. You hurt is the last thing I wanted."

Am I not enough? The question roared in his head again. *Want*. How silly. If Linc *wanted*, none of this would have been an issue.

"Pretty words, Linc. I almost believe you."

"What do you want from me?" Linc wrenched off his shirt, tats rippling. He shoved his clean clothes in the locker, but didn't pull out his gear.

"I told you already. Everything." On that, Jacob wasn't going to budge. He was done settling for scraps and almosts. Almost a date. Almost a couple. Almost love. Forget it. Forget all of it.

"I'm sorry." This time Linc whispered it, more anguish behind the words, but all it did was enrage Jacob. This was all so fucking needless.

"If you're going to be sorry, mean it, damn it. Put some action behind it. Show me. Otherwise it's as pointless as—"

"Sims says be ready for— *Whoa.* How are you guys still not ready?" Garrick burst back into the room.

"Sorry. Give me five." Sighing, Linc started pulling on gear.

Effectively dismissed, Linc's answer plain as a Vegas billboard, Jacob did the same and somehow they were ready at the hangar in time to finish gearing up and to check their cargo.

Garrick did his cross-check instead of Linc, hands impersonal as he checked Jacob's parachute rigging. Once on the airstrip, waiting for the plane, Linc shifted his weight from foot to foot, standing apart from the rest of them, looking like he was one stiff breeze away from rattling apart. Or possibly puking.

Damn it. Jacob hated himself for caring and hated the situation for making them so reliant on each other right when space was what they probably needed. Distance. Perspective. Anything other than this helpless caring. Finally, he couldn't stand it anymore. Pacing over to Linc, he stared him down.

"What the fuck is your problem?"

"Nothing. Just…you sure your connection points are good? That one buckle…"

"Oh, for fuck's sake." Because of course that was it. Of course Linc cared, even though he didn't want to. Of course it was concern over Jacob making him so agitated. Damn it. This would all be so much easier if Linc didn't care so deeply. Defeated, Jacob stretched his arms out. "Go ahead. Check me over. Better safe than…"

"Sorry." They both whispered the word in unison, and something passed between them as Linc did his cross-check. Not forgiveness precisely, but an understanding maybe. A shared regret. Despite everything, they still had that shared grief, always would, Wyatt tying them together even as his memory continued to shove them apart.

"Plane's coming in," Garrick shouted. Finishing his check, Linc moved away, emotion etched on his face.

"Fire's kicking up. Fucking wind," Ray said as they regrouped together. His shrewd gaze said he hadn't missed the tension between them. "Gonna be a tricky one. Need our heads about us. *All* of us."

Jacob nodded even as he tried to ignore the gnawing in his stomach. He hadn't prayed in years, but right then, all he wanted was to survive the shift, nothing else to go wrong.

Chapter Nineteen

The plane headed into the smoky sky, a familiar route which should have calmed Linc down, but somehow today the smoke seemed that much more ominous. The combination of unseasonably warm and dry and windy made the fire hard to predict and far more dangerous for all involved. Their assignment would involve some digging of hand line, and for all he was mixed up, he was glad Jacob was on their crew as he'd already proven himself capable of digging line to keep back fire like a machine.

And Linc had no doubt that Jacob could turn off all that anger and be professional in the field, be that mechanical firefighting machine. He hadn't wanted Linc's apologies, had been, if anything, even angrier than last night. *Put some action behind it.* Damn it, what was Linc supposed to do? He'd been close to grabbing Jacob, hauling him in for a kiss when Garrick had interrupted, but that would have been just as pointless as his words. Bottom line was that he simply couldn't give Jacob what he thought he most wanted, and that fucking sucked. For all of them.

The plane made a practice pass, approaching the

drop zone, allowing them to recheck the winds, then circling back to drop the cargo away.

"Gotta trust this weather holds," Garrick shouted as they deployed the cargo.

Something about the way he said *trust* made the word linger in Linc's brain. He wasn't much good at trusting these days. He'd trusted his mom to stick around forever, and then the universe had taken her way too soon. Ditto his brother. Ditto Wyatt. And he had too many years of experience to ever trust a fire. Too many times where he'd done everything right and it still all went to shit to trust anything, let alone something as mercurial as wind conditions.

But you trust Jacob. Unbidden, memories of the night of Jacob's birthday slammed into him. He *did* trust Jacob, on a fundamental level that went far beyond the physical. When Jacob had told him it wasn't his fault Wyatt had died, he'd listened. It had taken months to internalize it, and he still struggled with guilt, but he'd listened far more than he would to any other person. Jacob's unwavering belief in him mattered.

Maybe you gave your word to the wrong guy? Jacob's years-old question dug into him as surely as a too-snug piece of webbing, burrowed under his flesh to the places where he'd tried to bury both doubts and longing. And if he had…well, what the fuck was he supposed to do with that sort of misgiving?

"Ready?" Ray's shout came from behind him before he could come to any good conclusions.

No. Nerves he hadn't had since before Jacob's first solo jump careened into him, out of place and totally unexpected. Jumping like this, leaving both too much

unsaid and too much aired between them, felt wrong.
But there was no time to regroup, no time even to panic,
just to—

Trust Jacob. And there it was again. He had to trust
that Jacob could handle the jump, that he wasn't too distracted to pull it off. And then he had to trust himself.
Maybe if he could do those two things, everything else
would fall into place.

And as he leaped on cue, he summoned every piece
of his years of training and muscle memory, and he
trusted as they flew out over the ashy sky, smoke sting-
ing even through his goggles and gear. As was often
the case, the landing zone was tiny, precision of utmost
importance as they descended, aiming for a sliver of a
narrow dirt road that they'd later use for packing out.

"It's your only good way out." Ray's voice crackled
over his headset. "Creek to the south, but we're hoping
to have you out well before we lose road access. Ground
crews are having a devil of a time with this wind."

"Understood." Linc was no stranger to situations like
this one, with no good plan B. He'd also seen what appeared to be the only option morph and change over the
course of hours on the ground, had made hard choices
relying on the current plan only for it to change in a matter of moments. So Ray's words didn't make him panic,
but they did make him think about life and roads and
how what looked like a path sometimes wasn't and how
"no way out" could be a personal challenge. Sometimes
one got out when they could, other times they waited for
a better plan to materialize, and sometimes…

Well, sometimes a guy just fucking made his own
luck. Refused to accept defeat. Took the damn creek if

that was what it took. Was he really ready to toss Jacob away because there didn't seem to be a good path forward? Was he going to spend the rest of his life knowing he wasn't worthy or was he willing to fight for a sliver of a chance that maybe, just maybe he could be? Something had to give, that much was clear, but as he came in for a landing, for the first time he was willing to entertain the possibility of another way out of this mess they were in.

Thump. Bump. Roll. More of that muscle memory kicked in for a safe, if bumpy, landing. The wind conditions meant that they'd landed a fair distance downwind from each other, but it didn't take long to regroup. And then they were in the thick of it, no more room for deep thoughts, only working quickly at retrieving the cargo, getting their shovels and saws and remaining gear and getting a move on with digging their assigned lines. It was hard, dirty, smoky work that left his muscles burning and his attention focused on the job at hand.

He did, however, keep more to himself, less on Jacob's case about little details, and something surprising happened. The more he worked that whole trust thing and didn't nag or rush to do a task for Jacob, the less Jacob dug his heels in and the more he actually listened to him and Garrick when they did speak. Maybe he wasn't the stubborn kid Linc kept trying to paint him as. And if he wasn't that—

"Heads up!" Garrick stopped him from letting introspection back in by tossing brush near where he was working. On the comm set, there was a lot of chatter about changing wind conditions.

"Might need you to cut short if the wind shifts again.

If the fire heads down the valley, we'll need to get you out in a hurry." Ray was back at the base, working with the fire command to determine the scope of their assignment. The priority was to strategically fell several trees, and they moved on to that with renewed haste. The air was smokier now, the risk of raining embers growing as the fire moved closer.

The normally still forest was loud both with the sounds of their work and crashing burning snags in the distance, signaling that the command had been right about the shifting fire. In the air, more planes flew low, both with more jumpers for other drop zones and with loads of retardant to dump on the fire itself.

While working on the second tree, a warning alert sounded on the radio.

"We're extracting all crews along your line," the comm set announced right as several almighty cracks sounded.

Linc looked up to see several widowmaker branches headed right for where Jacob was crouched, bringing Garrick, who had been in the tree, down with them.

"Move!" Linc yelled, even as he was already diving for Jacob, shoving him out of the way. And then everything blurred together, a spectacular concert of swift movement and crushing pain.

"Jacob!" he called, but his ears rang too loudly to tell if he'd actually shouted. And had he saved him? Was he too late? Too late for both of them? God, he hoped not, his last conscious thought a prayer that Jacob be okay.

"Move!" Linc's shout reached Jacob almost simultaneously with an ominous cracking from above and a godawful yell from Garrick. And then Linc's body, all his considerable bulk, was crashing into Jacob, shoving him several feet back as pine needles and debris rained down on them, branches and Garrick hitting the ground with sickening thuds.

"Garrick! Linc!" Fuck. Jacob's wrist hurt from hitting the ground weird, mud was dripping down his face because his helmet was askew, and his ears rang, like he'd taken a roundhouse kick to the chin. But he was relatively unscathed while the other two were sprawled on the ground, and he didn't know who to run to first.

Think. He needed to think. Evaluate. Assess. Neither man had answered him, the sound of his own pulse roaring above the forest noise as his heart clamored for him to rush to Linc first. However, he started with Garrick—he was closer, and also Jacob wasn't sure he trusted himself to keep a clear head if Linc was bad. He had to pick branches and debris off Garrick to get a better look, including a heavy one off his legs that strained his aching wrist. Fuck. This wasn't good.

But Garrick's helmet was still on. Seriously dented, but on. Legs… *Deep breath. Stay calm.* The worst of the debris had landed there, and it wasn't pretty. But Jacob forced himself to focus on one task at a time, checking for a pulse while trying not to jostle him too much.

"Come in?" He rushed to make contact with the command center via his comm set.

"Go ahead, Hartman." Ray's voice was filled with static, but relief still swamped Jacob, made it so that he had to swallow hard before continuing.

"We've got a situation here. Garrick Nelson just fell from a tree. Nasty drop. We're going to need a medical evac for him ASAP. He's breathing, but…" *Hold it together*, he reminded himself, pausing for another breath. "It's bad, man. And Reid's hurt too."

"Hartman?" The comm set crackled again. "Did you hear the last order? We're pulling crews all along your line. We needed your crew heading to the extraction point."

"You're not listening." Some panic started to seep into his voice. "No way is Garrick walking out of here. His legs… We need a C-collar and a backboard and—"

"Understood. We're working on an alternative plan. Stand by. What's Reid's status?"

Okay. No choice but to go investigate. He held his breath as he stumbled to Linc, who—

"'M alive." A pile of small branches tumbled to the side as Linc sat up with a pained groan.

"You're…" God, Jacob was having to work hard to not weep only from the sound of his voice. But he forced himself to breathe through the wave of emotions and think.

"Here." Linc wobbled, head unsteady.

"Easy now." He reached out to ease Linc back down. "No fast movements."

To the comm set, he said louder, "Reid's conscious, but a second backboard wouldn't be a bad idea. He's got a bump on his head." That part didn't look good—he'd lost his helmet at some point, probably diving for Jacob. An ugly purple knot at his hairline jockeyed for real estate with some facial abrasions and scrapes.

"No…stretcher. Just…wind…knocked outta me." Linc didn't sound the best either, speech slow and labored.

"Where does it hurt?" Jacob scanned for more visible injuries. His limbs were intact, no weird angles or pools of blood. "Can you wiggle your fingers?"

"Yeah. Toes too. Ankle must've rolled or something. Knee too. Stiff. Hurts like a bastard." Linc's voice still wasn't normal, sounding like each word was taxed, but at least he was talking and making sense. It was a start, and Jacob would take it. "How's Garrick?"

"It's bad," Jacob admitted.

"Fuck." Linc's heartfelt curse pretty much summed up Jacob's feelings too. Ignoring Jacob's efforts to keep him still, he sat up again. "How soon till a chopper?"

"Come in? Do we have an ETA on evac?" Jacob spoke into the comm set again.

"That's a negative on a chopper to your current location," Ray reported. "Wind is too high now, visibility dropping. We're scrambling a jump—medics with supplies—but we've got to get you out of there ASAP."

"You're telling me." Satisfied for the moment that Linc wasn't imminently dying, he rushed back to Garrick. "Garrick's still unconscious. And there's blood. His legs…"

"Assess for bleeders." Ray's voice calmed him back down.

"Fuck. Bad gash on his thigh. Not sure direct pressure is gonna be enough."

"Tourniquet." Linc was already crawling to their supplies, which included a rudimentary first-aid kit. With so much saw work, bleeding was always a risk, so a one-handed tourniquet was part of their gear. He tossed Jacob the kit.

"Fuck. My wrist." Jacob missed the catch, but

quickly retrieved it. Another more detailed check of Garrick's wounds told him that the tourniquet was the best option. Somehow he managed to get it on.

"Nuh." Garrick released a pained groan, the first sound he'd made since the accident.

"It's okay, buddy." Jacob pitched his voice low and soothing. "We're getting you out of here. You just hang on. You'll be okay."

The last was more prayer than promise, and Linc made a warning noise like maybe Jacob shouldn't be making any guarantees. Fuck it. Jacob would lie if he had to. Keeping Garrick calm and fighting to survive was the most important thing. He'd lost a fair bit of blood, and shock was the biggest risk right then. Jacob reported the time of tourniquet application to Ray for him to tell the medics.

"There's a possibility of needing you to shelter in place. Prepare to deploy emergency shelters, but don't move Nelson yet. We've got a crew incoming, but if they can't jump…" Ray trailed off, voice uncharacteristically thick with emotion. And for good reason. Sheltering in place was a wildland firefighter's last resort, often with dire results even with the flame-proof tent for protection.

"Jacob can pack out." Linc had retrieved his own comm set at some point and was talking directly to Ray, not even looking at Jacob who was right fucking there. "Set up the shelters for us and head for the creek—"

"Hell no." Jacob put a stop to that idea. "We're a team. No way in hell am I leaving you two alone."

"Reid might have a point. We're having a devil of a

time predicting the fire with this wind. If we can get you out—"

"Nope. Nothing doing." On this Jacob was prepared to use all of his well-earned stubborn reputation. "Get that crew here. They'll need my help packing out with the stretchers."

"Your wrist—"

"Is fine." He cut Linc off before he could go giving the impression that Jacob was injured too. "Just get help here."

"We're trying." Ray's voice was resigned, like he wasn't going to push again on Jacob leaving, but Linc wasn't as quick to concede, growling at Jacob.

"Go. You've got a good shot at saving yourself, and I want you to take it."

"You can keep talking or you can help me set up shelters." Jacob wasn't losing this fight, and he also wasn't having it with Ray listening in. It didn't matter how angry he'd been at Linc earlier, no way was he abandoning him now. He couldn't switch off his heart that easily.

"I should have an update on the rescue jump crew shortly. They're en route," Ray reported.

"Good." Jacob stared Linc down as he checked on Garrick's vital signs again. He let out the occasional groan, but he hadn't opened his eyes and his pulse was threadier than earlier. The tourniquet was holding though so there was that. He covered Garrick with a space blanket before turning his attention to the emergency shelters—each sausage-shaped aluminum structure held a single firefighter and was designed to trap breathable air.

Working together with Linc, who still couldn't put weight on his leg but who had two working wrists, they fell into their old cooperation and figured out a way to potentially cover Garrick with minimal moving if it came to that. But when Linc switched off his comm set, Jacob knew he was in for another lecture.

"You should—"

"Save it." Gentling his harsh tone somewhat, he added, "And save your energy. I think you've got a concussion."

"Quit worrying about me." Linc held up his gloved hands. "I can't have you putting yourself at this kind of risk when you still have a chance."

"And I can't leave you. I just can't."

"Why?" That one word seemed to carry all of Linc's anguish, the grief of the past year, his steadfast refusal to admit to what was there between him and Jacob, his dogged determination to keep to his idiotic plan, and the sadness Jacob had seen in his eyes that morning.

"You know why." Jacob didn't break eye contact, held steady, tried to let his gaze say the words he couldn't. Not here. Not now. He refused to do any deathbed declarations—he wasn't giving up on their survival no matter what.

"Yeah." Linc's shoulders sagged. "Damn it, Jacob. I hate this."

"I know." And maybe that was also why he couldn't say the words. Fearing that maybe Linc didn't want to hear them, not really.

Making a frustrated noise, Linc lunged for him, hands on Jacob's upper arms. "Would it help if I said—"

"No. No crazy talk. We're in this together." Pulse

galloping, he seriously wasn't sure he could handle whatever desperate thing Linc was about to say.

"You're really not going anywhere, are you?" Linc held his gaze again, tone suggesting he was talking about far more than packing out.

"Nope." Jacob answered for all possible meanings. He wasn't leaving Linc and Garrick here, wasn't going to abandon his quest for more from Linc either. He could see that now. He was frustrated and angry and fed up, but he still wasn't giving up. Not yet. Linc had quite possibly saved his life, no thought to his own. And that meant something. Was worth something. And at that moment, he had to believe that they would make it through. On all levels.

"I—" Linc's words were cut off by the drone of an approaching plane. The sky was still hazy with smoke, and the wind appeared to have changed direction slightly but not died down. He flipped the comm set back on. "What's the status?"

"Crew did a practice pass. No go. They're doing another one now," Ray reported, voice clipped. "Fire is shifting. We're expecting more reports shortly."

Never had Jacob prayed as hard as he did in the next few minutes. Not only for himself, but for Linc and Garrick, especially. Garrick might not make it if the rescue crews couldn't reach them, even if the fire shelters held. His color was awful, a pale greenish-gray, and his skin was clammy to the touch.

"Okay. Four jumpers and cargo are away. They're being pushed downwind of the drop zone. Could have a hike to get to you, but their spotter is trying to keep them out of the trees."

Jacob glanced up in time to see little dots on the hazy horizon, each representing all his hopes for Linc and Garrick. *Please let them find us in time. Give us enough time to get this right.* Next to him, Linc grabbed his uninjured hand, squeezed, and Jacob had to believe something out there was hearing his unspoken pleas.

Chapter Twenty

Linc had been in some close calls before and made it through some harrowing tales, but he'd seldom cared so deeply about making it through. All of them. Garrick, who was going to survive even if Linc had to bargain with a slew of demons to secure his future, and Jacob, who was being an idiot, but was still the idiot Linc needed like the region needed rain. If Jacob wasn't going to listen to reason and pack out on his own, then Linc was going to make it through if only to shake him for being so damn stubborn. Again. And still Linc grabbed his hand, held on, as they watched the rescue crew parachute in. Somehow all his rules about personal contact on the job seemed irrelevant now.

The shapes got bigger before disappearing, another tense wait for news. Meanwhile, he eyed the emergency fire shelters, knowing there was still a good chance they might be needed. On the ground, Garrick groaned again, and Jacob released Linc's hand to go check on him.

"We're getting you out of here," Jacob told him, far more upbeat than Linc could have managed under the circumstances. "You just hang on, okay? Four jumpers are on their way. They should be touching down any second and making their way here. Wind's turning. I can feel it. All you have to do is hold on."

But when back at Linc's side, his eyes were grave, mouth a hard, thin line. "I'm not lying about the wind, but he's not going to make it if we can't pack him out ASAP."

"He's a fighter." Linc had seen many a fighter go down over the years, but it seemed like the thing to say, both for Jacob and also himself because fucking hell this sucked. He hated whatever was going on with his leg, rendering him unable to help Jacob as much as he wanted. And it wasn't just his leg—his head swam like he'd pounded shots for hours, a massive headache that made talking harder than it needed to be. And the combination of the leg and head meant that the burden of action was all on Jacob. Even if moving Garrick without a backboard were advisable, which it wasn't, he was too much for Jacob alone to carry, even if Jacob was one of the more fit jumpers. So, here they were. Stuck. Fire bearing down on them. Waiting for—

Crackle. Buzz. The comm set sputtered to life again. "We've had contact with the crew on the ground."

"Thank God," Jacob exhaled hard, sagging against Linc.

"Yup." Ray sounded far more upbeat than he had a few moments earlier. "They got carried almost a mile off the landing zone, some even farther down, and one got treed, and there were some cargo issues. But they're en route to you now. We're looking at a limited window for a chopper if you guys can haul ass to an evac point we've marked downstream from the creek. Road's a no go."

"I'm ready to run," Jacob promised. "Just get us those stretchers."

However, that request turned out to be easier said than done as the first of the rescue crew arrived, a heavily geared man and woman he'd known for years. Knowing how experienced and competent they were made Linc that much happier to see them, pulse speeding up as making it out in time seemed like a real possibility now.

"Well, Reid, what'd you get yourself into this time?" The woman, Duski, rushed toward them.

"Not me. Nelson." He gestured at Garrick's prone form, movement making his head pound again. "See to him first. I'm just a bum leg and a couple of bruises."

"That bump on your head looks pretty nasty," Cyrus said as he joined Duski in kneeling by Garrick. "The others are bringing more equipment, but we've got a situation. Cargo burst open. One backboard and C-collar survived the jump, but we're left with only one of the two field stretchers."

Linc could already tell where this was going. His rather empty stomach turned to a lead-lined pit of dread.

"Nelson gets the first-class ride out of here." He flexed his leg, testing. He'd gotten by earlier with a sort of half-crawl, but that wasn't going to get him very far. "You get him loaded. I can maybe hoof it."

Slowly and painfully, but he could do it. And he could already tell by the tilt of Jacob's chin that no way was he even entertaining the idea of leaving Linc behind. But he didn't say anything aloud, instead helping them prepare Garrick for transport, stabilizing him as best they could with the first-aid equipment on hand. Jacob wasn't kidding about Garrick's legs being in rough shape, and Linc had to look away at one point as they moved him. Not because his stomach was weak, but that was his friend, his buddy, and it was killing him to see him like this. And also knowing how easily that could be Jacob lying there weighed heavily on him. Fuck. All it would have taken was one stubborn insistence from Jacob that he be the one to climb and...

Bitter acid rose up in his throat before he could even finish that thought. And if it was Jacob over there, fighting for his life, then Linc might have truly lost everything. All day, his mind had been whirring, trying to get him to a place where he could both give Jacob what he wanted—*deserved*—and still live with himself, but now...

Well, now he knew, with painful clarity, there was no living without Jacob. Hell, he'd been one-hundred-percent okay with giving his life to save Jacob's. And if there was no life without Jacob, then maybe his many principles could be reduced down to one simple truth. He lo—

"What's our status?" The arrival of the other two jumpers interrupted his introspection and spurred a new flurry of activity. One of the new arrivals was clearly hobbled from the tree landing with a pronounced limp, but everyone worked together while waiting for the final word as to whether they would shelter in place or try for an extraction.

Jacob and Cyrus fashioned Linc a crutch from one of the fallen branches while the others worked on Garrick. Finally, Command decided that the wind and fire conditions were such that they could make the trek to the creek, then take it to the designated spot where they were going to try to get a helicopter in, but they were bringing the collapsible shelters along in case the fire turned on them.

"Ready? You sure you don't want us to carry you?" Jacob stuck close to Linc while the others transported Garrick.

"I've got it." Linc hoped he wasn't lying as he tried to match the pace set by the stretcher bearers and not wanting the other guy with a twisted ankle to outdo him. They were a ragtag crew for sure, trying to out-race both the fire and their own limitations. The terrain was rocky and uneven, especially tricky without the road to guide them, relying instead on compass work and the guidance of the command center. Not used to a crutch and head still fuzzier than a ten-year-old sweater, he stumbled more than once, but each time Jacob was there to steady him. They drifted farther behind the group with the stretcher, but Linc tried to keep his focus on each step.

The boulders became bigger obstacles as they neared the creek, and he struggled to get around stones he would usually bound over.

"You can do it," Jacob encouraged.

"Trying," he gritted out.

"Let me help more."

"I've got it." Frustration made him snappier in the face of Jacob's unending patience.

"I know, but we need to pick up the pace, and like everyone always says, we make a good team. Lean on me."

They did make a good team. Linc flashed back to the weeks of training, building the play set for the kids, and dozens of other memories over the years. They'd always worked well together, an effortless team. *Partners.* And it was a bond and level of cooperation that went beyond friendship, beyond coworkers. He wasn't ever going to find this with another soul.

"Okay." He let Jacob assist him over and around the next rock formation. Even with Jacob's help, he slipped and slid. "Fuck." Then, as he righted himself, he glanced up at the smoke rolling by. They still weren't clear of danger by a long shot. Renewed urgency surged through him, but not simply about their destination. There were things that needed saying. "I'm sorry. About everything. And when we're back—"

"Not. The. Place." Jacob gave him a hard stare. "Just let me help you without you feeling obligated in return. This doesn't have anything to do with…*that.*"

"Not feeling guilty. More like I'm realizing—"

"Let's get out of this and then you can see if you're still feeling so…apologetic."

Fuck. It hadn't occurred to Linc that he could figure his shit out and Jacob not believe him, not rush to make up, and not seem particularly inclined to listen.

"I hurt you and—"

"Next drop is the creek bank," Jacob interrupted. "And yeah, we've got some talking to do. *After.* Right now, focus on making that evac flight."

Jacob's tone was just this side of patronizing and made it clear that he still assumed that Linc was prepping some sort of deathbed confessional. But there was no time to correct him, because they were dropping to the shallow water, and the rocky creek bed made walking with the crutch even more difficult.

The other group was already farther down the creek, but Cyrus doubled back to them. "We've made contact with the chopper. We're looking at a very tight load window. Need to pick up our pace."

"Trying." Linc sloshed through the water with more effort.

"Let us carry you." Cyrus nodded at Jacob, who was quick to agree.

"Yeah. It's the best option and you know it." And Jacob being Jacob, he didn't wait for Linc to come to terms with this change of circumstances, simply scooping him up along with Cyrus in an impressively coordinated chair carry. And then they were on the move, it glaringly obvious how much Jacob had been holding back to keep up with Linc and the crutch as he and Cyrus easily plowed through the water. They made up ground with the sort of determination most recruits reserved for their first timed pack-out test.

Meanwhile, Linc struggled to keep his pride in check. It was one thing to know he might have to be stretchered out and another to be bodily carried, realizing there wasn't a damn thing he could do to make this easier on Jacob and Cyrus who were both huffing with exertion. And yeah his head still ached, but he was conscious enough of every movement, every bounce and jostle. But then they caught up to the stretcher, and one look at Garrick put all that pride to shame. This was nothing. A little indignity, but he wasn't complaining, not with his friend fighting for his life right next to him.

"I hear something!" Jacob's voice was breathless but excited. "What's the word from Command?"

"ETA five minutes," the comm set reported, Ray's voice even more filled with static. "The creek widens a little around this bend, and that will give them enough room for a tight landing."

The drone of an incoming helicopter increased as they all sped up, the sound giving everyone a renewed burst of energy. They reached the wide, flat section of creek bank, and after setting Linc next to Garrick, the rest quickly prepped for the helicopter landing.

"Hang in there," he said to Garrick, trying to summon all of Jacob's usual upbeat energy. "Come on, buddy, just a little longer."

"Yup." Jacob came to crouch in front of Linc. "Listen, here's the deal. And you can't have a fit, okay?"

"Okay," he reluctantly agreed.

"Because of how bad off Garrick is and because there's seven of us to evac, they're updating the plan. They're sending a second chopper. First chopper's going straight to the hospital in Bend. Cyrus and Duski want you on that chopper—no one likes the look of your head bump even if you are talking okay. We've all seen latent head injuries go bad fast. You need checking out."

"And you too. Your wrist—"

"Is fine. Even after carrying your ass, I'm fine." He gave Linc a hint of a rascally grin. "Just a sprain."

"You need an X-ray."

"And I'll get one if the medics say so." Jacob kept his voice low and patient. "But they're balancing loads, and I'm on the second chopper. No fits, remember?

"Fuck. *Jacob.*" He held Jacob's gaze, trying to get

him to see reason, knowing it was pointless, but needing to try nonetheless. "If the fire shifts... If they can't get a second chopper in..."

"We've got our shelters. We're near the water. And I'm tough."

"You're..." *My heart. My everything.* The words were right there, but then Jacob looked away.

"Here it comes!" he shouted, standing up, helicopter noise increasing now, drowning out whatever Linc might have tried to say. To Linc, Jacob nodded. "Just trust me, man."

"I do. Always. Find me. After." Linc had to yell to be heard.

"Always."

And then Jacob was gone, rushing over to the others as the chopper swooped low. Garrick was loaded first, two uniformed medics taking charge of his stretcher. Next Linc was transferred to a second gurney, leg strapped up. They were airborne almost before he had a chance to grab a breath, Jacob a pale dot on the creek bank, Linc's heart left right there next to him. The crew working on Garrick kept up a constant chatter of medical jargon, but all Linc could focus on was the smoky canopy beneath them. If the fire took Jacob...

God, he couldn't even finish that thought. Not before they talked. Not before he made things right. Not before he said all the things. Every thought Jacob hadn't let him finish and all the others rattling around in his increasingly foggy brain. So much left unsaid. All he needed was a chance. A chance for Jacob and the crew left behind. A chance for himself. And a chance for them, a chance that maybe everything wasn't already lost.

Chapter Twenty-One

Jacob hadn't let Linc complete any of what he'd wanted to say. He'd had good reasons for not wanting to hash things out in the middle of a crisis, not wanting Linc to say things he'd later regret. However, as he watched the chopper leave, all those missing words loomed large in his mind.

Be okay, Linc. We'll talk later, he promised the ashy sky as the helicopter disappeared over the horizon, and the rest of them settled in to wait for the second evac attempt. And for all he'd been short with Linc, he did intend to have the sort of lay-it-all-out conversation they were way overdue. He wasn't giving up Linc without a fight, but he also couldn't deny that he was still hurt and angry and frustrated and not sure he could trust heat-of-the-moment apologies. If Linc said what he most wanted to hear and then took it back…

Well, he simply wasn't sure he could cope with that. The thought alone made his wrist ache worse and made his stomach churn to the point that when he was offered a protein bar he had to decline. He'd let his fears keep Linc at bay, and now that he was faced with the very real possibility of never hearing what he'd been about to say, he was almost sick with longing. Fucking fickle brain.

The helplessness of the wait got to him too. There was not much any of them could do to increase their chances of rescue. They were at the mercy of the wind and the fire, and they had to trust the other crews to do their best with the unpredictable conditions. After two aborted helicopter landing attempts, he wasn't surprised when the call came down from Command to pack out farther, another long slog of hoping Linc was okay and that Garrick was alive. Everyone was similarly somber, not much small talk as they pressed on.

At the second extraction point, word came that Garrick had been stabilized in Bend and was on a life flight to Portland for further surgery. No word whether he'd lost the leg—Jacob knew he'd done the right thing with the tourniquet but it also increased the risk of amputation and permanent damage the longer it was in place. And no word about Linc's condition either. Jacob presumed he wasn't on the life flight, but there was a wide range between life-threatening beyond what the regional hospital could handle and out of danger entirely. He'd promised Linc he'd go to him, and he intended to keep that promise, but it was another two evacuation tries before he was en route to base on a bumpy ride over a fire that was increasingly contained, no thanks to the wind.

Then after the world's fastest shower and clothing change, he had a debriefing with Sims and Alder about what had gone so wrong.

"Any new word on Nelson?" he asked cautiously as their questions came to an end.

"Touch and go." Sims's face was grave, her usual sternness blanketed with a heavy layer of concern. "His family's been reached. We've got a retired jumper driving his father up to Portland, and his mother and sister are coming from Eugene."

"And Li—Reid?"

"At the hospital in Bend. Ray's family is seeing to his dogs. Speaking of Bend, we need to get your wrist x-rayed, no matter what you say about it being minor. It's too late for the urgent care here in town. I'm heading to Bend to check on Reid. I'll drop you at the ER." She nodded like this plan was entirely reasonable, which it was, but hell if Jacob could rush to Linc with his boss on his heels. He'd have to actually go through the motions of getting his wrist looked at and hope for a sliver of quiet moment when he could see Linc.

"Do you want to call your mother now or after we know more?" Sims's voice wasn't without compassion as they made their way to the vehicles.

"After." He didn't need Mom freaking out quite yet. Not before he saw Linc. If he called her, she'd come right away, and then he'd be that much further from being alone with Linc. Besides, he'd much rather call with a report that his wrist was a minor sprain and that Linc and Garrick were out of the woods than with a lot of uncertainties.

"Fair enough." Like the rescue crew out in the field, Sims wasn't inclined to chitchat on the drive to Bend, which was helpful as night finally fell and the long day didn't appear anywhere near over. While they drove, a call came in that Garrick was still in surgery in Portland, still fighting for his life, but holding steady.

"My X-rays can probably wait," he said to Sims after the call ended, the urge to be near Linc reaching overwhelming levels, even if it meant sharing him with others and not being able to speak freely.

"Nope." Her reply was pretty much as he expected. "I've seen permanent nerve and ligament damage from delayed treatment on what looked like a minor injury before. Tell you what, I'll text you what I find out on Reid."

"Thanks." It was something at least, but it was cold comfort for a long wait in the ER where he was understandably low priority on a busy night with multiple smoke inhalation cases and the usual assortment of car accidents and other injuries.

"It's a sprain," he confidently told the young female doctor when he was finally shown to a cubicle. "I'll be back on the job shortly, no problem. Maybe we don't need to bother with radiology? Just give me a splint?"

He'd heard enough from the nurses to know that X-rays were another lengthy wait, but the doctor just clucked and muttered something about hairline fractures before ordering X-rays. His phone finally buzzed with a message from Sims while he was cooling his heels, waiting to be taken to radiology.

Reid is stable. Being kept for concussion observation. Room 218. How's the wrist?

Well, that wasn't much to go on, but he supposed it was better than nothing. And now he had a room number at least. Heck, he was tempted to ditch the X-rays and head right there, but then the orderly showed up to escort him to radiology. Resigning himself to more waiting, he kept refreshing his phone after replying to Sims, but no more news came in about either Garrick or Linc.

And when the doctor came back in with an imposing black rigid cast with Velcro straps, he didn't even protest too much.

"I can't believe you hauled your buddy how far?" The doctor shook her head as she applied the cast. It was a damn fracture after all. Barely even a line on the X-ray and it didn't seem worth the cast to him, but he accepted it with a minimum of grumbling because it got him out of there faster.

Finally, he was on his way to room 218, which he was relieved to see was not an ICU room, just an ordinary hospital room, and as he reached the right number, he almost ran into Sims.

"I see I was right about the break." She nodded at his arm. "You need a ride back to base? Or your mom's house?"

"Uh…" Fuck. He needed to see Linc. But there were some things he couldn't confess to Sims.

Sims released a tired sigh like she didn't have time for his fumblings. "Or you think you can arrange a ride? I figure you're chomping at the bit to see for yourself that Reid's in one piece."

"Yeah. I'll work something out." He seized the opening like a life buoy, not disagreeing that he needed to see Linc.

"I stayed while they were running various tests, but he seems done for the time being with that. He's supposed to be resting, but I suppose you might be the right kind of distraction."

Right kind of distraction. Jacob had to smile because that pretty much summed up his summer thus far. Not that he could admit that to her.

"I won't keep him up," he promised. "And I know you want to get back yourself. It was a long day for all of us. I'll figure out something."

"That it was." She rubbed her temples. "And it's not over yet. I don't know much—HIPAA and all that— but Nelson is in ICU now in Portland with chances high that he'll need further surgery sooner rather than later."

"At least he's alive." Jacob chose to cling to that ray of hope.

"Yes, there is that. And you're on medical leave until we can figure out some light duty for you. So don't worry about clocking in tomorrow."

"Yes, ma'am." He honestly wasn't sure if that was a relief or not. He mostly wanted to be here with Linc, but part of him felt like he was letting his crew down, not being able to go out with them, see this fire through. Hopefully he'd be well enough for some mop-up duty.

Once Sims was on her way, he took a minute to take a deep breath, steeling himself for seeing Linc, for the talk they needed to have, but also for all his mixed emotions—relief that he wasn't more seriously hurt, guilt that it was saving Jacob that had injured him, hurt that it took near-death to get Linc willing to talk in the first place, and a bunch of other things he was refusing to label. His shoulders tensed and despite the late hour, his nerves clanged with leftover adrenaline.

The nearest bed in the room was empty, curtain

pulled back, and a weary-looking Linc in the second bed. Jacob's eyes burned, and he had to lean into the wall, stop himself from rushing to him.

"You awake?" he asked, voice rough.

"Thought I might have heard your voice." Even with his tired eyes and pale skin, Linc still managed half of a smile. He gestured at Jacob's arm. "What's with the new accessory? Wasn't that you who was rather insistent that you weren't hurt?"

"Yeah. Apparently, I'm a crappy judge of a non-displaced scaphoid fracture."

"Damn it. I'm sorry."

"You saved my freaking life. I'll take the broken wrist." He shrugged, not wanting to dwell on the injury, and not wanting Linc to feel guilty about it either. "It'll heal. They say I probably won't need surgery for it. Tell me about your leg?"

"Sims didn't tell you?" Linc groaned and gestured at his strapped-up leg, which was propped up on pillows. "Sprained ankle. But the knee… It's my ACL."

"Oh, fuck." Jacob had been around sports enough years to know that injury always sucked. "All those years of work and jumps, and one lunging tackle did it? Damn. I guess you're lucky football didn't do you in. Surgery?"

"Yeah. That's coming. It's not the worst type of complete tear, but they still want surgery. I'm on concussion observation first. They say I got away with a mild one, but they're being cautious."

"Good." Jacob dragged one of the visitor chairs over to the bed, not wanting to continue to loom over Linc, and also not being in a hurry to leave. "You let them be cautious. That bump still looks nasty."

"Yeah. Ruined my chances of modeling." Linc laughed, then grimaced. "Only bad part of being under observation is they're limited in what they can give me for the knee right now."

"I'm sorry. Fucking sucks. I'd give anything…" Jacob sighed and shook his head. "You saved my life, like I said. And now…surgery. And then recovery. It's not fair."

"Fuck that talk. Not fair is Garrick right now. This…" Linc pointed at his leg. "Is nothing. I'll be back out there. Eventually. And if it saved you, I'd give both knees. Hell, take a kidney. You safe is everything. I wasn't going to let those branches take you out. Not before…"

And there they were, back to the whole need-to-talk thing.

"I wasn't going anywhere," he said gruffly.

"Yeah, you were." Linc's voice was surprisingly gentle. "And with good reason. Like you said… I was a cowardly bastard."

"Maybe not quite *that*." Jacob winced at his own words. "And maybe I was a little hasty with the ultimatums. And maybe now isn't the time to rehash all of that. What matters is that you're okay."

"No, what matters is that I hurt you." Linc stretched out a hand. Jacob spared a glance at the door before taking it. "And I'm sorry."

"You did. But I don't want you all worked up over that tonight."

"Maybe I do." Linc made a frustrated noise. "Damn it, why won't you let me apologize?"

"Because perhaps it's not needed? I mean, I appreciate you being sorry. But I also see now that I can't make you feel things that maybe you don't. Can't force you to change your priorities. And it's not just about me. I get that I can't make you choose me, but I also can't seem to make you choose *yourself*."

And that right there was why he hadn't wanted this conversation earlier. Still didn't want it. Wasn't sure how he got to a place where he could trust Linc's apology or accept it, because if nothing real was going to change, maybe it didn't matter how bad Linc felt about hurting him. As he tried to figure out how to explain that, his phone buzzed at the same time as Linc's.

"Garrick," they said in unison, a joint prayer lifted up, cutting through their disagreement. But when Jacob checked his phone, the message was from his mom.

"Fuck. My mom just heard about Garrick and the accident. She's pissed."

"Uh-huh." Linc groaned. "Blowing up my phone too. Wants assurances that we're okay."

"I better call her in a minute." He typed out a fast reply to that effect. "I'm telling her we're okay, but she's gonna want to hear my voice."

"Are we?" Linc's eyes were serious. "Are we okay? I know you need to call her, but I don't like leaving things like this. You've put me off all day, tried to keep me from telling you that I want another shot. Give me a chance to make things right. Please."

"This is near-death talk. You're full of regrets and reflection right now, but you don't really want…" He trailed off, unable to keep voicing his deepest fears, even as part of him thrilled to Linc's words.

"I love you." Linc's tone was deadly serious, eyes hard. "And I knew that before today, so stop with me not knowing my mind."

"Yeah? Well, if you loved me yesterday, why the hell wasn't that enough?" Jacob's voice broke on the question, and he had to drop Linc's hand and look away. And fuck, Jacob had waited *years* to hear those words. He should be fucking giddy. But now that they were here, Linc actually saying them, he was anything other than ecstatic. Couldn't trust it to be real. To last. To matter. "Why wasn't that enough before we had to almost fucking die?"

"Because I am a cowardly bastard. You were right about that. But I want a chance to be something more than that. I'm not asking you for things to go back to how they were. Just give me a shot to be what you need. To show you that I'm serious about changing. Don't leave. Not now."

"I'm not leaving." Jacob scrubbed at his hair. Hell if he could ignore a plea like that even if he was still hurt and angry and more than a little confused. "I mean, I need to go find enough signal to call Mom. But I'll be back."

"And?" Linc prompted.

"I guess we'll see. I can't go back, Linc. I just can't. Not now. I wish I could. But I also know I can't quit you, can't give up hope that maybe…" He inhaled sharply, hating how each word felt like jagged metal against his tongue, truths that hurt to share.

"Just don't quit me, okay?" Linc reached for his uninjured hand again, and Jacob let him take it. "We'll work it out. All of it. Just don't give up. Not yet."

"I won't." And as he squeezed Linc's hand, he knew he wouldn't. Wouldn't give up on Linc, not yet, maybe not ever. Wouldn't give up hope until the last pebble of it was crushed and scattered to the wind, but hell, this was gonna hurt if Linc was wrong, if he woke up tomorrow and all his old reasons and concerns took priority again. Trust was in short supply, but even so, his heart knew what it knew. He wasn't going anywhere.

Chapter Twenty-Two

"So…how much trouble are we in?" Linc forced a smile as Jacob returned to the visitor's chair after calling his mom. He'd come back as promised. That was what mattered right then.

"Had to work overtime convincing her not to make the drive right now. I'd put money on her coming to see you first thing. I'm not sure who she's more upset about honestly, you or me. You always were her favorite." Jacob gave a weary shrug. "And of course she's broken up about Garrick. She's grieving Wyatt all over again too, I'm sure. And fuck, I hate making her worry like this. I wish what I want for me didn't have to be so bad for everyone else."

Linc knew he wasn't just talking about smoke jumping and his career choice. "Hey, now. It doesn't."

"I hate hurting people. Her. May. You."

"What you want…that's not that unreasonable." He cast around for Jacob's hand again, gratified when Jacob let him take it. "You're allowed to have wants and needs. Big dreams even."

"Yeah." Jacob met Linc's gaze and held. "I've wanted this for so long."

Again, Linc knew he wasn't only talking about his job. "I know. And I'm sorry. For all of it. For not being more supportive of you joining the smoke-jumping team. For making you wait so long for...everything else."

"You did," Jacob agreed, voice milder than Linc probably deserved.

"I'm sorry. And I don't have the all answers. But I'm working on it. And I'm done making you wait," he said firmly, squeezing Jacob's hand in a light massage. He'd showered at some point, was back in rumpled civilian clothing, and he looked utterly exhausted.

"Thanks." Jacob yawned and shifted in the chair. "And it's not all on you. Maybe we can find the answers together."

"Yeah. And speaking of answers, how are you getting back to your place?"

"Dunno." Jacob stretched his legs in front of him. "Don't much care. Someone from the crew will turn up sooner or later. I'll catch a ride back. Or mom in the morning. I know she's not going to be able to hold out checking on you. You said you're under observation. So consider me here to observe."

A kinder man than Linc would have sent him packing, would have made him go search out a bed at least, but after the day they'd had, Linc was honestly glad of the company. And if bad news came about Garrick, at least he wouldn't be alone.

"Maybe you can get a room near here later. But shut your eyes for a while first? Like you said, we don't have to work everything out tonight."

"Okay." He gave another yawn as Linc used his controller to lower the bedside light. Not dropping Linc's hand, Jacob slumped in his seat, not quite sleeping but not talking either, and Linc let himself revel in his presence, in the fact that they were *here*, that they'd survived, and that Jacob had promised him a second chance.

They dozed together a time, but then a red-haired nurse came in, quieter than most, rousing Linc for a vitals check, while Jacob snoozed on at his side.

"Your friend needs to go," the nurse whispered to Linc. Plump and motherly, she reminded Linc a little of Jenna. "Technically, we have visiting hours…"

"Don't kick him out," Linc pleaded in a low voice, surprising even himself by how much he needed Jacob there.

"Sometimes we make exceptions for immediate family, but not usually friends."

"Please. He's…" Linc took a deep breath. He'd told Jacob he was going to do better. And that meant being honest, including with himself. "He's the closest thing to family I've got. Don't make him go."

"Oh." She made a noise of startled understanding, eyes drifting down to their intertwined hands. "It's like that, huh?"

The old Linc would have stumbled and faltered at the direct question, unsure how much to reveal. But the new him simply nodded. "Yeah. It is."

"Okay. I'll make a note in your chart that he's good to stay as long as he's not interfering with your rest. Is he who you want as next-of-kin if we have questions about your care?"

Another question. Another step. Another easier answer than he would have thought. "Yeah."

"All right. I'll make it happen." She gave him a tired smile on her way out of the room. "You stay out of trouble. Keep resting."

Next to him, Jacob groaned and stretched. "Funny how they want you to sleep, then go and make that impossible with all their checking."

"Yeah. You…uh…you were awake?"

"Wasn't all the way asleep." He offered Linc a sly smile. "Next-of-kin, huh? You do know she was assuming something other than…brotherly between us, right?"

"Believe you're the one who said there's nothing familial about us." He stroked the back of Jacob's hand. "Except I meant what I said too—you're the closest thing to family I've got now. Not brotherly, but…" He trailed off, not sure exactly how to say all the words clogging his throat. "Important. You're important. More important than anyone else. And I'm sorry—"

"Shush. We can't have you apologizing every ten minutes."

"But it's true."

"I'm trying to believe you." Jacob worked his jaw, eyes still weary. "I'm just saying, I don't need constant apologies. We'll work it out from here, okay?" Leaning out of the chair, he brushed a kiss across Linc's forehead.

"Okay." That ghost of a kiss went a long way to calming Linc down. Maybe there was still a chance for them after all and that made him smile, despite all the uncertainty that remained. They drifted back to silence, and after the next vitals check, Linc made a concerted effort to get Jacob to go find a nearby hotel room to try for some real sleep for himself.

"We're already halfway through the night. Waste of money," Jacob grumbled. "Besides, I wanna be here. Stop trying to get rid of me."

"I'm not." Linc tried to tell him with his eyes that he wasn't going to get rid of Jacob at any level, and apparently the message was received because he got another quick kiss in return, this one on the lips.

"Mmm." Linc used a hand on the back of Jacob's head to keep him close when he would have pulled away. "Needed that."

"We're not getting up to anything here," Jacob warned, even as he had a soft grin for Linc and moved to perch on the side of the bed. There was something about being together like this, alone in the middle of the night, when they'd come so close to never having this again, that made Linc's insides bubbly.

"Trust me. Certain checks my body can't cash tonight anyway. Just… I missed you. That's all."

"I missed you too. So much." Jacob gave him another kiss, more lingering this time, and Linc kept it going a nice long while. For what felt like the first time, it wasn't about getting off or accompanied by other emotions like guilt and shame. No, it was about comfort, plain and simple. It had been a long damn forty-eight hours, and they both needed this. Having Jacob so near, he was able to let go of some of the fear still churning in his gut. They'd come so damn close to losing it all.

A startled noise, part squeak, part cough, made them break apart in a hurry. Jacob's mom was there in the doorway, and just like that all their cozy intimacy evaporated. Jacob sprang back to his chair like he'd been yanked by an imaginary arm. Then he was up again, grabbing the second chair, and babbling as he motioned his mom forward.

"Sorry. Uh. That…yeah. Chair? What are you doing here? At this hour?"

"I couldn't sleep. Not a wink." Jenna waved Jacob's questions away and ignored the offer of a chair. "I kept picturing you hurt and alone…both of you… But then… what's the meaning of this? Lincoln, explain."

It didn't escape his notice that she'd asked him, not Jacob, to explain. He was the older one, the one who was supposed to be in charge, to know better, and to not be kissing her youngest in a hospital room or any other place. And all damn spring and summer, he'd dreaded this moment, being caught, all their secrecy for naught. And now that it was here, he was…

Calm. Relieved even. No more waiting for the inevitable confrontation. But in his relief, he took too long to reply and Jacob made a frustrated sound.

"It was nothing."

"It was too," Linc corrected him while meeting Jenna's scandalized gaze. "I'm sorry you had to find out like this—"

"Find out what precisely?" Her voice rose, then fell as she seemingly remembered where they were.

"Noth—"

"We're together." He shot Jacob a "please be quiet" look as he answered Jenna. "We've been…seeing each other."

The euphemism was the best he could do. He didn't want to declare them in love when Jacob hadn't exactly welcomed that sentiment from him earlier, and calling them a couple seemed similarly optimistic, but he was also done pretending and hiding.

"Seeing?" Her eyes went wide. "You're gay? Or bisexual? Well, obviously I missed *that* piece of news. You didn't think there was anything I needed to know the last twenty years or so, Lincoln?"

She sounded so hurt that Linc had to look away before he could answer. "I'm sorry. It wasn't… Not that I didn't want to. Just…complicated."

"I'll say. And Jacob? *Exactly* how long has this been going on?" Her tone made Linc's jaw clench. He hated being right about her reaction and assumptions. And yeah, some of that was on him for sneaking around and her finding out like this, but still he'd warned Jacob she might not be thrilled.

"A…" Jacob shot a look at Linc which did nothing to make them look less guilty.

"Couple of months." Might as well go with honesty, even if that horse had long since left the barn.

"Months?" Her mouth pursed. "Months and neither of you thought it might be a good idea… Well, never mind that. Obviously you weren't thinking. About anyone. Or anything either. Your work? Wait." She swiveled to Jacob. "Is that why you insisted on taking the job?"

"No." Jacob sighed, disappointment at her reaction clear in his eyes. "You both tried to talk me out of that. At length. This was…after. And it was me who started it. Not Linc. I had a crush for…a long time. Wasn't exactly a state secret."

"It was both of us." Linc wasn't going to let him take the blame like that.

"Yes. I…suspected you had some sort of…puppy adoration thing going on. When you were a *kid*."

"I wasn't that young. I was nineteen the summer his dad died and I kinda got…obsessed. But nothing happened then anyway. And I'm not a kid now."

"Yes, you sort of are. And this…it's wrong." Jenna shook her head and leaned on the back of the empty chair, still not sitting down.

"Wrong?" Jacob's voice was low but deadly. "Wrong? You've been supportive of me since I came out. You really think it's wrong of me to have a relationship? To care about someone?"

"Of course I support you. You're my kid." Worrying her lip with her teeth, she exhaled sharply. "I just mean…this. I'm not sure I can approve of this with Lincoln. The age difference alone—"

"Is nothing. I have friends with far greater gaps. And they're happy. Why don't you want me happy? You love Linc."

Linc wasn't so sure about that. He wasn't one of her kids, wasn't owed any loyalty. The most loyal person in his life other than the dogs might well be Jacob, and even then, Linc wasn't sure he deserved him as a champion.

"I do want you happy." Jenna sounded more exasperated than sincere. "But… I just don't know. I need time. You almost *died* today. Both of you. Don't ask me to deal with this now."

"Not asking for your approval." It was one of the hardest sentences Linc had ever had to utter, but it was true. He was past needing permission to care about Jacob. "Not gonna lie, it would be nice. But I love him.

I'm not giving up this thing we've found together without a fight."

Jacob huffed like he'd been holding his breath for years, and his expression was part wonderment and part gratitude. It was getting easier to say the words, even if Jacob hadn't said them back, easier to share the truth of what had been in his heart for a long time.

Jenna made a sound like a house creaking, like she'd finally reached her limit of what she could handle. "Jacob. Can we go? You need some rest, and we can talk about this later. Privately. We'll let Lincoln sleep."

Like sleep was happening. And he'd been expecting the shut out from her, but it still stung.

"I'm staying here." Jacob's chin had that stubborn tilt that drove Linc crazy, but this time he was grateful for it. "We can talk later, like you said. It's late and we're all emotional, but I'm staying with Linc."

"Your mom shouldn't drive back alone." Linc appreciated the offer, more than he could easily express, but he also was practical. "And you do need sleep."

"Not leaving." Jacob's fiery eyes dared him and Jenna to disagree. "I love you, Mom. And I'm sorry you were so worried today. But I'm staying."

"Fine. Have it your way." Jenna rubbed her face. "I'm too tired to deal with you right now. Very, very tired."

"Go sleep at Jon's. Don't drive back yet." Jacob's voice was gentler now.

"Yeah. That's what I'll do." She rolled her shoulders. "And we *will* talk again."

Apparently satisfied that she'd had the last word, she left on that note, leaving behind a tension thicker than pea soup fog.

"Hell. That was *not* how I wanted that to go." Jacob slumped forward once she was gone. "Although, it could have gone worse. That's gotta count for something, right?"

"She said she'd think. Maybe all she needs is time." He wasn't so sure, but seeing Jacob sad made him want to offer up whatever reassurance he could. "And she does love you. She's not going to shut you out."

"Yeah. But if she tries to turn on you, I'm not having that either. You chose me. Least I can do is return the favor."

"I didn't choose you," Linc corrected him.

"What?" Jacob's eyes narrowed, hurt flashing there. "I thought…"

"It wasn't ever about choosing you over the family or anyone else. I know you thought it was, and I'm sorry for that. It wasn't about whether you were enough. You always were. It was about *me*. I had to choose me, like you said. I had to choose to put myself first. Had to decide that I was enough, not you."

"Don't be stupid," Jacob said thickly, squeezing his arm. "You are. You're one of the best guys I've ever met."

"Thanks. You thinking that about me…it means a lot. But anyway, I had to decide that me being happy matters. My needs and wants matter too. Not only everyone else's."

"Yup." Jacob nodded vigorously. "And I make you happy? For real? You want me around long-term? Everything that brings with it?"

"Always." Linc tried to roll toward him and had to wince when his various injuries reminded him where they were and why. "You've always made me happy. Took me a long time—maybe too long—to decide I was worth that. That it was okay to let down others if it meant me happy and with someone I care about."

"You're not letting anyone down." Jacob moved to sit on the side of the bed again, tenderly touching Linc's face. "Quit thinking that way. Anyone who has a problem with you happy or us together can deal."

"Yeah." Linc would have to work on believing that one, but he understood what Jacob was saying. "And I'm not asking you to choose me over your family or anyone else. That's not how this works. Doesn't have to be all or nothing. You can have both."

"But if they won't have you—"

"Then we wait them out." Linc wanted to believe that maybe time would thaw some objections. And if it didn't, they'd still cope. Together. "I meant what I said. I'm not giving you up."

"And the other... You meant that too?"

Linc knew what he was asking, knew what he wanted to hear again. Maybe if he said it enough, Jacob would start to believe it. "I love you."

Jacob's eyes fluttered shut, almost like he was inhaling the words, absorbing them at some cellular level. Good. Linc didn't expect him to say them back, not yet. But Jacob believing him would be a good start. And when his lips found Linc's again, a good start seemed like more than enough for both of them. All they needed was a start.

Chapter Twenty-Three

"I'm not made of kindling," Linc grumbled as Jacob helped him get settled in the truck. His pinched expression said that his leg was already aching, not that he was about to own up to it, not even after the nurse handed them the discharge paperwork and wheeled away the now-empty chair.

"Just let me help." Jacob was frustrated too, both with how his own cast made helping Linc hard and with all the red tape surrounding Linc's discharge.

"Fine." Linc was still too pale, bumps and bruises on his face stark, and giant black leg cast an imposing presence. It had been a long couple of days—first the observation for the concussion, then the ACL surgery, then recovery from the surgery. Jacob had stayed with him that first night, but the second Linc had chased him away, sending him back with McKenna and Kelley who'd come to visit Linc.

They hadn't had much alone time at all, due to a steady stream of interruptions from nursing staff and doctors and endless visits from their concerned coworkers and families. His room had filled with balloons and flowers from well-wishers to the point that Linc had sent the balloons to the children's floor and asked for the flowers to be given to geriatric patients in need of some cheer rather than try to haul them home.

And then they'd be alone where they could talk freely about the future at last. That future still felt a bit… nebulous, a low-hanging smoke cloud that defied efforts to predict its path. Oh, Linc said all the right things, especially after Jacob's mom had left in a huff the other day. And Jacob did believe he'd changed. It was more that Jacob was still working on trusting those changes to stick around. He hated how off-kilter he felt, like a carabiner with nothing to hold. He was still off work until the following week when he'd be on light duty after the orthopedist cleared him. Not having work and being in this strange, new place with Linc was just weird.

By some unspoken agreement, they still hadn't told anyone from work. Some people might have suspected something based on how Jacob had glued himself to Linc's bedside, but that simply couldn't be helped. He wasn't going anywhere. And if Jacob's mom had shared the news, it hadn't filtered back to him. He'd had a few terse texts from her checking on how he was feeling and decidedly not mentioning Linc. But she ended each with *love*. So maybe not all hope was lost there. Like Linc said, they had to wait his family out. But, fuck, how he'd hoped all along that Linc would be wrong and that things would be easier.

"Do you want food on the way back?" he asked as he headed for the highway. Driving stick with his wrist cast was tricky but not impossible. Still, he was glad he'd had time earlier to figure out workarounds without an audience. The vibrations from the truck made his arm ache, but he figured he still had it pretty easy, considering.

"Nah. It was late enough when they finally cut me loose. I wanna get back." Linc shifted in the seat, which he had all the way back and still not adequate room for the leg.

"I should have grabbed your truck. It's bigger. You would have more room."

"Yeah. Remind me to give you a key. Not like I'm going to be driving it any time soon."

"Yup." Jacob liked Linc's ready agreement even if it was likely rooted in practicality, not any relationship-milestone type sentiment. "Dogs are going to go nuts to see you."

"I bet." That got a bigger smile from Linc. Linc's neighbors as well as Ray and his family had been taking care of the dogs. Jacob had checked in that morning himself, throwing the ball for them even as they kept searching around for Linc. It had felt damn weird, being there without Linc. Still, he'd taken the chance to get things ready for Linc's homecoming and recuperation—managing to put on clean sheets even with his cast and setting up the grab bars and shower stool in the bathroom. He'd grabbed Linc a change of clothes and noted that the freezer was already full of casseroles from friends.

"And there's cake. The lady you get your eggs from dropped off some carrot cake while I was there checking on the dogs."

"You can help me eat it." Linc groaned, flexing his leg again, pained tone doing nothing to settle Jacob's mind.

"Hey, weren't you supposed to take a pain pill for the leg?"

"I don't like feeling stoned."

"Well, you're taking one as soon as we're back at your place."

"Yes, sir." Linc managed a little laugh before they settled into a comfortable silence as the familiar countryside raced by. As they got closer to Linc's house, he shifted in his seat again. "Hey, your phone just buzzed. Want me to check and see if it's Garrick news?"

"Yeah." Jacob tried to quiet the dread that raced up his spine. Garrick still wasn't out of the woods, having survived surgery but still in the ICU in critical condition.

"It's from Kelley. She heard that he's doing better today. They're holding off on more surgery for now, and apparently he said a few words."

"Oh, thank God. No brain injury would be huge." He drummed his fingers on the wheel. "Should have been me in that tree. You *know* I'm a better climber."

"No, it shouldn't have." Linc sounded resigned, as if he'd been wrestling with similar doubts. "And you can't go feeling guilty about it. It was an accident, plain and simple. You're the one who told me that after Wyatt, over and over until it got a little easier to believe you."

"Yeah, I know it wasn't anyone's fault, not really. I just feel bad. I only didn't argue about who was climbing because I was still in a bad mood about our argument the night before. He's an innocent party."

"He's an experienced smoke jumper and firefighter. He knew what he was doing. And if you were pissed about us fighting, then that's more on me than you. Be mad at me, not yourself."

"Can't stay mad at you," he admitted.

"Then don't stay mad at yourself either."

"Okay. I'll try." He turned down Linc's long drive. "Let's get you in the house, then I'll free the beasts. And you're taking those meds."

It was a slow process with the crutches and uneven path to the house, and they could hear the dogs going nuts in their run. Eventually though he got Linc settled on the couch with a big mug of water to take his pills with and saw to the dogs who hurtled toward Linc like he'd been gone two years.

"Hi, mutts." Even though clearly exhausted, Linc handed out head pats and didn't scold too loud when they tried to get up on the couch with him. He gave them attention until Jacob brought him food that he only picked at.

"Okay, to bed with you. We can figure out a shower for you tomorrow."

That Linc didn't argue showed how worn out he really was, and he accepted Jacob's help stripping down to his boxer briefs. But when Jacob would have left the room, he made a noise of protest.

"You're not tired?" Linc asked as he settled on the bed.

"I should make sure the dogs and dishes and stuff are set for the night. Figured I'd sleep on the couch so that I don't jostle your leg in the night."

"You won't." Linc opened and shut his mouth, expression strangely vulnerable. "Stay and talk? For a while at least. Just…weird mood. Tired but brain won't shut off."

His forehead crinkled as he looked away, the request clearly costing him a little of his considerable pride. Jacob wasn't about to make him ask again, pulling off his own clothes, leaving on his underwear because he doubted either of them was up to anything resembling sex. But even so, damn it felt good to stretch out next to Linc, cautiously cuddle up to his uninjured side. Linc tugged him closer, pulling Jacob's arm across his chest until they were spooning in earnest. Usually when they lay like this, it was after bone-melting sex and Linc was often on the outside. Felt strange but good, being the one to hold Linc and having it be more about closeness than anything sexual.

"Better?" he whispered.

"Yeah." Linc's breathing was already starting to even out. "Missed you."

"Missed you too." Jacob dropped a kiss on the back of his neck, feeling settled himself for the first time all day.

"I need you and I hate needing anyone, but…damn. Glad you're here. Thanks."

"Anytime." Jacob's throat was tight. There were still a lot of uncertainties, but this right here, it made it all worth it, the sheer rightness of being together.

"I know you think I'm gonna change my mind, but I meant every word I said in the hospital. I want this to work. Even if it's hard."

"I don't want it to be hard for you." Jacob spoke directly to a doubt that had been making him antsy all day. He wanted to make Linc *happy*, not be another obligation for him.

"Feeling what I feel for you…caring about you, that's not hard. I meant everything else." Linc yawned and pulled Jacob tighter against him.

It was the everything else that made Jacob worried even as his pulse gave a hopeful thrum. He wasn't ever going to get tired of hearing Linc say he cared. Maybe he simply had to trust that the everything else would work out, difficult as it was to summon that belief. And as Linc drifted off to sleep, he stayed awake, letting himself have the joy in holding him and being there. Everything else could wait.

"Last time I had you naked and wet was a lot more fun," Linc joked to distract himself from how awkward showering was, even with a cast cover, shower seat and Jacob's help.

"I know. We'll have to work our way back to that." Jacob had started clothed, but quickly lost his shirt when it got soaked. Getting clean felt amazing and Jacob's torso was as inspiring as ever, but it was far from the sexy showers they'd shared in the past.

"Soon." Linc hoped he could keep that promise. They'd shared some sleepy kisses that morning, but then the dogs had interrupted, and his leg had been acting up enough that he'd taken a pain pill with breakfast, which while effective had the side effect of making sex less likely. "You want a shower when I'm done?"

"Nah. I want to get a run in while it's still not roasting. The dogs need it almost as much as I do. I'll shower afterward and then see about some brunch for you?"

"You don't have—"

"Quit trying to talk me out of taking care of you. Or apologizing." Jacob helped dry him off before assisting him out of the shower. "And I know resting sucks, but maybe you can find us something new to watch on the TV."

"I'll try," he promised as he pulled on stretchy shorts to accommodate the cast. He followed Jacob to the living room and resigned himself to a day on the couch. "Don't let the dogs pull on your arm. You sure you're cleared for running?"

"Well, they didn't say *not* to run." Jacob offered his classic devilish grin, something Linc was beyond relieved to see again. "I won't be long, okay?"

He gave Linc a fast kiss on the head before heading out with the dogs. Linc watched preview after preview, nothing holding his interest, nothing that seemed ideal for bingeing with Jacob, who continued to be in an odd mood. Understandable really—Linc had put him through the ringer, then the near-death stuff with the fire, and Garrick being hurt, and him being off work. He was bound to be out of sorts, but still Linc worried about him, about what it meant for their future. He was almost grateful for the knock at the front door, even if hoisting himself off the couch and figuring out the crutches was a job and a half.

"Coming," he yelled as he made his way to the door. "Hold your horses."

Sims stood on his porch, covered casserole dish in hand, and usual stern expression in place. Heck. Maybe the TV was the better option after all than having to en-

tertain his boss. But he couldn't exactly turn her away
either.

"Sorry. I…uh…didn't know it was you." He ush-
ered her in.

"No worries. I had time off, so I thought I'd check
in on you," she said breezily as she found her way to
the kitchen, where she set the casserole on the counter. "It's some sort of chicken and Spanish rice dish.
My husband made it, not me, so you can be sure it's
edible."

"Thanks." He offered a smile even as he was trying
to figure out how to gracefully go for a shirt.

"Has HR been in contact with you yet? Your case for
temporary disability is straightforward if you need it.
Shouldn't be much of an issue, but I'm sure there will
be forms for your next doctor's appointment." Sims
never was much for small talk, which Linc appreciated.
It meant this visit might be on the short side, which
was good.

"No. I'll call tomorrow, get the paperwork started for
leave or whatever." Fuck, he didn't want to think about
how long he'd be off work. They'd told him in the hospital that he was looking at anywhere from six to nine
months before he was back at pre-injury strength and
range of motion, which meant he was for sure missing
the rest of this fire season as a jumper, and at least several weeks before even light duty became a real option.
"I've got plenty of sick days built up. Guess I'll start
with taking that."

"Yes, that's a blessing, although we've tried for years
to get you to take more leave." She gave him another
sharp look.

"What? And miss jumps? No way." Like all jumpers, he hated using his vacation and sick time during the season. But after all these years with the forest service, he did have enough to fall back on, at least while he was on crutches and dealing with the initial rehab process.

"Well, now you've got no choice but to take it easy. Don't rush it back either. I've seen too many knee issues turn chronic when people try to rush the rehab." Leaning against his counter, she pursed her mouth. "And you out on leave means more time for us to deal with—"

"Hey, we're back!" The back door banged as Jacob came through the mudroom, dogs rushing ahead of him. Jacob was shirtless again, using his T-shirt to mop his face. "Shower. Then eggs. I bet you can talk me through those at least. And then, it occurred to me that unlike me, you've got two working hands…" He trailed off, voice going from seductive to startled as he lowered the shirt. "Oh, h-*heck*. Hi, boss. Didn't notice your car."

"That," Sims said, voice as dry as August dirt around here. "As I was saying, more time for us to deal with *that*."

"Me staying here? Helping Linc?" Jacob wasn't much good at the whole feigning-ignorance thing and he yanked on his shirt like a guilty teen, but Linc appreciated the try.

"Do I strike you as particularly unobservant, Hartman?" Sims asked.

"No…" Jacob's mouth quirked. "No, ma'am. Sorry."

"This is apparently the season when we finally come up with a comprehensive fraternization policy." Sims pinched the bridge of her nose. "I've got…what? Three crews with people dating. It's past time we had a policy on file. Amendment to the anti-harassment one."

"It's on me." Linc was fast to take responsibility before Jacob could speak up. "If you're planning consequences, give them to me. Jacob's one of the best jumpers you have, even as a rookie. He deserves to be back out there as soon as he's medically cleared."

"Thanks." Jacob shot him a grateful look, eyes warm and mouth soft. "But it was both of us. I knew it wasn't the best idea for work, but I still pursued it. I'll take whatever discipline you think that needs."

"I'm not sure." Sims's expression was uncharacteristically uncertain. "I don't know as it's fair to do retroactive discipline even though that might send a strong message discouraging such behavior. It's more important what we do going forward. There will be long discussions about whether we can have couples in active relationships on the same crew, especially for small operations. We need a policy we can point to for everyone. So that's something we'll try to have in place before Reid is back. Luckily, we have some time."

"I understand. I mean, I hate the idea of splitting us up, but I get where you're coming from." Jacob sounded like he was having to work hard at finding a reasonable tone. "We work well together. No reason to stop that."

"You do work well together. No one is disputing that." Sims voice was level, calming. "But we have to think across the board. Situations where losing a crew could mean a family losing both parents. Or where relationship discord spills over into life-and-death decisions. And unless we one-hundred-percent prohibit relationships, that's the sort of implication we need to be ready for."

"I get it." Jacob sounded defeated, but Linc got Sims's dilemma. The management team had to be fair to everyone and consider all possible contingencies. Jacob's gaze met Linc's, and Linc hated the disappointment there, hated knowing that them being together might have real-world consequences for them both.

"It's going to be months before I jump again." Linc could be more pragmatic than Jacob. He'd been expecting worse, honestly. "But if the decision is made to prohibit relationships, I'll be the one to leave."

"No. You can't do that. You've got years and years—" Jacob was starting to get red in the face and Linc cut him off.

"You're more important to me than the job. Period." It had taken him damn long enough to realize that, and no way was he letting some policy tear them apart now. He gave him a hard look before turning to Sims. "I'll rehab like I'm coming back as soon as possible, but if you make me choose, I'm choosing him. Every time."

"I don't think it's going to come to that." Sims's tone was gentler now. "We'll keep you posted on the policy, same as I'm doing for the others. You're two of our best. We want to keep you."

"Good." Jacob still didn't sound satisfied, but he kept his mouth a thin, closed line as he nodded.

"Thanks." All Linc's muscles protested and he had to shift his weight on the crutches before he could add anything else. He'd been standing far too long and was going to pay the price for that later as well.

"Hey, let's get you back to the couch." Jacob must

have picked up on his discomfort because next thing he was guiding Linc back to the living room, Sims and the dogs trailing behind.

"I won't keep you any longer," she said as Jacob helped Linc prop up his leg on a footstool. "If you enjoy the casserole, let me know. Estevao has fun trying new things he finds on the web."

"Will do." Jacob showed her to the door after some more promises to keep her updated on their respective medical appointments, then came to collapse next to Linc on the couch. "Well, that wasn't *terrible*, but what the hell, man? You're not giving up jumping. No way. Or…" His eyes narrowed as he turned to give Linc an appraising stare. "Is this still about you thinking you need to sell this place? Some sort of a fresh start? New work situation?"

"No." Putting a hand on his thigh, Linc was fast to assure him. "Not like that. I don't need a new start. Not now. You're my fresh start. You. This. I don't need to run anymore."

"Good," Jacob said firmly. "But if you did need to get away from here, you better have room for one more on the road. Because I'm going too."

"Thanks." Warmth spreading across his chest, Linc appreciated his words more than he could ever say and had to lick his lips before continuing. "And yeah, I'll always have a spot for you."

"Promise?" Eyes serious, Jacob placed his hand over Linc's.

Linc took a breath because this wasn't a tiny thing. He took his word damn seriously, which Jacob well knew. "I promise. I'm not letting you go. And I'm not leaving either. That…wasn't my best plan. I belong here."

"With me. And doing your job," Jacob added, squeezing Linc's hand.

"It doesn't matter what job I do. What matters is us together for all of it. And I want that. The rest of the future can work itself out with time."

"I hope so." Jacob sounded surer than he had in recent days, which counted for an awful lot as far as Linc was concerned, and he pulled him close.

"I know so," he said right before he claimed a kiss. Jacob had been the certain one for so many years now, the one who had known that come hell or high water they were meant to be together. Linc had been the one intent on resisting the truth his soul had known for a very long time—Jacob was the one for him. If Jacob needed him to be the confident one for right now, Linc could do that for him, could wait for the moment when Jacob was as convinced as he was that this was the right course of action.

Chapter Twenty-Four

"I don't want to go." Jacob had jumped out of perfectly good airplanes, faced back draft, done days of mop-up duty covered in ash, and publicly had his ass kicked in MMA matches, and even with all that history, one lunch with his family filled him with more dread than any roundhouse kick or fire flare-up.

"You're going." From his place on the couch, Linc gestured at the front door. "And the sooner you go, the sooner you can be back here and we can finish that movie we started last night."

"I hate that she didn't invite you. I say you should come anyway." Jacob's mother had texted, summoning him to an after-church meal at her place. He supposed it was an olive branch of sorts, but it killed him that Linc hadn't received a similar message. She hadn't *specifically* said to come alone, but also hadn't suggested he bring Linc, which led Linc to assuming, probably correctly, that Mom wanted to see him alone.

"And I say give it time." Linc's voice was far more patient than Jacob felt. "This is a step. She loves you and wants to see you. Maybe she still needs to sort out how she feels about me."

"Bullshit. She's loved you for what…thirty years now? She can get over herself about objecting to us being together or thinking that you're taking advantage or anything else ridiculous."

"Just go. See what she has to say. If it's too awful, leave early. I'll heat up another casserole if you leave hungry."

Jacob sighed, knowing he'd lost the battle. For all that Linc had stood up to Jacob's mom and Sims, his family was still a touchy subject. And he understood. It was a loss for Linc, and Jacob would do anything to take away that pain along with magically healing his other injuries. No matter what Linc said, it did feel like Linc had chosen him over the family, like he was picking Jacob over Wyatt's memory, and Jacob was still working out how he felt about that.

Linc saying all the right things helped a little, all his promises to keep Jacob around. Because if there was one thing everyone knew about Linc, it was that he kept his promises. Linc said they were together no matter what now, and Jacob wanted desperately to believe him, to trust his word and trust that shared future, but it was still hard.

Still, as he drove to his mom's place, he replayed every tender thing Linc had said the past few days, let each sweet word lift his mood. Maybe he'd been a little naive in assuming that being together would be easy, but even if the reality was harder than he'd predicted, he still wasn't trading it for anything. If there was one thing he didn't doubt, it was his feelings for Linc. Those had only deepened over the spring and summer as he'd replaced his fantasy guy with the flesh-and-blood real person.

Privately, he could admit that a lot of his fantasy of being with Linc had been lust-driven, but after they'd given in to that, his emotions had become a lot more complex as he'd seen other sides of Linc. The playful guy with the dogs. The good cook. The careful gardener. The DIY house-rehabber. The snarky TV watcher. The late-night cuddler. The hot-water hog.

So, yeah. He might have his doubts about whether Linc would change his mind, but his heart was all-in, had been for weeks now. And he wasn't letting anyone, even his family, drive them apart. He almost turned the truck around when he saw Jon's Tahoe, kids swarming all over the play set. Damn. It was going to be hard enough with just his mom and May. His other siblings were another layer of complication he didn't really need.

For a change, his mother opened her own door.

"You came!" Her voice was bright but her smile was too wide, too toothy to be mistaken for her genuine one.

"Yeah. Linc helped me make his deviled egg recipe." He handed her the small platter. It was supposed to be a dozen, but a few had suffered peeling mishaps. And then he'd made Linc keep two for himself. So it was a paltry offering, but his mom likely had enough food to feed the whole crew at the air base. The eggs weren't the point.

"Thanks. You…uh…you're staying over there?" Her cautious tone matched her carefully schooled expression.

"He had ACL surgery. Needs help keeping the weight off his leg. He shouldn't have to deal with that alone."

"No, he shouldn't." His mother worried her red lips with her teeth. She was still in her church clothes—a summery printed dress that almost seemed too cheery for this conversation. Under ordinary circumstances she would have been first on Linc's porch with food and probably would have tried to insist he come here to recuperate. "I… Come eat? It's sandwich fixings—too hot to really cook, but I made that potato salad you like."

"Thanks." Jacob had seldom felt less like eating, but he followed her to the kitchen, where she added his platter to the assortment of chips, salads, and heaping plates of cold cuts and cheese. The brothers-in-law and Jon had some sort of car race on the TV, and May and his sisters were outside with the kids. Same as a million other Sundays, but none of the usual cozy feeling. He dutifully went through the motions of grabbing a plate and added a tiny scoop of the potato salad and a roll to put some turkey on.

"Not hungry? Did they check you for an infection?"

"Broken wrist. Not a big infection risk." He gave a tight laugh as he held up his cast. "Nah. Just a big breakfast."

"Oh." She flushed as if he'd made an off-color joke.

"Pancakes, Mom. Pancakes. We made them together when the dogs woke us up insanely early and Linc's leg hurt too much for him to go back to sleep. I can't flip them one-handed that well, but they were filling."

"Oh." Her shocked expression stayed firmly in place. Fuck. He didn't want to have this conversation, but here they were, and his frustration leached into the force with which he ripped open his roll.

"I'm sorry. Am I supposed to pretend I'm not over

there? That we're not together? That we're not sharing a bed?"

"Watch your mouth." Jon came into the kitchen, face flushed and eyes narrowed.

"You too?" He groaned and set his plate aside. "The kids are all outside. I'm not allowed to say *bed*? Or is it the implication that I have sex? That not allowed now either? You've known for almost six years that I'm gay. Is that only okay if I'm not actually in a relationship?"

Jon's mouth moved like he might be about to agree with that statement, but his mom spoke first. "Of course you can be in a relationship. I want you happy. I mean, I wouldn't want to confuse the kids, but—"

Jacob cut her off even as Jon was nodding along with her. He made a frustrated noise at both of them. "Does it confuse the kids when Jon and his wife kiss under the mistletoe? When Joy and her husband sleep on the couch bed together when they visit? There's nothing dirty or wrong about me having someone."

"You're right." His mother sighed. "You're right, of course. This is just all so new."

"Six years," he reminded her.

"I don't mean that. I mean this." She made a vague gesture with her hand. "Lincoln. You know. *This*. Whatever you think you've got going."

"I'm still trying to wrap my head around how long he had me fooled…" Jon shook his head.

"Fooled? Fooled. Because he didn't share something personal with you? Like you really think he was trying to *trick* you? Fu—"

"Boys." His mother interjected in the same tone she'd

used when they were younger. "This isn't serving anything."

"Exactly. It's so pointless. Linc should be here. He's
part of this family too. And you're punishing him, why?
Because he dared to fall for me? Another adult, I'd add."

"You were a kid when you first started hanging
around him." His mother twisted her silver bracelet.
"It's just not right. If he—"

"I was nineteen. Nineteen. And I was nearly twenty-
five when we actually kissed or did anything about it.
I'm as adult as him. As much to blame as him. Like
you said, I'm the one who had the crush on him. I finally wear him down and you blame him? That's some
messed up sh—*business.*"

"Maybe you have a point," his mother allowed. "It's
also that he's family. Like you said. It's…"

"Weird." Jon rolled his jaw. "He's like…an extra big
brother or something. And we trusted him—"

"Trusted him? Am I some classic car to be protected
from careless hands? Really, listen to yourself. This
is Linc. Linc, who sobered you up, night before your
wedding. Linc, who's built everything needing put together here from sheds to Christmas presents to light
fixtures. Linc, who's worked side by side with all of us.
Mud. Snow. Dust. Linc the baby whisperer. You seriously think you can't trust *him*?" As he finished his ti-
rade, sweat rolled down his neck.

"Oh." His mother swallowed loudly.

"Yeah. Oh." Maybe he hadn't convinced either of
them, but he'd sold himself. If he couldn't trust Linc
with his heart, then who? If he couldn't trust Linc of all
people to keep his word when he said he was keeping

Jacob around, then there wasn't anyone worth trusting anywhere. He was the best, most loyal, steadfast person Jacob had ever known. And if he said he loved Jacob, then he needed to be believed.

And now he seriously couldn't wait to get back to him and tell him exactly that. But first, he had to deal with stupid assumptions.

"I get it. It was a shock or whatever, but you need to get over yourselves. This isn't going away. I love him." It occurred to him about twenty seconds too late that he probably should have said those words to Linc the first time he dared say them out loud. But he would. Soon. "And he loves me. If you can't support us in that, then you're not the people I thought you were. And that's just sad."

"I…" His mother's eyes filled with tears, and he had to look away, especially as her voice broke. "I'll try. Okay? It's going to take some getting used to. I don't want to lose you over this."

"Maybe you should worry a little about losing *Linc* over this."

"Fair enough." She pulled on his sleeve, tugging him into an awkward hug. He was still upset, but he didn't pull away.

"I mean it." He met Jon's eyes over his mother's back. "I love him. I'm not giving him up, not for any of you. And you all owe him a great deal. And a lot better treatment than you've managed the past few days."

"Okay." Jon's pinched expression said it might be the holidays before he completely thawed. Which, okay. Jacob could wait him out, like Linc said. But he was also gonna keep on calling him on it when he was an ass.

"You came!" May and a pack of kids came rushing in. She looked brighter than he'd seen her in quite some time, in a pretty yellow dress. "Junior wanted to see your cast. He's still outside."

"I was just going, actually. I'll show him some other time. I need to get back."

"Okay." May came over and touched his arm as he pulled away from his mom. Jon drifted back to the couch area, apparently having said his piece. "Jacob?"

"Yeah?" His voice came out warier than intended, but God, he could not handle one more lecture, one more disappointed face.

"I'm happy for you."

"You are?" He inhaled sharply. The first person in this whole saga who seemed genuinely to care about him and Linc, and it was May, who had lost so much. It was almost more than he could bear, his throat tightening.

"He's the best guy any of us know." May gave a wistful little smile. "And so are you. Can you take him one of the cinnamon rolls? He always likes those."

"I can do that." His voice was rough as he hugged her. He let his mom fuss over making a container of leftovers for them, her working too hard to please him with the food choices, but it was something. He left with several plastic boxes of food and two foil-wrapped cinnamon rolls, and a new conviction that he needed to trust Linc. If he was lucky enough to get to keep Linc, then he was going to enjoy this. Enjoy him. And he was going to somehow find the courage to tell Linc the words he'd waited years to say.

* * *

Still not used to these long stretches of free time with nothing to do but rest on the couch, Linc dozed while Jacob was gone, but he woke up at the dogs making a ruckus. He stretched as Jacob let the dogs out back into their run before making his way to Linc.

"That was fast," he observed mildly, glancing at the living room clock.

"Yep." Jacob settled next to him, hips touching. He brushed a lingering kiss across Linc's lips. "It was. But they sent you cinnamon rolls. So, you know, not *terrible*."

"Tell me you didn't give them some kind of ultimatum." He wasn't an idiot. Jacob was vibrating with tension, there in his lips even.

Jacob's mouth puckered, a breath whistling out. "Not exactly."

"So you did." Linc groaned. "I am not worth you sacrificing your relationship with your family with. They love you and—"

"They love you too. And if they love us so much, then they can damn well be happy for us." Jacob had that stubborn expression that dared Linc to argue with him. "I'm not going to listen to their lectures or them fretting over something stupid like our age difference."

"It's not stupid. They care about you. They want to make sure I'm not taking advantage." Hell, Linc had spent years worrying that same thing. He got where the family was coming from even if Jacob didn't.

"Well, you're not. If anyone is, it's me. I'm the one who finally got you to give in…"

"Hey now." Linc reached over and cupped his face.

"You are not. I don't want you thinking the rest of our lives that you… I dunno…made a pest of yourself. This isn't you wearing me down until I gave in and gave you what you wanted."

"It's not?"

"No. This is you being persistent, yes, but you didn't create this out of thin air. This was me giving myself what *I* really wanted, not giving in to you. I mean, don't get me wrong, I do like making you happy, but you didn't force me into this at all. I wanted it. All of it."

"You really mean it, don't you?" Jacob's voice was full of wonder, but there was a trust in his expression, a warmth in his eyes that hadn't been there before.

"I do. And I'm sorry that I made you doubt it, made you feel so alone in this. I wanted it. Even back then. Even when I was so sure that you'd change your mind eventually."

"Not happening." Turning, Jacob straddled him in an easy motion that kept his weight off Linc's legs but still effectively pinned Linc to the couch. "I'm going to stick around." Jacob's demeanor had all the confidence of a bull rider determined to make bank and for once Linc couldn't disagree, not when he wanted this just as much.

"Me too."

"And if that means telling my family off, then that's what I'm gonna do."

"It's okay with me if they just want to see you alone for a time."

"Nope. We're a package deal now." Jacob bent down long enough to give him a firm kiss. "Like I told them,

I love you and you love me and if they can't support us, then that's their problem, not mine."

All the oxygen in the room seemed to evaporate in an instant, and he had to cough. "Say it again."

"You love me and—"

"Not that part."

"Oh, the part where I told everyone that I loved you." His eyes sparkled. "Yeah, about that…"

"Just because I said it doesn't mean you need to." Some old doubts crept back in.

"I love you, Linc. I've crushed on you since I was nineteen, but this time together showed me a different level to how I felt. Deepened it. It's not just some infatuation now. It's the real deal."

"Yeah." He had to agree with that. Tugging Jacob back down, he paused with their lips centimeters apart. "It's real all right."

Not letting Jacob reply, he claimed his mouth with the sort of possessiveness he no longer had to keep in check, loving how Jacob practically melted into him as he met him kiss for kiss. They kissed with a new sort of urgency—not their previous hurry to cram as much into as short a time as possible, but rather a drive to connect, to express these big, scary feelings they were finally starting to sort out.

Jacob tasted like he'd sampled the cinnamon rolls, sweet and familiar, and he welcomed Linc's explorations with playful, almost joyous, nips and licks from his generous mouth and strokes of his roving hand. His injured arm rested against Linc's shoulder, the cast a reminder of all they'd survived. For the first time in days, Linc's body burned with need, primal demands overriding any lingering discomfort in his leg, even as Jacob settled more firmly against him.

"This okay?" Jacob's voice was low and breathless as they ground together. "Don't want to hurt you."

"It's all good." Linc nuzzled into Jacob's jaw, loving how his head tipped back, putting all that delicious flesh at Linc's mercy. He rained kisses down the cords of his neck, finding all the spots that made Jacob gasp. Carefully, he bit at the juncture of his shoulder and neck, relishing how Jacob moaned and moved against him.

"Make a mark," Jacob whispered, the dirty demand going right to Linc's cock. They'd been so careful for weeks to not leave evidence, holding back that last scrap of self-control. And now, freed from the secrecy requirement, his fingers dug into Jacob's ass as he sucked hard. "Oh, holy fuck. Feels so good."

"Yeah it does."

Jacob rocked insistently against him as he did it again. "Fuck. Almost think I could come from that."

"Yeah?" Both intrigued and turned on beyond all reason, Linc pulled back to look at him. Lips swollen from the earlier endless kissing, cheeks flushed, eyes wide. "You got a werewolf fetish I should know about?"

"Nah. Just a you fetish." Jacob laughed as he parroted Linc's words back to him. "Do it again."

"Mmm. In a minute." He skimmed his hands along Jacob's torso, pulling up his T-shirt as he went. "Want skin first."

"You too." Laughing as their various casts got in the way, Jacob eagerly grabbed at Linc's clothing, shedding his own jeans and boxers along the way and pulling Linc's shorts down and off until they were back, skin-to-skin. An armful of warm, naked Jacob was possibly the greatest pleasure Linc had ever known and he had to groan.

He yanked Jacob down for a kiss, this one more demanding and purposeful, urging Jacob to move against him until they were both panting. Their cocks were trapped between them, and soon Linc was going to need more friction than their bodies allowed, but right then it was perfect. He returned his mouth to Jacob's neck and shoulders, thrilling to each of his gasps and moans, getting more aggressive as it became clear that was what Jacob craved.

"Ugh. Linc. That… Think I'm…" Jacob pressed harder against Linc, cock painting a wet stripe across his abs.

"Yeah. Do it. Whatever you need." Watching Jacob go became his singular goal, no sunset, no Super Bowl touchdown able to compete with the sheer beauty and adrenaline rush of feeling Jacob get closer and closer to the edge.

"Need you." Jacob's fingers dug into Linc's arm. They'd both have marks later, something that made Linc's cock pulse.

"You've got me."

"Now. Oh, fuck. Now." Closing his eyes, Jacob plastered his body against Linc, moving urgently now.

"That's it. Come on me." Linc grazed his teeth down Jacob's neck, waiting until his breathing changed, those little warning noises that were almost enough to pull Linc with him. At the first of those sounds, he sucked hard, a sharp bite that was rewarded with Jacob crying out as he came.

"Oh, fuck." Hard shudders racked Jacob's body as he spurted between them, the warmth and slick getting Linc closer too, especially as Jacob whispered, "Love you."

"Love you too," he groaned. Fuck, it was too much. He slid a hand between them, fisting his cock, Jacob's come the perfect lube.

"Gonna let me help?" Getting the hint, Jacob leaned back so Linc could work. He trailed his fingers along Linc's balls, little licks of electricity.

"Not gonna take much." Trusting Jacob, he moved his hand, let Jacob stroke him there.

"Good." Jacob gave a satisfied growl as he found a rhythm that had Linc's hips pushing up. "Wanna get you off."

"You are. Fuck. Like that." His head hit the back of the couch as his hands held Jacob tight.

"Come on," Jacob urged, speeding up his strokes until Linc had no choice, climax slamming into him, waves of pleasure tinged with sweet emotion that left him breathless. Laughing, Jacob flopped down next to him on the couch.

"Leg doing okay?"

"What leg?" He didn't even bother opening his eyes.

"I'll take it to mean that didn't suck."

"Oh, hell, baby. That was something else." Linc hauled him in close enough to kiss.

"Baby?" Jacob laughed against his lips.

"Give me time. I'll find a better pet name for you." His voice was sleepy, a silliness he didn't know he had invading his brain until he too was laughing.

"Never in a million years would I have thought of you as the pet-name type."

"I'm the you type." Linc's whole body felt heavy, wrung out, drunk on Jacob and his nearness and everything that had come before this moment and everything that would come after.

"Tell me again." Jacob poked him in the ribs when he might have been content to chase his fluttery thoughts into another nap.

"I love you." He held Jacob's gaze. "Never gonna let you go. I promise."

Licking his lips, Jacob nodded solemnly. "Me too. Love you."

Linc let himself see what had been there all along—that Jacob's word was just as solid as his, that he meant it as much as Linc did, that he wasn't going to grow and move on. Instead, they'd grow together, arms around each other. Maybe he'd known all along that Jacob was it for him, heart and brain fighting this until it was almost too late. But now, he wrapped that certainty around him, a parachute ready to carry them both into the future, finally equipped to meet whatever it brought.

Chapter Twenty-Five

Six months later

Jacob's hands were already cold, which made his newly healed wrist ache, and he had to shuffle his feet to keep warm as Linc checked the position of the crate in the truck bed, reaching in to test one of the bungee cords.

"We're going to be late," he complained.

"We've got the star of the show. Think they can wait for us for cake and singing." Linc offered him a patient smile, probably because he knew Jacob was more than a little antsy about Junior's birthday party.

"True. Hope he gets some cool presents from everyone else." Poor kid was saddled with a holiday birthday—between Thanksgiving and Christmas, when everyone was crazy busy with holiday get-togethers and school concerts and the start of the ski tourism season. But his family wasn't one to ignore the chance for a party, and Mom and May were combining his family party with a chili cook-off and movie marathon.

"Ours is better," Linc said confidently as he climbed into the passenger seat of his truck. He was technically cleared to drive now, but they'd fallen into a habit of

Jacob chauffeuring him around. It would take some getting used to Linc being fully independent again, but his physical therapy was almost done and he'd clocked several miles on the treadmill the last session.

"I can't believe Mom and May are letting us do this." Now that they were underway, the giddiness returned. Junior was going to *freak*.

"They trust us, I guess." Linc shrugged like it was no big deal. But it was. Thanksgiving had been weirdly tense until the four of them had hatched this plan for Junior over pie. His mom had run hot and cold like that all fall—reserved one day and showing up with cookies the next. Maybe they were all still figuring out how the pieces went together in the new reality where he and Linc were a couple, but this joint project had been good for all of them. Linc especially. He'd never say, but it mattered, him being treated like one of the family again.

"Are we still on for seeing Garrick tomorrow?" he asked.

"Yeah. He sounded upbeat on the phone. Said we'd be a good distraction from PT hell." Garrick's recovery was long and slow, but Linc and Jacob tried to do everything they could to support their friend.

"Remind me to dig through my boxes of winter stuff in mom's garage."

"Why don't we just load all your stuff in the truck after the party? You don't have to use her as storage anymore, you know."

"Seriously? It's more than just the one box." Jacob had been so used to the tight confines of his trailer for so long that he'd built up a fair collection of stuff at his mom's, mainly off-season clothes and sporting equipment.

"You haven't slept at the trailer in months," Linc pointed out as Jacob took the turn toward his mom's house. "Other than getting mail there, you've been living with me and the dogs ever since the accident. Even those mismatched dishes of yours migrated over. Probably past time you let the space rent go, honestly."

"You want me, my stuff from mom's and my trailer on your property?" As he braked for a stop sign, he blinked at Linc.

"The trailer might be useful for camping come spring. I'm getting too old to do tents. And as for the rest of it, yeah, I do. I've got the room." Only his fingers drumming against the window frame gave away that Linc was anything other than casual about this offer.

"You're keeping me through to spring?" he teased as he resumed driving. "What if you get cabin fever come January or February?"

"Not happening. And if you're the one itchy for... warmer parts, I'll just have to chase you down in Aruba or wherever, drag you home."

"Promise?"

"You know it." Linc's confidence was back, and with him making promises like that, it was only too easy to agree.

"Okay. I'll do the official change of address thing and make arrangements to move the trailer over to your place."

"Our place," Linc corrected with a grin as Jacob pulled into his mom's driveway, finding a parking space among the other assorted vehicles.

"Our place." Jacob liked the sound of that, a lot. "Come on. Let's make Junior's year."

May came bustling out of the house as they were carefully unloading the crate. "You got it?"

"You doubted us?" Jacob faked being wounded. "Sorry if we're late."

"You're not." She rubbed her hands restlessly. "And your arrival will distract everyone from me being the subject of all the gossip."

"You? Gossip?" Linc's head tilted.

"I…uh…" May looked out over the horizon. "I might have brought a date. Sort of. Accidentally."

"You accidentally brought a date?" Jacob was pretty sure his expression mirrored Linc's wide-eyed confusion.

"Who is he?" Linc demanded, all bristly and apparently more than ready to do the whole protective big brother thing for May.

"Be nice. He's the new gym teacher at Junior's school. He suggested Junior play in the little kids' basketball league over break and I…uh…might have invited him." She shrugged even as her cheeks turned pink and her eyes sparkled.

"So this is like a new habit you've got going? Accidental dates?" Jacob couldn't resist a little teasing.

"Maybe." She gave them both an arch look before crouching in front of the crate. "Let me get my camera ready. I can't wait to see Junior's face."

"I better carry it in." Jacob scooped the contents of the crate into his arms before following her and Linc into the house.

"Oh, birthday boy!" she called out, causing a pack of kids to come running. "Uncle Jacob and Uncle Linc have a surprise for you."

Junior made his way to the front of the crowd, and for the rest of his life, Jacob was going to remember the expression on his face. Not to mention Linc's deeply pleased look as he registered Junior's excitement.

"It's a puppy!" Junior shrieked.

"Well, technically, she's a year old." Jacob knelt down so Junior could meet the dog, a spaniel mix who was surprisingly gentle and calm despite the unfamiliar surroundings. "Your mom and Grandma wanted us to find you a friend who was already housebroken, so we searched all the rescues in the area until we found just the right one. We've had her at Linc's—*our* place for about a week now, making sure she knows some rules."

"And tricks?" Voice hopeful, Junior petted the dog's silky head.

"She can come. And sit. Sort of." Linc's soft smile did all sorts of things to Jacob's insides. "And you get to name her, okay? So choose well. They called her Lady at the shelter, but you can train her to whatever you'd like."

Junior's little face scrunched up as he thought hard. "There's a YouTuber called—"

"No YouTube!" May laughed, and man, it was so good to see her light and happy. The dog was going to be good for all of them, he could already tell. And he had a further feeling that the quiet guy looking like May was his personal holiday gift was going to be good too.

"Are your guys going to miss having the company?" Jacob's mom came over to ask. And that was nice too, the way she addressed both of them, not only Linc. Like the dogs were shared now, which he supposed they sort of were, especially if he was officially moving in.

"Yup. She'll have to come visit. It was fun having her." Jacob moved away from the herd of kids, toward the kitchen where vats of chili were bubbling away.

"What he actually means is that there was this over-grown terrier at the rescue, and he keeps telling me how easy three were." Linc's fond look was almost as nice as the arm he threw around Jacob. And that was good too, him feeling comfortable enough to do that, which hadn't been the case their first few visits.

"It wouldn't be that hard. Another dog bed—"

"That will get ignored." Shaking his head, Linc laughed.

"Is that a yes, we can go look again?" He batted his eyes and tried to look convincing.

"You always do seem to get your way." Linc tried for a stern voice, but the affection in his eyes gave him away.

"And you like it that way," he countered. He trusted Linc now when he said that Jacob hadn't talked him into this, that he wanted it too. He had months of proof built up, each day, even the hard ones, filled with little reminders that Linc cared in a way Jacob had scarcely dreamed possible.

"Help?" Linc looked at Jacob's mom, who simply shook her head.

"Oh, no. Not me. He's your problem now." His mother's gentle banter might be as close to approval as they were going to get, and Jacob's chest went warm and tight.

"That he is." Then Linc stunned him with a fast kiss on the head, right there in his mom's kitchen, and Jacob was pretty sure every dream he'd ever held came true in that moment. He'd won the heart of Lincoln Reid. And maybe he sometimes wished their path to right there together had been easier, but he wouldn't change the destination for anything.

Linc found Jacob out by the firepit, exactly where he'd expected him, draped over one of the lounge chairs, watching the flickering and spitting flames.

"Baby asleep?" Jacob sounded drowsy. He was undoubtedly tired. On top of the extra responsibilities with Junior's dog, he'd been working long hours doing winter work for the forest service, having lucked into some seasonal employment before the next smoke-jumping season.

"Yeah." Linc had offered to do bedtime so that May could say goodnight to her gym teacher friend. That and he wasn't going to turn down time rocking Willow, who was getting bigger by the day now. "She went down easy. Song and a bottle and she was out like a light."

"Linc, the baby whisperer." Jacob smiled and gestured at the other chair. "Sit."

Linc dragged the chair closer to Jacob's.

"Let's offer to keep the kids overnight some weekend soon."

"Boy, ask you to move in, and all of a sudden, you're throwing parties?" Linc pretended to be put out, but probably didn't do the best job of it. He'd been nervous that Jacob might not agree to move the trailer and the rest of his stuff. Some people might say it was a little too soon. But those people probably hadn't waited as long as them. Or been through as much.

"Hey, you heard my mom. I'm your trouble now."

Jacob laughed, then sobered, turning toward him. "Seriously, though, you okay with sharing your place with me? You've worked so hard on it…"

"Not that hard." Linc waved away the praise. "And… maybe the place needs you."

"Oh? How do you figure?"

"It's waited a long time to be a home again, not just a place to live or a collection of memories. I might have a lot of past with that house, but you give it a future."

Cheeks darkening, Jacob nodded sharply before looking off into the fire. He was silent a good while before softly adding, "I can't erase the past you had before me. The one you shared with Wyatt, especially. And I don't want to. Not for anything. And I know I'm not him, and I'm never going to make up for his loss, but I'm not sorry that I get your future either."

Linc sucked in a hard breath. They didn't talk about Wyatt much at all, but he was always there, an uncomfortable conversation waiting to happen. But for once, Linc wasn't going to shy away from the topic.

"You don't have to make up for anything. You're… This is different."

"I know." Jacob's tone was sadder and more resigned than Linc liked, so he reached over, touched Jacob's face.

"I never felt anything for him like what I feel for you. Not even remotely the same ballpark. He was my best friend, but you…you're my…everything."

"Thanks." Tilting his head, Jacob kissed Linc's fingers. "But you miss him."

"Of course I do. We all do. But I'm done feeling guilty for choosing to be with you. I hid my feelings behind my friendship with him way too long. It almost cost me you. I've had a lot of time to think these last few months…"

"And?"

"I like to think that even if he was around, I would have found the courage to be with you. To stand up to him. Because you, what we have together, it's important. Sure, the promises I made to him mattered. But the ones I want to make to you, maybe those matter a little more."

"You want to make promises to me?" Jacob's voice was little more than a puff of air, but the hope there was enough to prod Linc to keep going.

"I do." Linc's hand shook against Jacob's skin, and he had to draw a shaky breath. "I mean, if you're gonna talk me into that third dog, I guess I better make an honest man out of you at some point…"

"Well, when you put it that highly romantic way…"

"I love you." Linc might not have many pretty, flowery words, but he had those and they meant something. "I love you, and I want to promise you forever. As long as I've got, I'm yours."

"Okay, that's more like it." Jacob's eyes were shiny, even in the dim firelight. He kissed Linc's fingers again. "I love you too. And there's no promise I wouldn't make for you."

"Same." Linc tried to tell him with his eyes how much he meant that. He was well and truly done running from what they had. Too many years he'd spent hemming and hawing about what was the right thing to do, when really there was only one right thing. Love. It was the answer to every question and doubt he'd ever had, the reason for his biggest regrets and the cause of his greatest happiness. And maybe that, more than anything else, was the biggest change of the past months. He was happy. Genuinely, abundantly happy. And that, that was worth darn near everything. Promising forever seemed like a bargain if it meant keeping Jacob by his side, keeping that happiness he'd found. He was worth it. They both were.

* * * * *

Reviews are an invaluable tool when it comes to spreading the word about great reads. Please consider leaving an honest review for this or any of Carina Press's other titles that you've read on your favorite retailer or review site.

To find out more about Annabeth Albert's upcoming releases, contests and free bonus reads, please sign up for her newsletter here or at eepurl.com/Nb9yv.

Author Note

Longtime readers know that I love my research. My research into the world of wildfire fighting and forestry led me down many wonderful paths. Rather than try to copy an existing smoke-jumping base with its specific procedures, policies, ways of handling rookies and so on, I combined various parts of my research into many different bases into one fictional base. (The especially eagle-eyed will note that I essentially replaced the Redmond, Oregon, base with my own, and mine is not intended to be an exact duplicate of theirs in any way. Likewise, Painter's Ridge is an entirely fictional central Oregon town.). In particular, different bases handle the assembly of teams differently—some have a policy of rotating small crews, others have a "first in, first out" policy of whoever is there that day and ready to go, and others have more established crews. Depending on the size of a fire, multiple crews may be used or larger crews formed as necessary—I simplified this for the purposes of the book.

Similarly, each program seems to handle rookie training slightly differently, and I took elements from several different sources to come up with what Jacob and the other rookies go through. Further, some air bases have jumpers who spend the season essentially living on base while other air bases have more seasoned jumpers who may live nearby as I have the characters do here. Often callouts for fires are multi-day affairs and may involve use of a base camp near the actual fire without time to return home, and it's not unusual for smoke jumpers to be sent far from home or even out of state to fight a particularly large fire. Fire management usually involves multiple agencies and interagency co-ordination. Again, some of these details were simplified to allow the focus to remain on the characters and their growth and their story, but I did try to include as much realism as possible. It's an arduous job that taxes the people who take it on, and many consider it a calling as much as a vocation. I tried to bring their amazing dedication and resilient spirits to the secondary characters as well as our main characters. I also tried to reflect the very real dangers the job brings. Every year, brave and valiant people die fighting wildfires and others are seriously injured. We owe a great deal to their service.

Any time you have a team of individuals who spend a great deal of time together, fraternization concerns become a real and complex matter for management to consider. The brief discussion of the matter in the book is not intended to represent how all government agencies handle dating between coworkers nor is it intended to make light of what can be a serious and complicated situation.

I tried to stay true to the region's feel as much as possible. From unique eateries to a vibrant crafting community to a rich and diverse tourism culture with many different things to do, it's truly a unique area and land-scape.

Oh, and longtime fans will spot the very small Easter egg for the Out of Uniform series. If you're interested in more stories with a "band of brothers" type team feel, be sure and check out that series. And if you're wanting to know what a particular couple is up to now, be sure and sign up for my newsletter, as I do updates on fan-favorite characters from time to time.

Acknowledgments

A brand-new series is a wild and wonderful adventure, and I'm so thrilled that so many decided to take the leap into this universe with me. I am truly blessed with an amazing team supporting me, especially at Carina Press and the Knight Agency. My editor, Deb Nemeth, wanted more adventure romance from me, and her support and enthusiasm led me to chase this new plot bunny with great excitement. As always her wise and careful stewardship of this book through the editing process made for a stronger story, one that I'm truly proud to bring readers. And for my readers, a giant thank-you for taking a chance on this series. I've heard from so many fans who wanted another series like Out of Uniform, and I so hope the danger, excitement, friendships and deep emotions of Hotshots delivers. I can't thank readers enough for their readership and encouragement over the years. Bringing you the stories of my heart is one of my greatest joys.

My behind-the-scenes team is also so appreciated. My publicist, Judith of A Novel Take PR, goes above and beyond with every release, and I am so very grateful to her. My entire Carina Press team does an amazing job, and I am so very lucky to have all of them on board. A special thank-you to the tireless art department and publicity team and to the amazing narrators who bring my books to life for the audio market. A special thank-you to Angela James who believed in this new series. And my beta readers are also so good to me. Abbie Nicole and Edie Danford had invaluable advice on pacing, and Wendy Qualls provided her usual amazing sounding board for plotting.

I am blessed with the support of so many friends, especially writer friends, and it would be impossible to name everyone, but I am so grateful for all my "friends in the computer" as my kids call the wonderful people I'm privileged to know. I am so appreciative as well of the writers who take time to give advice and support via the various writing groups I am a part of. My real-life family and friends put up with a lot during the drafting of this book, and I'm so thankful for their patience and understanding. We went through some challenges as a family during this draft, and I'm truly grateful for the ways in which my family pitched in, especially in regards to making writing possible for me. I know I'm missing people who undoubtedly deserve appreciation—know that I am so grateful for every person in my life who helps me do what I love. And no one makes that possible more than my readers. Thank you so very much for the gift of your readership and your support via social media, reviews, notes, shares, likes and other means. You make it possible for me to live my dream job, and I don't take that for granted!

About the Author

Annabeth Albert grew up sneaking romance novels under the bedcovers. Now she devours all subgenres of romance out in the open—no flashlights required! When she's not adding to her keeper shelf, she's a multi-published Pacific Northwest romance writer. The Hot-shots series joins her many other critically acclaimed and fan-favorite LGBTQ romance series. To find out what she's working on next and other fun extras, check out her website www.annabethalbert.com or connect with Annabeth on Twitter, Facebook, Instagram and Spotify! Also, be sure to sign up for her newsletter for free ficlets, bonus reads and contests. The fan group, Annabeth's Angels, on Facebook is also a great place for bonus content and exclusive contests.

Emotionally complex, sexy and funny stories are her favorites both to read and to write. Annabeth loves finding happy endings for a variety of pairings and particularly loves uncovering unique main characters. In her personal life, she works a rewarding day job and wrangles two active children.

Newsletter: eepurl.com/Nb9yv.

Fan group: www.Facebook.com/groups/annabethsangels/

Chapter One

"Come on, honey. You gotta let me help you." Garrick liked to think he was good at sweet-talking people, but his track record of success was in serious jeopardy here.

Woof. The dog danced away from him again. Balanced on crutches, he was limited in his ability to lunge for her. A year ago, his fast reflexes would have made his words irrelevant, but now he pitched his voice low and gentle.

"Sit? Can you sit?"

Miraculously, the dog plopped her fairly sizable behind down on his porch. She appeared to be some happy mix of pit, rottie and lab with a short brownish coat and white and tan markings on her nose and chest. No collar, which was alarming enough, but it was the bloody paw prints on his porch and scrape on her side that had him truly concerned.

He took a few steps toward her, but she quickly backed up. Damn it. It was probably the crutches that were scaring her.

"Me too, dog. Me too." Industrial gray with heavy forearm cuffs, the crutches made a heavy sound with each step. They were a necessity that made his life far easier than the underarm variety had, but he couldn't deny that they were probably intimidating to the scared dog. He needed a better plan. She was probably only fifty or sixty pounds, but he wasn't going to be able to even grab her scruff, let alone lift her.

"Can you stay?"

The dog cocked her head like she was actually listening, which made Garrick laugh for the first time since discovering her barking at his front door. Obedient even if skittish, she stayed in place while he went back into the house. He traded the crutches for his wheelchair and retrieved his phone from the dining table.

Hell. He hated needing help, had needed so much of it in the past year, but he couldn't let his pride get in the way of helping a wounded animal. His neighbor Shirley had dogs, two of them, little white yappy things. She'd have a leash and know a vet to call. She didn't answer when he dialed her number, but he could see two cars in her driveway. Probably had company, and he hated interrupting, but it really couldn't be avoided. If she wasn't home, he'd have to try another friend or his dad, but this would be quicker.

Pocketing the phone, he rolled back out to the porch where the dog waited right where he'd left her.

"Good girl," he praised, but when he scooted closer, she backed up again. "Okay, okay. I'm getting help. Stay."

He used the wooden side ramp his friends had built for him to navigate the two porch steps, then zipped down the driveway and across the cul-de-sac to Shirley's house, a neat little seventies ranch, same basic size as his own. Hers was a friendly shade of lilac, while he'd gone for gray. It was an older neighborhood of smaller homes but decent-sized yards, and close to both a park and Garrick's favorite sports bar, where he used to hang out all the time.

And the air base, but he was trying not to think about that. Gorgeous blue sky, not a cloud in sight, fresh spring air, perfect day for a training jump or two. But not this year. *Next one. You'll get there*, he reminded himself as he navigated Shirley's driveway, which had more of an angle than his.

No porch for Shirley, but the single step in front of the front door was always a challenge. He should have brought the crutches, but he'd been in a hurry. Stretching, he managed to reach far enough to rattle the storm door. "Shirley? Shirley? It's Garrick."

"What the—" The door swung open to reveal a younger man, undoubtedly one of her many grandkids, and that would explain the extra car. And of course it would be one of the gorgeous guys who starred in the pics all over Shirley's fridge—riot of curly chestnut hair pulled up, brown eyes and a lean dancer's build in a shimmery blue shirt. "You need something?"

All of a sudden, Garrick was acutely aware of his dingy sweatpants and grubby T-shirt advertising a triathlon from five years back. He'd been going through his physical therapy exercises when he'd heard the dog barking. And it had been months since he'd last worried what he looked like, so God only knew the state of his hair and face, but something about this guy made him care. And like with the dog, he did not seem to be making a good first impression, judging by the guy's scowl.

"I'm her neighbor," he hurried to explain. "From

across the street? The one who built her garden beds in back. We're friends. I need her help with a dog situation."

"A dog situation?" The scowl dropped, leaving in its place a more speculative expression, one that showed off the guy's full mouth and high cheekbones. "She's mentioned you. She's resting right now though. Said she had a bad arthritis night."

"Heck. Yeah, don't wake her up. But there's a dog on my porch, a hurt stray, and I need to figure out what to do with it. It won't let me close."

"On your porch?" He gestured behind Garrick. A quick swivel revealed the dog at the bottom of Shirley's driveway, looking expectantly at him.

"I thought I told you to stay!" Garrick said to the dog, then turned back to the young man, who was laughing now. Dimples. Because, of course. "Yeah. That's it. Seems friendly enough, but I don't have a leash and I'm not sure what to do once I catch her."

"Okay, hang tight. Let me make sure Mimi and Molly are secure, then I'll get a leash and some treats." The guy disappeared into the house.

"Come on now. You don't need to be afraid." Garrick rolled toward the dog, hand outstretched. She let him get closer than she had on the porch, then started backing up.

"Cookie? Who wants a cookie?" Shirley's grandson reappeared with a black leash and a packet of bacon-and-peanut-butter-flavored biscuits. Mouth cracking into a doggy grin, the hound ignored Garrick's hand in favor of limping toward the treats.

"Guess you're Mr. Popular now," Garrick joked, following her.

"Oh, you know that word! *Cookie! Don't* you? Smart cookie!" The guy had a great voice, friendly and musical, not overpowering at all, and for a second, Garrick wouldn't have minded being the one showered with praise. Which was odd. Not the attraction—that happened some, or at least it used to. But it hadn't since the accident. Not even hookup apps or porn of any stripe held much appeal these days. But apparently golden brown eyes and bouncy hair and really bad timing did the trick.

"She knows *sit* too," Garrick provided as the dog gobbled down a treat. "Sit."

Obediently, she plopped down on the concrete driveway. *Woof.*

"Someone wants another cookie?" This time the guy was lightning fast, the sort of reflexes that would be at home on any engine crew, as he lassoed the leash around her neck, clipping it in place. He doled out another biscuit as he straightened. "She's hungry. Probably hasn't eaten in a while. Want me to get some water while you call Animal Control?"

Garrick had to laugh. "This is a small town. *Very* small town. There's no dog catcher or pound."

"None? Police nonemergency number maybe?"

"I don't think they handle stray dogs that aren't a threat. Fish and Wildlife will come for wild animals like bobcats on your property, but not dogs."

"Thank goodness you're not a bobcat." Giving a nervous laugh, the guy glanced off into the hills before patting the dog again.

"There's an animal shelter in Bend, about forty-five

minutes away, but I think she needs a vet first. I'd go door-to-door to find an owner but that paw has me worried about walking her too much."

"Good point."

"Rain? What's the commotion?" Shirley emerged from the house, walking a little slower than normal, but looking pretty with her long gray hair spilling down the back of a dress dyed the colors of an Oregon sunset.

Rain. He had to be one of the Portland grandkids—they all seemed to have hippie names. Rain, Skye, Lark and so on. And he was clearly used to bigger cities than Painter's Ridge, where no one who worked for the town was coming out for a lost dog.

"Your...uh...neighbor found a dog." Still holding the leash, Rain walked over to her. The name absolutely suited his lithe frame and natural grace to his strides.

"Garrick." He offered a handshake after Rain transferred the leash to his other hand. He hadn't grabbed the wheelchair gloves he usually used for longer treks, so his bare skin met Rain's. And there it was again. Sparks, sure as a flint meeting steel, right when he could least do a damn thing about it. And because Shirley undoubtedly wouldn't appreciate him macking on her much-too-young grandson, he glanced away.

"I'm gonna get that water. You think you can hold her?" Glancing down at Garrick's chair, Rain offered the leash somewhat reluctantly.

"Yup. I'll put the brakes on." Garrick engaged the locks for his wheels. He was still getting used to all the bells and whistles on this one. It was a nice chair, far better than the old-fashioned clunky things he'd first had at the hospital. Ultralight. Racing style they called it, though that was a bit optimistic as far as he'd found. The thicker bicycle-like tires and red trim added to the sporty appearance. He'd been reluctant to give up the rental chair, get this one custom fit when he wasn't sure how long he'd need it, but the insurance, which could be a bastard about some things, had paid up.

"I don't know if I like the look of that dog. Too big. And you never know, might be aggressive." Shirley shook her head.

"Seems like a sweetheart to me." Garrick kept his tone light, not too argumentative, but the dog, who was currently twisted around trying to get at her scrape, seemed more scaredy-cat than fighter.

"Don't let Rain talk himself into keeping her here. Mimi is downright territorial over her house. And we have to watch Molly at the park. She's always goading bigger dogs."

It wasn't really Garrick's place to be preventing Rain from anything, but he nodded. "Well, hopefully we'll find the owner quickly. You've never seen this dog around?"

"No. But I can make some calls. And I'm on that neighborhood group thing." She whipped out her phone, a newer model that one of the grandkids had talked her into.

Garrick largely avoided the online neighborhood group, which tended to complain about package stealers, lawn ornament movers and inconsiderate parkers, but it might be useful for something like this.

Shirley snapped a picture of the dog and got busy on her phone as Rain came back with a mixing bowl full of water. The dog waited patiently for Rain to set it down, then gulped down most of the water, tail wagging, still paying no mind to the leash. Yeah, she was a sweetheart all right, and someone had to be frantically looking for her.

"The vet will be able to tell us if she's microchipped." Rain patted the dog on her head.

"Yes. Cherry Pet Care on Main is where I go. They take walk-ins," Shirley added, not looking up from the phone.

"Do you want me to take her?" Rain's mouth quirked as he glanced between Garrick and the dog. "Or do you want to come? The vet might not…uh…do pro bono work on strays."

"I'll come." Garrick got it. He'd been a broke college kid once upon a time too, and Rain didn't look much older than twenty-two or so, which was a nice reminder not to go perving on his good looks again. "I've got a card the vet can use if needed. I'll just need to grab my wallet."

"Thanks." Relief was evident in Rain's wide eyes.

"No lost dog notices from the neighbors," Shirley reported. "And you better hurry. The vet only has short Saturday hours. You sure you're up for the outing, Garrick?"

"Nothing better to do," he said lightly, but it was true. Weekends were the worst. No physical therapy. Fewer visits from his dad, who worked long hours at his Western-themed shop, which did a ton of tourist business. Friends were busy with their own lives, and inviting himself along was far more complicated than it used to be, as was finding his own fun. The dog was the most exciting thing to happen in a while, and that was just sad. "Besides, Rain said you were feeling under the weather. You rest and check the app, and we'll handle the dog."

It felt good to take charge of something again, even if it was simply logistics for the dog. He sent Rain to fetch old towels to protect his car from the dog's wounds while he headed back to his place for his wallet, keys and crutches, which went in the holder on the back of his chair, another spiffy feature that helped. No time to change clothes though. Not that he needed to care what sort of impression he made on Rain or the vet or anyone else.

Rain met him at his car, a small SUV, with the dog waiting on her leash.

"So…dog goes in the back seat and your wheelchair in the cargo area? That sound okay?" Rain asked, not told, which was nice, especially when he continued after Garrick nodded. "Can you tell me how best to help you? Is the car too tall for you?"

A lot of people would have made assumptions and started doing things at this point, but Rain gave him space, both literal and figurative, which Garrick appreciated.

"I can stand to transfer." Pulling up even with the passenger door, Garrick demonstrated. "Tall is actually easier. If you want to fold the chair and stow it, that would be great."

"No problem." Rain wheeled it around to the back of the SUV.

"It's pretty sturdy," Garrick called as he hefted himself into the passenger seat, suddenly weirdly on edge.

"It collapses by pulling on the seat cushion, but don't try to force anything."

"I've got you. Not my first time folding a chair. You're safe with me, promise."

"Thanks." Strangely, Garrick found himself nodding. He did feel comfortable with Rain, even though he was younger and a stranger and his car was old enough to not exactly inspire confidence. And the gentle way that Rain loaded up the dog helped too. He didn't have the brashness Garrick associated with a lot of guys his age. And he seemed good-natured, the way he'd rolled with having his Saturday upended by Garrick and the dog. All in all, Garrick could have done a lot worse for an unexpected rescuer, and despite the seriousness of their task, he found himself almost eager to spend more time with him.

Danger. Abort. Bad idea. Nice as it was to remember what attraction felt like, he wasn't up to flirting let alone anything else, and Rain was the trifecta of probably straight, too young and way off-limits. Better he simply focus on the job at hand and not let himself get carried away with anything else.

Grandma's neighbor was hot. Like distractingly so, with broad shoulders and biceps for days coupled with a movie-star-worthy face—chiseled facial features and piercing green eyes and shaggy hair that danced between dirty blond and light brown. But Rain was supposed to be focusing on the dog, not Garrick, and on driving through a town he'd only visited a couple of times since his grandmother moved. She refused to call it a retirement, but buying a house had been her admitting that maybe her years on the art festival circuit were coming to a halt, and providing her fabric crafts to a nearby touristy place was more her current speed.

"So you visiting for the weekend?" Garrick asked as Rain followed his phone's GPS directions toward downtown.

"No, I'm supposed to be here for a couple of months. I took the spring term off college, thought I might see what seasonal work I could find around here, help Grandma out at the same time."

"That sounds nice. I'm sure she could use the hand."

"Eh. She's like her dog—rather territorial about her place. It was my mom's idea, so we'll see if it sticks." Rain did love Grandma, but so far she hadn't let him anywhere near her sewing machine or dye buckets so he wasn't sure how much help he was actually going to be. "I had an interview this morning for a bartender gig— that's why I'm dressed up—but I don't think I passed it."

"Oh?" Garrick didn't sound judgmental, merely curious.

"Yeah. It's the clubhouse at the golf course south of town. I didn't know half the drinks they quizzed me on, and they asked how I felt about a haircut."

"Ouch." Garrick laughed. "Yeah, don't do that. Keep looking. Plenty of other seasonal jobs."

"You'd know, right? I thought Grandma said you were a smoke jumper?"

"Yep." Garrick didn't seem inclined to elaborate, instead looking out the window, and Rain couldn't blame him—he'd get the scoop from Grandma about Garrick's injuries rather than bug him for gory details he probably didn't want to share.

"That's cool. I've got some applications in with the forest service and other places since some of my classes were pre-fire academy. I didn't get a slot for this year though, hence taking a term off." He kept his voice casual. The Portland Fire Academy was notoriously competitive so he was trying hard not to take it too personally, but man it had hurt to not even make the short list of applicants who would be considered for fall placements. Oh, well. On to the next adventure.

"You can park up here." Garrick pointed to a lot next to a brick building with a cheerful sign with dogs and cats on it. "And don't let it get you down, kid. Don't give up on the dream."

Kid. Okay. So much for Hottie Neighbor. No one called him *kid* these days and got away with it. Quietly seething, he found the closest spot to the door. He might be irked, but he was still careful with the wheelchair and crutches as he unloaded them for Garrick.

"Need my arm?" He knew better than to hover, but still wanted to make the offer if Garrick needed assistance.

"Nah. I've got it." Garrick smoothly transferred from the car to the chair, then waited for Rain to unload the dog. "That's a good girl." Garrick stuck out his hand and this time the dog sniffed it, even without a treat. She seemed to be warming up to both of them, even though she was noticeably skittish as they approached the door. Once inside, she plopped down, almost like she was trying to hide behind them.

"Now, who do we have here?" A receptionist in kitten-print scrubs and pink glasses peered over her desk at them. Garrick explained about finding the dog, and the receptionist nodded sympathetically. "It shouldn't be too long a wait for the vet. I'll need a name for her though, just to start a chart."

"Name?" Garrick looked over at Rain like he might have the answer, which was nice, being consulted like that. Usually take-charge guys like Garrick didn't slow down long enough to solicit other opinions. Which Rain had.

"If they can't find an owner, you want her to have a great shot at adoption. Pick something fun and gentle for her maybe? Approachable? She looks all tough, big black dog, but really she's almost shy. Aren't you, sweetie?"

As if she knew she was being talked about, the dog crept forward to nose at the treat bag Rain was holding.

"No, you can't have another cookie," he said firmly.

"Cookie." Garrick smiled, and it was a great smile, wide and welcoming, the sort of easy charmer who probably had tons of friends. "That's it. At least we know she'll come to that. And you can put my address for now."

After the intake information was handled, they were shown to a little room with a window facing a garden and a cheery mural on the wall.

"You and your son can wait in here while I take Cookie for her weight and temperature," the receptionist said to Garrick, making Rain snort. The dude wasn't *that* old. Mid-thirties maybe. His messy hair and facial scruff made him look older, but he didn't have any gray yet. For himself, Rain was used to looking young. Probably one of the reasons the bartender gig had fallen through. The manager guy had sounded like he didn't trust Rain to not be slipping drinks to underage buddies.

"Not the son. Just another neighbor," Rain said quickly before she could leap to her next assumption that Garrick was the sugar daddy with the credit cards. Not that Rain would necessarily mind, but this was a small town, and Garrick had "sports-loving dude bro" written all over him.

"Ah. Well, Cookie is lucky to have you both. I'll check on a microchip while we're in the back."

"Man, I hope she's got the microchip and a nice owner on file," Garrick said as the receptionist and Cookie left, leaving Rain to take one of the seats in the room.

"Yeah, she's a great dog." Personally, Rain didn't have as much hope of an owner—no collar, and despite a sturdy build the dog looked like she hadn't had a good meal in a few days.

"So, tell me about these firefighting classes you were taking. What certs do you have?" Garrick asked like he actually cared about the answer and not like he was just looking to kill time. Which made Rain give him a real answer, one that kept them talking about his rather eclectic collection of community college classes until a vet tech brought Cookie back.

The tech was followed by a woman around Garrick's age who had to be the vet, judging by the stethoscope around her neck. "I have good news and bad news," the vet said as she shut the door behind her. Cookie now sported a white mitt on her paw and a shaved patch around the scrape on her side, but seemed in good spirits. "Which do you want first?"

"Good," Rain said, right as Garrick said, "Bad."

"Okay. Both it is." The vet laughed. She had kind eyes and short dark hair, and Cookie was already nuzzling up to her, looking for treats. "Well, no microchip for one. No lost dog calls here either. But good news—she's been spayed and other than a large thorn in her paw and the scrape on her side, she's pretty healthy. I'd guess she's a year or two old. We've cleaned her wounds, and she'll need to keep the mitt on her paw for a couple of days. I'd like to do a round of antibiotics because the side scrape did look somewhat infected to me, but that's largely out of caution."

"What's the rest of the bad news?" Garrick sounded like a guy who had heard more than his share of it over the years, not reacting to the better news about Cookie's health beyond stretching out a hand for her to warily sniff again.

"I'm assuming you're hoping to get her off your hands, but our kennel is full of patients who need overnight care. Lydia called the shelter in Bend, and they're full as well, including foster homes that could handle an injured animal. They can stick a picture of her up on the found page, but they're not sure they can get her a place before they close tonight. A number of the rescues are in a similar boat—either they're very breed- and size-specific or they aren't taking new animals right now. I'll be honest—her size and her breeds along with the injuries are going to make her a tough placement, especially on a weekend."

"Heck." Wide shoulders deflating, Garrick studied his hands, which left Rain to pet Cookie.

"I can work on Grandma. Maybe by Monday, her owners will be found."

"She said no," Garrick reminded him. "And she's got the other dogs to think about. It makes sense. My friends in the country would be good, but they just added a third dog—I doubt they're going to be up for one more already. I can see who else might be able to help."

"How about you?" Rain turned on the sort of smile that usually brought him good luck.

"Me?" Garrick blinked.

"Yes, you. You'd be perfect." Nodding, he leaned forward, waiting for Garrick to embrace the obvious.

Don't miss
High Heat by Annabeth Albert,
available summer 2020 wherever
Carina Press ebooks are sold.
www.CarinaPress.com